102

His most unforgettable mission.

Cover Art by Luis Flores

ISBN: 978-1-7345815-0-8
ISBN: 978-1-7345815-1-5

Printed by KDP in the United States of America.
First printing, Jan 2020. The events and characters portrayed in this book are fictitious. Any similarities between real persons, living or dead or real life events, is coincidental and not intended by the author.
102 : a novel / by Victoria Diaz. —2nd ed.

1

STRANGERS AND STRANGE ROOMS

(Zara)

The summer heat wakes me again. I'm soaked. The air conditioner has been out in my apartment for over a week now. With no sign of repair in sight.

The daily forecast calls for beautiful skies and extreme temperatures. Not to anyone's surprise but the sun has really stuck around this year in California, even though it's borderline fall.

Outside the birds are chirping and I hear a lawnmower growling as the landscaper trims the grass. It's somewhat soothing, actually.

I live in a small suburb of Los Angeles called Harper. Population of around one hundred thousand people. A particularly small city, yet filled to the absolute rim with busy, always-in-a-rush humans. But what do you expect? It's LA.

"Three more days," I say to myself as I stare at my reflection in the mirror. Pulling down my eyelids with my fingertips and causing my eyes to bulge out of my head.

Ugh, I hate September. I think to myself.

No, I don't hate summer or fall or anything, I'm not a complete weirdo. There's a back story, a tragic one. Both of my parents died in September. Three days from today, twenty-four years ago to be exact.

Every year around this time, I'm plagued with crippling anxiety and paranoia. Then come nighttime, the torment shifts in the form of nightmares. Dreams so terrifying I wake up screaming and drenched in sweat. Once I'm up, though, I never seem to remember what the dream was about.

"Just three more days," my eyes close softly, taking in one last deep breath. "I can do this."

Hoping the pep talk worked, I head back into my bedroom to leave. Constantly trying to remind myself that all I have to do is survive these next three days, and then the torture will be over.

Before I head out the front door, I slide into my work shoes. They're scuffed up and old but they get the job done.

Apart from being a traumatized orphan, I am also a registered nurse. During most of my free time you can find me at Silverstone Health Memorial. Not my favorite job, but it pays the bills. Silverstone Health is one of the largest healthcare providers in the country, with over 400 hospitals and almost 7,000 medical offices nationwide.

Why do I know this and how is it of any importance? It's not, and it's just what I do. On my spare time, when I'm not working to barely make ends meet, I like to research useless facts nobody cares about. Storing them in a special part of my brain until the perfect occasion arises where I'm finally able to use them. You could say I'm a bit of an outcast.

I have one friend and a cat named Binks. I'm not much of a cat person actually, if it were up to me I'd have a dog. But my apartment complex doesn't allow any dogs. Just cats.

Stupid rule if you ask me.

Not that it's stopped me from trying, though. I've smuggled in a few dogs here and there. But Hector, the maintenance guy, he always catches me. I swear, the guy should work for the CIA. He'd be a real top dog.

No pun intended.

As I arrive at the hospital, my Jeep pulls almost knowingly into the employee parking lot and squeezes into it's usual spot. Right next to the dumpster.

Okay, I know what you're thinking. But it's a spot I put very much thought and consideration into. You see, I can conveniently dump things into it if need be and the best part is, it's very far away from the cars of the other employees. Although, as incredible as this all may sound, there is one slight drawback. It's inconveniently located very far away from the building I work in.

After the song that's playing over the radio ends, I shut the engine off and dig through my bag, searching for my earbuds. It's become a custom that I walk through the parking lot with my earbuds in. Not necessarily to listen to music as much as to avoid small talk with anyone in the unfortunate circumstance that I do bump into someone.

It's actually a great technique I've gotten down. Sometimes I even forget to play anything at all, but when someone speaks, I just mouth, "I'm sorry" while pointing to my magical earbuds, and they go away. It's borderline genius, really.

As I'm jamming out to my music in the elevator, waiting for my stop, I mentally prepare for my day. The doors open and I take another deep breath before I exit. As introverted as I am, sometimes I wonder why I chose a career that requires so much *extrovertedness*.

When I step out, I'm pleased to find my friend, Ripley Wells, already there waiting for me. Ripley is the longest friendship I've ever had and the closest thing to a sister I'll ever be blessed with.

And she has snacks.

In less than a second, she's swiftly by my side. Ready to update me on the latest hospital gossip. Which I didn't ask for, but she's always happy to share with me anyway. Often I wonder if she imagines herself as the main character in a romantic sitcom like Grey's Anatomy. Which also happens to be one of her favorite TV shows. Because she sure does act like it sometimes.

What could it be today?

Is nurse Khloe still sleeping with the new intern from the 3rd floor? Or is it Dr. Smith this time, who got caught last week fooling around with the janitor?

"He's baaack," Ripley whispers to me in a sing-song voice. While she simultaneously slips me a freshly baked croissant as if she were doing a drug deal.

"I'm sorry, *who's* back?" I reply then take a bite of my still-warm pastry. Closing my eyes in ecstasy as the buttery flakes melt on my tongue. "Wow! This is *incredible*. Thanks, I'm starving," I manage to say.

"You're always hungry. I honestly don't know how you survive," she complains as she lifts my arm in disgust. "Skin and bones."

"I survive just fine, thank you," I roll my eyes at her then scarf down the rest of my croissant.

Ripley's face lights up when she spots

something down the hall behind me. Naturally, I turn around to see what it is.

"Mr. Silverstone!" she calls out before I even get to see the culprit.

Shit!

Without a second thought, I quickly dive behind the nurses' desk, hoping he didn't see me. It's Liam Silverstone. Name sound familiar? He's handsome as they come, I'll admit. But God went heavy on the A-hole with this one. And to top it off, he made him rich! The nerve. God really does have favorites.

Liam also happens to be heir to the company. Fortunately for him, he's the sole grandson of the man who founded this place. *Thee* Mr. Silverstone himself.

Or is he the great-grandson?

I'm not quite sure actually, I've never been curious enough to look up the specifics of his family. Or him for that matter. But basically, he owns the place now.

"Goddamn it!" I hush-yell towards Ripley. "Not this again! Did you already tell him I was here?" I can see the silhouette of his reflection on the glass windows that line the halls as he approaches. "He's coming! Damn it, Rip!"

"He didn't ask!" she hush-yells back in a defensive tone. She looks like she's arguing with a chair.

"I'm finding that very hard to believe right

now," I whisper to her with gritted teeth.

"Whatever! He must have checked the schedule and saw that you'd be in today. I didn't say anything! Why do you always have to blame m—hey!" she changes her tone instantly.

I see his feet reach the desk and I dart to the opposite side, into the hallway. Making my escape.

Yes! I made it!

"Phew, I don't think he saw me," I mumble to myself as I continue on.

Slowly, I crouch lower, then crawl towards the emergency stairway on all fours until I reach the door. My hand swipes above my head a couple times blindly until it finds the door knob and with a little struggle I manage to get it open. Then I squeeze through, into the stairwell. Carefully closing the door behind me.

Once I'm all alone, I get back on my feet and sprint to the fourth floor. Almost flying down the single flight of stairs. When I push the door open, my body freezes.

Shit!

Someone's here.

Two someones actually. I squint my eyes, attempting to catch a glimpse of a face while they smash up against each other in passion.

"Looks like it's nurse Khloe from pediatrics." And she's making out fiercely with a young blonde by the elevator. "And *that* must be the new intern. I guess this spot is taken." I close the door again.

The 4th floor has been my secret hideout since they closed it down for maintenance three months ago. A little before Liam took over. But nothing has really gotten done, and no one even comes down here. So I hide here sometimes, no big deal. Take a nap or two in the meeting room under the table. But I'll have to find somewhere else now that nurse Khloe is going to be having make-out sessions in here. I snap out of my thoughts quickly and get back to my mission. But before I take off, I glance above me, then back down below.

Which way do I choose?

"Seven is known to be a lucky number, right?" I ask myself. "And I've never been up there before…okay, the decision is made. Up we go."

After conquering two floors, the level of exhaustion I'm feeling surprises me. But I pull myself together and drag my legs up the final steps to the seventh floor. Pushing the door open with minimal strength, while simultaneously trying to catch my breath.

Wow, we're out of shape.

My head pokes through first and I do a quick visual sweep to see if the coast is clear before going in.

"Score! No one is here!" I celebrate, fist pumping the air. Still cautious, I tiptoe around, looking for a nice room to crash. When I hear something. "Not again!" I scowl.

**Ding*! The elevator sounds.

My head instinctively turns towards the elevator that's in the same direction I just came from. Then I hear the door open. The sound is soon followed by voices.

Men's voices.

And one in particular rings a very familiar tone.

"Is that Liam?" I whisper to myself. Panicked, I open the first door I see and rush inside. "Is he following me?" I stare out the small window on the door. Watching for the men.

Once my nerves die down, I look around the room to inspect. There are rows and rows of filing cabinets all around me. And a massive wooden table that stretches through the center.

"I guess I'll hide here," I slide underneath.

Down the hall, the voices are getting closer and the footsteps are getting louder. They seem to be heading my way. "Are they coming in here?" I begin to panic again. The men are now just outside the door.

They are *coming in here!*

My hand flies over my mouth, in an attempt to quiet my heavy breathing. When the door flies open. From underneath the table, I watch as the two men walk inside. A loud gulp tries to escape my lips, but I quickly clasp my mouth tighter.

They exchange hushed words between themselves as I try desperately to strategize a plan to get the hell out of here. Without losing my job. But while I'm swimming in my own thoughts, the volume of their discussion begins to elevate. The men are now arguing too loud to continue to ignore. I've never been much of an eavesdropper, but the argument piques my curiosity. So I start to listen in.

"Look, I don't care what my father said. I want all the information. *I'm* in charge now, and I have the right to know. I don't see why Operation Red Robin has to be any different. It's about helping small communities nationwide, right? Why can't I know the details?" one man argues.

I think it's Liam. But who is he talking to? I've never heard the other man's voice before. His accent is very thick and not American at all.

Russian maybe?

"Liam—um. I mean—Mr. Silverstone," he corrects himself, "your father just wants to keep this little project to himself, okay? It's his last opportunity to do a good deed before he retires. And it's important to him that he do it alone," the Russian guy says. He doesn't sound very reassuring.

He sounds rather suspicious if you ask me.

My conscience adds her usual two cents.

"Yeah, because that sounds like something my father would do," Liam remarks almost poetically. I sense sarcasm in his tone.

"Cut him some slack, Liam. He just doesn't want to burden you with the hassle of charity work. That's all I know, kid," the Russian complains.

Kid? What happened to "Mr. Silverstone"?

"Paul, I've known you my entire life. When have you ever known my father to do anything out of kindness for *me*? Or anyone for that matter. *"If it isn't making me money, it's wasting my time."* was my nursery rhyme at bedtime. You expect me to believe he's doing charity work?"

"What do you want from me, kid? He's the boss. I just follow orders, and that's what I was told."

"I just have a bad feeling about it, that's all," Liam says in a strange tone.

A bad feeling, huh?

I think to myself.

"Do you have any other questions for me? Or can I go now?" The man sounds annoyed.

"As a matter of fact, I do," Liam responds in a snarky tone. "When does this campaign actually begin?"

"Briefings about new company policies

need to be started this fall. No later," he urges. "So that by the end of the year, it can all be normalized."

Normalized?

Nothing he's saying makes any sense to me. And frankly, it's starting to bore me. When suddenly my ears begin to ring, diverting my attention from their discussion. Then chills start to creep at the nape of my neck.

Not this again.

My anxiety is back. The same torturous feeling I've been fighting all morning, has come to revisit me yet again. And at the worst possible timing. With a shake of my head, I try to clear it, when my attention is suddenly diverted elsewhere. Making me forget about my anxiety altogether.

There's a person standing by the window at the door. His eyes fixated on the two men talking.

Now, who do we have here?

I catch myself staring at him with the same intensity that he's using on them. More fascinated by him than what ever conversation the two men had going on. When he finally looks my way I let out a gasp.

He must have felt me staring.

But I can't look away. Our eyes glued to each other like magnets. Pulled to one another for what feels like minutes, because I can't seem to look away. And I don't think he can either.

Which doesn't make any sense because I've never seen this man before in my life. We continue to stare. Then without warning, he's gone. Disappearing before my very eyes with a flash.

What the fuck!

I shake my head. Blinking rapidly as if trying to reset my vision. My mind can't seem to comprehend what it just witnessed.

Did that really happen?

What did I see?

The man didn't just disappear like you would if you ran off or ducked. He literally vanished with a flash of light. Like some type of magic.

Am I going crazy?

This is the last thing I need right now. I thought I'd have a few more years at least before the screws came loose upstairs. My aunt Lucy made it to the ripe old age of thirty six before she lost it. Is my fate worse?

Well, maybe her mental deterioration had something to do with her sister and brother-in-law dying tragically and leaving her a four-year-old little girl to raise.

Yeah, that could do it.

I snap back to reality, remembering what

I was doing in the first place. I really should get back to my eavesdropping.

"Well, that makes sense, for flu season, right?" Liam is talking again. "I read through one of the new memos going around that we will also be conducting drive-thru immunization clinics, free of cost?"

An immunization drive-thru clinic for charity?

Well, that's nice of them. Maybe the Silverstone family isn't so rotten after all. I didn't know that they did charity work. I even like the name of the project.

Who doesn't love Red Robin?

"Uh, yes, sir. Your father is very passionate about providing free or affordable public health care to all those who can't afford it. Or to those who have trouble getting access to it. Hence the drive-thru," Paul explains.

"Hmm. Makes sense," Liam has run out of arguments.

"Will that be all, sir?" Paul sounding increasingly annoyed. But Liam doesn't respond. The door just opens and one of them exits the room. But the other stays behind.

I'm not sure which one though. The room is so deafeningly quiet, I can hear his phone vibrating in his hand. He starts typing. Then the shoes are on the move again. Going towards the filing cabinets along the wall.

What kind of shoes was Liam wearing?

My memory always seems to fail me at the worst moments. Damn it, were these the ones I saw earlier? I don't think so. I'd imagine these shoes with those little red buckles would be hard to forget. Those definitely weren't the shoes Liam was wearing earlier.

A noise above the table startles me. The *click-clack of a lock being twisted around by a key. Then the rustling sound of papers. The man, who I can now confirm to be Paul with the mysterious accent, shoves something back into the cabinet. Then slams it shut, doing the *click-clack with the lock again. And just like that, the shoes and their little red buckles are gone. Leaving me alone once more.

Quietly, I sit under the table.

Motionless. Listening. Waiting.

After I'm sure I've heard the elevator do it's elevator ding two times, I crawl out from underneath my hiding place. Hoping this time I'm really alone.

"Man, this floor is way more interesting than the 4th floor," I make a note to myself.

And it has ghosts!

As I tiptoe down the hall, I try my best not to run into any more people. The elevator looks more inviting than the stairs this time around, so I head that way instead. When I get in, I stand there, taking a minute to decide which floor to go to next.

Should I: **A.** Go back to the 5th floor where I work and where there's probably a nurse waiting for me to relieve her so she can go home?

Or do I choose **B.** And go straight to the 3rd floor to Psych for an evaluation after seeing that ghost?

I weigh my options carefully then hit five.

"It's the responsible thing to do," I declare proudly to myself. "Also, now I'm kind of super late."

(102)

Did she see me?

"No, I don't think so," I begin to argue with myself. "I had my invisibility on. She couldn't have seen me." I'm trying desperately to make myself feel better. "I don't think she was a Halfling." I'm pacing around an empty janitorial closet like a mental person, talking to no one.

Then why did she look at you that way?

My conscience presses me.

This is the last thing I need right now. I'm already on thin ice as it is. I press my thumb and index finger into my eyes and rub them firmly until I see stars.

"Looks like I may be hallucinating again," I half convince myself. "I really need to get back to work."

Somehow I manage to stay on task for the remainder of the day. But images of the girl are still flooding my thoughts.

2

DO ALL DOGS GO TO HEAVEN?

(Zara)

After surviving a crazy shift and successfully avoiding getting fired for showing up almost an hour late, I still managed to have a decent day. But I've got to admit, I haven't been able to get that mysterious man out of my head all day.

"Hey Ripley, can I ask you something?" I begin, already regretting what I'm about to say.

"Yeah, sure," she responds.

"Do you think I'm crazy?" I ask, making her roll her eyes.

"Here we go again," she mumbles. But I ignore her reaction and continue.

"Like, out of all the people you know. If there was a crazy scale, where do I lie right now at this moment?"

Ripley narrows her eyes at me. I think she's either on to me or she's so used to my nonsense she isn't even taking me seriously anymore.

"Really? That's what you wanted to ask me?" she raises an eyebrow.

"Yes?" I wince.

"Nope—," she begins, shaking her hand at me. "Not today."

"Just hear me out!" I stop her as she starts to walk away. "Hypothetically speaking—."

"Hypothetically speaking?" she turns slowly.

"What are the chances that you'd believe me if I told you something, let's say—not so rational?"

"How irrational are we speaking?" She seems interested now.

"Like, me seeing a disappearing man?" I spit out the words then brace myself for her reaction.

"Uhh—," Ripley begins. "You mean, like a ghost?"

"Yeah, we could say a ghost," I smile. This conversation isn't going half bad. Ripley looks pensive, as if she's crunching numbers. "Let's say I saw a ghost."

"Okay, I think I got it now," she nods. "So, the scale, one through ten right?"

"Right," I smile.

"Right now, at this very moment. I'd have to say—a *nine*. A level nine crazy," she raises her brow. And I frown at her in disappointment.

"What?" I sigh.

"Are you feeling okay, Z?"

"That hurts," I cry as I clench my chest in pain, jokingly. "Good thing it was hypothetical."

We both laugh. But deep down I wonder if I really did see a ghost or if maybe I am just losing it. Ripley opens her mouth to begin talking again, but we are interrupted by someone. And I let out a sigh of relief.

"He's gone, fret no longer, ladies. Just saw him walk out of the lobby," our visitor announces. It seems like everyone is spying on everyone these days.

"Who did you see?" Ripley asks.

"Well, I didn't technically *see* him," he admits. "But I knew it was him because his Tesla was waiting out front for him like some kind of spaceship. What level of douche do you have to be to not let the valet drive your car just to avoid tipping? The dude is a gazillionaire."

That's Kevin Sing, he works in Radiology. I guess one of the perks of working on the 1st floor is that you get to see everyone that comes and goes. But it's a wonder he sees anything at all these days since he's always on the 5th floor it seems.

Visiting.

But I believe Miss Ripley Wells may have something to do with that.

"You know, they've been paging Radiology for the past fifteen minutes. Shouldn't you be there? You know, working? Taking X-Rays?" I remark. Then dip my hand into the bag of chips he's holding and grab a Cheeto puff.

"Oh? Maybe they should check the 4th floor. I might not be the only one they find," he glares at me and I glare back, munching on my puff.

"Touché, my friend. Touché," I nod as I steal another Cheeto and leave them to their flirting.

(102)

Mr. Silverstone has left the building and now I'm debating whether I should follow him home or not. This guy is turning out to be a dead end. I've gotten virtually no information off him.

But just as I'm about to head out, I spot the Earthling again from this morning. The one that was hiding in the meeting room with Silverstone.

The one you've been looking for all day.

My conscience snaps.

"Shut up!" I snap back. Embarrassed at the confession I've just made to myself. "She must be a nurse," I note, glancing over to the clock on the wall. "But why is she still here? It's after 3:30. She should be off by now."

Not that I know what time she gets off or

anything.

I'm beginning to sound like some kind of stalker. Seeing her now, though, makes me feel silly. She looks fairly well for the amount of worry I've been lugging around all day. But you can never really tell these days.

"You know what? I'll just check on her one last time before I go. Better to be safe than sorry." I slide behind a door and continue to spy on her. Listening closely as she converses with her friends.

They chat for several minutes and I rejoice when she finally starts saying her goodbyes and her friend walks off. But she remains.

What now, Earthling?

The girl starts digging through her bag then pulls something out. "Earphones?" I shrug. Still intrigued, I watch as she pops one end of the wire into her phone and the other two ends with the buds into her ears. She presses something on her screen that sets a sound off in her head. A pleasant melody begins to play and she nods along to the beat as it blasts from her ears.

"Man, she's beautiful," the words leave my lips without permission. But I don't take them back.

Shamelessly, I continue to gawk at her. Her dark brown ponytail hypnotizing me as it bounces up and down. Envious every time it brushes up against her slightly pink cheek when it goes up. Wishing I could feel her skin, too.

I close my eyes, swimming in the vibrations that are coming from her earphones and I drift away. Following close behind her as if I'd lost control of my body. When an alert sounds in my head and the spell I'm under seems to break. It's an IM from the Commander at the Galaxy Defender Headquarters in Xia.

IM is our primary source of communication in the galaxy. IM is short for Internal Messaging. Which is so much more convenient than cell phones that blast tons of radiation into your brain. Honestly, I don't know why Earthlings choose to make themselves sick over simple technology that we are all already preprogrammed with.

I listen to the message. The Commander is requesting an update. Worst timing possible right now, but I quickly send him a brief summary to fill him in. Attaching a small clip of the meeting so he can identify the other man. All while trying not to lose track of the girl.

What about the girl!

My conscience reminds me.

"I'm getting there," I shake my head. I was hoping to keep her a secret, but apparently even my brain is preprogrammed to blindly follow orders. I obediently send a second clip of the Earthling girl that I found next.

Or that found you.

There's just something about her. But what makes her so fascinating to me? No Earthling has ever intrigued me. Not enough to make me want to know more about them.

"But this girl—she makes me want to know *everything* about her," I say out loud.

Wow, I sound insane.

I can't believe myself.

"What the hell is wrong with me?" Although I may seem to have an infatuation with the Earthling girl, I still don't know why she was in that room with Silverstone. I'd never imagine her to be involved with someone like *him*. I may not know her, but a gut feeling tells me she's innocent in all of this. Which leads me to the second topic I need to discuss with the Commander.

Protection for the Earthling.

Commander: "What of this Earthling?"

He starts first.

Me: "Sir, it seems she may have been at the wrong place at the wrong time. And heard too much. I fear they might come looking for her."

Commander: "Very well. You know what to do, make sure she remains safe. I don't need any casualties this time. Is that understood?"

Me: "Yes, sir."

I respond diligently.

A smirk spreads across my face in accomplishment. And I do as I was instructed to do. I continue to follow her.

The Earthling leads us to the parking lot where I assume her vehicle to be. We get to her car and when she drives out, I head out with her.

But I don't go inside. The last thing I want is to risk being caught in case she actually can see me. Instead, I hover inches above her car. Stealthy and undetected. Flying from left to right as she swerves and swivels in and out of traffic like a maniac.

Is she lost or something?

After taking two detours, for whatever reason, we finally arrive at her place. Or what I assume to be where she lives since it's her last stop. This place looks more like a prison than a home, though.

"Why is everything always gates and chains with these people? Always trying to keep someone out or keep someone in."

Earthlings and their trust issues.

Whatever the case, this girl is a horrible driver. I'm just glad I don't have to sit inside the car with her.

If a hitman doesn't get her, her own driving sure will.

My conscience is being an insensitive smart ass. After she parks, I jump off the car and hide behind a garage, still watching her. Waiting patiently for her to get out of the car so I can plan my next move. But why is she taking so long? What is she doing in there?

Through the rear window, I can see her fidgeting around with something. She does this for several minutes. Then she stops moving. Just when I think she's taken up residence in there, she reappears. Slamming her door shut as she exits her vehicle and runs off as lights flash behind her and the car beeps.

Why is she running like that?

"Maybe she *is* in on it?"

Why else would she be acting so suspicious?

"What if she thinks someone's out to get her because of what she overheard?" I argue with myself. Trying to defend this complete stranger that I know nothing about. Then I nod. "Yeah, that's definitely it." Proud at how brilliant I am and how fast I can come up with rational conclusions. Another loud slam startles me. Coming from her apartment upstairs. I assume she's safe inside now. "She's a feisty one, this one." Before I go up, I take one last look around to make sure no one followed us here.

(Zara)

After surviving nearly two accidents with my reckless driving, I miraculously manage to make it home in one piece.

I think we lost him.

"Or her?" I correct myself. "Well—whoever was following me."

If someone was.

Maybe I'm just being paranoid.

But then why do I still feel eyes on me? If someone is watching me, I hope they know I'm aware of them. And they can't have me. Not without a fight. I know their plans. They want to murder me and sell my organs for a quick buck.

"Organs go for a lot of money on the black market, you know?"

I read that somewhere.

I lock the doors and sit in my car safely while I gain some courage to get out. Meanwhile, I formulate a plan. Do I run? Or do I walk?

Deep down I know this is just my yearly September paranoia talking. But there was something about that guy in the window. Why can't I get him out of my damn head? Maybe I just need a distraction. Something to get my mind off things. I pull out my phone quickly and text

Ripley.

Me: "Hey Rip, can you come over after work?"

I sit there with my phone in my hand, anxiously awaiting a response. When I see the three little bubbles pop up at the bottom of the screen. She's already responding. I'm sure even if she does have plans tonight, she'd blow them off in a second. And not even tell me just so that I don't feel guilty about it. I sigh heavily, then start writing out another text before she finishes typing hers.

Me: "Never mind, gonna head out later, I forgot. I hope you have a good night at work with Kevin (smooch emoji). Thanks again for covering for me. See you tomorrow!"

I hit send. But here I am, still sitting in my car. My Jeep is already cool from being off for so long. I remove the key from the ignition, then fumble with my key chain until I find what I'm looking for.

"Gotcha!" I hold out my apartment key, then jam it in between my fingers like wolverine's claws. "Now I'm prepared for a fight."

Or flight.

"We don't know how I'll feel yet," I shrug.

All I know is that if someone *is* following me, they'll sure get what's coming to them. And in this instance, it's my apartment key. I hold it up to demonstrate how I will scare off the murderers, peering at myself in the rearview mirror. Then I swipe my hand around violently.

Pretty terrifying if you ask me.

I open my car door slowly. Just wide enough for me to slip through, then I slam it shut. Hitting the lock button as I run off to my apartment door. Everything inside me is screaming. Then I fly up the stairs as if I actually were being chased.

After quite a struggle, I finally manage to get my door open. It's hard to unlock a door with a key in weapon position. Once I'm inside, I shut the door and lock it as fast as I can. Then shove a chair under the knob.

Yeah. That'll keep them out.

My conscience snaps with sarcasm.

I take a step back and admire my makeshift security system with pride.

"Take that, organ stealer. I'm not afraid of you!" I yell at the top of my lungs. Okay, that was a bit far. I hope no one heard me. I drop my things on the kitchen counter.

"I really need a shower," I shake my head.

And a chill pill.

(102)

"Looks like the coast is clear," I zap myself

closer to her door, but stay downstairs. Pacing back and forth while I babble with myself. "Should I go in?" The Commander was very clear. I need to stop being so impulsive and think before I act. I can't let what happened last time happen again.

Better just wait out here.

There's a loud banging coming from upstairs where the Earthling girl lives. But as much as I want to zap myself up there to satisfy my insatiable need to act, I convince myself not to worry. That's until I hear her scream.

"Did she just yell for help?" I stop pacing. "That's my cue." I zap myself upstairs to rescue her without a second thought.

But when I get inside. She's not there.

"Where are you, Earthling?" My heart pounds with both worry and adrenaline. I don't know what to expect. Using my thermal vision, I scan the apartment. It's small, so she's easy to find. "There you are." A smile spreads across my face. She doesn't seem to be in any type of distress after all.

Shocker.

"Will you shut up?" I tell my conscience. "Always ruining the moment."

Now that I know the Earthling is safe, I cave into my curiosity and snoop around. When I spot the wooden chair pressed up against the door.

For some reason it makes me smile and not laugh in ridicule. As if it were cute instead of stupid. Which isn't like me to find something which could debatably be called stupid, cute. What's going on with me? I wiggle the chair a bit and it falls over.

"Shit!" I curse. Then catch it quickly before it hits the ground and blows my cover. "I'll fix this for you, free of charge." I push the chair back up against the door, this time making sure it's secure.

That was kinda cute.

My conscience agrees with me. Suddenly taking a liking to her as well. Another loud thud sounds from her bedroom, stealing my attention.

"The Earthling!" I zap myself over to the other side of the wall without thinking.

When I see her, my eyes become almost glued to her. Instantly making me forget what I even came in for. She's okay. She's just sitting on the edge of her bed. Her hair is down and falling freely over her shoulders in a web of waves. I can see her earphones hanging from her ears again and it somehow fills me with warmth. A strange feeling of comfort.

Her head is bopping to the sound coming from them and her lips mesmerize me as she lip sings the words to the song. I can't help but stare.

She giggles loudly at her phone. Making

my grin grow. I admire her laugh. It's deep and hearty, like she means it. The way her cheeks turn the slightest shade of pink when she smiles, giving her already perfect olive skin an envious blush. I can't seem to get enough.

"What is happening to me?" I shake my head. "Why am I acting like an idiot?"

Anytime I find myself in her presence, I continue to surprise myself by what a mindless idiot I can become. How does she captivate me this way? This—*Earthling.*

Images from earlier today start to flood my mind. Of that cute ponytail bouncing on her shoulders. And I smile again.

Cute?

"Since when do I find things *cute*?" I can't believe the way I'm acting. This isn't me. She clicks her phone off and the music stops suddenly. Then she yanks out the earbuds, tossing them on the bed. "What is she doing?" I continue to watch her as she pulls a foot up onto her knee and yanks her sock off, then proceeds with the other one.

Maybe she's going to bed already?

"At 4 P.M.?" I roll my eyes at myself. The girl stands up, moving her hands to her waistband next and starts untying her scrub pants. "Oh!" I quickly realize what's going on and try to take a step back, in an attempt to get out of there quickly. But I'm flustered, and it causes me to bump into a chair. I don't react fast enough and it falls over loudly.

Shit!

She heard. Her eyes, big as saucers, dart my way. And I zap off in a flash.

"Did she see me that time?" I really need to be more careful.

(Zara)

As I'm rinsing out the remainder of the shampoo from my hair, I hear my phone chime repeatedly from inside the shower. I try to ignore it but then it chimes two more times, making it seem urgent.

"It must be Ripley, shit!" I reach my arm out through the curtain, dripping water all over the floor, and scoop up my phone. Struggling to unlock it with wet fingers.

Ripley: "So...what's up? You still need me?"

Ripley: "Hello??"

Ripley: "Okay...I'm sorry, you are not a level 9 crazy! Only a level 7..."

Ripley: "Joking! Come on, text me back!"

I read her messages then shake the water off my fingers to reply.

Me: "I'm fine! I'll see you tomorrow."

I shut the water off, shivering as I step out of the shower. The air is chilly on my wet skin, making it instantly cover in goosebumps as soon as it touches it.

As I dry myself I think about my day, recalling every odd occurrence all over again. Who was that man Liam was talking to? And who was that guy in the window? But my demeanor suddenly changes.

"The chair," I gasp. Remembering that it randomly fell over just before I got in the shower. The memory sends a chill up my spine. "What if the ghost followed me home?" I gulp.

The thought of a ghost in my room surprisingly scares me more than the thought of a murderer. I search every corner of the room, not exactly sure what I'm hoping to find, but find nothing.

"I'm watching you," I whisper to nothing, narrowing my eyes at it. But my standoff comes to a sudden halt when my stomach rumbles in a protest for food. "I'm starving. I'd better get some dinner," I talk to myself. Hurriedly, I get dressed to head out.

"Should I walk or should I drive?" I debate. "If I'm going to die, might as well get a little exercise in, right?" I shrug. I told myself this year that I desperately needed to get myself back into shape. I'm nearing thirty, and I don't feel as young as I used to.

I commit to the walk, heading out the front gate, starting onto the main road. There's a diner right up the street passing two street lights. It isn't too far so I decide to go there.

The walk alone takes me only twenty minutes. When I arrive, I drag my exhausted and out of shape butt over to the teenager at the cash register and order a burger and fries. Then my phone chimes again.

Ripley: "Okay, great, because I have a date with Kevin later. Can you believe it? Kevin! Who would have thought?"

I laugh loudly to myself making everyone in the diner turn to stare at me. My face turns crimson, but I shoot them a glare in annoyance. I'm not going to let them ruin my mood. Not today.

They look away instantly, just as I expected. I'm sure they can sense the threat I've been building up inside for those creeps out there, following me. They don't look back, and I could have sworn I saw one lady hush her small baby and tell him to turn around also.

Now I feel bad.

Me: "Not Kevin the X-Ray man? You're kidding! Have fun, and be safe. Call me when you're in."

I respond to Ripley then stick my earbuds

back into my ears, hitting the play button on my phone. The place empties out and I take advantage of the solitude, finishing my food in peace before I also get up to leave.

(102)

My boots stomp loudly with each step as I march back and forth nervously. Pacing the halls at Xia's Department of Defense. Still unable to get that damn Earthling girl out of my head. You'd think with all the shit I've had to deal with in the last 24 hours that an Earthling would be the last thing I'd want occupying my mind. I have a buzzing brain with emergencies I need to get to, but all I can think about is her.

All I want to think about is her.

"Miss Lara," I sigh like some lovesick schoolboy.

The Commander looked her up, and that was all the information he gave me on her. Due to her lack of crimes, her file is closed and secured, unable to be opened by anyone. Privacy is a big thing in the universe. But that doesn't help me when I need to know her name.

Want. Want to know her name.

"I wonder if she's okay," I stop marching. "I did leave in such a hurry. What if the chair frightened her and she didn't shower after all?

What if she left the apartment because she got scared? Or worse!" I gasp. "What if someone kidnapped her!" I clasp my mouth before someone hears me talking to myself. Okay, okay. Maybe I'm being irrational, but the Commander did leave me personally in charge of her safety. "I'll just swing by to make sure that the chair I left stayed in place."

Yeah, sounds rational.

I zap off.

(Zara)

"Maybe that burger was a bad idea," I groan as I hold my stomach.

And our feet are our ride back.

"Shit," I slump out the door, dreading the walk home. Contemplating why I even decided to walk here in the first place. When something distracts me. And a smile instinctively spreads across my face as I pull the earbuds out of my ears and shove them back into my bag. "No freaking way. Is that a dog?"

It must be my lucky day.

My mood instantly changes. And I think my stomach ache even goes away. But the poor thing looks terrified and as I get closer, I spot something blue around it's neck. Believing it could be a collar, I cautiously walk over to find out.

"I was right," I conclude nearly reaching the dog. "Well, looks like I have to return him home. He has a family, and it's my obligation now," I convince myself. When the shaggy, blonde dog spots me, his tail goes into a frenzy. Swinging violently from side to side making his entire body convulse with excitement.

"Woah! Take it easy, big guy. I'm going to help you find your family. Just let me take a look at that tag there," I assure him, slowly moving in to touch his fur. It's soft and feels clean and fluffy, a sign that he hasn't been in the streets too long.

When I scratch his chest, his body relaxes. "That's a good boy," I tell him. "See? That was easy. Nurse by day, dog rescuer by—almost night."

We should make business cards.

As I continue to scratch him, I twirl his collar around his neck with my fingers but don't see a tag on it.

Shoot.

"I guess I'll just have to take you home with me until I can find your owner," I explain to the dog as if he could understand me. "I'm sure Hector will understand— right?" Trying to think quickly, I search through my bag for something I could use as a leash so that I won't lose him. But find nothing but useless junk and old wrappers. "Shit." I look around and think for a moment. When a light bulb goes off in my head.

I dive back into my bag, searching frantically. Then rip out my earphones. "It was nice knowing ya," I shrug. Then I squat down next to Fred.

That's his name, we just named him that.

But I'm really struggling to get the wires through his collar because he won't stop moving. My technique of holding him with one hand while trying to loop the wire with the other has proved no success.

"Sit still, Fred! You don't want me losing you again, do you?" I warn him, mid-wrestle. But apparently, that's exactly what he wants because his collar rips out of my hand just as he darts off. Sprinting full speed ahead. "No! Fred! Come back!" I yell and before I can even think, I take off after him. Running as fast as I can. Full belly and all. I ran track in high school, I can catch a little dog easy. "Please don't throw up. Please don't throw up," I chant in an almost prayer as I run.

Yeah, good luck with that.
You haven't run in ten years!

(102)

I'm back inside her apartment. But it's

eerily quiet this time. The place looks deserted.

"She's—gone?" I half ask myself, half proclaim.

Where'd she go?

The chair I secured at the door is gone, too. I rush into her bedroom but find it also empty. Then I check the bathrooms, still nothing. "What if someone took her?" Thoughts about the worst things imaginable start to surface in my brain. I zap myself outside.

Cranking up my sensitivity as high as it goes. Trying to catch her scent anywhere. But I can't get anything. It seems she's been gone for a while now.

"Her car," I immediately note it's lack of absence, then I really start to panic. "Where could she have gone? Why would she leave without her car?" Did someone take her? I'm getting worried now.

Why am I getting worried?

I set up a radius around her apartment, estimating the distance she must have stayed in. Accounting for the time I've been away and how far I think she could have gotten on two feet. I zap myself high up, trying to find something that could point me in the right direction. When miraculously, I catch something. A brief scent.

I zap myself from lamp post to lamp post, surveilling the sidewalks and roads. Still no visual. But I know I'm getting closer, I can feel it. I get a strong scent and look over towards a small diner across the way. That's when I see her walking out.

"Gotcha," I smile. It looks like she's heading back towards the main road.

Did she walk here? Why didn't she take her car?

This girl has me puzzled. But I follow her nonetheless. She walks through the parking lot, towards me. But then gets distracted and wanders off the opposite way.

What is she doing?

I take a seat on a lamp post and watch her as if I were watching a live action play. As she goes from petting a random street dog to suddenly chasing the animal down.

Why is she chasing a dog?

I get up quickly and start chasing her too.

We go on for about a mile. Surprising me at how much speed she has. The squirrel is leading the show and I guess I'm part of it now. We're like a train of dummies. Not really sure where we're going but we're going anyway.

"This is a killer chase," I admit struggling to keep up. The dog dips under a branch that's hanging low from a tree, and he gains some distance. "Ooh!" I wince as the branch smacks the girl right in the face. "Ouch! That's got to hurt."

But it doesn't slow her down. She goes even faster and I speed up too. Oh no, the dog is getting close to the intersection. Is it gonna stop?

Uh-oh.

"Hello! Girl! Are you watching the road ahead of you!" I shout.

3

NOT TODAY, DEATH.

(Zara)

I speed up, adrenaline racing through my veins. I've almost got him. Fred gets to the street. "Oh no," I gulp, but keep running. There's a bus headed the way he's headed. Going into full throttle, I jump forward trying to catch him but miss. Then he takes off even faster. "Shit!"

Fred has almost gotten to the other side of the road, and I encourage him to continue. The bus is still a distance away, I think we're actually going to make it. "Go! Faster!" I shout. I'm catching up quicker than anticipated. Inches away now, I reach down and go for his collar. "Gotcha," I whisper to Fred, just feet away from the sidewalk now. "We made it boy," I loosen my grip to try to tie him down with my earphones.

When all of a sudden, without warning, the bus driver starts to blare his horn at us. Fred gets spooked and manages to escape my grasp. And is now running back into the road again.

"No! Fred!" I scream, trying to make a run for it again.

The bus lets out a ear piercing screech as he floors the brakes. My hand reaches down and snatches Fred up by the collar once more. When something pulls me away. Making me fly a good ten feet up into the air. But somewhere between the take-off, Fred's collar slips out of my hand, and he runs right back into the direction of the bus.

"No! Fred!" I yell as I start falling. It all happens so fast. I brace myself for my landing while inevitably watching the accident unfold before me. When I land gently on the grass.

What the hell?

The scene fills quickly with people. Everyone is now huddled in a circle around me and some around the dog. I force myself up while everyone tries to push me back down. Insisting that I stay still and wait for the paramedics to arrive. Just in case I may be paralyzed.

Can't be paralyzed if I can stand, people.

I look over the crowd, trying to find Fred. When I see him, lying lifeless on the pavement. My earphones still hanging from his collar and a pool of blood beginning to form around his beautiful golden head.

"Oh, Fred," I sigh. A tear rolling down my eye.

The poor guy didn't make it. The bus

driver rushes over immediately and apologizes. Pulling something out of her wallet. She jots down her information and hands it to me. "Just in case," she says. While insisting that I get looked over by a medical professional. I grab the note and thank her, sticking the piece of paper into my front jean pocket then getting back on my way.

"Wow, lady, that was awesome! Where did that dude come from?" A young guy in a red beanie and giant headphones stops me.

"Dude?" I question him.

"Yeah. He just appeared out of nowhere!"

Apparently, he was sitting at the bus stop when the bus hit the dog and witnessed my escape from the clutches of death.

"It was a woman bus driver, actually. Figures," I laugh at the irony. "But yeah, I know right." I walk off. Returning to my trip home, trying not to get into any more trouble before I get there.

(102)

"That was way too close," I shake my head. "But you see? She didn't see me." Somehow in my delusional state, I still find myself proud. Still trying to convince myself like an idiot that I've actually changed.

But that Halfling kid saw us.

My conscience always seems to point out the things I'm trying to avoid.

"Great." Now I have to go find him and get rid of that memory. I zap myself high up into the sky until I spot him.

But before I go, I shoot one last glance down at the poor dog I wasn't able to save. There's still a crowd formed around him.

I'm sorry, Fred.

Zap*

(Zara)

The adrenaline's beginning to wear off, and now I'm starting to feel uneasy about what happened. What I felt. Or thought I felt.

How did I do that?

"I jumped like *really* high," I say out loud. Beginning to wonder if maybe I was hallucinating the whole thing. But at some point, I could have sworn I felt a grip on my arms as if someone was lifting me off the ground.

Like a guardian angel?

I laugh at myself. "That's insane. Completely ludicrous," I shake my head. But how did I land so gently? I'm more sore from that branch that smacked me in the face than I am by that fall.

Today is weird. And I need to get home fast before it gets any weirder.

"Maybe today is just my lucky day?" I half smile. Trying to make myself feel better. But seriously, what else could I get into at this point?

As I walk up the familiar street, my apartment gates finally come into view. I'm almost there. This walk took a lot longer than anticipated, that ten minute chase really drained me. But I've somehow managed to make it home safe while also managing to not get abducted by aliens.

Or worse, human traffickers.

My body tenses up in response to my thoughts. I'm getting that feeling again, like someone's watching me. My eyes pinball around, trying not to move my head. Then I take a breath, readying myself for a sprint.

"Leave me alone!" I yell as I take off like my life depended on it. But I'm stopped before my feet even get a chance to leave the pavement. Crashing head-on into something that wasn't there before. And scream a bloody scream, right into the face of a stranger.

"Woah, not so loud," the man tries to cover my mouth.

"Hey! Back off, man," I push off my attacker. I can't believe I was right. But I'm prepared. I've trained for this.

No, you haven't.

"Please, I'm not going to hurt you," he assures me, still trying to touch me.

"Get your damn hands off of me! Help!" I continue to shout. "I have pepper spray!" I add.

Yeah, good idea—lie!

"Really?" he chuckles.

"Yeah. And a gun too! In here," I point. "Inside my bag. Don't make me get it out, or I will. Don't test me!"

Wow, I'm impressed. You're beginning to scare me.

The man noticeably holds back a laugh.

"Is this amusing to you?" I narrow my eyes at him.

"Look, girl, I don't want any trouble," he responds.

"No, *you* look, *boy.*"

"Boy?" he chuckles.

"Man—boy, whatever! I just found out today that I may or may not be crazy, so if you don't mind. I'm in a very sensitive place right now," I take a step back, staring down my attacker.

"Are you finished?" he laughs again.

"Wait a minute," I step towards him. "I recognize you. You're the guy I saw at the hospital. You were peeping on Liam Silverstone, weren't you?" I grin letting my guard down for a brief second.

"No—I."

"Who are you! Who sent you? Are you here to steal my kidneys?" I point my invisible gun at him from inside my purse.

"I'm not gonna steal your kidneys," he smiles at me genuinely. And I shoot him another glare.

"You're not?" I rebuttal.

"No. I have my own, thank you. Here, let me help you with that gun," he reaches out towards me. Sending me into a panic.

I fidget around inside my bag. Looking for a weapon of some sort to defend myself. When I find my key. Grasping it tightly, I close my eyes and swing. Stabbing something. The man grabs my arm as he hollers in agony. But when I open my eyes to inspect the damage, nothing could prepare me for what I see.

"What the fuck!" I shout. "How did I get in here?" I'm inside. In *my* apartment.

"Was this really necessary?" The strange man says as he points to his gashing eye. My key chain still dangling from it like a decorative earring.

"You're here too?"

"Uh—yeah," he responds as if it were a dumb question.

"How did you get us here? And why do I feel dizzy?" I grab my head while my balance starts to give out.

"I'm sorry, I had to do that. Here," he pulls a chair out at my kitchen table for me to sit. "It may feel a little weird when you teleport for the first time. Might want to take a seat."

"Teleport?" I repeat in a surprisingly calm tone. Now I'm equally terrified and intrigued.

I brush my back up against the wall, keeping my eyes on him at all times as I squirm my way to the couch. Then take a seat there. Away from him.

Maybe he should go get that eye looked at.

I did get him pretty good.

"Now, if you don't mind, this is really starting to irritate me," he casually reaches up to his face and yanks the key from his eye. Blood gushing like a river down his face and dripping onto his shirt.

Forcing my eyes away in shock, I hold back a gag. I'm a nurse, and even this is too much gore for me.

"What the hell, man! What the hell!" I stomp. "You couldn't do that in the bathroom or something? I just had a very big dinner that I'm not planning to share with you," my head begins to spin again.

I think we need to lay down.

"Hey? Girl? Are you okay?" his words echo faintly in the background, until I can't make them out anymore. Everything turns into a blur, and the room slowly darkens until everything is pitch black.

"Hey, what's—?" I try to speak, just before I pass out.

(102)

"Fuck. I killed her." Her body is toppled over her chair.

Is she dead?

I check her pulse.

"She's alive!" I shout. Jumping up and down. "Okay—we're okay," I scoop her into my arms and carry her to her bedroom. "She just needs to rest. Everything's going to be okay."

I fight the panic that tries to set in. I've never teleported an Earthling before. Or let one see me. Not since—.

What did you do?

"The Commander will understand, right? It was necessary. She was almost killed!"

But how does that explain why you let her see you?

Shit. Shit. Shit.

"It's okay. I'll think of something," desperately trying to make myself feel better. "For now, she has to get some rest, and I'll be right here when she wakes up."

Maybe we should get that key cleaned?

I shrug my shoulders.
"Maybe."

4

COWBOYS AND ALIENS

(Zara)

My head is pounding when I wake up. I sit up, leaning my back against the headboard of the bed. Trying to pinpoint exactly where the hell I am. The wood is cold on my hot skin. I can feel it through my thin shirt and it somewhat soothes me.

What time is it?

I search frantically around for my phone. But it's too dark to see anything. My cat, Binks, pounces on the bed, startling me. But causing the screen on my phone to light up. Then starts meowing uncontrollably.

"You found my phone!" I grab it and check the time. "It's 3A.M.?!" I shout when I see it. My cat ignores me and continues to meow at me. "What's wrong, Binks? You hungry, boy?"

I scoop him into my arms and together we head into the kitchen. I pop open a can of cat food and dump it into his bowl. He purrs happily and starts eating. I scratch his head then go fetch myself a glass of water and some aspirin for this headache.

But I almost lose it and let out a scream without warning. There's a man sitting casually at my dining table. Watching me.

"Not this again," he sighs.

"What?" I pull a drawer open and go for a knife. But he grabs my wrist first, stopping me. "Who are you?"

Why am I getting déjà vu?

After I manage to slip out of his grasp I grab the knife.

"Woah, take it easy with the screams. Someone's going to think you're being murdered," the man says as he puts his hand out to calm me.

"Don't touch me!" I swipe at it with my weapon, causing him to retract it. "Who are you? Why are you in my apartment?" I eye him from top to bottom.

Do I know him?

"Come on, let's just put that knife down before someone gets hurt again."

"Again?" I frown, dropping the knife slightly. Why does he look so familiar? Foggy memories begin to surface, and I shake my head as his face appears in them. "Hey! I do know you. I saw you in my dreams." I walk around him, towards the front door. Still in a menacing stance.

"Dreaming about me already, are we?" he smirks at me. I reach down quickly and pick up the shoe that's lying on the floor beside me and toss it at him.

"Shut it!"

"Ouch! I'm joking! Geez," he rubs his head. "It wasn't a dream, it really happened."

"What? What really happened?" I ask. Kind of afraid to hear the answer.

"It was me who saved you from that bus earlier. Before you passed out. Now here I am getting this very warm thank you. After saving your life. You Earthlings, I swear. Always resorting to violence."

Wait, what?

"Earthlings?" I pause, scrunching my nose. "And what do you mean you saved me? No one saved me. I saved myself. Clearly, you need to get your eyes checked."

Speaking of eyes, now I remember!

"Yeah. Thanks for the advice," he points to his eye.

"Hey—what happened to your eye?" I ask, looking around for my key.

"My eye, uh—it got better," he grins.

"Oh?"

"No offense, Earthling, but did you really think you made that jump all alone?" he scoffs and turns his back to me. "The Halfling saw me, you know. He told you himself."

"The—*what*?" I question. Not sure what he's referring to. He reaches for something on my kitchen counter, and I stick out my knife to defend myself. "Hey! Not so fast there. What are you getting?" I point my knife at him again.

"Here's your key," he shrugs. Flashing me what looks like a dimple.

Why am I oddly attracted to this weird guy?

"Thanks," I snatch it from him. Then I inspect him more closely.

He is a pretty good-looking guy. He's tall and tan with gray contrasting eyes. Some slight stubble on his cheeks. He's wearing a black t-shirt that you can still see dry blood on from when he pulled the key out of his eye. A mossy green buttoned-up shirt with the sleeves cut off rigidly, and left completely unbuttoned hangs casually off his shoulders. There's a funny fanny pack draped across his chest and a pair of dark khaki cargo pants are securely tucked into his black leather boots.

"Done checking me out?" he smirks.

"Wait a minute," I begin. My head spinning as images of the bus crash flash through it. "That was—*you*?" I look down and think back to what happened. What I *felt*.

"Yup," he stands there proudly with his hands at his waist.

"Were you grabbing my arms?" I inquire curiously, "I felt that. But why couldn't I see you?" Trying to wrap my head around it, but it doesn't make any logical sense.

"Because I didn't let you see me," he says.

"What? What do you mean you didn't *let* me see you?" I question him. "And how did your eye just get better? What are you, some kind of alien or something?"

"Alien?" he scoffs. "I am *not* an alien, sweetheart. I am a human *being*, just like *you*."

That seemed to hit a nerve.

"But—how? You can't be *human*?"

"Of course I can," he rolls his eyes. "What? Did you really think you were the only humans in the Universe? Come on."

He's really getting a kick out of this.

"No!" I snap back. I'm a huge fan of Ancient Aliens in case he didn't know. "I knew there was something out there. I just didn't expect it to look like, well—like *me*." I walk around him and poke his back. "You look so—*real*."

And not half bad for being an alien.

He rolls his eyes again. "What is that supposed to mean? I *am* real!" He starts getting defensive again and zaps himself to the couch to sit away from me.

"Woah! How'd you do that?" I shriek.

"That?" He disappears then reappears. "I just teleported. All humans can do that."

"You see, that's where you're wrong, Alien Dude. Us real humans *can't* do that. We don't have magic powers," I get closer to him. And take a seat across the couch that he's on. Cuddling up on the orange loveseat.

"I don't have magic powers, Earthling. These are abilities all humans have. You just don't use them. For whatever reason," he explains, standing up and starting to scope out my apartment.

What is he looking for?

I stand also, quickly trying to hide the mess that's lying around before he sees it. Then I toss it on the couch behind him.

"So—if it isn't magic, then what is it?" I interrogate him. Very intrigued now.

"Well, it's a force of some sort. Like energy."

"A force?" I raise my brows, very pleased in the way this conversation is going.

"Yeah. Haven't you ever watched Star Wars? It's kind of like that," he explains.

I can't believe this.

I must still be asleep. I pinch myself but when the shock of pain radiates up my arm, I know this isn't a dream.

Maybe I hit my head somewhere, and that's why I have a headache? But he's very real. I touched him with my bare hands and everything. I narrow my eyes at him.

How do I know he's not lying?

What if this is all just some prank?

Well, one thing I know for sure is there certainly is a force of some sort that allowed him to zip across my apartment like that. And to have saved me from the bus without even being seen? The alien stands up and starts walking into the hallway.

"Okay, Alien Dude, let's say I do believe you." I follow behind him as he peeks into my bathroom.

"You're gonna have to stop calling me that."

"Hey!" I run in front of him. Shutting the door and sprawling myself over it. "A little privacy? Geez. Do you not have boundaries out there on Mars?"

"Mars?" he smirks.

That smirk that's making me not want him to be a stranger anymore.

"What?" I scoff. Trying to remember what we were talking about. "Why are you laughing?"

"You're funny," he grins. "So, let's say you do believe me. Can we get back to that?"

"Ah! Yes," I continue, remembering what we were talking about. The smirk distracted me.

Or was it the dimple?

"Hello?" he waves his hand in my face.

"Let's say I believe you," I begin again. "Why are you here?" He's still standing over me in front of my bathroom door. I clear my throat, and he backs away.

Boundaries, Alien Dude.

"Sorry," he begins. "I'm here to protect you, Miss Lara." His face is serious now and his tone seems genuinely concerned.

"Protect me from what? Or who? And how do you know my name?" I question, walking back into the kitchen, just in case I need a weapon again.

Not that it would do me any good. The whole key in the eye situation tells me this guy won't be going down too easily.

"Something big is going on, Miss Lara. But I'm here to make sure it doesn't happen and that you're safe," he assures me. Why do I believe him?

Of course, you do.

Is that your mouth talking or your vagina?

"Something big? Like what?" I inquire curiously.

"That's all you need to know," he warns. "The less you know, the better. I don't want anyone putting a hit out on you."

"A hit! For me?" the thought terrifies me. "Why would anyone want to kill me!" I'm crying now.

Why am I crying?

"It's okay, Earthling. You don't need to be afraid."

"Look, I don't know anything about anything, okay? Who could possibly want me killed? I'm just a nurse! I don't even own a car! It's a lease!" I drop to my knees and begin sobbing into my hands. When he comes down to my level and pulls my hands into his.

"Earthling, nothing is going to happen to you," he assures me, his eyes peering dangerously into mine. "Even if you don't see me, I'll always be there. Protecting you. I promise," he smiles warmly.

"Really?" I sob.

"Yes," he puts his hand up to my face and wipes my tears away with his thumb before they roll down my cheek. "I won't let anything happen to you. I swear on my life."

Are humans allowed to be attracted to aliens?

"Thank you," I mutter in a shaky voice. Humiliated now at my reaction. He gets to his feet and offers me a hand to help me up. I accept.

His hand *feels* human. It's a little rough, but it's warm. I wipe my tears with my sleeve when I get to my feet. And he gives me a warm smile.

"Do you feel better now?" he asks. I nod

my head.

"So, what planet are you from then? Since you didn't come from Mars and clearly, you're not an Earthling like me," I go sit back down on the couch. He waits for me to turn back over to him. Then he clears his throat and starts again.

"May I sit, Miss Lara?" he gestures towards the seat next to me on the couch. Uncomfortably formal.

I really wish he'd stop calling me that.

"Yeah, sure," I blush and quickly move the junk I gathered there earlier when I was trying to clean up. Then he sits.

"First off, it's the year 2020, and you still think Earth is the only planet with intelligent life?" The look of confusion on my face answers his question. And he lets out a small laugh before he continues. "We'll save that conversation for another day. I come from Xia."

"Xia?" I repeat.

"Yes. That's my home."

"What's it like there?" I question.

"It's beautiful," he explains. "Green, untainted and peaceful. Nothing like Earth."

"Like Earth? What's so bad about Earth?" I frown.

"Well, for starters, I'm surprised any of you have even made it to a hundred years with all of this pollution. It's horrible here."

Excuse me?

This alien is really starting to irk me with all this smack talk about Earth. It may not be the best place in this Galaxy, but it's *my* home.

"Hey, can you take a chill pill with the insults, ET? I happen to live here."

Who does he think he is?

"I'm sorry, but it's true," he shrugs.

"If Earth is so bad, then why are you even here?" I'm unnecessarily angry now. "Why don't you just let Earthlings like me get hit by buses or die of natural causes like all the other friendly aliens on all the other planets?"

"Okay, okay. I'll stop," he promises. "I apologize."

"Good," I scoff. "So, tell me. What exactly *is* Xia, anyway?"

"Just another world in your galaxy," he explains.

"Like Earth?"

"Yes. But it's weird, you only live in one section of Earth that you've made inhabitable. The rest is closed off."

"Closed off? For what?" I raise an eyebrow at him. Unsure whether to believe him or not.

"Heck if I know," he shrugs again. "You Earthlings are very strange."

"Oh, *we're* strange?" I snort. "You're one to talk."

"Let me ask you something, where do you think people got the technology to build the pyramids back in ancient times?" he raises an eyebrow back at me.

I think to myself for a second, I've never actually thought about that before. But I won't admit it to this smart ass alien know-it-all.

"Strength?" I answer quietly. And he laughs. "Okay. Tell me then, what else is out there in *my* world that I don't know about, smart guy?"

"A whole lot of world," he puts his hand on my shoulder.

"And how does one get there?" I ask.

"By traveling through space. That's how you get anywhere. All I'm going to say is, those stars out there aren't all that they seem."

"Travel through—space?"

"*Teleporting.*" He says it so casually as if speaking about star travel were normal.

"That's unbelievable. It makes sense though. I've actually always kind of thought that's how it worked."

"Really? You've thought about this before?" He gives me an incredulous look, as if he doesn't believe me.

"Yes, of course. I've always been interested in space travel. I've just never had the time to look into it before."

Note to self: look this stuff up!

"Too busy saving animals, I presume?" he teases, raising an eyebrow again. We both laugh, and whatever tension was left between us, dissipates.

"Something like that," I chuckle. "More like people. Not as cute, but still pretty rewarding." I make him laugh.

"You're funny," he mentions a second time.

"Anyway," I change the subject before I get lost in his dreamy eyes again. "Is this about that secret meeting you saw me crash? Is that why you're here? Because honestly, I was just trying to hide from this guy—and then they came in. Before I knew it, they were talking about red birds and flu shots. I heard nothing else. Honest."

"Inoculations?" he mumbles something under his breath.

"What was that?" I ask, unable to understand him. He looks like he's thinking. Then he looks away from me and down at the ground, shaking his head. "What is it?" I question him again. But he ignores me and heads into the kitchen.

What the hell is going on?

Alien Dude must have broken down, because he can't seem to hear me. He just sits down at the table, facing the front door. Either deep in thought or out of juice. Because he's not saying a word to me.

"What is it!" I shout again, this time with more urgency.

"They're planning to use inoculations," he

murmurs to himself. "That has to be it."

"What? Do they not have vaccines in space?" I question. But before he answers me, the door begins to jiggle.

"Were you expecting someone?" He looks at me.

"Shit." I'm suddenly reminded just as the door swings open. "Ripley!" I yelp in genuine surprise.

"Hey, weirdo. Who are you talking to?" She looks around, tossing her keys onto the counter.

I turn back quickly to Alien Dude. But he's gone.

Darn, I still had so many questions.

"I—uh. No one," I lie.

I'm becoming such a liar these days.

She raises an eyebrow at me, clearly not buying my bullshit. But I change the subject quickly before she presses any further and I end up spilling the beans on accident.

"Sooo—," I begin. "How was your date with Kevin the X-Ray Man?" I tease her for a change.

Her face softens and she gives me a smile. Then she hops onto the big couch in the living room and calls me over. Tapping the seat next to her.

"I thought you'd never ask," she raises an eyebrow. "Sit, I will tell you everything."

"Hold that thought," I sneak back into the kitchen and pull out a carton of ice cream from the freezer and pluck a couple of spoons from the silverware drawer. Then I walk over and sit next to her. I hand her a spoon and she takes it happily. "Now, tell me *everything*," I say.

5

PRINCE CHARMING

(102)

"You did *what*, 102?!" the Commander's thundering voice rattles the room. I cringe, trying to keep my distance on my side of it.

He's about to rip you a new one.

"I'm sorry, sir. But like I said before, the situation was completely unavoidable," I lie.

"Do you really expect me to believe that?" he fumes.

Was it really unavoidable, though?

"Shut up!" I snap at my conscience.

"What did you say, 102?" The Commander is pissed now. "Did you just tell me to *shut up*?"

Great. Now I've done it.

"Absolutely not, sir. I said—I got the kid," I lie again. If smoke could come out of someone's nose, I think I'd be seeing it right now.

"I really hope you didn't screw this up, Sergeant," he closes his eyes and rubs his temples.

Shit.

"I didn't," I defend myself as if he didn't already know me. "I erased only the memory of him seeing me and that's it. And no one else saw me. Sir," I add for good measure.

We are never allowed to go into an Earthling's mind. Or anyone's mind for that matter. Especially not someone who is defenseless and unable to mentally protect themselves. In other words—*Earthlings!*

"Are you certain no one else saw you?" the Commander continues to interrogate me.

"I'm positive," I assure him without actually being certain of it myself.

"And the Earthling girl? Is she safe?" He lets out a grunt as he pulls himself up from his giant chair.

He's a massive man. He's much older than I am and looks it. The equivalent to his appearance is that of a middle-aged, Earthling man. They say he chose this age to seem more intimidating.

He was right; it is.

There are some Galaxy Defenders who are in command that decided to stay looking like teenage boys. It's hard to take them serious sometimes.

But hey, who am I to judge?

“Um—yes, sir. I left as soon as I was sure she was safe.”

“Very well then. Nothing we can do now. I want you back at Silverstone Health at 0500 PST, understood?”

“Yes, sir,” I nod.

“Will that be all?” he groans.

The inoculations.

My conscience reminds me. How could I have forgotten?

“Actually, yes. I do have something else.”

“Well, what are you waiting for?” He smacks his thigh in annoyance, making me wince.

“Earlier, when I spoke to the Earthling girl, she mentioned that after I left the secret meeting, Mr. Silverstone was discussing something about inoculations,” I inform him.

“Inoculations? Like for Earthling children?” he frowns.

“I believe so.”

“Why didn’t you mention this before?” he turns around and starts fumbling with papers.

“Sorry, must have slipped my mind,” I confess. Realizing that this girl has really been crowding my mind lately. I’m not thinking straight.

“That has to be it,” he mumbles to himself, examining one of the papers he’s holding. “I don’t know how I didn’t realize this before. It’s genius!"

"A little evil," I nod. "But genius. I agree." At least we're thinking the same thing.

"Did she say anything else?"

"Nothing specific. But it did get me thinking."

"Thinking about what?" his eyes narrow to slits.

"Well, I've been doing a little research. Do you think maybe this could be connected to why so many humans on Earth have been losing their light force in the last decade?"

"That's a big accusation. We'd have to check time—."

"It lines up," I interrupt. "I looked up the timelines." The Commander's eyes widen then he turns away from me, looking towards the huge window in his office. Trying to hide his expression.

"How did you—," he begins. Then shakes his head. "Never mind, that will be all, Sergeant. Now rest up. I want you to see what else you can find out about these inoculations."

Why did he react like that?

Is there something *he's* not telling *me*?

"Yes, sir," I nod.

"And make sure that clumsy Earthling girl stays alive. I told you, I don't want anymore casualties," he warns again.

My pleasure.

I'm just about to zap off when his thundering voice calls out to me again. Making me freeze in my tracks.

"One last thing, Sergeant!"

"Yes—?" I turn slowly to face him again.

"Stay out of people's minds, 102," he scolds.

"Yes, sir," I salute. Giving him a wink. He rolls his eyes and that's my cue to go.

(Zara)

I've secretly been looking for my mystery man all morning. With no luck. Did he already complete his mission on Earth and go back home to his world? The thought saddens me. I was really hoping to see him at least once more. I still had so many questions I wanted to ask.

That face is nice to look at too.

"Ripley, I promise you, you don't need to get me breakfast every day. As much as I appreciate it, I know how to make my own food."

Or buy it. Whatever.

But I grab the croissant and eat it anyway. It's so warm, so flakey and so delicious. Then I continue to pace back and forth at the nurses' station. Occasionally peeking down the halls while nibbling on my pastry.

Where does she get these from?

"Here, someone left this for you," Ripley hands me a small box with *Nurse Lara* written across it.

"Who's this from?" I question.

A patient, maybe?

"I don't know. It has no 'from' name. I already checked. And who the heck are you looking for?" She notices my lack of eye contact. "You looking for your man?" she teases, making kissing noises at me.

Am I that obvious?

"My man?" I respond nervously, examining the box.

"Is *that* who you're looking for?" She points behind me. Could it really be him?

Alien Dude?

My heart flutters with hope.

"Speak of the devil," she crosses her arms with a smirk. Something tells me it's not Alien Dude.

When I look over, the disappointment is plastered on my face clearer than a summer day in August.

"Don't you dare," I begin. But she continues on anyway.

"Liam! Over here!" she calls out to him ignoring my warning.

"Shit, Ripley! Not again!"

That's it. We're disowning her.

I shove the box into my bag and yank on her shoulder to force her face into mine. I grit my teeth and give her the stink eye.

"What the hell are you doing? He's coming over here!" I scold her. "Count your chickens, Rip," I threaten before I let her go. Not really sure what I'm threatening exactly. When I turn to face Liam, he's already grinning stupidly at me.

"Sorry," she mumbles to me.

Too late.

He's seen me. There's no hiding now. I wave at him as I look around for something or someone who can save me. But I was right, it is too late.

"Good morning, Mr. Silverstone," Ripley exclaims, walking closer to him. I stay at the nurses' station, where I can have a desk between Liam and me.

"Good morning, ladies," he responds, while only looking at me. He can be decent looking sometimes, I guess.

Oh, you think so?

That's not what you were saying on his first day here.

Is everyone's conscience a dick? Or did I just get lucky?

"Can I talk to your friend in private, Ripley?" he finally acknowledges her existence.

I do hope I'm not the friend he's referring to though.

I lock her leg with mine, making sure she isn't leaving me alone here with him.

"Oh no you don't, sister," I mouth the words to her. Then she gives me a look that assures me she's on my side. That I can trust her. So I make the stupid decision to let her go.

"Anything you say to her, you can say in front of me," she tells him, clearing shit up for us.

Thank you, Rip. Thank you!

"Okay—," he continues before she cuts him off.

"She's going to tell me what you say as soon as you leave anyway—Ouch!" she shrieks when I kick her under the desk.

"I'm sorry, Liam. I'm actually swamped right now," I grab a couple random papers and pretend to read them. "What is it?" Then I start typing gibberish on the keyboard.

*Click clack click clack

"dhshbdccnsebbfmsjgbknnsdf"

is what my word document is reading so far.

"Um," he looks at Ripley then back at me.

"I was just kind of wondering—," he lowers his voice to a whisper then comes closer, leaning into me. Ripley follows as he does and leans into me also. Flipping through random papers, acting like she's incredibly busy. He looks at her again then back at me and continues. "I was just saying, if you weren't busy tonight, maybe we could go out for some dinner?"

"Uh—," I don't know what to say.

"Doesn't have to be food. It can be coffee. Or whatever it is that you're into consuming," he scratches his head. "I'll do whatever you want."

Whatever I want?

Ripley lets out a snort behind me. I turn around and give her a death glare. She jumps then sticks her nose back into her papers.

Busy busy.

"Are you asking me out on a date, Mr. Silverstone?" I ask, trying not to laugh but still keeping my eyes glued to the computer screen.

*Click-clack!

Shit, what do I say?

"She's free!" Ripley blurts out, shoving me over. "She's so free. And even if she wasn't, I'm sure you could afford her," she teases and shoots him a wink.

You slut!

"Ripley!" I'm appalled.

"So, what time were you thinking? Seven tonight?" she negotiates with him as if I weren't even there.

"Uh—yeah? Seven works," Liam responds. Smiling from ear to ear as if he just won the highest bid on a prized pig.

"Perfect. She'll be ready," she grabs a sticky note and jots something down. "Here's the address. Pick her up there," she points to her pink sticky note with her address on it, scribbled hardly legible in purple ink. And hands it to him.

This feels illegal.

I gather all of my strength to force a smile, but I'm still not giving up without a fight.

"But Ripley, I have a double shift today. Maybe another night," I plead with my friend whom I used to love like a sister.

"No, you don't, silly. That was yesterday, and I covered for you. Remember?" she corrects me, giving me *the look.*

Man, I hate the look.

I shut up and smile at our visitor. And *boss.*

I give up.

"I guess I'll see you at seven then," I tell Liam probably not hiding my disappointment very well.

Then I flare my nostrils at Ripley. I can only hope she's prepared for the wrath that's about to be unleashed on her as soon as this guy leaves.

"Perfect! Wow," he beams, maybe not catching my expression after all. "It's settled then. See you at seven!" He turns on his heel and almost skips away.

"Oh God, Ripley! What did you just do? I had plans tonight," I complain.

Well, not really. But I was hoping I did.

"Girl, you and I both know you don't have any plans. Binge-watching a docuseries on pyramids until you pass out is not really a plan to be declining real plans over," she assumes. And I gasp dramatically.

"Those are *real* plans! You know what, Ripley?"

Here it comes.

I'm about to tell her where she can shove that opinion!

"Yes?" she glares at me. Eyebrow raised.

"I'm going to go on this date—," I begin. *Come again?* "And I'm gonna have fun!"

"Go on," Ripley encourages.

"And I'm gonna eat good food. Probably tiny, expensive food. But I'm going to dress nice, and I'm going to enjoy it!" I proclaim. Who is talking? Is this still me?

Hello, hello? Mayday, mayday!

"That's the spirit, sweetheart," Ripley

grins.

(102)

What are we up to, today Mr. Silverstone?

My annoyance with this guy is hard to hide lately. I narrow my eyes as I watch the spray-tanned, dusty blonde-haired man approach the nurses' station. Where my Earthling—I mean—*the* Earthling girl is.

"Why is she talking to him anyway?" I complain.

Am I jealous?

I zap myself closer so I can listen in on their conversation better. Her body language tells me she's uncomfortable. But he doesn't seem to catch on, because he's getting even closer to her.

Why the hell is he getting so close to her?

"Is it getting hot in here?" I fan myself. I'm starting to get a little heated with the lack of distance between them.

Wait a minute.

"Is he trying to ask her out?" I laugh to myself. "How does he not get it? She's not interested."

Why am I sweating?

I continue to listen. She's trying to turn him down but her friend is ruining this for us. I mean—for *her*.

"Wow. You've got to be kidding me."

This Ripley chick just accepted the date for her.

Are we going to have to worry about you, miss Ripley?

After stalking the Earthling for as long as my schedule would allow, my day then starts to drag. No matter how hard I try to focus on work, I just can't help but wonder what this guy's deal is with her.

And why is he always trying to get her alone?

(Zara)

"Are you coming, Ripley? I'm not gonna hold the elevator forever. This lady and her baby want to go down!" I holler from across the hall. The lady with the baby glares at me then rolls her eyes, still bouncing the inconsolable infant in her arms. "I'm sorry—you can go," I tell her, then get out before an eye roll isn't the only thing I get.

Yikes.

She takes the elevator down and I stand there to wait for the next one. Giving it a couple minutes before I press the button again.

I really need to get new earphones.

I look around casually, whistling a toon while I rock myself on the balls of my feet. "Come on, Rip, what's taking you so long?" When something down the hall catches my attention. A familiar flash of light. I stop rocking instantly.

What was that?

I follow the light I saw. Or thought I saw. "Did I just see—?" But where did it go?

"Boo!" Ripley appears in front of me. "Who you looking for? Liam?" she laughs.

This joke is getting old.

"No! Go away," I push her aside.

"Is that who that box was from?" she interrogates me.

The box! I totally forgot.

"*No*," I reply in a mocking voice.

"Gosh, attitude much? Are you ready to go?" Ripley changes the subject.

"I've been ready," I scoff. "Let's go, I have to shower and make myself look somewhat decent before tonight."

"You ain't lying," Ripley mumbles.

"By the way, why did you give him your address?"

"What?"

"You could have given him mine, you know. I have nothing to hide. I'm not ashamed of where I live," I fold my arms across my chest and frown.

"Girl, no one is saying you have anything to hide. I just don't want you to have a stalker if things don't work out. You already work for the guy."

"Now you think about this stuff, Ripley? After you've already pimped me out?"

"Sorry," she cringes. "At least this way, if he does try to stalk you, my security will stop him."

"I guess," I admit and she nudges my arm.

"Look, your man is leaving. Say goodbye," she motions to Liam with her head, trying not to make it too obvious. But also not trying very hard. And cue the kissing noises.

Is she twelve?

The valet pulls her car up as she walks out the front doors. The same guy that parks her car every day tosses her the keys as she slips a crisp $100 bill into his back pocket. Then she slides into the driver seat of her Mercedes and we all watch as she speeds off.

She sure is something.

I don't know much about cars, but I know her car costs more than what I make in a year. And that was just her graduation present from her father. I continue to stand there like some kind of fan girl whose favorite celebrity just signed an autograph for her. But just when I thought I was all alone with my thoughts, destiny comes strolling my way again.

Shit! Why is he coming over here?

"Hey, Mr. Silverstone," I manage.

"Please, call me Liam," he responds with a smile.

I'd rather die.

My thoughts are loud, but I keep them to myself and do as he says. Even though I gag every time I say his name.

"Okay, *Liam*," I struggle with the words. "Well, I have to go. I'll see you later." I head back inside.

"Wh—wait!" he calls out to me but I ignore him, continuing faster.

I speed past reception, hoping Liam didn't follow me again. When I pass the front desk, I cover my face to hide from Kevin. He's standing around talking to someone and luckily doesn't notice me. I glance up quickly to find my way around and get to the emergency exit. When I spot something above me.

There he is again!

He's in the elevator.

"It's really him," I mumble.

Alien Dude.

The elevator is composed entirely of glass, minus the floor. This allows you to see the lobby from every level when you're inside. Which also means I can see every stop of the elevator from precisely where I stand. It stops on the fourth floor, and I follow it.

My floor? Why is he on my floor?

I scurry to the employee stairway before anyone spots me. Taking on two flights of stairs like a champ. Once I reach the top, I'm completely winded.

"What floor is this?" I question myself. "What! Three? Barely!"

Ugh.

I take a couple of long, deep breaths and start my final feat. Dragging myself up the last few steps.

"I made it," I pant. I push the door open with my remaining strength and continue to drag myself down the hall towards the elevator where I thought I saw him.

But he's not here.

The entire floor seems empty. I must have missed him. I turn back around to head down the hall again, while peeking inside every room. Just in case. Searching hopelessly for this stranger I know nothing about.

"Looking for something?" A deep, masculine voice makes me jump about a foot up off the ground.

"Damnit!" I shout.

Why is everyone scaring me today?

I compose myself then turn to see who the

handsome voice that nearly caused me to shit myself belongs to.

Please be him. Please be him.

My conscience has her fingers crossed for the both of us.

"It's you!" I shout, then cover my mouth quickly.

"What?" he laughs. I smooth out my scrub top then take a step back because I feel like I might fall over.

"Nothing. I—uh. I was just—," I stutter. I have so much I want to say to him, but now that he's finally here I stumble in my thoughts and can't find the words.

6

HELLO, DEATH? SORRY I MISSED YOU.

(Zara)

"Hey! There you are!" someone interrupts us.

Who the hell is it now!

My conscience snaps. And I thought she didn't like Alien Dude. When I turn, I'm morbidly disappointed at what I find. It's Liam.

Stupid, stupid Liam!

"Liam?" I respond innocently.

What in the hell is he doing here!

When I turn back, Alien Dude is gone. Again. And all because stupid Liam showed up.

Stupid, stupid Liam!

"Hey there! Did you get lost?" Liam responds, continuing towards me.

"No, I —," I begin. But he doesn't let me speak.

"I didn't think anyone came to this floor.

We're starting construction on a new ward up here," he informs me. Seemingly desperate to get me out of here.

"I can see that," I remark. Trying not to let him touch me.

"We should really get out of this place. It's a mess, I wouldn't want you getting hurt," he insists, rubbing the back of his neck. He seems uneasy.

"I think I'll be fine," I assure him. Wishing he'd just leave me alone. "Did you need something from me?"

"No," he responds. Still waiting, I'm assuming for *me*. "Come on, I'll hold the elevator for you."

"O—kay," I continue awkwardly. "I—I was just looking for someone." I look back, hoping he gets the hint. But Liam herds me into the elevator with him anyway.

"Who were you looking for?" he questions me. Breaking the silence.

"Uh—," I blank. "They already left." I give him a smile. He smiles back then hits the button for the lobby.

We stand in silence as the elevator goes down. Both of us watching tentatively as the numbers change above the door. When the door opens, I decide I'll make a run for it.

"Boy, it's getting late," I begin.

"Yup," Liam grins, glancing at his watch.

"Gotta rush home," I add. Waiting for the

elevator to stop. The ding sounds, and I wiggle my way out of the door before it's even entirely open. "I'll see you tonight, okay?" I respond. Then take off like a racehorse.

You really know how to make an impression, don't you?

My conscience is always throwing shade.

I roll my eyes and ignore her.

"Bye!" Liam calls out to me.

"Bye!" I yell back. Everyone at the hospital is staring at us now.

So much for trying to keep it low key.

On the jog to my car, I inspect my surroundings. Still searching for Alien Dude. Still hopeful. But I still don't see him anywhere. What is his name anyway? I don't recall him ever giving me one. It's probably something foreign and strange, like Zeen or Krypton.

Yeah, I'm sure it's something like that.

My conscience teases.

I really need to start asking for people's names.

When I get in my car, I hurriedly lock the doors and buckle myself in. Aside from the anxiety brought on by my new alien friend, I'm also suffering from my yearly paranoia. I'm sure it will save my life one day, though.

The paranoia. Not the alien.

I'm just about to turn the ignition when

I hear a rustling sound in my back seat. Leaving me frozen in fear. I turn around slowly.

"For fucksake!" I shriek.

That's it. I'm definitely dying from cardiac arrest.

My heart can't possibly take any more of this.

"I'm sorry. Did I frighten you?" The alien begins.

"You think?" I put my hand to my chest. "Why do you have to do that? Why can't you just walk up like a regular person?" My heart is still pounding.

"I said I was sorry. Isn't that how you apologize on Earth?" he wrinkles his nose.

"What are you doing in my Jeep?" Not that I really care. I'm just glad he's here.

"So. Liam Silverstone, huh?" he responds.

"What?" I'm confused.

"That's the guy? *Liam Silverstone.*" Why is he talking about Liam?

And why is he saying his name like that?

"I'm sorry. Did I miss something? Why are we talking about my boss?"

"You couldn't have picked a better guy than *him*? Seriously?" he scoffs then folds his arms over his chest.

Is he upset?

"A *better* guy? What are you talking

about?" I question.

"Like, out of all the Earthlings out there that you could have chosen to mate with, this is the one you've chosen? A *Silverstone*?" He continues in a disgusted tone.

"Mate!" I grimace at him. "What's wrong with a Silverstone anyhow? And can you please stop saying his name? I'm afraid if you say it one more time he might actually appear."

I pull out of the parking lot and wave to Emilio at the gate. He makes a strange face at me as we pass. I think he's wondering who I'm talking to.

"Is he looking at me like that because he sees you in my car, or is he making that face because he thinks I'm talking to myself?"

"I think the latter," Alien Dude responds. "Where are we going? I haven't been in a car in *decades*." He rolls the window down then sticks his face and hands out like a toddler.

"Hey! Get back in here! You'll lose a head!" I shake my head then roll it back up, forcing him inside.

"Okay. Okay," he slides into the seat beside me and pouts.

"You said *we*?" I scoff. Pretending to be annoyed by his presence. But secretly I wish I could take him with me.

"Yes, *we*. I *am* in the car too," Alien Dude remarks.

"*I*," I emphasis. "*I* am going to my friend

Ripley's house. To get ready for—uh," I stop. Wondering if I should even be mentioning this. He obviously already knows. And what does he care anyway?

We don't even know the guy.

"Get ready for what?" he presses.

"My date," I state confidently, "with Liam." His wide smile disappears and he zaps himself to the backseat.

"Oh," is all he says.

"Can you stop doing that while I drive? It's distracting," I tell him. And he just shrugs.

"Is your shower broken or something? Why do you have to go get ready at your friend's house?" he starts up again. He's starting to get on my nerves with all these questions. Is he my dad now or something? Doesn't he have a galaxy to defend?

Or some shit.

"No," I respond. "Not that that's any of your business."

"So—are you two a thing now or something?" He adds.

"Liam and me? It's only one dinner," I reply defensively.

Why am I even explaining myself to him?

"Uh-huh," he nods his head.

"And you really shouldn't be eavesdropping," I inform him. Making a left turn at the light. I'm almost at Ripley's place.

"Look, I didn't mean to hear that. I was simply just listening in to make sure he wasn't suspicious of your listening in on his secret conversation. That's all," he explains.

What?

His words form a tangle in my brain. He's crazy. But why don't I seem to want him to leave?

"You don't know what you're talking about. You need to call off whatever plan you have because it was a false alarm. Operation Red Robin is about charity. And public health. Stop being paranoid, this is a good thing," I educate him.

"A good thing. Eh?" he scoffs just before he disappears again in a flash.

"Alien Dude?" I'm left speaking to myself again. Just like that, he's gone. Almost as quickly as he came.

I wonder where he went now?

I pull up to the driveway of Ripley's father's house. The massive iron gate runs 20 feet high and is sure to keep anyone out. Even Liam. I inch myself closer to the intercom box and press the red button.

"Uh, hello? It's Ripley's friend. Can you let me in?" I speak into it.

"Hey, loser," someone answers me. It's Ripley. "Let me buzz you in," she says and the gate opens. I drive in and make my way up the driveway to Ripley's house.

The long driveway goes out for almost a quarter-mile, then it wraps around a giant fountain and comes back to the same road. But I take a detour to the right for Ripley's cottage. One of her drivers starts walking out towards my car, motioning for me to stop and let him take over. But I wave him off.

I can park my own car, thank you.

I'll never get used to that.

"What took you so long? I thought you were right behind me," Ripley remarks with a hand on her hip. Already waiting with the door open for me.

"I took a little detour," I confess. And she shakes her head.

"Let's go. We still have to find you something to wear," she snaps, pulling me inside by the arm.

Yay. Dress up.

"Can we please keep it PG Or PG-13, at least?" I plead. She is excellent at fashion. But some things, only she can pull off.

"What's that supposed to mean?" she glares at me.

"Nothing! I just don't want anyone thinking Liam is paying me to be there. If you catch my drift." I joke. But like my usual jokes, she doesn't get it.

"What? What size are you now?" Ripley

ignores me as she tosses clothing around in her bedroom sized closet.

And off she goes into her own little world of fashion and clothes too expensive for me to even be looking at. When she's finished, I try on about twenty dresses before finally finding one that I feel comfortable in.

"I think this one is it, Rip. I can't imagine wearing one of *those* dresses," I point to the pile of dresses worth more than my life. "This one is simple. And looks like it doesn't cost as much as the rest," I reach for the tag, but Ripley smacks my hand away before I get the chance.

"It's fine! Leave it," she snaps at me.

I chose a black dress. Soft like satin, and showing a little more skin than I'm usually comfortable with. But what the heck. If I'm going to go out, I might as well look good.

Right?

"What time is it?" I inquire as I strap in my heels. "I really don't want to wear these shoes, Rip. What happens if I fade the red on the bottom sole? Am I supposed to walk a certain way to avoid that?" I am genuinely concerned. I don't know how much these shoes cost, but I know I can't afford to replace them.

She laughs and rolls her eyes. "You'll be fine. It's a quarter to seven." She scans the Apple watch on her wrist. "I'm counting on him getting here, maybe around 7:15 or 7:20. Guys like him like to make you wait a little. Make an entrance."

"Whatever," I roll my eyes right back at her. "How do I look?" I straighten up and take a look in the mirror. Impressed is an understatement.

"Amazing!" Ripley pushes me towards my reflection.

"Wow, Rip. Is this really what I'm capable of? Or what you're capable of?" I tease, and she tosses a pillow at my head. Her phone rings in the distance, and off she goes to fetch it.

Must be Kevin.

While I wait, I prop down on a small bench she has in her bedroom and pull out my phone. Scrolling social media to pass the time. When my thoughts begin to wander.

Do aliens have phones?

Surely, they must. How else do they use Instagram in space?

(102)

Alright, what did I miss?

When I get to the Earthling's friend's house, I spot her Jeep right away. Which I believe is a good sign. It means she might still be here.

"Now, where are you my little Earthling?" I don't even try to hide my delusion anymore. I catch her scent and follow it. Her aura is always so strong, I feel like I can spot it anywhere now. I walk around the cottage, peering through windows. Hoping to catch a glimpse of her before she leaves. When I finally spot her.

"There you are," an automatic smile spreads across my face, "and you look absolutely stunning."

Her black dress is hugging her curves in all the right places. The fabric has a subtle sheen that catches the light as she moves, drawing my eyes to her neckline and making me gasp, "wow."

Her hair is swept up in an elegant yet messy bun, soft locks of hair falling freely on her face. But revealing the delicate curve of her neck that alone makes me weak in my knees. The black dress was the perfect choice, emphasizing her natural beauty and sophistication, yet commanding the attention she deserves. All without actually demanding it. She's the type of woman to leave an impression that lingers in the minds of anyone who'd be fortunate enough to see her.

"Look at her, frying her beautiful brain, scrolling through that death bomb they call cellphones."

I can't seem to get enough of her, no matter how long I look. She's just so cute. The way she slightly squints her eyes because her phone is too bright. The way she twirls her hair with her finger when she's concentrating too hard. Or the way her lip curls just the slightest to let me know something that she saw on her phone amused her.

She's so intoxicating.

So—*beautiful.* The kind of beauty that translates into multiple worlds. I gaze at her with lovesick eyes, staring mindlessly at her.

Then I zap myself inside to get a closer look.

(Zara)

A sudden wave of chills run down my spine and send my body into a shiver. I thought I saw a shadow by the window from the corner of my eye. But when I look over, there's nothing there.

You're just being paranoid. Nothing is here.

But the all too familiar feeling overwhelms me again. The feeling that someone's watching me. Ripley is on a phone call in the other room, but the silence around me is starting to become deafening.

"Are you in here?" I whisper. "I can feel you, ya know?" He has super alien hearing; I know he can hear me.

If he's here.

"Who are you talking to?" Ripley cuts

in. Making me jump. Then I let out a sigh of disappointment.

"No one," I reply. Wishing that wasn't my answer.

"Well, Liam's pulling in. Are you ready?" Ripley asks as she stands back to take one last look at me. "Damn, you look good," she lets out a yelp of excitement. I really don't know how she gets a kick out of this.

"As ready as I'll ever be," I inhale deeply. "Let's get this over with."

And let's have some fun, dammit.

"Liam is going to freak when he sees you," Ripley adds. Making me even more nervous.

(102)

"She feels me?" What does that mean? "Was she talking to me?"

Well, duh idiot, who else would she be talking to?

Another alien she knows?

Did I just call myself an alien?

Oh God, this girl is starting to rub off on me. But I can't say that I mind it. I watch her as she exchanges a few more words with her friend then they both walk out of the room together. I zap myself closer to follow them. Someone's at the door.

I peer out the window to find a pearly white Tesla Model X parked out front. "Nice car, but what is he wearing?" I scoff at her date's choice of outfit.

It's the douche.

She couldn't have chosen a bigger loser. The guy is wearing penny loafers and sunglasses. *Sunglasses*. At 7PM.

"Idiot," I laugh. Trying to mask the uncontrollable jealousy I'm feeling with humor. But it's not working.

Together they walk off and I watch as he reaches for her hand. Smoothly trying to hold it. My gut twisting as his fingers brush hers. Then smile when she surprises me by brushing his hand away and continuing on without him.

That's my girl.

"Damn it," I hear Liam curse under his breath. Then scrambles to catch up. Even though he's making a complete fool of himself, I can't say I'm not still drowning in envy over his position right now.

Still a douchebag though.

(Zara)

He doesn't play any music.

Who doesn't play music in the car?

I'm beginning to question this whole entire thing. This definitely qualifies as sociopathic behavior. I air drum my thigh as I stare out the window. Wishing he'd say anything to drown out this god awful silence.

After the short, not too pleasant drive, we finally arrive at the restaurant. And I'm pleased to say that the place actually looks incredible.

He's really pulling out the big guns here, huh?

As we step inside, I'm immediately struck by the opulence of the place. The walls are adorned with ornate gilt mirrors, and the most exquisite crystal chandelier hangs from the high ceilings above us. Casting a soft, warm glow over the room.

The hushed sounds of classical music fill the air, creating a serene ambiance. Oh god, I really hope he's not expecting me to sleep with him. Because that's definitely *never* happening.

Like ever!

My thought bubble is suddenly burst by a server.

"Right this way, sir," his velvety voice almost sings to Liam, then he nods in my direction, "ma'am."

Even the staff seems to be above my class. Instead of sitting in the same class I'd usually be seated at. I feel so out of place. But I suck it up and pretend.

We follow the server as he guides us to our seats. Sauntering casually past a full house of elegantly dressed rich people. And heading straight to the back.

Where are we going?

We come to a halt before two grand doors, adorned with a lustrous golden iron frame and handles to match. Peering through the glass, I catch a glimpse of the world beyond and let out a small gasp. The view is breathtaking.

But once he opens the doors for us to go through, that's when I'm really at a loss for words. From the outside, the doors are entwined with verdant vines that spill over onto the walls. Enveloping the entrance in a wild embrace. It's a stunning contrast to the elegant and refined interior, as if the beauty of nature has reached out to claim the space as its own. I can't help but marvel at how different it looks from out here.

There's a soft glow from the twinkling lights that hang above us like icicles.

Now this I like.

A lingering scent of flowers and herbs wafts by as a warm breeze blows through. Adding a touch of nature to the already idyllic scene. The entire balcony is set up for only us two. The table draped in crisp white linen and flickering candles dance in the middle. Creating a soft, romantic atmosphere. And the city skyline that stretches out before us, is just the cherry on top.

It's kinda dark, actually.

"How will we see our food?" I mumble under my breath. Then turn over quickly when I hear snickering coming from a bush in the corner. "Did you hear that?" I nudge Liam.

"Hear what?" he responds. Pulling my hand to our seats. "We'll take a bottle of the grand cru, please." Liam orders without even opening the menu.

"Excellent choice, sir. I'll be right out with that," the waiter hands us our dinner menus then waltzes back inside.

Grand cru?

I pull out my phone and quickly do an internet search on what the hell a grand cru is.

A $5,000 bottle?!

"Geez," I mumble quietly then take a sip of my water. But at the first taste, I cough. We just ordered a $5,000 bottle, and they gave us tap water?

Can't have it all, I guess.

When I look up, my eyes catch Liam's staring back at me. I think he might have caught my expression.

"Is something wrong?" he questions, starting to fume before I even give him an answer. "Did they give us *tap* water?"

He says it as if it were poison.

"What? No. Well—yes. But tap is fine. Mmm, so good," I mutter as I pretend to take a sip. "Okay, it's gross. But please be ni—hiii, sir." The waiter is back.

"Is everything okay?" the waiter asks with a smile on his face. Liam begins but I interrupt him.

"Could we get two bottled waters, please?"

"Why, of course," he responds.

"Poured into fancy glass receptacles? If we may."

The waiter hides a laugh. "Well, of course you may, ma'am," he replies. "I'll be right out with those *glass receptacles*."

"No ice!" Liam yells out to the waiter who's already half way back inside. And I eye him. "Please!" he hollers again. "What? They make the ice with tap water," Liam informs me.

The waiter gives Liam a thumbs up letting us know he received the message. Then reappears moments later with two glasses filled with flat, iceless water and two empty Veen bottles as proof. Another waiter follows with our bottle of wine and a corkscrew.

"Look, the wine is here! Let's drink!" I sound like a borderline alcoholic, but I feel like that's more acceptable these days than someone having a mental breakdown. The waiter pops off the cork and pours the expensive burgundy liquid into our glasses. I take a sip.

Barf.

Why does expensive wine taste so horrific? You always assume the more expensive the bottle, the better it will taste.

Or at least I did.

Like some kind of magical fairy potion of goodness. But it's false advertisement, ladies and gentlemen. Stick to the $15 bottle of sugar. That's where it's really at.

"It tastes absolutely lovely. I adore it," I lie, speaking in a voice I've never used before.

What the hell is wrong with me?

I try not to flare my nostrils as they both look at me in anticipation. Waiting for me to take another sip just so they can watch me enjoy once again what may very well be the most expensive wine I'll ever taste.

I hate this.

I'm sobbing internally. But I swallow the room temperature, bitter-tasting fluid, and feel every drop burn it's way down my gullet. Praying that it doesn't come back up.

I should have stayed home.

Why am I being tortured? The waiter is satisfied with my response and leaves.

"Isn't it great?" Liam inquires, "it's my favorite wine."

"It really is. I just wish we had more," I lie again.

Don't throw up. Don't throw up.

"I can order another bottle if you'd like? Waiter!" Liam yells out as he jumps up from his seat.

Why don't I just keep my mouth shut from now on?

"No, no! It's fine. I'm joking," I yank him back down to sit, but it's too late. The waiter is already coming back. He needs to stop taking things so literal. I take a giant swig of wine and force it down.

Let's just get this over with.

I scour the menu quickly so I can at least order my meal when the waiter gets here. But first I have a brief meeting upstairs with the brain cells. Should I get, the Skinny Girl Salad, or the meal I really want, but know will probably get messy?

Eh, what the hell.

We decide on the burger. If he's gonna go all out on wine, I may as well let him know what he's in for.

"I'll take the burger, please. Medium well with fries on the side," I grin. The waiter raises an eyebrow at me as if he's surprised at my choice and then turns to Liam.

"Impressive," Liam agrees and folds his

menu over, handing it to the waiter. "I'll have what she's having."

I guess we'll both get messy.

"If the World Was Ending" by. Jp Saxe is being played on the piano inside. And all I can do is think about Alien Dude.

I rest my chin on my hand and daydream as I stir my wine around with my knife. Not seeming to be able to get him out of my head. I wonder what he's up to right now?

Probably fighting crime or something cool.

My conscience decides.

I really need to get his name next time I see him.

Next time I see him.

The thought comes so naturally, I begin to wonder what in the hell makes me so certain I'll even see him again in the first place. I hum the lyrics to myself and continue to drift off into my thoughts.

My thoughts about *him.*

(102)

"Is this what all dates are like on Earth?" I remark.

Snoozeville.

I begin to nod off when I hear the song

playing inside. Recognizing it from one of her playlists. I don't know why, but it makes me smile. And the way that the pianist sings it—it almost makes you feel like the song was written just for you.

"Would you love me for the hell of it. All our fears would be irrelevant. If the world was ending —"

"I would love you. I'd love the hell out of you if you'd let me," The words slip from my mouth as if they weren't mine. Then I snap myself out of her love spell and frown.

What the hell is the matter with me?

Why do I burn with jealousy over this—*Earthling.* Or is this not jealousy that I feel but —something else? Or what if it's *both.* Why does my heart and my mind seem to think that this Earthling is now the most precious thing to ever exist?

"This idiot doesn't deserve her," I complain. When an alert sounds in my head, distracting me. It's an I.M. from my buddy Logan.

Logan: "Are you still drooling over your new assignment?"

He teases.

Me: "Get out of my head, fucker!"

I respond.

Apparently, brain snooping is okay if it's your best friend. I must have forgotten to lock my mind back up. That's how distracted I've been lately. I ignore my friend and get back to my girl and the idiot.

Is he trying to hold her hand again?

"Nice move, bro. You already tried that last time," I laugh.

(Zara)

There's that sound again!

"What is that?" I ask Liam. Knowing there's no way he didn't hear it this time.

"I don't hear anything, babe," he responds as he downs his second glass of wine.

Babe? Oh, gosh.

As soon as I catch a glimpse of our food arriving, my eyes light up with excitement, and I can't help but do a little happy dance in my chair. Although he seems to enjoy the dance, he hasn't witnessed my burger-eating skills just yet. Which I know will most likely result in some level of embarrassment.

Here we go.

With a hand on either side, I go in for the first bite. However, before I can even taste it, my phone begins to ring, interrupting the moment.

"It's Ripley," I mutter. A little confused. She wouldn't call me unless it was an emergency. She's a strict texter. So, without a second thought, I pick up.

"What is it, Rip?" I speak into my phone. She's frantic on the other line. "How! Shit. Okay. I'll be right there," grabbing my things as I stand.

"Is everything okay?" Liam questions.

"No, I'm having a bit of an emergency, actually. I have to go."

"Why, what happened?" He quickly gets to his feet to stop me. Honestly, I don't even know myself. How *could* this even happen? I left my car parked inside her house.

Some security system, Rip.

"It's my car," I begin. "Someone stole it."

"*Stole* it?" The tone of his voice suggests that he doesn't entirely believe me.

"Trust me, if it wasn't an emergency, I wouldn't be leaving." I assure him. Knowing damn well I would have actually taken any excuse to leave at this point.

"But—I can take you home if you need a ride after this?" Liam attempts to help. Not really grasping the seriousness of the situation.

Rich people.

"Thanks, but Ripley is already waiting for me out front. There's a police report that needs to be filed and such. I just have to go," I push my way back inside. Liam still chasing behind.

"Just—wait!" Liam shouts.

I ignore him, rushing out the same way we came in. Storming out of the building and onto the chilly outside. The sudden realization hits me that I should have brought a jacket. I take a step onto the pavement and begin to make my way towards the parking lot when I'm blinded by headlights.

"Ripley?" I mutter, but as I look up, I realize it's not her. It's too late to move out of the way, and I'm frozen in the SUV's headlights like a scared deer. The vehicle is still going too fast, and the blaring horn only adds to the chaos. As the sound becomes faint in my ears, I close my eyes, bracing myself for the impact.

It was only a matter of time before death came back to claim me.

I've seen Final Destination. I know how this works.

7

DIDN'T MOTHER TEACH YOU NOT TO STEAL?

(Zara)

I don't feel anything.

My body is numb, and I can't tell whether I'm alive or dead.

“Wow, death isn't too bad,” I mutter to myself, slowly opening one eye to test if it still works. “My eyes still work!”

The confusion sets in. Am I dead? Is this heaven or hell? I quickly begin to recall my past, trying to decide if anything I've done is bad enough to warrant an eternity in hell. After a moment of thought, I shrug, realizing that I haven't been too bad.

“Why is it so dark?” I begin to inspect my surroundings, and it becomes clear that I'm outside somewhere. I can't be in hell since there's no sign of fire, nor is there a little red guy with horns.

I look up to gauge my location and realize

that I'm very high up. I walk over to the brick ledge for a better look. "Very high up!" I conclude, feeling a sense of fear creeping in.

I gaze up at the sky, and darkness swallows me. The vast expanse is filled with millions of sparkling balls of fire that illuminate the night, sweeping over the distance and lighting up the city below, if only slightly. I can see people dancing on the dirt road below, and the stars glow like a soft blanket over them, looking so vibrant that it feels like I could grab one.

"Heaven is so beautiful," I gape, awestruck.

Below, there's water that looks like an ocean. The moon is reflecting beautifully over it, and I close my eyes, listening as the waves crash rhythmically into the glowing sand.

"Where am I?" Still confused, I look up at the dark sky again, this time reaching for one of the balls of fire. Almost believing I can actually grab one.

My thoughts immediately wander to Alien Dude and what conspiracy theory he might have enlightened me with had he been here. Perhaps about what the stars really are and how us Earthlings are being lied to about that too.

"Why would they lie about something like that anyway? What's the point?" I think out loud.

"We gotta stop meeting like this," a deep voice startles me, almost causing me to fall over the ledge.

God? Is that you?

My conscience is already getting way ahead of herself. I turn around quickly, ready to meet my maker. But it's not God. I gasp loudly as I come face to face with the handsome alien I haven't been able to get out of my mind all day.

"It's you," I smile instinctively.

I guess it may be heaven after all.

"You don't seem surprised," he mirrors my smile.

"Where are we?" I respond, looking around at my new surroundings. Alien Dude's nonchalant response to my question only makes my curiosity worse.

"Take a wild guess," he says with a smirk.

I can't help but laugh at his response. This is gonna be a regular thing now huh? Teleporting.

"On a roof?" I guess, completely unsure of where we could actually be.

"We're in Greece," he whispers from behind me, his breath sending shivers down my spine. "On a roof. *Correct*." His warm smile on my cheek makes my heart flutter.

But my joy becomes short-lived as soon as I remember the reason for my urgency. My car and Ripley.

"Shit," I curse, breaking away from Alien Dude's hold. "I wish I could stay, but I really have to go. Ripley just called me and said my car—."

"That was me," he interrupts, a mischievous grin on his face as he hides his hands behind his back.

My confusion quickly turns to anger. "What do you mean it was you?" I demand, my eyes narrowing to slits. My phone rings again, and I see Ripley's name flash across the screen.

I answer.

"Hey, Rip! Sorry, I'm on my way. I'll be there in a second, I just—," I begin, but I'm interrupted again, this time by his voice through the phone.

"*Testing Testing,*" he chants jokingly. My blood is now ready to boil over.

"How?" I clench my jaw in anger. "But most importantly, *why*!" I shout. I'm furious.

"Woah, I'm sorry!" he tries to calm me.

"You know, you scared me half to death!" I yell. "And *Liam*! Poor Liam! We didn't even get a chance to eat."

"Liam is fine," he responds in annoyance. "He can afford it."

"What about my car?" I add.

"Your car is fine, too, don't worry," he assures me.

"This isn't funny. You can't joke like this," I scold him as I fold my arms across my chest.

"It was just your car, relax. It's not like I said somebody was dead or anything. I'm not that immature."

"Oh, really?" I raise my eyebrows at him.

"Yes," he assures me. "I made sure everyone was okay first. Ripley is out with that one guy, what's his name? Kevin the X-Ray Man. And your cat is also fine," he adds.

Has he been listening to me more than I thought, or does he just call him that too by coincidence?

Or are we both dead?

"Not a pretty big list of people to have, huh?" I laugh.

"Not really. And one of the two is a cat... so," he chuckles. It seems like everyone and everything is safe and accounted for. I might as well stay. Right?

You know you want to.

My thoughts aren't always wrong. I really do want to stay. And I must admit, I don't want to leave him either. I want to stay here. With *him.*

"I *guess* I can stay," I give in without needing much convincing.

"Great!" He's all smiles again. I peak over the rooftop one more time just to get a better view.

"Scary!" I remark, "but absolutely gorgeous. I've never been to Greece before."

I've never traveled anywhere actually.

As I turn back to Alien Dude, I am taken aback by what I see. A table has magically appeared beside him, complete with two garden chairs tucked neatly underneath. The table is draped in a cream-colored tablecloth with white lace trim, and on top rests a crystal vase holding a single red rose. The air is thick with the sweet scent of the one flower, which seems incredibly strange. Several white candles are scattered around the table, already burning brightly, though they were not there just moments before.

"What's all of this?" I inquire, my eyes scanning over the perfectly set table.

"You said you didn't get a chance to eat," he replies, a mischievous glint in his eye. "You are hungry, aren't you?"

"I'm famished," I reply, still in disbelief at the sight before me. It's as if we've been transported to another realm where anything is possible.

"Perfect!" he grins, pulling out a chair for me. "Then none of this will go to waste."

I hesitate for a moment, wondering if this is all some sort of trick or illusion. But as I lower myself into the chair, I feel its solid weight beneath me. He pushes my chair in and takes a seat opposite me.

"Did you do all of this?" I question, still trying to wrap my head around the situation.

"Of course. Who else would?" he replies with a smirk, flashing me a dimple that sends a warm sensation through my body.

As we sit down to eat, my head spins

continuously from the strangeness of it all. I press my palm to my temple, trying to ease the pressure that has built up there. But as I take a bite of the delicious food that has appeared before me, I can't help but feel grateful for the unexpected company of Alien Dude. "When does the vertigo get better? Or do you just get used to it?" I ask him.

I hope I still look okay.

Teleporting is kind of strenuous sometimes.

"Sorry—um, I'm not really sure actually. You'll get used to it, I guess," he assures me, not so confidently.

"This is amazing, by the way. Did you have to take me to Greece, though? The US is fine. So is California. But I am impressed," I can give him that at least.

"Sorry—*again*," he responds. Rubbing the back of his neck. "I guess I need to make a list of rules, or something," he chuckles.

"So, is this how you wine and dine the alien girls back home on Xion?" I question him.

You had to ask that, didn't you?

Now he's going to think I'm a psycho.

"It's *Xia*," he laughs. Repeating it back slowly so I can get it right. *"Zzzziaaaaa,"* he emphasis.

"Zzzzzia," I repeat.

"No alien girls for me," he responds.

"Huh?"

"Your question," he laughs. "*No* girls, for that matter."

Fuck. Is he gay?

"Oh? And why's that?" I inquire. Trying to be cool about it.

"I'm far too busy with work," he admits. I let out a sigh of relief. Not that I care if he's gay or not. I'm just really thrilled he's not.

He didn't technically say he wasn't, though?

Curious, I decide to change the subject.

"So, what exactly is it that you do?" I inquire.

"I'm a Galaxy Defender," he replies, matter-of-factly.

My eyebrows shoot up in disbelief. "A what?" I chuckle. "You can't be serious."

"I am serious," he retorts with a frown. "I've been defending the galaxy for as long as I can remember."

"I have never heard of such a thing. How old were you when you started?"

"It's hard to say for sure. The force took me in when I was just a small boy," he explains.

"A small boy? And your parents let you join?"

"My parents were dead," he states bluntly. I nearly choke on my food. "Are you okay?"

"They died when you were just a boy?" I compose myself.

"Yeah. I've pretty much been on my own for most of my life," he explains. And the realization hits me hard. We're more alike than I thought.

"I'm sorry to hear that," I say sympathetically. "It must have been horrible being all alone."

"It was," he admits. "Except for my buddy, Logan. I met him when I joined. He's been the only family I have."

I nod, understanding his struggle completely. "Sounds like we have the same amount of people," I joke, trying to lighten the mood.

I get a chuckle out of him with that.

"Yeah, I guess so."

"Was Logan all alone too when he joined?" My curiosity starts speaking for me.

"Yeah, he was worse off than I was actually. They brought him in shortly after me. His parents died too. You could say I kinda took him under my wing."

"Sounds like something you'd do," I respond, as if I knew him well enough to know what *something he would do* even was.

"Someone had to do it. He was tiny back then." He laughs. "We got really close and as the years went by he became more like a brother to me."

"That's nice," I smile. "Like the little brother you never had?"

“I’d say little, but boy did he grow. The guy is six foot three and almost three hundred pounds now.”

That laugh.

A melody so sweet. A song that's quickly climbing to the top of my favorite songs list and he’s not even music.

“Are all Galaxy Defenders orphans?” I inquire, my curiosity piqued.

“Of course not,” he replies, with a sly wink. “Only the exceptionally gifted ones. Some orphans are given the choice to join the force instead of being placed in a home. But not many choose this path. We did.” As he speaks, two plates appear before us at the snap of his fingers.

A burger and fries materialize before me, and I can’t help but exclaim. Then suspicion sets in. And I eye him.

“Were you listening in on my date?” I question, my guard raised.

He tries to play it cool, shrugging with an innocent expression, but he’s not convincing anyone. “Okay—maybe?” he finally admits with a smirk. I narrow my eyes again.

“That was you in the bushes, wasn't it?” I accuse him, yet already knowing the answer. He chuckles, this time with a mischievous glint in his eye, and takes a bite of his food. I really should have known.

“Can I ask you something serious?” I

change the subject, a question that's been burning in my mind for some time now.

He appears nervous, swallowing his food harshly then taking a huge gulp of water. "Sure. What do you want to ask me?" He inquires nervously.

"What's your name?" I inquire, holding back a grin because his response was payback for his hijacking of my date. He lets out a laugh of relief.

"Need a name to go with those dreams?" he teases. Then he takes a bite of his burger, ketchup spilling onto his chin. Making him look almost boyish. His innocence is cute. "It's Ronan," he responds with a grin. "Ronan 102, if you ever want to mail me a letter or something."

I can't help but chuckle at the absurdity of the situation. "Ronan? That's oddly normal," I remark.

"Yeah, I'm pretty normal," he nudges my arm. "What about yours? All I got on you is *Lara-Female*, No criminal record," he confesses, and I let out a giggle.

"My name is Zara. Is 102 your last name?" I question just before taking the first bite of my food. The taste of the burger sends me into a state of ecstasy, and I exclaim, "Woah, this is the best burger I've ever had!"

Ronan beams at my response. "You like it?" he asks.

"Like it? It's incredible! What kind of

animal is this?" I ask, taking another bite and making a mess of myself.

"It's cow," Ronan laughs. Which I can now confirm is my new favorite song indeed. "I put it all together back home for us. The meat is from my farm," he reveals.

As I continue to chew, I bring up the question I had earlier. "You didn't answer my question. What kind of last name is 102?"

"It's an assignment number," Ronan replies.

"An assignment number?"

"Yeah," he confirms. "We all get them."

"So, that's what you're given at birth? A number instead of a last name?" I ask.

Ronan chuckles. "Of course not. I had a family name when I was born, but after I became an official Galaxy Defender, I was reassigned to be the new number 102."

"The *new* number 102? What happened to the old one?" I ask, chewing my food.

"He died," Ronan states continuing to eat also.

"What?" My mouth falls open, and I stop eating for a moment. "He *died*?"

"Yes," Ronan nods. "It's unfortunate, but it happens."

"Wait a minute. You can die doing what you do?" I blurt out. "I thought you were immortal for some reason."

Ronan chuckles. "Why'd you think that?"

"I don't know. I guess the eye thing?" I shrug, making him laugh again.

He shakes his head. "Nope, we're not immortal. It's all part of the job. When we join the Galaxy Defense, we know that we might not make it out alive."

"But why?" I ask. "Why would you want to give your life up like that?"

"To defend the galaxy from all threats, foreign and domestic," he replies with a serious tone. "And to keep universal peace at all costs. It's a hard job, but someone has to do it. We all know the risks when we sign up."

"That sounds... fun," I say sarcastically.

Ronan grins at me. "Zara Lara," he sings softly. As if I couldn't hear him. I glance down at the ketchup on his beard and hand him a napkin to clean himself up.

"I'm sorry about the old 102," I say as he wipes his mouth.

"It's okay," he assures me. Meanwhile all I can think about now is how much I wish I were that napkin. "I didn't even know the guy." My mind drifts off as I daydream about his lips.

"So, do you like your job?" I ask, trying to keep myself on task. He nods, finishing off his burger.

"I actually love it. Kept me happy enough for the past 1,200 years."

I nearly choke on a fry. "1,200 years?!" He quickly hands me a glass of water as I cough.

“Are you sure you’re okay?”

“Yeah, I'm fine.” I respond after swallowing my food. “Man, you're old.”

“Thanks,” he laughs. “So, how old are you exactly?” I question, kind of afraid of the answer.

“I should be around 1,235 years old. I don't really keep track anymore, to be honest. I've never even celebrated a birthday.”

“You're kidding,” I reply in disbelief.

“Nope," he shakes his head, lips pursed. “Those are 1,235 Earth years, that is. We measure time differently in Xia, so I'm technically not *that* old.”

“That's an awful long time to be alive,” I remark.

“Yeah, it actually hasn’t been that great," he finds humor in my honesty. “But I've had no complaints either. I’m a simple man. I've never needed anything more than I've had, and I've never really felt like I was missing out on anything.” He seems so nonchalant about it all, but I can't help feeling a little freaked out.

“So, over 1,200 years and you've never had a girlfriend or boyfriend before?” I ask, still trying to get a definite answer on that.

“Boyfriend?” he chuckles. “Neither, actually. I mean, there were a few female friends throughout the years. *Companions* of sorts.” He air quotes. “But nothing serious.”

“Interesting,” I take mental notes, trying to hide the slight sting of jealousy.

“Anyway,” he changes the subject. “That’s another thing you Earthlings don't seem to have a grasp of,” he slips in as he plucks extra fries off my plate.

“And what's that?” I ask.

“Longevity,” he responds. “I can’t believe most of you down here don’t even get to a hundred years old.”

“What do you mean?” I ask.

“Human beings have the ability to live for hundreds of years, some even thousands,” he informs me, taking a sip of his water.

“All humans? How?” I cross my arms.

“We just can. Humans have the ability to self-heal and regenerate in most cases,” he explains.

“I think you're messing with me.” I start to become skeptical.

“Don't you remember my eye?” he points to a perfectly healed, perfectly perfect, beautiful gray eye.

“I guess you're right.” I then recall stabbing it. “Now, tell me more.”

“Okay,” he grins eagerly. I think he’s rather enjoying himself. “Did you also know that we have the choice to stop aging physically whenever we want?”

“You're kidding,” I gasp in disbelief. “We can stop aging?” So many thoughts running through my mind.

“Yup,” he confirms. “Or you can choose to

age and grow old, but that's up to you. Although we do age a lot slower in other worlds." He frowns. His mind notably beginning to wander as well.

"That's amazing."

"Indeed, our human minds really are amazing," he agrees. "In the universe, we have a saying, *'If you can dream it, you can achieve it.'* I want you to always remember that. Because that's exactly the way life works."

After dinner, Ronan clears up all the evidence we left behind. Then he pulls me into his arms and zaps us back home.

Ronan and I stumble onto my kitchen floor, our bodies intertwined. We blush, but don't let each other go. Although I'm trying, I can't help but feel a little giddy from the night's turn of events.

"Thanks for tonight, Ronan," I smile, looking up into his eyes. "It was honestly amazing."

"It was my pleasure," he replies, a soft smile playing at the corner of his lips. "I'm just glad your night turned out as amazing as it should have been in the first place."

We stand there for a moment, our bodies still entwined, before I finally pull away. Even though it's the last thing I want.

"I should probably go to bed," I say, feeling a sudden wave of exhaustion wash over me.

"Of course," he responds. Taking a step back. "But before you do, can I first ask you something?"

"Sure," I reply, both curious and nervous for his question.

"I know we just met, and this might be a little forward, but...can I see you again?"

I look up at him, my heart racing with excitement. "Yes," I say, without hesitation. "I would love that."

"Great," he responds with a smile that illuminates my heart and makes it skip a beat. The way his dimples dig deeply into his cheeks the wider his smile spreads, just for me. I can't help but smile back at him, feeling lucky that out of all the Earthlings in the world, he bumped into *me.*

"You're really going to have to teach me how you do that, you know?" I say to him.

"Do what?" He asks.

"Teleport." I grin. "We are the generation of instant gratification, right? And I really do hate driving."

The dizziness isn't so bad anymore either.

"We'll see," he says as he readies himself to leave.

"Wait, you're leaving?" I accidentally try to stop him. My heart unexpectedly heavy with just the sudden thought of his departure.

"Yeah," he responds in a tone just as

melancholic. “I guess I’ll see you soon.”

“I doubt that,” I confess, struggling to hide my disappointment. Why do I feel this way? He already asked to see me again.

Are we already attached to this stranger?

Are my daddy issues really that bad? Or is it just because they’re also combined with mommy issues?

“You never know,” he winks. “I may bump into you at the hospital or something. Maybe try to save you from being killed again?” He grins, a beautiful dimple filled grin. “You seem to have a habit of that.”

“Stay,” I say, surprising both him and myself. Am I crazy?

We barely know him. What if he’s dangerous?

“What?” he asks, taken aback.

“I want you to stay.” I don’t seem to care if he could be dangerous after all. “Can you stay?” I plead.

“I don’t know—I really shouldn’t,” he replies, rubbing his neck.

“We could watch a movie or something,” I continue. “You know what a movie is, right?”

His stern expression softens, and a smile graces his lips. “Yes, I know what a movie is, Earthling.”

“So?” I insist. “What do you say?”

“Okay,” he agrees, smiling. He hesitantly

makes his way over to the couch where I'm sitting.

If something goes wrong, it's all on you, Zara Lara.

I turn on the television, searching for a movie to watch. *Zombieland* seems like the perfect choice, so I select it. We sit close to each other, watching the film in silence, occasionally glancing over at each other like shy teenagers. A pillow resting between us almost serving as a barrier. I watch from the corner of my eye as he creeps his hand up and lays it on top of the pillow, his hand open.

Is this an invitation?

My palms begin to sweat. I cautiously slide my hand on top of the pillow and inch it closer to his. I can feel the heat emanating from his body as I near his skin, but he suddenly jumps up from the couch and stands up.

(102)

"Do you have a bathroom?"

Of course she has a bathroom, you idiot!

Stupid choice of words, I know. But my nerves are getting the best of me. I *really* like this girl.

"Uh, yeah. Over there," Zara points down the hall. "Remember?"

Yes, I remember, I'm just nervous, okay!

I walk down the hall and enter the bathroom, closing the door behind me. I stare at myself in the mirror, wondering what the hell I'm doing here. Then run my hands under the faucet, splashing cold water on my face. Somehow hoping it will calm me.

Meanwhile I'm scrambling my brain for an excuse I could give the Commander that would possibly compel him to tell me to stay. But I can't find any.

Ugh, I hate leaving Zara.

"It is pretty late, actually. Maybe I should get going," I begin to talk to my reflection like a crazy person. "Why are you being a little chicken shit?" My reflection insults me.

I continue to analyze the pros and cons. Then I consult myself again. "What if I just stayed? Just tonight? What could happen?" I stare harder at my reflection, hoping it will tell me the answer I'm looking for. "No one has to know," it assures me.

"Whose side are you on?" I ask myself, unsure of anything anymore. "We're staying." We decide. Then I double and triple check to make sure my mind is locked.

I flush the toilet and wash my hands before stepping out of the bathroom. Then stroll back over to the couch to the spot next to Zara.

The pillow that was lying between us is still there, so I pick it up and toss it onto the love seat and out of our way. I prop down next to her and grab her hand confidently, lacing her fingers into mine. I catch a slight smile on her face in the light of the television.

What are you doing, man?

My conscience finally decides to make an appearance again, but we're already in too deep. I ignore it and lean in closer to her. She moves in closer to me too, and then her head falls to my chest. And within minutes, we're both fast asleep.

8

ARE WE WIZARDS NOW?

(102)

One week later.

"Oh shit!" Zara's shrill cry jolts me awake. She's always been fixated on the clock, and I can tell from her frenzied demeanor that something's up.

She leaps out of bed and snatches her phone from the nightstand. "What's wrong?" I inquire, but she's too preoccupied to respond, frantically searching for her charger.

Glancing at the time, I realize I might be running late as well. "It's 8:15," I offer, though she's the one with the watch on her wrist. "Do you have somewhere to be?" I know I do, but it can wait.

For her it can.

(Zara)

"Yes. I have to go to work. Ugh," I groan as I force the charger into my phone, squeezing it so hard that my fingertips turn white in the hope of making it charge faster.

The logic?

My conscience starts mocking me. "Shut up!" I say out loud.

Ronan looks up, surprised. "I didn't say anything," he responds.

"Sorry," I apologize, realizing how irrational I sound. "I didn't mean for *you* to shut up. It's just—." Why am I even trying to explain this to him?

"Just calm down. What time are you supposed to be there?" Ronan asks, but I ignore him, desperately shaking my phone and waiting for the Apple logo to appear.

"I'll just pretend I'm not here, then," he says, sensing my agitation.

But then I see that I have twenty-five new text messages, and my heart sinks. I open up the ones from Ripley first, ignoring the rest.

> Ripley: "Where are you? I'm already at the hospital about to head out. Do you need me to cover for you?"
>
> Ripley: "Hello?"
>
> Ripley: "Hello! Are you alive? I swear you better be dead! You owe me!"

Ripley: "Jk I don't hope that you're dead. Love you, bye!"

She sent that three hours ago.

I text her back as fast as I can, my fingers lighting up the screen.

Me: "I'm so sorry, Rip! Thanks, and I do owe you. Whatever you say, I will do it! I'll explain later. Love you. Gotta go!"

"Everything okay?" Ronan asks again, concern etched on his face.

"I'm good now," I tell him, relieved.

What did I ever do to deserve Ripley?

"You sure?"

"Yup. It looks like my schedule just cleared up. Are you busy today?" I turn back to Ronan, hoping the plans for his day match mine.

Please say no. Please say no.

"Just have to go home and wash up. Why? You up for an adventure?" he asks, flashing me his dimples. I almost forget about the fifteen messages I have from Liam.

Don't be a dick! Text him back!

"Fine," I respond mentally to my conscience and quickly text Liam to let him know I'm not lying dead in a ditch somewhere. I toss my phone into my bag and turn back to Ronan.

"Meet back in 30 minutes?" I propose with

a smirk.

"Make it fifteen," he counters, giving me a side smile before disappearing.

"Shit!" I bolt to the bathroom and hop in the shower, hoping I can get ready in time.

(102)

I ponder over my options as I quickly wash myself and mentally plan my outfit. Although I'm not known for being particularly creative in that department.

"She said not to take her out of the country, so I assume that means I can't take her out of her world either?" I talk to myself. But, to be honest, she's not ready for that kind of trip yet.

"She did say to stay in California," I continue the inner dialogue. "But there's nothing fun in California!" I exclaim. "I got it!" I think I've come up with the perfect place. And I enjoy the irony in it.

Once I'm dressed, I teleport back to her apartment. A few minutes too early. I can hear the shower running loudly in her bedroom, along with her usual loud music. I strain my ears to listen, and I recognize the soft, slow tune of the Dixie Chicks. I've been learning a lot about Earth music just from hearing her playlists from afar.

I wait in the living room, with her cat on my chest, purring deeply. I've never been fond of cats, but this one isn't so bad.

Finally, the shower shuts off, and I wait for her to come out. "Zara, can you hear me?" I call out to her.

Her head pops out, damp hair flowing wildly around her face, and I can't help but admire how stunning she looks. Taking a mental picture to save forever.

"What is it?" she asks.

"Dress comfortably," I tell her. "And turn up the music. I like this song." I bop my head to the beat, while her cat meows back at me.

(Zara)

Excited to be going on an adventure, I waste no time dressing up. "He said dress comfortable. I'm not going to argue with that."

I quickly slip on a pair of old blue jeans, throw on a green t-shirt, and tie my hair into a ponytail. A little makeup, including a hint of blush and mascara, does wonders to brighten up my face. After grabbing my favorite sneakers, I walk into the living room, ready to go. But my companion is snoring loudly, and I have to shake him awake.

Binks wakes up first and jumps off him, stretching loudly. Ronan, on the other hand, looks disappointed that I woke him up.

"We're going on an adventure, right?" I ask with a sad face, hoping he hasn't changed his mind.

"Of course we are, ready?" he replies, holding out his hand. I close my eyes and nod, taking it.

Here we go again.

He transports us to a small lake on a tiny boat. I am disoriented but thrilled to be here. Wherever *here* is. As I look around, I spot a buoy moving gently in the water, and an old wooden dock with a massive dead shark hanging from a hook above it. I turn to ask Ronan where we are, but he's pale and seems fixated on something behind me.

"Are you okay, Ronan? What's wrong?" I'm afraid to turn around, but I do it anyway. And to my horror, a huge fin is coming towards us. "Why are there sharks here! Where the hell are we!"

Ronan still isn't responding.

In a panic, I look around frantically for paddles to steer us out of harm's way, but I can't find any.

"Ronan! I need your help!" I try to shake him, but it's like he's frozen in shock. "Fine, I'll figure it out myself."

I try to turn on the engine, but it says we're out of fuel. "Shit," I curse. When I realize that there's a fuel station ahead. But I have no idea how to get there.

The fin is getting closer, and I'm still screaming for Ronan to wake up. When suddenly, there's a massive explosion. And now flames surround us. The leaking oil has now caught fire, and the shark is only a few feet away.

"What do we do." The words leave my mouth in an almost whisper.

Are we going to die?

In the worst three ways imaginable?

Burn, drown *and* get eaten by a shark.

My thoughts are becoming cryptic. When Ronan finally wakes up.

"There are no paddles. Watch out!" He points behind me, and I see that the shark's jaws are now inches away from my face.

And that's when I notice that its teeth are fake. I feel disappointed.

Why are you disappointed? Did you want to die?

Ronan laughs hysterically, and I am angry with him for playing such a cruel prank. As I look around, I begin to realize that everything is fake, and we might be on a movie set. "Where are we?" I begin to ask Ronan when a loud voice starts speaking over an intercom.

"Quick, someone's coming!" We hear a vehicle approaching, and Ronan grabs my arm and zaps us away before anyone sees us.

When I open my eyes, we're in the Old West.

"Okay, seriously. Where the hell are we!" I question Ronan.

"We're at Universal Studios," he explains.

"Universal Studios?"

"Yeah! It's in Hollywood. You've never been?"

"Surprisingly, no," I shrug.

"Really? Well, it looks like I'm going to have to give you the VIP Presidential, Exclusives only tour then, won't I?" he proclaims. Making me laugh.

"I guess you will," I blush. "But first, can we go to Harry Potter World? I've always wanted to go to Hogwarts!" He smiles at me and nods.

"I'll take you wherever you'd like," he offers his arm. "Come on, Earthling."

(102)

Zara's hair has a captivating fragrance that always draws me in for a whiff. As we arrive at Harry Potter World, we slip into the crowd unnoticed, grateful to have avoided the attention of Earthlings. The sight of long lines forming near wooden carriages parked in the middle of the alleyways intrigues me.

"Do you want one of those things?" I ask Zara. Unaware of what the *things* actually are.

"What is it?" We decide to investigate. I slide my hand into hers and lead the way.

If there are that many people lined up for it, it must be good.

I brought a bag full of currency with me, to get her whatever she'd like. I have no idea how much Earth's goods cost, so I opted to bring a safe amount of $20,000 USD.

After waiting in line for fifteen minutes, we reach the front and learn that the wooden cart is selling "Butter Beer."

"Butter Beer?" I read.

"What is a butter-beer?" she mumbles to herself.

"I guess we're about to find out."

As we order two iced butter beers, I notice Zara reaching for her wallet. "No, no," I stop her. Pulling out my giant wad of cash. She looks surprised and puts her wallet away.

A friendly teenager hands us our drinks. "Cheers," she clinks her glass into mine then takes a sip. Foam forming matching mustaches over our top lips. To my surprise, the taste of the butter beer is sweet like soda but creamy like ice cream. Zara is equally impressed with the taste and downs her mug quickly.

Earthlings sure do enjoy their sweets.

"Come on! Let's go on this ride!" Zara points excitedly towards a giant castle up ahead, urging us to go. She takes my hand, dragging me along as we rush towards the castle.

"Okay," I let her.

I could get used to this.

(Zara)

"I can't believe I've lived here my entire life and this is my first time ever coming here," I exclaim, my excitement palpable. "It's so magical! This is probably what kids feel like at Disneyland."

As we step into the castle, I'm awestruck by the dark and cold corridors, accompanied by the familiar tune from the film playing softly in the background. My attention is immediately drawn to the Mirror of Erised from the Philosopher's Stone, and I can't help but gape in amazement.

I stand in front of the mirror, imagining how cool it would be if it actually showed me something. I know it's only just a movie prop and it doesn't actually work, but it's exciting to try it anyway. As I squint my eyes and focus harder, Ronan comes up beside me.

"See anything worth seeing?" He nudges me. I smile at his reflection and reply.

"I do."

As we rush through the dimly lit halls, I gaze up at the moving portraits above, trying to admire them as quickly as I can while trying to catch up to Ronan. We finally make it to the front of the ride, and I suggest that we sit in the front row to get a good view of everything.

Ronan nervously asks if I'm sure, but agrees. Once we're seated and buckled in, Ronan pulls out a disposable camera from his bag and snaps some pictures of us.

"Where on Earth did you find that?"

"What do you mean?" He's clueless. "I'm trying to save these memories forever, for you. So you'll never forget me." His response surprises me. I give him a kiss on the cheek and he captures it forever with a flash.

This guy is dangerous.

My conscience isn't entirely wrong.

When we get to the end of the ride, Ronan suddenly takes off before I can catch up, leaving me to wonder if he's abandoned me.

"Ronan?" I shriek when he taps me from behind.

"I just barfed my guts out," he complains, holding his stomach. "Remind me to never go on that ride again."

"Ditto," I laugh.

"Come on, let's go get us some magic wands. For our spells and whatnot."

“Move a little to the left,” I gesture with my hand. "A bit more, just a tiny bit. Yes, there, perfect!” I shout, hitting the timer on her phone before rushing back to Zara before the ten seconds are up.

Finally, we're both in the frame, capturing an epic picture I've been trying to get all day. It's a moment I want her to remember forever.

Just as I will.

“Perfect!” I exclaim, admiring the photo. “This one's a keeper for sure.” Zara comes up behind me as I kneel on the ground, resting her chin on my shoulder.

“Absolutely,” she agrees. “Definitely a keeper.”

Yes, you definitely are.

9

ALIEN MOUNTAIN

(Zara)

A month later.

As I stroll to my car, I count the jack-o-lanterns guarding every door along the way. Marveling at how quickly Halloween is approaching. This year has flown by in a blur, especially since meeting Ronan. A smile spreads across my face just thinking about him. But it's quickly replaced with guilt when I remember that I've been keeping him a secret from my best friend, Ripley.

"Speak of the devil." My phone buzzes with yet another call from her. I screen it, instantly adding to the guilt. "I'm sorry, Rip. I wish I could tell you," I whisper to my phone as I put it away.

How do I tell my only friend I can't hang out with her because I'm hanging out with a guy I haven't even told her about? A guy that I've kinda been hiding for over a month now. And that according to everything she knows to be true, doesn't really exist?

I've been driving aimlessly down Route 66 per Ronan's instructions, for over an hour now.

"Make a left at Willow Parkway and then a right at the pink mailbox with the kangaroo," those were his exact words.

That's a very odd description of a mailbox.

As I squint to read the street signs in the barren desert, I wonder how I'm supposed to find anything out here. When finally, I spot a beat-up travel trailer and a peculiar pink object in front of it.

"Is that the mailbox?" I'm completely taken aback. It's a pink spaceship with a kangaroo perched on top, complete with a mustache and aviator goggles. I chuckle to myself, wondering how Ronan ever found this place.

As I pull up beside the spaceship flying kangaroo, I notice Ronan standing in the middle of the road, cradling something in his arms. "There you are," I exclaim before realizing what he's holding. "Is that an animal?" I gasp, quickly parking my Jeep.

“Ah, she made it,” I can finally breathe. I’ve been anxiously waiting for hours, concerned that she might have gotten lost since she's not the best with directions.

Or driving.

That, too. But I had to bring her somewhere secluded where no one could see us. And that meant sending her to the middle of nowhere.

Knowing she's usually unprepared, I brought her a warm jacket and special hiking shoes I picked up for her in Xia that allow for extra efficient climbing and grounding with the Earth - unlike most shoes made here that actually prevent grounding. Which honestly makes me wonder if they're designed that way intentionally.

Earthling’s are an odd bunch.

Zara parks the Jeep behind the old trailer, then rushes towards me. Seemingly preoccupied with what's in my arms.

“This is for you,” I hand her the items, and she eagerly unwraps the jacket and shoes. But her smile fades.

“Shoes?” she sighs, sounding disappointed.

“What's wrong? You don't like them?” I ask, unsure.

“No, they're fine. Thank you,” she

responds, still seeming glum.

"Okay," I reply, still unconvinced.

Did I get the wrong color?

"So, what's this stuff for?" she questions.

"You'll need that jacket for our hike; it gets pretty cold up there," I point to the top of the mountain across the desert. "And you'll need those to climb up," I say, pointing to the shoes.

"Oh," she responds simply.

"What's the matter? You don't like them?"

"No, it's not the things," she explains. "I just thought you were holding something cute and alive." She makes me laugh. "So, what's this about a mountain?"

(Zara)

So bad news, it was not a small animal.

It was just some boring shoes.

"These shoes feel funny," I complain.

"Funny how?" he responds.

"It feels like I'm not wearing any," I wiggle my toes.

"How is that funny?" he chuckles.

"Because why doesn't anything hurt my feet then?"

"Cool, right?"

"Yeah, they're weird. I kinda like 'em."

The hot desert makes it challenging for us

to cross, with dry ground crunching beneath our feet. The air feels thin, and I'm already struggling to breathe, even though we haven't reached a high elevation yet. As we trek, a vulture buzzes over our heads. Probably waiting for one of us to drop dead so he can eat us.

After a grueling hour, we finally arrive at the mountain. Ronan hands me a bottle of water from his fanny pack, and I down it thirstily, marveling at how he managed to fit it in there. We start climbing, but it's not long before I'm panting and feeling drained.

"Hey Ronan?" I try to catch my breath.

"Yeah?" he responds.

"How far— up—are we— going?" I manage to say. "I don't— know—how much— longer—I can— take." I can barely even breathe.

And my calves are on fire.

"Just ten more miles," he explains casually.

How is he talking so easily?

"What!" I stop walking. "Hell—no. I'm— out." I shake my head and turn around. Starting back down towards the direction that isn't ten more miles up off the ground.

"Get back here!" he snaps and comes after me.

I know he can just teleport us up there. So what is he playing at here? Is he purposefully trying to make me suffer? This isn't fun for me. I don't enjoy coming this close to death.

"I can't—climb— all the way— up there, Ronan. I'm not— like you. I'm—*tired,*" I sigh. Trying to catch my breath still. He reaches for my hand and holds it tightly in his. Then gives me a warm smile.

"You're tired?" he asks.

"Yes," I pant. Is he joking?

"Well, why didn't you say so? You never asked me for help," he chuckles.

Oh no, he fucking didn't.

"What do you mean—I didn't ask for help? You didn't offer—or I would have—gladly taken it. But also," I mutter, drilling the tip of my toe into the dry, cracked dirt. "I thought maybe I could do it," I confess.

"And what makes you think you can't do it now?" He narrows his eyes at me.

I'm out of shape, for starters.

"I don't know," I pout. "I'm just exhausted. That was a very long walk through the desert alone for someone who hasn't worked out in years. I'm just ready to call it a day." He's really starting to irritate me. What kind of adventure is this anyway? Why can't we just go somewhere fun?

"But you only gave up once you found out the distance you had left," he tells me.

What is this? Some kind of test?

"What are you trying to say?" I glare at him.

"Nothing. Just that you didn't even give yourself enough time to try to see how far you could go."

Ugh. He's right.

No, he's not. Shut up!

"That's not true!" I exclaim defensively.

"No? Well what if I had told you we only had one mile left, would you have continued then?" he questions. And I roll my eyes. "What about two? Five? What was the limit you were willing to aim for?"

Okay. This is definitely a test.

"I don't know," I admit, hanging my head in shame. "You're right. I did give up because I thought I couldn't make it. Can I try again?"

Wow, I'm proud of you.

I can't believe I actually admitted that. Nor can I believe the fact that I'm about to attempt a ten plus-mile hike.

He smiles. My most favorite of smiles. The one where his dimples carve deeply into his cheeks and his perfect white teeth contrast flawlessly against his swarthy skin. The mere sight of him energizes me, giving me a sudden rush of confidence and I decide to take the lead this time. Grabbing his hand and pulling him along behind me.

We're gonna make it to the top, even if it kills me.

As long as I get to die next to him, I'll be happy.

We continue for another couple hours and I'm still going strong. I'm no geographical mathematician, but from the looks of it, I'm pretty sure we're almost halfway there.

But after another hour, the exhaustion finally starts to kick in again and my legs begin to quiver in surrender.

"Oh, no!" I shriek. Just before I start rolling backwards. But Ronan catches me. Stopping me from tumbling down the mountain to my death.

"Maybe we should take a break?" he insists. He's been offering me a break every mile or so, but I've refused every one of them. I've been too determined to stop. But it seems like the toll has finally caught up to me and I should probably take him up on the offer now.

"I'm—fine," I attempt to lie.

"No you're not. Sit," he demands, pointing to a large rock behind me.

That was definitely not there before.

I do what he says and sit. Not because I want to but because I literally can't even stand on my own two legs right now.

How am I going to get back down?

It's starting to get dark out. And the panic begins to set in. Ronan notices the worry on my face almost instantly. He puts his hand over mine and rests it on my lap. Instantly making it all disappear.

How does he do that?

His warm, magical hands always find a way to bring me comfort.

"What's wrong?" he questions me with concern. But I just shrug. He chuckles nervously then lets out a breath. "You're doubting yourself again, aren't you?"

"Alright, Mr. Myagi, I've just about had enough of this," I scoff.

"Mr. Myagi? Is this one of your references I know nothing about?"

"Ronan, we're not even halfway up. You can see for yourself that I have not given up. It's my body that literally can't take another step. Not unless it's tumbling downwards," I chuckle.

"Can you do something for me?"

"If it can get us out of here. Sure," I agree. "Anything."

"You have to trust me, okay?"

"Anything that starts with that usually ends badly."

"Please? You know I'd never hurt you."

"Fine," I accept defeat. "I'll do what you say."

"Great!"

"But I'm going to need you to zap me back down the mountain after, deal?"

"Really?" Ronan laughs.

"Yes. Because I don't think I'll survive the fall." I proclaim, getting another chuckle out of him.

"Okay. But only if you still want the help after," he suggests. "Deal?"

"Ha," I scoff. "I still will. Trust me." I shake his hand.

"Now close your eyes," he instructs. I side-eye him. "Please?"

"Okay," I sigh. "My eyes are closed. Now what?"

"Now relax," he speaks softly. "Breathe."

I do as he says. But I don't feel very relaxed.

"I'm trying," I fidget. "It's just really hot and I'm sticky."

"Stop fidgeting, Zara. I need you to concentrate."

"Okay, okay." I try my best to clear my mind and focus. And I think I've got it.

"Now, I want you to feel the Earth at the bottom of your feet. Do you feel that?" he whispers softly.

"Yes, of course," I reply.

"Good. Now breathe," he instructs. "What else do you feel?" his voice soothing and calm. My focus sharpens, and I feel a sense of relaxation wash over me.

"Uh—it feels like—," I squeeze my eyes tightly and concentrate on the pulsing sensation shooting up my feet. "Electricity," I say.

What the fuck kind of alien shoes are these?

"Good," he continues.

"Ronan—why do I feel electricity?" I begin to panic.

Then he slowly slides his fingers into my hand, and all the panic drains away.

"Inhale that electricity, Zara."

"Inhale it?" I laugh. Opening an eye.

"Focus, Zara!"

"Sorry. What do you mean inhale it?"

"With your body. Not your lungs," he explains.

Yeah, that makes more sense.

"What? How am I supposed to do that?"

"Concentrate," he scolds me. "You need to focus again. Get in your zone."

"Okay," I sigh. And close my eyes.

"Breathe," he instructs. And I breathe.

I take a deep breath and focus again, slipping into the same state I was in before. "I'm ready," I breathe, feeling more at ease now. Ronan's voice lulls me into a deep, sedative state, and my body begins to radiate with energy again. And I inhale it.

"You're doing it," he exclaims. "Now, guide that power and send it to the tips of your fingers."

My fingertips start to pulsate, and I feel a sense of power coursing through me. "Now, feel the energy as it pulses up your spine and into your head," he continues.

"I feel it," the words leave my lips like a flutter of butterflies. Drifting far and fading away. And my fingertips pulsate. They feel almost—*powerful.*

The light in front of me grows brighter and brighter, but it doesn't blind me. I become overwhelmed by unexplainable emotions, and a tear escapes my eye. Touching my skin and evaporating almost instantly.

"Open your eyes," Ronan whispers into my ear. I peel my eyes open slowly.

For some reason, my body no longer aches and my mind is no longer worried. For once in the past twenty four years, I feel—care-free.

Holy shit!

"Did we just do an alien thing?" I laugh.

"Kinda," he laughs. "How do you feel?"

I feel incredible, actually. The exhaustion has all just about melted away, and I feel completely recharged. Ready to take on the rest of this mountain. I might not even need a ride back down after all.

But I'm not going to say all that.

"I don't know. You tell me," I give him a playful push. "Race you to the top!"

"Hey! Wait up!" he shouts, chasing after

me. Struggling to keep up.

10

TIME TO PAY THE PIPER

(Zara)

December.

The rain is pounding outside, and the freezing temperature makes me glad that I no longer have to walk or drive in this weather. As I'm getting ready for work, I hear Ronan call out from the kitchen.

"Zara, are you ready?" He's waiting to take me to work.

I know what you're thinking. So let me first say, yes he has kind of been sleeping here every once in a while.

More like every night.

My conscience reminds me.

Okay—he's been staying here every night. But there's a valid reason for it, Ronan thinks that I could be at high risk due to some new breakthroughs at work.

Ronan is just being Ronan. As usual, being

extra precautious. And you know what? It's really none of your business anyway.

That's what he would have said.

I honestly don't know how he does it. He denies it, but I know he's been staying up all night. I've caught him because I'm a terrible sleeper and it's not coincidental that he's also been up every single time I wake up. Despite his claims to the contrary.

But Zara, what about when he leaves?

That's a good question. But he never leaves. The only time he ever leaves me is for work. And his constant communication and quick return make me wonder when he actually does sleep.

Maybe he does that thing we did on the mountain?

"Yeah! Coming!" I yell back.

Although I hate the cold, I do love Christmas. I've never had a real Christmas before though. You know, with all the family and stuff. Ripley gets me tons of gifts every year, even though I beg her not to. She just can't help it; she's a giver. And she always says, "What else am I going to do with all the money I earn?" People with hearts like Ripley deserve to be rich in both money and happiness.

I hate thinking about my parents because it depresses me. But I know before they died, they used to go all out for me. I still have some memories. And most are good.

My apartment is as festive as it can be for the size. Not much décor, but I have my little Charlie Brown Christmas tree crammed into a corner of the living room, and that's all I need for it to feel like Christmas. Ronan trudges towards me, clearly exhausted, and zaps us both to Silverstone Health. We land gracefully on the 4th floor in a matter of seconds.

Sans vertigo.

"Do you think they'll ever finish this floor? It feels like they're purposefully not finishing it. Why do you think that is?" I inquire, knowing that there will probably be many more questions to follow.

Ronan puts on a serious face and begins to respond, "Well," he starts, pausing for a moment before continuing, "So we could keep it all to ourselves, of course." He winks, making me blush.

As I reflect on the past three months since meeting Ronan, I can hardly believe how much my life has changed. Or that I had lived so long without him before then. Ronan being in my life feels like the missing piece that makes it all complete. I couldn't imagine my life without him now.

"I have to go!" I exclaim, giving him a quick kiss on the cheek before rushing off to catch the elevator. Despite spending three long months together, I can't help but feel like we're just friends. I thought that our relationship would naturally progress into something more, but I think I've been friend-zoned.

Or Earth-zoned.

Either way, I know that I need to stop overthinking and take action. Maybe tonight, or even right now. But before I can do anything, Ronan is gone. "God, he's fast," I mutter to myself, wondering where he's off to today.

I head back to the elevator. Disappointed and already missing Ronan. I press the number five on the panel and take my trip up a level to my floor. My eyes have a hard time staying open as I watch the number above the door change from four to five. Then the elevator opens to let me out.

Ripley is already there, punctual as usual. Leaning over the nurses' station desk talking to Kevin.

And she's spotted me.

"Hey, girl!" Ripley shouts, leaving her conversation and rushing towards me.

"Hey Rip. Good morning to you!" I mirror her chipper tone. But the next words out of her mouth are the last ones I want to hear right now.

"Remember that favor you owe me?"

"Yes—," I gulp audibly.

This can't be good.

"Well, I'm cashing that sucker in today." Ripley pulls me aside, raising an eyebrow. I groan inwardly.

"Really, Ripley? Today?" I complain. "But it's so nice out."

"Yes, today," she confirms, and I glare at her.

"What is it?"

"So, there's this party tonight," she begins.

"This already sounds like torture," I whine.

"Well, it's more of a fundraising event my daddy's company is hosting for charity," she clarifies.

"That doesn't sound too bad," I concede. "Okay. What do you want me to do? Wait some tables or something? Gladly," I offer.

"No, not exactly," she laughs. "I wanted you to attend, silly."

"Of course!" I exclaim, relieved. "That doesn't really sound like a favor," I say happily, feeling the Christmas spirit.

"Great! I'm also going to need you to be Liam's date to this thing," she drops the bomb, and my bubble of happiness bursts.

"Excuse me? You can't be serious, Rip," I protest.

"I am?" She attempts a smile.

"But why?"

"Before you say no, hear me out!"

she pleads. "Liam's grandfather has very deep pockets, and we'd really appreciate the extra donations for the fundraiser."

This can't be happening right now. "I had plans for later," I inform her. Plans I really didn't want to reschedule for even a second more.

And especially not for Liam.

I think to myself, desperately searching for a way out. Is it too late to take back that 'anything' I was throwing around so freely what feels like a century ago?

"Come on, Z," Ripley pouts, her eyes wide with puppy dog eyes.

"I can't!" I whine.

"Really?" She shakes her head at me in disappointment and walks away.

"Please don't be upset," I go after her. "Come on, Rip! Anything but that! Please!"

"Oh, I'm sorry," she apologizes sarcastically, interlacing her fingers in a manner that I know means business. "What happened to 'anything,' Ripley? You got it, Ripley?" She's mocking me.

"That's not what I sound like," I defend myself. *She has the words right, but the tone is all wrong.*

"Please, just this one date?" she pouts again.

"Okay, fine!" I give up. "I guess I can go."

"Thank you!" Ripley hugs me.

"Not like I have a choice," I shoot her one last desperate glance, hoping to see a hint of mercy. But even my best puppy dog eyes are in vain.

Does he even want to take me, though?

"I knew you'd say yes! You're the best. He'll be so excited when I tell him."

"Ripley, you do know I haven't responded to any of Liam's calls or text messages since our date, right?"

"When was that again?" She asks.

"Three months ago. I don't think he'd even want to go with me, in all honesty." I make one last attempt to get out of it.

"Nice try. But he was here earlier waiting for you so he could ask you himself," she retorts.

"You've got to be kidding me."

"No. He waited a while actually, but he said he had to leave."

"Great. So you're telling me I dodged one bullet just to be shot in the back by my own best friend?"

"That's a terrible way to put it," she responds, "But yes. Stop being so dramatic. He asked for a favor and I agreed."

"Yeah, and I'm sure it took a *lot* of persuading on his part," sarcasm in my tone.

"He was very adamant about it. I had to help the poor guy out," she defends herself.

"Oh really?" I snort.

"Yes, as a matter of fact it felt like my job depended on it, actually," she pulls my strings.

She has jokes now?

"Oh, you don't say?"

"Yes, I do say," she starts to laugh, breaking our serious streak.

"Ugh. And here I was, almost convinced I'd heard the last from him last week. But I guess I was wrong. Turns out, he was just warming up."

"Just give the guy a chance," Ripley tells me.

"Okay, fine. One hour! But we are going strictly as friends."

"Okay, whatever you say."

"Make sure he's aware of that. What time is this thing, anyway? And I don't even know what to wear," I add, shaking my head.

"Leave that to me. I'll make sure you look stunning," Ripley assures me. I roll my eyes but can't help the small smile that tugs at the corners of my mouth. "Come home with me after work today," she starts to plead her case.

"I can't, I have stuff—."

"Come on. I can let you borrow a dress. It might be hard to top that last one, but I'm sure we can find something."

"How do you have so many dresses my size?" I ask, starting to get suspicious. "Honestly, I can't."

Her face drops instantly. All the

excitement that was there just a second ago, now drained. I have a feeling she already had this all planned out beforehand. But I have some plans of my own I need to make happen with Ronan later. Plans that can't wait another day.

"What? Why not?" Ripley's tone is sad.

"Well, I can. Just not right after work," I add. And her expression lightens up.

"Okay. Then when?"

Geez, give me some time to think.

"I'll meet you there—around six?" I suggest. She's nodding.

Good.

"So, whats the deal?" She presses me. "What do you have to do?"

"Nothing," I lie.

"Oh, it's nothing now?"

"I just have someone I need to meet up with real quick," I admit. "Then I'll be there."

"Hmm." She raises an eyebrow at me.

"You can pick out my dress and everything." I add a smile on my face for decoration. "No complaints!" She's grinning uncontrollably now.

Wait, what have I done? Can I take that back?

I gulp.

"Fine," she agrees. She seems pleased.

"So, about the dress?" I attempt to take

back my words.

"I hope you know I'll be taking you up on that."

"Great," I sigh. She walks off before I can argue. Back over to Kevin. Their conversation continuing right where they left off, without even skipping a beat.

Shit. What did I just do?

The entire work day I'm dragging. Dreading what's to come tonight. But mostly I'm dreading having to explain this to Ronan. He's going to be upset.

It's 3:30 P.M. on the dot, and I'm already on the 4th floor waiting for Ronan. I've been practicing my speech all day. I'm going to tell him how I feel, and then I'm going to lay one on him.

A kiss. That's what I'm going to lay on him.

He's taking an awful long time to get here today. I pull my phone out to check the time.

"Two minutes late."

Where is he?

"Damn it, Ronan. I just gave up a ride with Ripley. How am I going to get home? I didn't bring my car," I say out loud as if he can hear me.

"Hey!" He creeps up behind me. "Sorry I'm late. I got a little caught up. Shall we?" Ronan sticks out his elbow for me to grab his arm. Will this ever get old?

I sure hope not.

"Why must you always scare me, Ronan?" I complain. He's always so serious yet so playful. He makes no sense.

But, God, I can't get enough of him.

"So, are you ready for your first lesson?" he smirks at me as I grab his arm.

"My first lesson?" I question.

What is he talking about now?

"You want to learn how to be superhuman, right?" He grins, his voice dripping with excitement.

"Uh—," I stutter. I wasn't expecting this. "Y—yes?"

"Then let's go!" Before I can ask anymore questions he pulls me closer and we are bolted far away from Silverstone Health.

When we finally land, I open my eyes again, feeling both disoriented and amazed. We're standing on a white platform in a colorless room.

"Woah, where are we?" I exclaim, my curiosity piqued. Ronan has never brought me here before.

"What do you think?" he inquires. Ignoring my question. The lack of floor kind of startles me. The walls look never-ending, and I can't tell where the wall and the floor connect. Or where they even end.

"What is this place, Ronan? Is this the

matrix?"

"Funny you say that." He squats down low before taking a giant leap backwards. Catching massive air. Time seems to slow down before my very eyes as he bends his back and propels himself backwards with his arms above his head.

"Ronan!" I shout, sprinting towards him. Strangely, I can still move at full speed.

What is happening here?

As I reach Ronan's body, I raise my hand to touch him, but it goes right through his movements as he executes a backflip in slow motion. "What the hell."

"Cool, huh?" he smirks, landing his backflip like a pro.

"This is insane! Where the heck are we?" I scan the never-ending white room until I feel dizzy.

"We're in Rhelm Zero," he replies, as if that's supposed to mean anything to me.

"Rhelm Zero? Wow!" I exclaim, still trying to process what's happening. "What's Rhelm Zero?" I inquire some more, hoping for an explanation.

"It's a training ground of sorts. We call it an Enlightenment Center," he informs me.

"An Enlightenment Center?" I repeat, still trying to wrap my head around it all.

"Yeah. It's the one place where everything goes. No rules. No limitations," he explains.

“So, you can do anything?” I question, my mind racing with possibilities.

“*Anything*,” he assures me. *“If you can think it, you can achieve it,”* he winks at me as he chants the familiar phrase I’ve heard him use many times before.

“And what exactly do you do at this Enlightenment Center?” I’m intrigued.

“Train,” he replies. “It’s a safe place to practice new abilities you’re learning.”

“Safe, huh? How dangerous can it get?” I scoff.

“You’d be surprised. Things can get pretty crazy. As you can imagine, aliens can get very creative around here,” Ronan informs me.

“Aliens?” I laugh. Sounds like I’m rubbing off on him.

“I meant *people*,” he corrects himself.

“So, that’s what you have an Enlightenment Center for? To keep everyone safe?” I continue with my 21 questions.

“Yes. Out here in the Galaxy, we’re always encouraged to keep learning new things,” he explains. “But we also like to make sure no one gets hurt.”

Interesting.

I mentally jot down a few questions to ask him later about that.

“So, why isn’t anyone here then? If they’re used *so* often and *so* creatively?” I mock him.

I hate that he thinks everyone is so much better than Earthlings.

"Funny you ask that," he winks. "There are actually millions of other people right here, right now. We just can't see them."

"Oh really?" I laugh. "How convenient."

"I'm serious," he chuckles.

"So, then where are they?"

"Rhelm Zero is infinite, Zara. It can be accessed from anywhere in the Universe. Just like stars in the sky, there are too many and too far away from each other to ever get close enough to actually see one another," Ronan explains.

"Hmm, can I do that too?"

"Do what?" he questions.

"What you just did," I reply before getting ready to backflip.

"Nope! Let's not do that quite yet," he stops me.

"What! Why not?" I question, disappointed.

"We'll get there soon, grasshopper," he jokes.

I'm going to give this guy a heart attack.

"So, this is some type of magic-free-for-all then, huh? I like it," I remark.

"I told you, none of this is magic, Zara. It's science. And practice. It's a force, remember?" he reminds me.

I know all of this already. I just love to hear him explain it to me. Over and over. "I have another question," I continue.

"Of course you do," he responds, smiling.

"If this is science, then why don't we learn about it like we do other things?" I inquire curiously.

"You did at one point. You're just no longer allowed to research it," he replies.

"Wait, hold the phone! Now I have some real questions," I exclaim, surprised.

"Real questions? Oh, no," Ronan teases as he begins to walk off. "Einstein was onto something, let's just say that. Come on, let's begin."

11

CHAMPAGNE AND LIGHTS

(102)

I really hope I don't regret this.

"Alright, sit down right here." I instruct, holding her gently by the shoulders and guiding her down to the ground.

Her soft, dark brown hair brushes against my cheek, her lavender scent enveloping me. I inhale deeply and I smile into her neck. Making her skin curl under my lips.

"Now close your eyes," I whisper in her ear, keeping a loose grip on her arms.

"Are we going to do that thing we did on the mountain again? Your alien thing?" she begins her interrogation.

Always joking, this one.

"Be nice," I glare at her and she concedes.

"Fine," she shrugs. Crossing her legs. "It was a joke, geez. The *human* thing. Is that better?"

"Yes," I grin. "Now, relax."

"I'm trying," she gives me a side smile.

"Sorry," I move my lips from her neck. "Now, forget everything you're thinking about."

"Everything?"

"Everything," I repeat. "Every thought residing in your mind, let them all go."

"Okay," she breathes softly. I feel her shoulders loosen, and her body relaxes under my touch.

"Now, watch as your thoughts escape from your mind and float out into space." I chant softly in her ear. "Watch them disappear. Do you see them?"

"Yes," she breathes.

"Now breathe deeply," I instruct. Squatting down behind her. "Remember that electricity we played with last time?" I whisper. And she nods anxiously. "We're gonna do that again." The intense energy radiating off of her skin is now beaming. "Find that energy, Zara. Breathe it in."

"Breathe it in—," she breathes softly.

"Yes. Inhale it deeply; let it fill your body. Let it overflow and seep out of your fingertips. Build a light," I whisper.

As she takes a deep breath, the energy radiating from her skin pulsates, synchronizing our breaths into a singular rhythm. Our lights intertwine, growing brighter and brighter, and I am overwhelmed by a sensation I've never experienced before. When I open my eyes, I see that my light is merging with hers in a way that is entirely new to me. It's a powerful and almost euphoric connection.

I close my eyes, reveling in the sensation. Our lights flowing together, in a rhythmic dance. They grow increasingly luminous, illuminating the entire room. The intensity of the energy between us is unlike anything I've ever experienced.

"Do you feel it?" I sigh. She nods, light cells beginning to form on her skin. Making it sparkle like diamonds. The room becomes blinding, and I shield my eyes as the light begins to change, taking on different hues of violet.

As her light grows, I crouch down to get closer to her, and I notice a strange blue glow forming on my skin as well. "What the hell?"

What is this?

The light is mesmerizing. The hues of blue my body is now omitting are breath taking. Her energy continues to radiate into me. Flowing in through my arms, and now I'm the one pulsing with electricity.

What's going on?

Our lights start merging into one solid light. They collide in an almost dance like explosion of violets and blues, shining even brighter than the white lights before. I close my eyes and become consumed by this whole new feeling that's over taken the last one. Then a frown of confusion wrinkles my face when a different sensation touches my lips. I open my eyes quickly.

She's kissing me!

"Zara!" I shout. Then push her away. Standing there frozen in shock.

Why did I do that?

My conscience is trying to snap me out of it but I'm still frozen and can't move.

Say something!

"I'm sorry," I begin.

You're sorry?

"You're sorry?" she pulls away from me.

"Zara!" I go after her but she's walking so fast.

"Don't," she scoffs. Her tone changed.

"Zara, I can't—and you shouldn't," I begin again. Not even sure where this is going.

We can't get attached to her.

"How do I get out of here?" her voice cracks, knowing she's on the verge of tears.

What if something happened to her?

My thoughts are so fucking loud right now. And they're flooded with images I never want to think about.

"Zara, please. You don't understand."

What will you do when she dies?

My conscience just won't stop. I can't seem to think straight, but I know I can't bear the thought of losing her. Not now. Not when I'm already invested.

"Then help me understand, Ronan!" she snaps at me. Tears filling her eyes.

"You can't be with a guy like me, Zara. I'm no good for you."

"Really?" she laughs. The tears streaming down her cheeks. Her beautiful, rosy cheeks. "You've got to be freaking kidding me, Ronan."

"Zara, I love—."

"Shit! I have to go," she cuts me off, checking the time on her watch.

"Wait, you can't leave yet," I attempt to stop her.

"How the hell do I get out of here, Ronan?" She asks not really looking for an answer from me. She pats herself down, searching for something. "Where's my phone?"

"Please, stay a minute. Just talk to me," I beg.

"No. I have to go, Ronan." Her words are like a punch to the gut. Why do I feel like I'm already losing her? When she's right here, right in front of me.

"Okay, can I just finish what I was going to say then?" I follow behind her.

"Why doesn't my phone work?" she ignores me. "Ugh! Stupid matrix white-room bullshit!" she yells.

"Zara, please!" I try again. But she pushes me away.

"I need you to take me back to Earth, somewhere I can get some reception." She's not going to listen to me now.

You need to make her listen.

"No, Zara," I begin. "Please, listen to me. Let me talk." I just need to get her to understand. I need to tell her how I feel.

"I don't want to hear it, Ronan. I have to go," she shrugs me off again. "Just forget the stupid kiss. It was a mistake. Just please take me to Ripley's."

"No," I back away from her. "I need you to listen." I try to talk to her again, but she grabs my arm then disappears. "What the hell. Did she just teleport by herself?" I mutter to myself, preparing to follow her. But an urgent message from work distracts me.

"Fuck! Not right now!" I stomp my foot in frustration. "I'll be back. I'll fix this."

I have to.

I zap off.

(Zara)

"I can't believe I just did that!"

What's wrong with me?

I feel a surge of self-loathing wash over me. He's not even from here, Zara. Why would he want you? When he can literally have any girl in the galaxy. I kick Ripley's bed. You thought you were special to him? You never were. You were only an assignment. What did you expect?

Take it easy, Zara.

My conscience adds. My thoughts are killing me right now and I can't seem to turn them off.

"I'm such an idiot!" I yell.

I'm hiding in Ripley's bedroom arguing with myself. Trying to fight back the tears. I'm just glad he sent me here alone and stayed behind. I couldn't even stand to look at him right now.

I'm so humiliated.

Ripley stammers into the bedroom and lets out a blood-curdling scream when she sees me.

"What the fuck, Zara! How'd you get in here?" she shouts.

I'm turning into Ronan.

"Ronan," I mutter under my breath. Then I feel my eyes begin to sting again. Just at the mere thought of him. But I get a grip of myself and shake him out of my mind before I really do start to cry. "Long story," I say to Ripley with a shrug.

"Well, you're late," she remarks in an annoyed voice. "Hurry, let's get you dressed."

"I'm sorry," I apologize. Then stand so she can take a better look at me.

"Wow," she scoffs. "*And* you're a mess. Wait. Were you crying, Z?" She tries to wipe the mascara smudges from under my eyes with her finger and then helps me take my jacket off.

"No," I lie. "It's just the rain. I forgot my umbrella and got caught in a downpour on my way to my car." She eats the story right up then continues with her orders again.

"Hmm," she gives me a side pout like she doesn't believe me but has no choice but to. "Come, get in. Hurry," she demands as she turns the shower on for me. Then waits for me to get in.

I look down at my clothes. I need to get undressed. But Ripley's mouth is still going a million miles per minute, and she doesn't seem to be slowing down.

"Kevin is picking us up in an hour. Liam is going to meet us there. He's already set up a donation fund. Eeeek! I'm glad we're only going for the after-party and don't have to sit through the boring stuff. I really can't tell you enough how much this means to me, Z. To us."

"Uh-huh," I reply. The water still running, and the mirror already beginning to fog. But she still doesn't seem to be letting off.

"And you really never know. You may

rekindle that flame with Liam," she continues. "Then who—."

Here we go again.

"Rip?" I try to stop her.

"—it's not like you're seeing anyone or anything. What do you have to lose?"

Nothing apparently.

She continues to ramble on senselessly about how Liam could be the one. The thought is laughable. Guys like Liam don't marry girls like me. They marry girls like—well, Ripley.

You should really shut her up before the house floods.

"Hey, Rip! Could you get out so I can take my clothes off, or do you want to watch?" I finally cut her off.

"Right," she chuckles then walks out.

But she does have a point, actually.

Not the part about Liam being the one, but the part about me not having anything to lose. I haven't been on a real date since the last time Ronan highjacked it. And well—Ronan is out of the picture now.

"Ronan," I sigh.

I undress while thoughts and replays of what happened earlier with Ronan course through my mind. Steam filling the room. I step into the scalding shower, feeling the water as it stings my skin.

"You know what? Screw Ronan," I mutter to myself. "Yeah, that's right. I shot my shot. I made my move. And he pushed me away. How could I have been so stupid? How did I get the signals so mixed up?" I continue talking to myself. "I thought he liked me too."

A wave of regret washes over me and once again I find myself fighting back tears. But then the sorrow turns to anger.

"You know what? I don't even want to see him anymore. Not now, not ever. Not for as long as I live!" I stomp my foot on the stone floor and make a small splash.

Easy there, tiger. You don't mean that.

"Yes I do. I can't believe I'd convinced myself he stuck around because he had feelings for me. *For me!* What an idiot!" I stomp again. "He was just doing his stupid job. But who was I even in danger of, supposedly? Liam?" I scoff.

Despite my frustration, I can't help but replay the situation in my head, wondering what I could have done differently. As I shampoo my hair, I catch a whiff of the luxurious scent and marvel at the quality of it.

Good God, this shampoo smells incredible.

"It must be expensive," I shrug. Then without warning I'm crying again.

This is going to be harder than I thought.

Tears begin to flow down my face, mixing

with the water as they cascade down my body. I wish I could wash away all the memories of him as easily as they wash down the drain. But tonight, I need to focus on moving forward and enjoying myself. Liam may not be perfect, but he's sweet and deserves a chance. Maybe Ronan and I were only meant to be friends, or even nothing at all.

I step out of the shower onto the heated marble floor, feeling the warmth beneath my feet. The dress and heels laid out for me are extravagant, but I can't help but feel hesitant. "Am I going to a ball?" I amuse myself, unsure if I can handle the towering heels.

But then I remember my promise to Ripley and resign myself to whatever she wants. "Whatever you want, Ripley," I remind myself.

The heels are about five inches tall, and I'm pretty sure I won't be able to walk, let alone stand in them.

I reach for the dress, and my fingers graze the soft velvet fabric. As I slip it on, it glides against my freshly shaved skin like a gentle caress. I take a step back to admire myself in the mirror, and a smile spreads across my face. "This is nice," I say to myself, the dress fitting me like a glove. "How does she always get my size right?"

The dress is a deep shade of red, reminiscent of a fine wine. Its tight fit accentuates my curves, and the two thin straps delicately rest on my shoulders. The neckline is low-cut, revealing just a hint of cleavage, while a daring slit runs up my left thigh, exposing my tanned skin. I feel a surge of confidence as I take in my reflection. For the first time in my life, I feel sexy. I've never felt sexy before.

Pretty? Every now and then.

Beautiful? Maybe on my best days.

But tonight, *sexy* is what I'm going for.

As I awkwardly perch on the edge of the bed, struggling to slip on my hooker heels, I'm grateful that this is not a lifestyle I lead, but merely a brief visit. "How do women do this every day?" I wonder to myself.

Finally, I manage to squeeze my feet into the towering shoes, but as I stand up, I realize that walking in them is going to be a greater challenge than I anticipated. With a deep breath, I steady myself and tell myself that I can do this.

However, as I take my first wobbly step, I resemble a newborn calf, swaying back and forth in an attempt to keep myself from falling over. "Uh-oh," I begin, "maybe I don't got this." I come tumbling to the ground.

"What the hell was that?" Ripley comes storming in after hearing my fall.

"I fell," I reply. Still on the ground.

"Oh, God. Get up!" She forces me to my feet again and makes me stand the entire time it takes her to paint my face.

I think I'm getting the hang of these

skyscrapers.

When she's all done doing my makeup, I strut down the hall like a supermodel to show Ripley my newfound skills. She applauds me proudly, but our moment is interrupted by the doorbell chime. Ripley's face lights up, and I know exactly who's at the door.

"That must be Kevin the X-Ray Man," I snort.

"Stop calling him that!" Ripley playfully smacks my arm. "We gotta go."

Reluctantly, I grab the clutch that Ripley insisted I borrow, even though I would have preferred my satchel. She insisted that it would clash with my outfit, and I don't want to risk upsetting her.

An angry Ripley is not someone to mess with.

Despite growing up in the hills and being born into privilege, she likes to boast that she's still got some street in her. It's unclear how she acquired this toughness, but I must confess, for someone as refined as she is, she can definitely hold her own.

"Eager to see your man, Z?" she teases.

"Actually, yes," I lie, but almost half convince myself.

The party is just next door at her parents' mansion. Despite the short distance, Ripley insisted on driving instead of walking, arguing that it's tacky to parade high fashion without an occasion.

There are so many rules with her.

As we arrive, a valet dressed in a sharp tuxedo greets us and opens the door after our brief ride.

"This way, ladies," he says kindly, nodding at Kevin, "Sir." He helps us out of the car, and we step onto a red carpet that's been laid out just for us.

It's for everyone.

It feels like we're celebrities. I'm not sure how to behave, should I wave or clap? What should I do with my hands? I awkwardly wave them around before slapping them firmly at my sides.

"Does your father throw this party every year?" I question Ripley as we walk through the grand entrance and into a palace.

"Every year," she replies nonchalantly. "But he didn't go all out this year like he usually does."

"This isn't all out?" I'm surprised. I can't imagine what *that* would look like.

As Ripley goes off to mingle with guests, I take the opportunity to explore the lavish house. A server approaches me with a tray of champagne, and I eagerly accept a glass. After taking a sip, I continue down the foyer, taking in the beautiful arrangements of white roses and gold painted vines decorating every corner.

I pass through a doorway, finding myself in a stunning ballroom, complete with a grand master staircase that reminds me of the Titanic.

"I need to get a picture." As I make my way towards it, a server bumps into me, causing me to spill my drink all over my dress. "Great," I mutter to myself as I stand there, drenched in my own misery.

Ripley witnesses the whole debacle and rushes over to me. "What happened?" she asks in an accusatory tone.

"I spilled my drink," I try to explain.

"I can't believe it," Ripley scolds me unfairly, as if I were a child who ruined her good church dress.

"How is this my fault?" I protest.

"Just go upstairs and take care of it," she instructs, clearly irritated. "There's a bathroom at the top of the stairs, first door on your right. Go clean yourself up. I'll be down here looking for Liam."

"But I've never been upstairs," I argue, wishing she'd just let me go home.

"Go!" she orders, cutting me off. "I'm sure you can find everything you need in there. And if not, we can sneak you out back to change at my place. But you are *not* leaving."

She must have read my mind. I refrain from arguing any further as she already seems to have a solution to everything. I pout and stomp my way up the stairs in an ungraceful manner.

The whole situation just sucks. I had hoped to have a good time, but now all I can do is scrub the stench out of my dress and keep hoping.

Halfway up the stairs, I suddenly remember where I am and realize that everyone can see me. So I straighten up and attempt to walk gracefully up the remaining steps, although it's not very successful.

When I finally reach the top, I rush into the bathroom, lock the door behind me, and stare at myself in the mirror with disappointment.

“What am I even doing here?” I question my reflection. “I'm a complete mess.”

I grab a hand towel and run it under hot water, adding soap and lathering it up. I scrub frantically at my dress, determined to get all of the smell out. Fortunately, I had already consumed most of the glass, so there wasn't much left to spill. I continue to scrub until my fingers turn red.

“I think I got it all out,” I say to myself as I remove the dress and rinse it under the water. Standing there in just my bra and panties, I examine myself in the splattered mirror. “Looks good enough,” I conclude, relieved that the champagne smell is gone.

12

HERE'S LOOKING AT YOU.

(Zara)

With a deep breath, I steel myself for what's to come. My nerves are jittering like a swarm of bees inside me.

Why am I so nervous?

"Let's get this over with." I inch my way towards the railing, trying to regain my balance.

As I scan the crowded ballroom below, my heart races. Finally, I spot Ripley waving at me and relief washes over me. But as I continue to survey the scene, my eyes land on Liam standing beside her. He looks surprisingly handsome in his sleek, black tuxedo with his hair styled to perfection.

My gaze meets his, and I can't help but smile at the sight of him. A bashful grin spreads across his face, and he waves at me eagerly. As I start to make my way down the stairs, I feel a flutter of excitement in my chest.

Maybe tonight wasn't such a bad idea after all.

But my joy is short-lived as I realize that every pair of eyes in the room is fixed on me. Suddenly, my confidence wavers, and I begin to feel self-conscious.

"Great," I mumble. Now that I know I have everyone's attention, I'm starting to get nervous.

Suddenly it feels like I've forgotten how to walk. I have to concentrate on each step and trying not to fall. As I reach the last step, I miss it entirely. But before I hit the ground, Liam jumps forward and catches me in his arms.

"Well, that went differently in my head," I chuckle, looking up at him.

"Hi," he responds, laughing in return. "Why are we laughing?"

"Maybe because I almost face-planted the floor?" I reply, feeling humiliated.

"What?" Liam replies, struggling to hear me over the music. But just as I start to repeat myself, the music fades, and my voice carries across the room, drawing even more attention to us.

Great.

"Oh, God. Let's go outside," I cover my face with my hands.

"I'll lead the way," he takes my hand confidently and guides me through the sea of people.

We find ourselves sitting on the garden wall, surrounded by the peaceful quietness of nature. Liam still holds my hand tightly, his touch soft and warm, while his scent fills my senses. Despite the chaos of the party, I strangely feel at peace with him by my side.

Our eyes dart around nervously, searching for something to talk about. As we both open our mouths to speak, our words scramble together inaudibly, making us both laugh and apologize.

"You go," I insist, making him blush. This is a side of Liam I've never seen before—nervous and vulnerable. He's always been confident, strutting the halls of Silverstone Health in his expensive suits and fancy watches. It's hard to believe this is the same guy who took me out on a date just three months ago.

Liam inhales deeply, gathering his courage. "Ripley told me there was no emergency," he begins, and I think I make a face. "Well, she didn't technically tell me."

"Okay, I guess we're doing this," I sigh, grabbing a glass of champagne from a passing waiter. "What exactly did Ripley tell you?"

"She didn't tell me anything," he assures me, but I'm not convinced. "I guess I might have asked the right question."

"And what question was that?" I inquire.

"The car," he says, and I nod in

understanding.

"Thanks for not saying anything," I reply, feeling grateful that he kept my secret.

"Well, it wasn't my place to say anything. I wanted to leave it up to you to tell her the truth or not," he says, his hands still shaking slightly.

"Are you okay, Liam?" I question, noting his nervousness.

"No," he admits. "I gotta be honest. Ever since that day, I haven't been able to get you out of my mind. Thinking about where you went, or with who. But it doesn't even matter. I just want you to know that I—I like you, Zara."

"You *like* me?" I repeat, surprised by his confession.

"Yes, like a lot," he admits, his voice full of sincerity. "And I don't know why."

"Okay," I chuckle.

"That came out wrong," he adds quickly, turning red. "I mean, I do know why. Obviously, you're incredible. I just—I've never felt this way about anyone. I don't know what to do, especially when the person I feel this for doesn't return any of my calls."

"I can explain that," I lie, feeling guilty for ghosting him.

"Look, if you never want to talk to me after tonight, then I'll never bother you again," he promises, looking genuinely hurt.

"Or bribe my best friend for a date?" I say under my breath, and he chuckles.

"I'm making no promises there," he jokes. "But can you just give me this one last chance, please? And I mean a real chance. Not just a pity date to shut me up."

"I don't do that," I say, offended by the accusation.

"Can you just do that for me? Please," he pleads, his eyes filled with hope.

"Only if you promise me one thing in return," I say, feeling a little more generous.

"Anything. You name it," he responds eagerly.

"You have to be yourself," I state firmly.

"That's easy. I can be me, I promise. Do we have a deal then?" he asks, offering his hand. His nerves seem to have vanished.

How can I say no to that?

"Deal," I take his hand, and we shake on it.

And now he's kissing me.

Oh boy.

(102)

I finish my assignment early and give the Commander a rundown on the Gullies. Notorious space travelers who wreak havoc wherever they go. They're like space pirates, except they possess incredible abilities, making them even more dangerous. Nonetheless, the task was easy, and I zap myself back home to freshen up for my evening with Zara.

After a quick shower, I root around my closet for my best suit, opting for a slim-fit gray ensemble. As I dress, I take my time, savoring each step to calm my nerves. Once dressed, I admire myself in the mirror and give myself a wink before realizing I almost forgot my shoes. After slipping them on, I give my beard a brush and rub my chin in admiration.

"I'll win her over again easily in this," I tell myself confidently. I'm planning to surprise her tonight. I speed off to Ripley's party, hoping I'm not too late.

I arrive at the scene in a new matte black Mercedes, drawing attention from the fashionable crowd. As I stride inside, everyone stares at me, wondering who I am.

Once inside, I scan the partygoers for Zara, eager to explain why I acted the way I did and apologize for my behavior. I'm desperate to find her, hoping she's there despite not telling me so.

"What the hell is wrong with me?" I mutter, still embarrassed by my actions around her.

This girl makes me act not myself sometimes.

Once in the ballroom, I look over the crowd. But I can't find Zara anywhere. I've decided to stay visible all night, so I'll have to look for her the old fashioned way. My plan tonight is to show her that I'm ready. That I will give everything up for her.

Now where the hell is she?

As a draft blows in, I catch her scent, a scent that I know all too well. My heart starts racing. "She's here," I sigh and follow the alluring aroma.

The party is packed with people. I push through the throngs of Earthlings, determined to find her. The scent leads me to the staircase, and I race up the steps, taking them two at a time.

When I reach the top, I find her lingering scent in the bathroom. My insides flutter at the thought of her being so close. I've never told her how I feel before, but tonight feels like the perfect opportunity. I look over the railing and scan the main floor below, which is now even more crowded with party-goers. That's when I catch a glimpse of something outside.

"Zara?" I mutter to myself, ready to zap myself to her side. But then I remember that everyone can see me, and I can't risk causing a scene. "Being an Earthling kinda sucks," I grumble. But I'm willing to suck.

For her I am.

As I hurry down the stairs, my eyes remain glued to the woman outside. I recognize her dark, long hair, and I'm almost certain it's her. She turns her face just slightly, and I can see her perfect nose and pink lips.

"It's definitely her," I tell myself, but then I notice the person beside her. "Who is that?" I wonder, unable to make out the figure clearly.

As I get closer, I realize with shock that it's Liam, the guy who always seems to be lurking around her. "This guy again?" I chuckle, deciding to watch from the patio doors before I intervene.

He's harmless.

But then, to my horror, Liam leans in and kisses her. And she lets him.

"No!" I yell through the glass. "Get him off of you! Don't kiss him!" My pleas turn into cries as my heart shatters into a million pieces.

I can't believe what I'm seeing. The pain is unbearable, and I feel like I can't breathe. My chest is tight, and I press my forehead against the glass as tears stream down my face.

"Zara—why?" I sob, unable to understand why she would choose Liam over me.

Just when I think things can't get any worse, she pulls him in and kisses him back. The tears start flowing uncontrollably. I can't take this anymore. I zap off, not caring who sees me anymore. I'm just desperate to escape the pain.

(Zara)

I close my eyes and taste Liam's lips, a

mixture of peppermint and champagne. His lips feel as soft as his hands, but the only face I want to see is Ronan's. I imagine him here, kissing me instead of Liam. I wish we could replay what happened earlier and that things could turn out differently.

But in the heat of my thoughts, I grab Liam and kiss him harder. However, the images of Ronan make my stomach turn and my eyes fly open. "Oh, no," I gag, feeling bile rising in my throat. I step back in disgust, hoping I don't puke all over Liam.

We break the kiss, and I can barely look at him. I feel guilty for thinking about another man while he kissed me, but I can't control my wandering mind. I feel like I'm cheating on someone, but who am I even cheating on? Ronan didn't want me.

My mind wanders back to Ronan, the way his lips felt when I kissed him, and the way he pushed me away. Tears start to sting my eyes, but I push them back. A cold breeze blows through my hair, sending a chill through my body. I look over at Liam again, and while it was a good kiss, it just wasn't with the person I wanted it to be.

God, I hate Ronan.

I don't want to think about him anymore. So I make the choice right then and there, I'm going to lock him up in the back of my mind for good.

Where he belongs.

"Are you okay?" Liam asks, trying to hide a smile.

"Does my pain amuse you?" I joke.

"Sorry, it's hard not to smile after that."

"I'm fine," I laugh. "I think the champagne just made me a little dizzy. I haven't drunk in a while."

Another cold breeze blows through, sending an uncontrollable quivering attack on my body. My teeth begin to chatter, and Liam realizes I'm not even wearing a jacket. He quickly pulls his off and wraps it around my shoulders, then pulls me in close to his warm body. His body heat stops the convulsions almost instantly.

"Come on, let's head back inside. I don't want you catching anything and missing work tomorrow. I'm looking forward to seeing that smile again." Liams words make me grin.

Maybe we should give him a chance.

My conscience is falling for this guy.

As we make our way inside, I steal a glance at Liam's face, admiring his exquisite features. Or maybe it's just the champagne talking.

The music is loud, and people are dancing and having a great time. I spot Ripley and Kevin in the middle of the dance floor and drag Liam over to join them. For someone who doesn't usually dance, I'm surprisingly good at it, swaying my hips perfectly to the beat of the music. I snag a champagne glass from a passing server and take a long swig, feeling a tingle in my toes. “This is going to be a great night,” I think to myself, momentarily forgetting about Ronan.

And who even is Ronan, anyways?

As the music dies down, I realize that Liam and I are the last ones on the dance floor. The servers are tidying up, and the band is still playing, but just for us. Dancing with Liam had been unexpectedly fun. I check the time and am surprised to find that we had been dancing for hours. Time flew by so quickly.

“It looks like the party’s over,” I tell Liam, noticing the disappointment in his face. He had been trying to make the night last as long as possible.

“Are you ready to go?” he asks, his voice low.

“I guess so,” I look around, knowing that we can't stay forever. “We should probably leave before they kick us out. Hey, have you seen Ripley?”

Liam shakes his head. “I haven't. But I can take you home if you need a ride.”

I consider my options, realizing that I can't drive myself home in my current state, and I hadn't brought my car anyway.

“Thanks, Liam. That would be great,” I accept, grateful for his offer. Then remembering Ronan teleported me here. “Ronan,” I whisper under my breath. It's like I can't seem to escape him, no matter how hard I try.

"What was that?" Liam questions, looking at me with concern.

"Nothing," I shake my head, trying to push Ronan out of my mind once and for all. I don't want to think about him again. Not today, and not ever.

The car ride is a peaceful contrast to the lively party we just left. I break the silence, trying to get to know Liam better.

"Now, tell me about yourself, Liam Silverstone."

"Okay," he replies nervously. "What do you wanna know?"

"Well, what do you think I need to know about you that I don't already know?"

"Depends, what do you already know?" he chuckles.

"Just that for fun you enjoy tormenting and frightening small sick children at the hospital you own." I tease.

"Hey! I do not! I need to straighten out your facts," he protests.

"The untold story of Liam Silverstone. This should be good," I announce, getting another laugh out of him.

"You're funny," he says, and for a moment, I'm reminded of Ronan, who used to say the same thing to me all the time.

"Okay, let's start from the beginning, I guess," I instruct, shaking off the thought.

"The very beginning?" he asks with a weak smile.

"Yes. Back to when you were just a wee boy."

"Okay," he laughs nervously. "Well, I was born on June 25th, 1989–."

"I did say the very beginning," I tease.

"You did," he blushes. "I'd say I had a pretty normal childhood I guess. Well—," he pauses, looking at me. "Normal for—."

"For a rich kid?" I suggest, knowing exactly what he means.

"Yes, that too," he admits with a weak smile. "But I meant normal for having witnessed *—the accident*."

"The accident?" I question, my curiosity piqued.

"When we lost my mother," he explains, and I feel a pang of remorse.

"I'm sorry," I sigh. Regretting my big mouth. "What was your favorite part of your childhood?" I change the subject.

"The horses," he replies, his face lighting up. "We used to have horses. Five of them when I was growing up. Zola, Lily, Stallion, Jeff, and Rosey," he beams, his voice full of nostalgia. "My mother used to take me out riding nearly every day. We were really close, my mother and I."

"What about your dad?" I ask curiously.

"My father didn't really care for the horses. He was strictly about business," Liam explains sternly. "We didn't see him very often."

"Did he work a lot?"

"A whole lot," Liam confirms. "My mother hated the business. She always wanted my father to sell and move far away to start a farm. And I always had the same dream."

Liam working on a farm?

It's hard to imagine.

"Why didn't you guys ever get that farm?" I question.

"My mother—there was a fire in the barn one night. That's when everything changed," he tells me, his eyes glistening with unshed tears. I regret my question quickly.

There I go putting my foot in my mouth again.

I softly inquire, "Was that when—?" not needing to finish the sentence.

Liam nods before continuing, "She ran in to let the horses out. And got trapped inside. I ran out to help her as fast as I could. But my father stopped me."

"You tried to go in!" My sudden outburst surprises even me.

Liam almost whispers, "Tried. He grabbed me before I could make it inside. I'll always regret that I didn't try harder."

"You were just a boy, Liam. It wasn't your

fault."

"I was fifteen, Zara," Liam clenches his jaw, "I was old enough. I could have saved her. But he went in after her instead."

"Did he find her?"

"Yes," Liam replies, "He tried to get her to leave the horses. But she wouldn't. She was trying to get them out but their gates were locked. The gates were never locked. My father was fighting her and that's when the entire barn collapsed on them."

"Oh, my God. Liam—I'm so sorry," I gasp.

"My father barely made it out," Liam tells me. "Sometimes I can still hear him calling out to her. I remember everything felt like it lasted for hours. But the whole thing went down in less than ten minutes. It all happened so fast." My eyes moisten, and my heart aches painfully for fifteen-year-old Liam.

"I'm so sorry you had to go through that, Liam," I offer comfort, resting my hand on his.

"Thank you," Liam grins, "You know, my father may not have been very good at showing it, but he loved my mother very much. She's probably the only thing he's ever loved."

"I'm sure that's not true," I try to reassure him.

He forces a chuckle, but I can see young Liam's need for his father's love inside adult Liam's eyes, "You don't know my father," he responds.

He's right.

Things aren't always what they seem from the outside looking in.

"Anyway, after the fire, we had the barn removed and never rebuilt it again. That was the end of my farm dreams."

"What's there now?" I ask, wishing sometimes I wasn't so uncontrollably curious.

"We had a giant willow planted there in her memory," Liam explains. "It's still there today. Beautifully magnificent, just like my mother."

"That's nice," I reply then try to change the subject, "Did you ever get any more horses?"

"No," Liam's smile disappears. "My father couldn't even stand the thought of horses after that, so we never had any again."

"I'm so sorry, Liam," I offer my sympathy, "I know I keep saying it, but that was all just awful. Did you have any friends to help you get through it?"

"No," Liam laughs, "I was actually homeschooled by my mother my entire life, so after her death, I was forced to go to regular school for the very first time."

"And how was that?" I inquire.

"That was a whole new adventure in itself," Liam replies with a nervous chuckle. "I didn't fit in. Especially starting in high school at an all-boys private school. Teenage boys can be mean. But rich, spoiled brats are a whole different type of terror. So, I guess you could say I was pretty popular. But not in a good way."

"That must have been hard," I sympathize. "What did you do to get through it?"

"I did everything I could to graduate early. I was already way ahead of my peers, so it wasn't too much work," he explains in the most humble manner.

"Show off," I tease. "What did you do after high school?"

"Well, I was only sixteen when I graduated, and I had gotten into every Ivy League college in the country," Liam boasts.

"Impressive," I acknowledge.

"Yeah. I figured this was my one chance to reinvent myself. To not be the nice, sensitive pushover everyone knew in high school," he shares. "This was college."

"It sure was," I agree jokingly.

"Hey, that was where I made a new name for myself," Liam continues.

"And what name would that be?" I inquire.

"Liam. Liam Silverstone. Not David's son or Silverstone Junior," he answers. "But *Liam.*"

"That's respectable," I compliment.

"Thank you. So, you need to understand, with my father handing over the business to me, I have to keep up the act now more than ever," Liam confesses.

"What do you mean?" I question him.

"I mean, even if it's just pretend. I need to gain respect from the men who work for me, who are much older and have been working alongside my father for many more years than I have. It's all just an act," he explains with a sigh.

"So, do I call you David's son? Or is Junior cool?" I joke, and he laughs.

"*You* can call me whatever you'd like," he replies with a smile.

"I'm joking," I clarify. "But seriously, how am I going to top that back story?"

"You think you're willing to give me a chance now?" Liam asks, forcing a smile.

"Look, I know you're a nice guy, Liam. I can see it now. I just wish you'd let other people see it too," I comfort him, rubbing his arm. He gives me a little smile.

"I know. But—."

"And you also really need to start tipping the valet at the hospital. Even if your car does drive itself. Remember, those five bucks can really make a person's day," I remind him.

"You tip people $5? And you call me cheap," he teases back. "I tip people in other ways. Ways they don't necessarily see right away. Maybe I'll tell you about it someday," he adds with a wink.

"Hey! We're not all gazillionaires. I'd be happy with $5. I'm actually not that hard to please. I'm a very simple girl," I retort.

Despite my partially intoxicated state, I manage to give Liam accurate directions to my home.

"I bet you've never seen one of these before, huh?" I tease as Liam drives us through the gates. He flushes, knowing it's true.

"One of what?" he lies poorly.

"An apartment," I laugh.

"No. Yeah. Of course, I have!" he stammers. His cheeks turn crimson.

"Oh, yeah? Where?" I tease.

"On television," he whispers to himself. I laugh and reach for his hand.

"Come on," I say as he parks his car. "I promise you, I won't let you get murdered or mugged. Now please, let me out of your alien car. How do I open this thing?" I search for a handle but can't figure out what opens what.

"Here," he laughs, pushing a button to open the Tesla door. I step out and frown.

"Now, how do I close it?" I ask. He pushes another button, and it closes on its own. "Gotta get me one of these," I joke.

"Hey, don't tempt me," he laughs. "It's almost Christmas, and I'm an excellent gift giver."

"Liam!" I playfully smack him. "You can't buy cars for people you barely know." I lead the way to my door, and he follows close behind, reaching out to hold my hand to avoid losing me.

We climb the stairs to the second story

where my door is. I unlock it and turn to him.

"This is me," I say, not inviting him in. I just wanted to see his reaction to where I live.

"Can I—?" Liam begins, and I cut him off.

"I'm exhausted," I yawn. "I should get to bed."

"Okay," Liam lazily closes his eyes.

Did he just fall asleep?

He starts moving towards me, and I think he's going in for a goodnight kiss.

"And I also need to feed my cat," I blurt out, just before his lips touch mine.

"What?" he opens his eyes.

"Goodnight," I add.

"Oh," he forces a smile. "Well, goodnight then."

"And thank you," I tell him.

"For what?" he questions.

"For tonight," I reply, making him grin. "It was surprisingly very fun. Let's do it again sometime?" His eyes light up, and I can't resist his cuteness.

"Really?" he asks excitedly. "Y—yes! I had an amazing time, also. Definitely, we should do it again!" He hugs me, and I don't reject him this time.

"Goodnight, Zara. I hope you sleep very, very well," he says.

"I hope you do too, Liam. Goodnight." I close the door and watch him walk downstairs from the peephole, noticing he has a little pep in his step.

“It’s bedtime, bud,” I say to Binks as he rubs himself on my leg. Vibrating while he purrs. “I'm really tired, and my feet are killing me.”

13

WHAT HAPPENS IN N.Y.

(Zara)

It's been over a week since the Christmas party, and I still haven't heard from Ronan. Did I scare him off with that kiss?

Clearly, he had his output signals mixed up because I know when a guy is into me. And he was into me! *Very* into me!

Okay, I'm not that great at telling, but this time I thought I was sure.

Oh, you think?

I shut the voice up in my head.

"I'm not stupid. He's stupid," I tell myself.

Yeah!

"Or maybe he really just doesn't like me."

My heart feels like it's skydiving and forgot the parachute. I wish I could talk to Ripley about all of this. She'd know exactly what to say. Or what to do.

Loneliness engulfs me, tearing me apart

whenever it gets a chance. And then come the flashbacks. Every night since he left, I've woken up drenched in sweat, realizing he's no longer there beside me, like he always used to be. Watching over me as I slept— protecting me.

"Why did you have to be so good to me, Ronan? Why did you have to make me fall in love with you!" I shout, tears streaming down my cheeks. I force myself to stop crying and try to forget about him. But it's not easy.

I can't eat, and I've been crying daily.

Maybe it's just a bad hangover?

No, it's more than that. I'm heartbroken.

Before heading to work, I do my daily self-training. Ronan taught me enough, but he didn't get to teach me everything. I sit on my living room carpet and close my eyes.

"Big light. Big light," I chant. I can do this alone.

We don't need him.

I arrive at work early and sit quietly at my desk, typing my nurses' notes into the computer. When suddenly, someone grabs me from behind. "Ronan!" I instinctively shout.

But it's not him; it's Liam.

I'm clearly disappointed, but trying not to show it.

"Who's Ronan?" Liam's eyebrows rise in surprise.

"Oh, hey, it's you," I turn crimson, "What's up?"

(102)

I'm so fucking tired of seeing them together.

It's like a never-ending torture. "Does he really need to be here all the time?" I ask myself, my frustration building. "He's not even doing anything productive. He just hangs out at the nurse's station all day, disrupting everyone's work!" I scoff, clenching my jaw, unable to take my eyes off them.

They're across the room, laughing and flirting, as if the world revolves around them. It's nauseating.

But today is my last day here. I'm being reassigned to his father, hoping to get better leads on the campaign and the inoculations they're planning. I hope it's not as sinister as we suspect. Despite my relief at no longer being the invisible third wheel, the thought of not seeing her at all hurts.

How could she move on so quickly?

Did she ever care about me like I do about her?

Or was she just stringing me along?

All day, my mind circles back to these questions. Tormenting me. But the memories are what keep me going. Every night, I watch them again. Reliving every moment. As if we're still together. Frozen in time.

It's a pathetic routine, I know. But I can't seem to break free from it. I watch him rub her shoulders as she types away, and it's like a punch to the gut.

"Why did you have to make me fall in love with you, Zara?" I snarl through clenched teeth.

The day is finally drawing to a close and Logan has picked his favorite haunt to crash. A small retro bar in the heart of New York City. As I enter the joint, I take in the shiny red leather booth benches, smooth stainless steel tables, and the waitresses zooming around on rollerblades, wearing tiny shorts.

It's no surprise why Logan likes this place.

The walls are covered with snapshots of celebrities and politicians from all over the world, sitting in the same booths. Clearly, this is a popular spot. I spot Logan sitting in a corner booth on the far right, engaged in conversation with two girls.

Great.

"Hey, brotha!" he spots me right away and bellows, as if I couldn't already hear him from outside the bar. I nod in acknowledgment and the girls turn to look at me.

"Ladies, meet Ronan the Mighty Warrior!"

Logan introduces me to his new friends boisterously, slapping my shoulder to emphasize that it's me whom he speaks of.

"Hi," I offer a polite wave as Monica and Carla greet me in unison.

It's easy to tell that they're both New Yorkers from their hoop earrings and the way they chew their gum. As I watch Monica chew, I can't help but compare her to a cow nibbling on grass.

Logan continues with his usual charade of bullshit, announcing that I'm a fireman who just finished a shift.

"Shall we sit?" I wait for him to finish before politely suggesting.

I could kill him right now.

I slide into the booth next to Monica. Not that I have a choice, really. She's kinda cute, I guess.

If only we could get her to spit out that gum.

Already annoyed, I send Logan an IM while I glare at him from across the table.

Me: "What the hell are you doing, man? I just wanted to talk to you. Alone!"

Logan: "Come on, bro. I can sense the sorrow. You need to live a little."

He's right. I really do need to get my mind off things. Off of Zara.

He sends me another I.M.

Logan: "And I'm also 100 percent sure you haven't gotten laid in months."

I kick him under the table.

"Ouch!" he yells. I shrug like I don't know what happened. I mean, he's not wrong. But, I wish it could be Zara instead. It's not like I wasn't going to go back to talk to her. I was! And I did. She was the one that was kissing that douchebag. And she liked it, too.

The same freaking day she tries to kiss me, she kisses Liam! Liam! Ugh! My blood begins to boil, and the pump sends a rush of adrenaline to the part of my brain that's in charge of fun and stupid decisions.

Me: "You win this one, man. Let's have some fun."

I tell him, leaving out the part where I desperately do need to get laid.

Hours later, we get into a stupor, and I can't seem to stop running my mouth.

I wrap an arm around each of the girls' shoulders, slurring my words and breathing whiskey on them.

"Do you know what the problem today is, ladies?" I ask. Logan shakes his head, anticipating trouble. "There's no such thing as real love these days," I proclaim, prompting frowns from the girls.

"I have to disagree," Monica argues.

"Well you're wrong. The young people now, just don't have the same type of commitment. As soon as you think you might be feeling it—splat! Someone comes around and squashes your heart," I explain, smacking one hand into the other as a demonstration and pointing to my chest.

The drinks I've been pounding are all starting to catch up to me. I stumble and catch my fall on a barstool. Then I sit and sway back and forth, still speaking when clearly I shouldn't be.

Can someone please come stop me already?

"Hey, are you okay, man?" Logan asks me but I shake him off.

"Come, come," I wave the girls closer and clear my throat. "It's story-time," I announce. The girls pull up a chair, their eyes wide as they listen attentively.

"Ooh! Story time!" Carla beams.

"So, this happened one night, many many years back," I begin. "One of our good friend's, he wasn't from Earth, he was from our planet—," I hiccup.

Logan: "Don't do it, man, we don't know these girls well enough. Watch what you say."

"He was the only one of us to find love. Then one day—," I gag, painfully swallowing a ball of vomit in my throat.

“One day what!” Carla presses. Wanting to hear more.

“He died,” I sigh. “Leaving her all alone. Can you imagine the feeling? To find the love of your life, then have them die before you?” My own grief over losing Zara resurfaces, and I realize that the pain I feel must be similar to what she experienced. It's a painful reminder that I have lost the only person I’ve ever loved. And not to death but to my own foolishness.

Carla leans in towards me, hope and anticipation written all over her face.

“Are you a romantic, Ronan?” she questions, eagerly awaiting my response. I know what she wants to hear, but the truth is, I’m not the guy for her.

“Not really,” I reply, trying to keep my tone neutral. “I've never even had a romantic relationship in my life.” I can see the disappointment on Carla's face. The story had given her false hope about my intentions.

“Oh? And why not?” she presses, continuing her interrogation.

“For starters, I've been in this galaxy for over a century and still haven't had that kind of luck. Not even once,” I explain, holding up my index finger to illustrate the amount.

“I find that hard to believe,” Carla counters, crossing her arms.

“You know what? You're right, Carla,” I

concede. “I actually did find that once.”

“Really?” Carla's friend Monica chimes in.

“Yes,” I confirm. “After all these years, I thought I had finally found the girl for me. The one I thought I wanted to spend whatever time I have left with. And I was going to tell her, too, actually.”

I take a sip of my drink, trying to compose myself. Monica seems annoyed that the girl I was speaking of wasn't her.

“Well then why isn't this girl here with you now?” Monica rolls her eyes. “Since she's so amazing.”

“Because she doesn't know how I feel, Monica,” I explain to her, my voice cracking with emotion. “I never got the opportunity to tell her. Obviously. Are you not listening?”

“Aww!” Carla cries, moved by my story. “Why not?”

“I tried! But when I went to go tell her, I found her kissing some other guy,” I admit, feeling a lump form in my throat.

Carla reaches out to wipe the tears from my eyes with a napkin. “Oh, sweetie,” she coos sympathetically.

Monica puts her arm around me, trying to comfort me as well. “Let's cheer you up, baby. It's alright. There are other girls,” she suggests.

“Other girls?” I grimace, my voice thick with sadness. “Like who?”

“Like me,” Monica offers, giving me a

goofy smile. "I may not be your dream girl, but I can help you forget about her for just one night."

She bites her lip seductively and slips her hand into mine, her blinking awkwardly out of sync.

"I have to go, man," I tell Logan, suddenly feeling a sense of urgency. "I need to go see her. I need to tell her that I'm sorry. Tell her how I feel."

"Maybe we should go," Carla suggests to Monica, her annoyance palpable.

"Yo, relax. Come here," Logan grabs me firmly by the shoulders. "Ladies, it's fine. I'm just going to take him to the little boy's room real quick and we'll be right back," he throws my arm over his shoulder and carries me off.

"Where are we going?" I muster.

"Come on, man," Logan drags me. "What the hell is your problem? That was guaranteed for both of us!"

"I want to go see, Zara," I complain. "Let me go!" I try to get away but he grabs me again.

"Ronan, get it together man! Monica was just about to take you to pound town. Don't you want to get laid?" he pleads with me as we stand in the middle of the men's restroom. But I can barely make out what he's saying. His voice sounds distant and keeps echoing in my ears.

"Yeah, man. It's cool, whatever," my words a slur.

I push past Logan and stumble towards the sink to splash my face with cold water. As I lean over the sink, I notice a guy standing beside us, pissing into a urinal. And we seem to be distracting him from doing his business.

"Enjoying the show?" I give him a hard slap on his back, causing him to pee all over himself.

"What the hell man!" he shouts.

"Oh, my bad. Hahahaha!" I laugh. The man zips his pants up and leaves without even washing his hands. Then he has the nerve to look back at me like I'm the crazy one.

"Gross! Wash your hands, bro!" I point to him as he walks out.

"Come on, man. Are you gonna be cool in there or what?" Logan shakes me. I puff out my cheeks and feel my mouth begin to fill with the drinks I was pounding earlier.

"Oh, no," I cry. Then I bolt into a stall and throw up every drink I just had. And then I throw up again.

When I can no longer get anything else to come up, I grab a wad of toilet paper and clean my mouth.

"Are you okay, man?" Logan storms into the stall where I've just emptied my guts. "That was fucking gross, dude," he grabs my hand and pulls me up.

I quickly wash my hands and face and rinse out my mouth.

"Alright, man. I think I'm cool now. Let's go back out there. But I think I want the other one," I wink at him.

"Ha! My man!" he winks back. "You got it. She's all yours," Logan slaps me on the back. Then shakes my hand as we walk back out.

Carla is looking really good right now.

14

CURIOSITY KILLED THE CAT

(Zara)

January.

The chill in the air seems to have settled in for good now, it's much colder than last month. Rain is now a constant, and it only adds to the gloomy atmosphere that's been following me around lately. It's been over a month since I've seen Ronan. I catch glimpses of him occasionally, or at least I think I do. Once while hiding out on the 4th floor, and sometimes when I'm with Liam. But those are just imaginary fleeting moments that vanish the instant I turn to look. I know it's probably all just in my head.

Maybe he didn't have a reason to stay anymore. He did tell me before that there was talk about being reassigned to someone new. Because Liam wasn't giving him enough information. But he always reassured me that he would still stay with *me*.

He promised me he would.

But that was weeks ago.

I try to hold back tears, but I miss him so much. Every night, I dream of him. Hoping to wake up to his looming presence, only to realize he's no longer there.

Not anymore.

He used to make me feel safe, protecting me from threats that weren't even real. At least, that's what I thought. I just want to get him out of my head. I want to stop seeing him everywhere I go, and not feel his presence with me when I know he's not here.

Not anymore.

"Not anymore."

My phone chimes loudly and startles me.

It's a text from Liam.

Liam: "Be there in five. XO"

Things are moving pretty quickly with Liam. Today, I'm going to meet his father for the first time as his girlfriend. But I'm not going to pretend to be someone I'm not. I'm going to wear my own clothes that I bought with my own hard-earned money.

After getting dressed, I admire my reflection. I'm wearing a pair of ripped blue jeans and a black tank top, layered with a mustard-colored cardigan. To top off my look, I slide on a black beanie and my rain boots, just in case the unpredictable California weather decides to act up.

Suddenly, I hear footsteps approaching my door, followed by a soft knock.

"Are you ready, Zara Lara?" Liam teases through the door. I give my hair a quick brush and grab my coat to leave.

"Bye, Binks," I pat the black fur-ball lightly on the head. "See you later! Well, that's if daddy Silverstone doesn't suck my blood dry," I joke, trying to lighten the mood.

When I open the door, Liam greets me with a kiss. "You look absolutely stunning," he admires. "Come on, babe." He takes my hand and leads me to his car.

(102)

What the fuck happened last night?

As I wake up, my head is pounding, and I can't remember a thing. All I know is that I'm completely naked, and so is the brunette lying next to me. I gather my things quietly, trying not to wake her up. I have no idea who she is or where I met her, and I'm not sure I want to know.

This has been happening quite frequently lately. There's a hole I've been left with that I'm not sure how to fill yet. But in the meantime, I've been filling other things.

Many other things.

"God, I'm a mess. I need help," I say to myself as I sneak out of her house.

Earth is great for one night stands. I never have to worry about running into anyone again. Every night a new city and every city, a new girl.

That's my new motto.

My new assignment has been great so far. I'm close to cracking the whole case. Douchebag Jr. still shows up from time to time, but working over his father means I no longer have to worry about running into Zara.

Although I must admit, the thought does cross my mind occasionally. But I quickly dismiss it, knowing that even a glimpse of her could undo all the progress I've already made in moving on.

Progress? Please.

"God damn it," I curse at my conscience.

I have to confess, I haven't made any real progress in getting over Zara. The mere thought of seeing her again fills me with uncontrollable emotions and could honestly send me spiraling once again. I'm just not ready for that yet.

On the bright side, David Silverstone has been a fascinating subject to investigate. This guy seems to have all the intel we need. According to him, they've been plotting to incapacitate the entire human race on Earth for decades. It's not surprising, but it's certainly alarming.

Shocker, right?

The old fart is upstairs bathing. Despite spending an hour in the tub every day, David still manages to reek of malt liquor. Which makes me wonder if he drinks while he bathes. Or maybe he bathes in the stuff? The thought alone is enough to make my stomach turn. I decide to stay put in his office, unwilling to venture upstairs to investigate.

As I wait, I decide to do some snooping around. I've had my eye on a particular filing cabinet for weeks, and now seems like a good time to break in and see what I can find. I begin scanning through the documents when a sound outside the door catches my attention.

Is someone here?

I listen closely as the front door opens and two mysterious visitors enter. They're quiet, seemingly waiting for someone. But their arrival is soon overshadowed by David's heavy stomping as he descends the stairs.

David is tall, heavyset, and has a thick, salt-and-pepper beard that I'm certain he gets professionally dyed. You can both hear and feel him coming. When he greets his guests, I strain to hear what he's saying, but their conversation remains elusive.

After a few moments, the visitors wander

off, leaving David to join me in his study. I've been patiently waiting for this moment, as he is scheduled to attend a very important meeting today - the very same meeting I am here to crash.

(Zara)

As Liam pulls the Tesla into the long driveway, I can feel my nerves rising. The European-style castle is simply breathtaking, with its perfectly crafted deep gray stone walls adorned with navy blue wood trimmings and neatly trimmed greenery. The tall set of stairs leading to the front door is particularly impressive.

Liam stops the car at the front steps and turns to me.

"Are you ready?" he inquires, taking my hand tightly in his. He kisses it, and I feel my heart flutter.

Smiling warmly at him I nod.

He gets out first. I watch him as he walks around to my side. Then opens the door to help me out.

"Ready to meet your future father-in-law?" he teases.

The mention of Liam's father being my future father-in-law makes me feel uneasy, and I try to push the thought aside.

"Have I told you how handsome you look

yet?" I reply, pulling him close and kissing him.

"Nope," he kisses me back a little too eagerly.

"Okay, okay, that's enough, Liam," I push him back. He smooths out his shirt and grins at me.

"What you do to me, Ms. Lara," he grins, looking flustered. "Let's go." He offers his hand, and I take it, letting him lead me up the steps to the giant front door.

The house smells of peppermint, and I can't help but notice that it looks like it hasn't been renovated in the past century.

Liam turns to me with a proud grin.

"What do you think?" he waits for my response.

"It's great," I give him two thumbs up. "Did your grandfather grow up here too?"

He nods eagerly, "His father did too, actually."

Note to self, be on the lookout for ghosts.

A tall, heavyset man comes stomping down the stairs, and I recognize him instantly.

But does he even remember my face?

David Silverstone never came around the hospital as often as Liam does. But I know for a fact that I've exchanged a word or two with him on numerous occasions. My palms begin to sweat profusely as he approaches.

Why am I so nervous?

Oh yeah, I forgot to mention, those words were not very friendly.

"Hello, uh—?" Mr. Silverstone begins, as he struggles to recall my name. But I'm relieved when he fails to remember me.

"Zara!" I quickly offer, shaking his hand. "Zara Lara."

"Hmm. That's funny," he responds before walking away without another word. David disappears into his den and slams the heavy wooden French doors behind him.

I'm left standing there with my hand still out, looking confused. I turn to Liam who is grinning and giving me two thumbs up. I'm not sure if he's serious or just mocking me from earlier. It's hard to tell whether this encounter went well or not.

Did this go well?

(102)

As I sink into David's plush office chair, my eyes remain fixed on his every move. He frantically shuffles through files in his cabinet, and as he reaches for his chair, I quickly jump out of it, not wanting to risk being crushed. I keep a close eye on him as he logs into his computer, unaware of my presence. I memorize all his passwords, knowing they'll come in handy later.

It's a gold mine. The files I've been searching for on the Livingstons, Kinghills, and even the Steeles are all here. I can hardly believe it. But my eyes lock onto a new name that wasn't part of my initial investigation.

Mr. X?

I knew there had to be more than one family involved in this conspiracy.

As David closes his files and rushes out of the room, I follow him and watch as he jumps into a black SUV and speeds away. It's clear he won't be back anytime soon. I quickly return to his office and continue to search for anything that could be useful before he returns.

With ease, I log into his computer without needing to hack it. Everything seems to be falling into place. I had a feeling this would be a night to remember.

(Zara)

“Wow, that went better than I expected,” Liam exclaims. But I'm left feeling confused.

Did I miss something?

“You think so?” I question, puzzled, wondering if we all witnessed the same thing.

“Come on, let’s go,” Liam replies, motioning to the back of the house. I cautiously follow him deeper inside.

We stop in the kitchen, where he hands me a small pink-striped shopping bag from atop the counter.

"Did you buy me underwear or something?" I arch a brow at him.

"No, silly, it's a swimsuit! I didn't know where else to find one," he replies. "Anyway, we're going swimming!"

"Swimming?" I shriek. "In winter?"

"Go in there," he points to a door down the hall. "And put that on." I shrug my shoulders and do as I'm told. I'm down for some swimming.

But it's a little cold out, don't you think?

I hurry into the bathroom and quickly strip down before pulling out the blue two-piece swimsuit from the bag. As I go to put it on, a hard and metallic object falls out and hits the ground.

"What's this?" I pick it up. It's a key. I look back in the bag and find a note.

"Just in case," the note reads, along with an emoji of a house.

Is this Liam's house key?

"It fits!" I shout.

"Good!" Liam answers from outside the door. When I step out, he's already dressed, waiting for me in snug, blue swimming trunks that stop just above his knees and have baby blue stripes.

"What's this?" I inquire, holding the key.

"I'm not asking you to move in or

anything. Don't freak out. It's just a spare in case you ever need it. I don't know," he explains.

"Oh," I say, slipping the key into my bag. "Thanks."

Liam grabs my hand and leads me down the hallway to a hidden stairway. It's dark and looks a bit sketchy.

"Where are you taking me?" I question wearily.

"It's a surprise," he whispers, looking back at me with a mischievous grin.

"Are you going to murder me?" I chuckle, trying to make a joke but also feeling a bit uneasy. Liam chuckles but doesn't deny the question.

What does that mean?

As we reach the top of the stairs, a long dimly lit hallway greets us, with large holes resembling garbage chutes running along its walls. The eerie atmosphere seems to be perfect for a horror movie.

"Take your pick," he offers, turning towards me.

"Oh my God, you *are* going to kill me!" I exclaim, attempting to flee back down the stairs. But he holds me firmly, refusing to let me go.

"Zara!" he chuckles.

"Help!" I shout, struggling to free myself.

"Shh, stop yelling," he tries to calm me down, still laughing uncontrollably.

What's so damn funny!

"Is this where you dump the bodies, you sick bastard!" I yell, hoping someone will hear my cries.

"I'm not going to kill you, silly. They're slides," he clarifies.

"What?" I stop resisting, confused.

"Like I said, take your pick," Liam replies, disappearing into one of the giant holes.

I rush towards the hole. And I see water gushing down a dark tunnel.

"It is a slide," I chuckle, grabbing onto the metal bar and sliding in.

The warm water feels like velvet against my skin as I slide down the slippery tube. Finally, I see the light at the end of the tunnel and brace myself for the impact. Splashing into the water.

I open my eyes but can't find Liam. I swim up for air and realize we're inside an indoor pool. This place is like a miniature water park, with towering palm trees and stalks of bamboo stretching up towards the ceiling. The air is humid and heavy with the scent of tropical plants that adorn every corner and crevice of the space.

The ceiling itself is a masterpiece, a massive window that dominates the entire area, offering a clear view of the full moon shining down from above. The soft moonlight casts a serene glow over the rippling water, lending a surreal and magical touch to the entire scene.

I look out and find Liam standing at the top of the steps above me, extending his hand out to me.

"Wanna go again?" he smirks.

"Hell, yes!" I take his hand.

(102)

"I've got it all," I proclaim triumphantly, a wide smile spreading across my face. "Everything we need to put David away for good."

But as I turn to leave, a nagging feeling tugs at the back of my mind. Who were those Earthlings that stayed behind? I never heard them leave. I can't resist the urge to investigate.

I zap back inside the house, my heart pounding with anticipation. I search every room, but they're nowhere to be found. Frustration builds inside me as I try to locate them.

"Concentrate, Ronan," I whisper to myself. And then, like a whisper in the wind, I hear something. Laughter. Coming from the back of the house.

The sound of their laughter grows louder as I make my way towards it. My mind races with questions. Who are they? Why are they here?

Finally, I come across a hidden stairway behind the kitchen. I've never seen it before, and the old man never mentioned it. My curiosity takes over as I ascend the stairs.

At the top, I'm met with a strange hallway lined with deactivated portals. My eyes widen in amazement. Is this a teleportation station? But something feels off.

I reach inside one of the portals, and my hand comes out unscathed. It's then that I notice the water flowing through it. I follow the tunnels, my heart pounding with excitement and fear.

As I near the end of the tunnel, I hear the voices again. And then, I hear her. Zara. My heart skips a beat.

What is she doing here?

I inch closer, trying to make out what they're saying. But I can't hear them clearly. My heart begins to race and I feel my palms get sweaty. But my instincts force me to search for her. I look around quickly, needing to see her. And as soon as my eyes catch a glimpse of her face, I'm stuck again. All the feelings I've been trying to suppress are now forcing their way back into my heart. And into my soul. I watch her like a mindless zombie as she climbs out of the pool. Seemingly in a rush. She looks like she's *running* from someone.

Where are her clothes?

I'm about to run over to her when Liam appears, and my blood boils at the sight of him.

Why did he bring her here?

Why is he chasing her?

My instincts kick in, and I'm ready to jump in to protect her when I realize they're just playing around. Zara is giggling, and my heart shatters all over again.

It's like watching a car crash, and I can't look away. She seems so happy, like she doesn't even remember me or what we had. And then Liam tackles her to the ground, and they start kissing. My stomach turns, and I feel sick to my core.

How can she be this happy without me?

"I should have never come back here," I snarl to myself as I storm off back home. I can't take it anymore. The pain is too much to bear. I wish I could just forget everything, erase the memories of her from my mind. But no matter what I do, I can't seem to escape her hold on me.

I've tried so hard to move on, to find someone else, but nothing works. No one can compare to her. She's engraved in my soul, and I can't shake her.

Why did I let her go so easily?

Why didn't I fight for her?

The self-hatred consumes me, and I'm left with nothing but the pain of losing her all over again. I know I need to get out of here, to escape the memories and the pain. So I zap myself to the bar, hoping to find some solace in Logan's company.

But I know even he can't distract me from the ache in my heart. I don't know what to do or how to move on from her. All I know is that I can't live without her.

And I don't want to.

(Zara)

Liam and I spend hours racing down the slides and playing in the pool. It's been the most fun I've had in a long time and a nice change from our usual routine. I feel like a kid again, but it's getting late.

"I think we should get going, Liam," I remind him. "Your dad should be back soon, and I don't want him to see me like this."

"Okay," he responds, seemingly disappointed. "You ready for the after party at my place?" Liam raises a hopeful eyebrow at me.

"I wish," I lie. "But I have to get to bed; I have work in the morning."

"Darn it," he sighs. "Maybe I can convince your boss to give you the day off?" He winks.

Good one.

"You know how I feel about that. We need to keep work and us separate," I raise an eyebrow back at him. "You promised."

"Fine," he throws his arms up in defeat.

"I'll get us some towels. Wait here."

After drying off, we head downstairs to get dressed, and my stomach growls loudly in protest for food. I can't even hide it. "Let's grab a bite to eat, then head home," he suggests.

"The ol' rumbling gut gave it away, huh?" I laugh. "All that swimming made me build up an appetite, I guess." Liam's face lights up.

"Me too," he laughs.

"How about In-n-Out?" I suggest.

"What kind of place is that?" he frowns as he wraps a towel around his head like a girl.

"It's a fast-food place," I assure him.

"Sure, I'm down with that," he agrees and picks up his keys. "Don't worry about my dad. He's already gone."

"That's too bad," I lie.

After waiting in a long line of cars, we pull up to a young kid in a uniform wearing a small, red and white cap. Liam rolls his window down, seeming confused. "Do I tell him what I want?" he whispers to me.

"Hi! Can I have two double-doubles, animal style and both with animal style fries, please?" I lean over him and order for us.

"You got it. And what would you like to drink?" The kid asks.

"Two chocolate milkshakes!" Liam adds, and I smile at him.

We continue to the window ahead, and

Liam doesn't once ask any questions. He just reaches over and hands the cashier his card and pays, then hands over the food to me in the passenger seat when we reach the second window.

"You're acting like we just bought drugs," I chuckle.

"I do have one question. But I'm afraid to ask," he eyes me.

"What is it?" I laugh.

"What does animal style mean?"

I burst even louder into laughter. He's too cute.

"You'll like it, I promise. I can't believe you've never had In-n-Out," I tease him.

"I'm sorry, we always had a cook growing up. We weren't allowed to eat out, especially not fast food," he explains, then parks the car.

I hand him his food, and he picks up his burger first, gripping it with his two large hands. The orange sauce oozes out as he takes his first bite. I watch him and wait for his reaction. His eyes widen as he nods in approval.

"Wow, I've seriously been missing out!" he exclaims, then takes another bite.

"Try the fries," I almost demand.

"Oh man!" he groans. Digging madly into his french fries that are pilled with cheese, grilled onions, and In-n-out's famous orange sauce.

"Do you like it?" I ask. Already knowing his answer.

"This is amazing! What did you say all of this extra stuff on top was called?"

"Animal style." I laugh again.

The drive home is silent, the only sound coming from the soft radio playing in the background. As I stare out the window, memories of Ronan flood my mind, making me feel like I'm drowning in a sea of emotions. Liam taps his fingers on the steering wheel, lost in his own thoughts, humming to himself. Unaware of the turmoil I'm in.

The melody of "The Girl" by City and Colour fills the car, taking me back to the day Ronan and I spent singing this very song during our short getaway. The memories are still vivid, and a smile involuntarily creeps up on my face. Suddenly, Liam's touch on my arm jolts me out of my reverie, and I jump in my seat.

"What's wrong?" Liam inquires, looking at me with concern. I squeeze his hand, trying to shake off the sadness that's weighing on me.

"I'm fine," I reply, managing a warm smile. But deep down, I'm torn.

Is it possible to love two people at the same time?

As we pull up to my apartment building, Liam turns to me with a hopeful expression. "Are you sure you don't want to stay over at my place tonight?" he asks.

"I can't," I reply, not really having a reason. "I have work tomorrow, and I haven't really been sleeping well lately."

"I understand," he mutters, his face falling.

"But I had a great time today," I add, trying to lift his spirits. "And thank you for introducing me to your dad. He's a great guy," I lie. Not able to tell much from our two second encounter.

Liam's face brightens at my words, but what he says next takes me by surprise.

"I love you," he says, his voice barely above a whisper.

I freeze, unsure of what to say. He's never said those three words to me before. My heart races as I try to process what's happening.

"I—thank you," I manage to say, feeling like a dick for not being able to reciprocate his feelings. The lump in my throat makes it hard to speak, and I can feel my eyes filling with tears.

Liam notices my hesitation and quickly reassures me, "It's okay. You don't have to say it back if you don't feel it. I just wanted you to know how I feel."

I nod, still unsure of what to say.

"I just want you to know that I would never do anything to hurt you," he assures me, his voice gentle but firm. "I care about you more than anything in this world."

His words touch me deeply, and I know

he means every one of them. I'm not in love with him yet, but I know that I'm falling for him. Without thinking, I lean over and kiss him passionately, letting him know how much I appreciate him.

“Goodnight, Liam,” I say, pulling away. “Thank you for being you.”

15

FORGOTTEN TREASURES

(Zara)

Four Months Later.

Liam is taking me out tonight to celebrate our five-month anniversary at a new restaurant. It's two days late, but he couldn't get a reservation until now. He said he's been trying to book this place since our very first date. I feel like celebrating every month is a bit much, but Liam insists, and who am I to argue?

I'm trying to catch up on my nurses' notes before the mandatory briefing we have to attend today.

"Hey, Rip, what time does the briefing start?" I inquire, looking up from my work.

"The memo says noon. Do they really have to cut into our lunch hour for this bullshit?" Ripley replies, grabbing her lab results from the printer.

She's only saying what everyone is thinking.

Our hospital has been undergoing many changes recently, as have hospitals and facilities nationwide. A new campaign for better health has taken root across the country, and it seems most of our patient care now revolves around giving vaccines.

Everyone has to get one or they can't even enter the building. So far, employees have been exempt, but there's been talk that we'll be forced to comply, or there will be serious consequences.

Meaning termination.

This briefing will update us on these new policies.

"This is some serious bullshit. We're completely healthy. Why should we have to get these damn shots too? We already complain enough about the flu shot as it is, and none of us even get that one," I argue, realizing that management doesn't care about what we want.

"I don't know what anyone else plans to do, but I sure as hell ain't getting anything pumped into me. Or my father will have something to say about it," Ripley declares, folding her arms across her chest.

I wish I had that kind of influence.

Oh, right, Liam.

"Z? You still with me?" Ripley waves her hand in my face, bringing me back to reality. "The meeting is starting."

As we leave the briefing, everyone is handed a list of vaccines they need to get before returning to work on Monday. "How can they do this?" I ask Ripley.

Ronan had mentioned something about this before, but I can't remember the details. Was it a good thing or bad? I can't imagine there being any ulterior motives behind this. The idea seems too ridiculous to be sinister.

"Can't you talk to Liam about this?" Ripley suggests. I even consider it myself.

But what if Ronan is right? What if I just put myself in danger by exposing my doubts to Liam? The thought sends shivers down my spine.

But Liam would never hurt me.

He's made that very clear.

But why? Why did he feel the need to make that clear in the first place?

Am I overthinking this again?

"It's settled," I proclaim. "I'll ask him tonight."

I trust him, and he loves me.

He wouldn't hurt me.

The rest of the day drags on with everyone around us complaining about the new policy changes. I finish my rounds and do my med count with the next nurse on shift. After we finish, I wave her off and bend over to grab my bag from underneath the desk when nurse Khloe from pediatrics pops up.

Great.

"Looking for something?" I scowl.

"Hey, Zara! I was looking for you, actually. Can you believe this crap?" Khloe begins, clearly upset.

"No, I can't. It sucks, doesn't it," I reply sarcastically.

"Can't you talk to your boyfriend about this? I'm sure this can't be legal. Or healthy? How do they expect us to get this many shots all at once?" Khloe complains.

This is my chance to tell her off.

I've waited for this moment for years. And now it's been served to me on a silver platter. And our boss being my boyfriend, just happens to be the cherry on top.

"But Khloe," I begin. "Aren't you all about vaccinations? You give babies those every day and talk down to parents who refuse them. I've never seen you question if that was safe. Actually, don't you refer to people who choose not to vaccinate as anti-vaxxers?" I scoff. "The irony, right? I guess that makes you an anti-vaxxer now, doesn't it, Khloe?" She glares at me and storms off.

Okay, maybe I was a little harsh. But I can't stand those needle-pushing nurses in maternity and pediatrics. I'm sure they're getting a taste of their own medicine now.

(102)

I approach the Commander with a sense of urgency. “Sir, this situation is moving faster than we anticipated. They’ve already begun nationwide briefings and plan to launch the campaign on Monday. What's our next move?”

Our spy was exposed and captured, and although they're not talking, they're aware of our presence, and they're trying to speed things up and stop us at any cost to ensure their success. The Commander takes a moment to process the news before responding.

“We have to deploy more defenders and act swiftly. I want one defender at each location and one on each person we know is involved. We need to monitor their every move. If they shit, I want to know about it. Is that understood?”

“You got it,” I salute.

“And remember, we need to end this without involving the public. We keep this strictly under Code 14.”

He can’t be serious.

“Code 14?” I repeat, feeling increasingly angry. “But sir, I thought—.”

“Is that understood, Sergeant?” The Commander raises his voice above mine.

“But the public has a right to know!” I

shout unexpectedly. "Don't you think it's time we stepped in and told them the truth?"

"You don't question orders, Sergeant. You out of everyone should know better," he reprimands. "There are rules that need to be followed, 102. And you need to follow them just like the rest of us."

"Really? Screw their rules!" I snap.

"That's enough, Sergeant!" The Commander shouts.

"But—."

"But *nothing*," he slams his fist into his desk.

"We're supposed to be their heroes," I respond softly.

"Heroes?" he scoffs. Mocking me. "You're naive to the situation on Earth, Sergeant. To them, we aren't the hero. We are and always will be the enemy."

The enemy?

The word echoes in my mind as I try to come to terms with the harsh reality.

Earthlings have been programmed to fear us since before my time. And there's nothing I can ever do to change that. So many thoughts are now circling my mind. But one in particular stands out from the rest.

Zara.

I have to warn her.

(Zara)

I flip through the handful of dresses I own, searching for something to wear. Liam likes to go out a lot, so I've grown my collection from zero to some. I've always resorted to borrowing something from Ripley just so I can feel like I fit in. But Liam is a gift giver and always buys me something new to wear every time we go out. It's so exhausting really. And I don't want to do that anymore.

For once I want to be comfortable just being me.

So with my eyes closed, I take my pick.

"Eeny, meeny, miney, moe," I chant.

My finger lands on a navy blue, long sleeve dress. The neckline swoops down into a U to expose my collar bone but not low enough to show any cleavage. I drop my towel and slide into the tight dress. It's knee-length and perfect for the chilly weather outside. Because here in California, we're still hopelessly waiting for some sun.

After I brush the knots out of my damp hair, I pull out the blow dryer to finish drying it off. Once it's dry, I wrap it into a small bun at the nape of my neck and fasten it securely with several bobby pins to keep it in place. Then I pull out a strand of hair in the front, letting it fall freely over my face. I pat some blush on my cheeks and search frantically for my mascara.

Where the hell is it?

"My bag!" I shout. Recalling leaving it there this morning when I had to do my makeup in Liam's car.

I rush to the kitchen counter and grab the bag, sifting through its contents to find the mascara. Instead, my fingers graze something hard and square. "What the—," I mutter.

It's a box that I completely forgot about, labeled "Nurse Lara." I tear off the wrapping paper, feeling a surge of excitement. Inside, I find a brand new pair of headphones, still in their packaging.

"Oh my God," I gasp, pulling them out and examining them closely. They're sleek and modern, with a soft cushion that promises hours of comfortable wear. But then I notice the note that's fallen out of the box.

"What's this?" I whisper, unfolding the paper with trembling fingers. As I read the words, tears prick at the corners of my eyes. And my heart begins to shatter all over again.

For my favorite Earthling. I'm sorry I couldn't save your last pair, I had something more important to save.

But I know how much you loved them. So, here's a new pair that I hope you enjoy just as much. May you never be burdened with small talk from strangers. – Alien Dude

The tears come streaming down my face before I've even fully processed what happened. I read the note over and over until my eyes are so filled with tears that I can no longer make out the words.

"How did he even know about my earphones?" I sob into the now soaked note. "Stop it!" I stomp my foot.

Now I'm angry.

I wipe my tears in a fury then I untwist my mascara and finish what I started. Memories of Ronan still blaring through my head, too strong to push away. But I won't cry for him. Not anymore.

November 26th.

"Good morning, beautiful," his words like honey. There he is, where he always is.

How can someone look this good in the morning?

"Good morning. Why are you up so early?" I rub my eyes then turn over so I can go back to sleep. "It's my day off, I want to rest."

"Come on," Ronan shakes me. "You up for an adventure?" He sticks his face right in front of mine, and I can't help but laugh.

"Hmm, it depends," I begin. "Will it be warm on this adventure, or will it be cold?"

"Why?" he raises an eyebrow.

"Because I'm tired of the cold," I complain. "So if this place is warm, then maybe I'm okay with waking up a little early." Now I'm kind of up for a short vacation.

"Say no more," Ronan replies. "Grab a swimsuit, and let's go."

"What? Really?" I jump up off the bed and frantically search through my dresser for a swimsuit.

Despite living in sunny Los Angeles, I rarely swim or go to the beach, so finding a suitable swimsuit is a challenge. But after some digging, I finally locate a red one-piece then hurry to the bathroom to shower and change.

And we gotta shave.

I'm in and out of the bathroom quickly. It's not the most flattering swimsuit, but it's all I could find. When I open the door, Ronan and Binks are curled up on the bed, listening to City and Colour on my phone. There's a song that Ronan has been playing on repeat, and it's stuck in my head now.

Ronan looks as handsome as ever. Even with minimal effort. He's wearing a backwards cap, a white tank top, and tan board shorts with red palm trees on them. His foot is tapping along to the music, and I run my fingernail down the bottom of it to let him know I'm here.

"Hey!" he squirms, extending his arm out

for me to come lay down in it. And I slide into his embrace happily. *"Please know that I'm yours to keep, my beautiful girl,"* he sings *The Girl* into my ear as we snuggle up tightly. My head rests on his chest and then off we go. Not sure where yet but I'm excited.

The anticipation is always my favorite part.

16

SO, DO YOU?

(Zara)

Present Day.

The doorbell sounds.

That must be Liam.

After I finish with my mascara, I slip into my knee-high boots and grab a sweater from the hallway closet before opening the door. We drive to the restaurant in silence, with only the soft hum of music in the background, which I find comforting. The fog outside is dense, obscuring the road ahead. I spend the entire ride staring out the window, observing the clouds. Watching as they grow darker by the minute.

It looks like it might rain.

Liam's fingers are gently drumming on my thigh to the beat of the song. He seems so happy. But I somehow can't keep my mind from wandering somewhere else.

To someone else.

The words in that note seem to be etched in my brain. Deep in my own secret thoughts, I contemplate what could have been with Ronan. Had he not left.

Did he even want to talk to me about what happened? Why did he just leave like that without saying goodbye? That's the part that hurts me the most. Even if he didn't feel the same way I did, we were still friends. And he just—left me.

When I loved him.

And as much as I hate to admit it, I still do.

I place my hand over Liam's, and his lip curls in response. He looks over to me, and I can feel the love pouring from his eyes. He gives my thigh a small squeeze and I'm instantly filled with guilt over my thoughts.

As we enter the restaurant, I notice that it's quite elegant, but nothing out of the ordinary for the fancy restaurants that Liam frequently takes me to in LA. None of this has ever been impressive to me. I find it rather wasteful, really. But I act surprised, letting out some 'oohs' and 'awes' to please him.

We're soon greeted by an elegantly dressed server who guides us down a dimly lit hallway. I can't help but wonder why fancy restaurants always have to be so dark.

What are they trying to hide?

Next, the server takes us up an old elevator shaft. As we step out, I notice that the hallways are lined with red satin wallpaper and exquisite white crown molding trimmings. It's a beautiful sight, but what catches my attention the most is the sheer number of doors that we pass by. I can't help but wonder what lies behind each of them.

Well this certainly is different.

We walk past what feels like hundreds of doors until we finally stop in front of one that's numbered 214.

"Here you are, sir," the server says as he opens the door for us to enter.

As I step inside, I can feel my jaw drop to the floor at the sight before me.

"Wow! Now I know why there are so many doors!" I exclaim a little too loudly. The entire back wall is a giant window, offering an unparalleled view of the city below.

There's also a table set for two, adorned with magnificent dishes and elegant silverware. The server leaves us and closes the door behind him, allowing us complete privacy.

"Where did you find this place?" I question. Actually impressed this time. He just smiles and pulls my chair out for me. Then he tugs at my hand when he sits.

"So, what do you think?" Liam inquires. His face seems particularly suspicious today.

"It's incredible!" I gape. "And this view—it's to die for."

"I'm glad you like it," he beams in his seat.

"To be honest, I thought this was going to be just like all the other places we go to. No offense," I add.

"None taken," he chuckles.

"But, this place is really something," I admit.

I get up from my chair and walk towards the window, placing my hand gently on it. The unexpected coolness of the glass sends a shock through my fingertips, and I shiver. Liam sees me shaking and wraps his arms around me, rubbing his hands on my arms to warm me.

"It's cold out there."

"It is," I agree. "Why is it so cold lately?"

I cross my arms in front of me and hold his hands in mine. His touch is like a comforting blanket. He pulls me closer, and I can feel the heat radiating off his body as he rests his chin on my shoulder. Then, he plants a soft, tender kiss on my cheek, and I can't help but revel in his sweetness.

"I love you, Zara," he whispers in my ear. "So, much."

I smile and turn to face him. Then I pull him close and plant a soft kiss on his lips. Holding him tightly as he melts in my arms. Then I let him go and walk back over to our table to sit back down.

“I’m starving,” I change the subject. “What do they have to eat here?” I skim over my menu and he grins. Coming to join me.

After we partake in a game of elimination, we settle on two dishes that we were both drooling over and insisted it was only right to order both and share.

“Liam, can I ask you something completely random and off topic?”

“Sure, what's up, babe?” he responds casually.

“I wanted to ask about the new hospital policies. What's up with the *'Vaccinate Everyone'* campaign?” I inquire. He seems unfazed by my question, which makes me feel good about asking.

“I'm not entirely sure, actually. It’s my father’s project. But I think it's a nationwide effort to increase vaccination rates and prevent outbreaks,” he explains.“Too many people are opting out these days. So he says.”

“That makes sense,” I reply, starting to feel even better. Then he shares something surprising.

“You know what's crazy? No one in my family has ever gotten a vaccine. Not one. And we own a significant portion of the nation's healthcare and vaccine stock.”

“Really? And why’s that?”

“Never needed any,” he flexes his arm as

evidence. "Strong genes."

I laugh, trying to hide my concern. "Wow, that's impressive. With all that access to the best medicine, you guys must really know what you're doing."

He chuckles, "Exactly."

Our dinner arrives and everything is great. But as the night goes on, I can't shake the feeling of unease. Why is Liam's family so opposed to vaccines, especially given their background in healthcare? The thought keeps nagging at me.

Why?

(102)

She's not here.

I pace the length of Zara's living room, unsure if I should wait for her or head to the hospital in search of her. My impatience grows, but I don't want to risk being seen. "How long do you think she'll be?" I consult Binks. He purrs, rubbing against my leg. I think he missed me too.

As I bend to pick him up, a lingering scent pulls me away. It's a scent I haven't smelled in months, but one that can stop me in my tracks anywhere.

Hers.

It's so hypnotizing that I can't help but follow it. The scent leads me down the hall and into her bedroom. The door creaks open, and I step inside.

The bed is unmade, as usual. And clothes are strewn about haphazardly. I want to tidy it up for her, like I used to. But the disorder comforts me in a strange way. It makes me feel as though she's still here.

My messy, disorganized Earthling.

I sit down on her bed and pick up her pillow, the one that's just the right amount of soft. It's too soft to lay your head on, but perfect for holding tightly against your face as you sleep.

Just like she did every night.

As memories of her flood my mind, old feelings stream in as if they never left in the first place. I drop my face into my hands, trying my best not to fall apart right here and now. When I glance up, I notice something red sticking out from under her nightstand.

“What's that?” I say aloud, and Binks purrs at me in response. I bend over to pick it up and pull it out.

“It's the red swimsuit Zara wore when I took her to Thailand,” I tell the cat, and the memory brings a smile to my face. “The one she swore to me she lost.”

I dive into the most sacred parts of

my memory to revisit that moment. The place where I've kept all my memories of her. Locked away and untouched, for the past five months. With trepidation, I scroll through the images, uncertain how I'll react to seeing her again. Then her face appears. She's laughing.

And I crumble to pieces.

That laugh. How I've missed that laugh.

November 26th.

"It's so warm, Ronan! Come on, jump in!" Zara yells to me from the other side of the stream. Just before she dives back into the water. The silhouette of her body moves rhythmically like a mermaid as she swims. The water is crystal clear and I've never been more thankful for that.

The sun beats down on us as we swim. The lush greenery surrounds us, tall trees towering overhead and colorful flowers lining the banks. The air is filled with the scent of tropical blooms and the chatter of exotic birds.

"Here I come!" I yell. I take a deep breath then dive in after her.

The water is cool and refreshing, the perfect escape from the heat. I swim as fast as I can towards Zara then jump out in front of her. She splashes me in the face playfully then dives back under to get away from me. But I follow her.

As we swim, we pass by a group of locals fishing in the stream. They wave at us, smiling, and we wave back. The water is so clear that we can easily see the tropical colored fish swimming beneath us. It's a serene and idyllic scene. A moment that I'll forever cherish being able to watch her experience.

When I come up for air, I see her climbing out of the water. She goes straight towards a tree and picks a banana off of it. "What is she doing now?" I go back under and swim over to her.

"You got hungry?" I ask, splashing her. "Should have told me, I would have brought us over some food. They have some amazing food here in Thailand."

"Is that where we are?" She questions, peeling open the banana. Then she cautiously steps over the large roots growing out of the ground and reaches up into the tree again.

"What are you doing?" I begin. When a small monkey reaches out towards her from the tree.

And that answers my question.

"Come on," she talks to the monkey. "It's okay, I won't hurt you. Here." The monkey is small in contrast to it's big, curious eyes. Watching us intently as Zara offers him another banana.

Leave it to her to find an animal to befriend.

Zara then goes back to the tree and grabs a large bunch of bananas. Tossing them next to me. She sits down beside me to eat and I smile at her. Watching as she pulls off a banana from the bunch and tears it open from the bottom like a primate. Then stops halfway in to offer me a bite.

"Want some?" she can barely speak through her mouthful.

"No, thank you," I laugh.

"These bananas taste unbelievable. Can I take some home after this?"

"Sure," I nod. "I don't see why not."

"Awesome," she grins, continuing to eat.

"We can take back whatever you'd like."

"Really?" she shrieks.

"Except for the monkey."

"Shucks, never mind then," she scoffs.

I love her, so much.

"I've never met anyone like you, you know," I tell her.

"Good," she grins. "I'm not interesting enough to have more than one of me." She finishes off her banana then dives back into the water. Swimming off down the stream—where there's an elephant getting a drink.

"Oh, no," I zap off after her before she gets herself killed.

Present Day.

(Zara)

After Liam and I devour our plates, we eagerly await our dessert. Every bite was divine, but now I feel like I could hibernate. I let out a big yawn, feeling stuffed to the brim. Liam looks equally stuffed, but he still insisted on ordering dessert. I can't imagine taking another bite of anything though. Not even ice cream.

Okay, maybe if it's ice cream.

"Are you feeling okay?" I question Liam, noting his clammy face. Maybe we overdid it on the food.

"I'm fine," he responds. "It's just really hot in here, don't you think?" Liam quickly sheds his jacket like it's on fire and flings it onto a coat rack, barely catching it. A knock on the door startles him, and I start to worry about his strange behavior.

"Are you sure you're okay?" I press him. "You're acting kind of funny."

"I'm fine," he insists, opening the door.

In walks the waiter with a beautiful serving cart covered in flowers and white rose petals. In the center of the cart sits a single plate with a shiny silver lid.

This dessert cart is something else.

"Zara?" Liam begins as the waiter leaves and shuts the door again. His voice is trembling.

Is he going to be sick?

"Are you sure you're okay, Liam?"

"I'm fine," he clears his throat and starts again. "Zara, please give me your hand, baby."

Oh. My. God.

Is he about to propose?

I fumble around, trying to find something to say, but before I can, Liam drops to the ground.

"Zara?" he asks for it again. But I still don't give it. The seconds tick by, and I still haven't said anything. "Zara?"

I gulp loudly, wondering if the people next door can hear us. Are they getting engaged too? Is that why the rooms are soundproof? I feel stuck. Trapped in this weird limbo where he keeps saying my name forever and ever and I just never respond.

"Zara!" Liam shouts again, desperation in his voice.

"What?" I snap out of my thoughts and back to reality.

Oh yeah. Shit.

"I know that we've only been seeing each other for a few months—but I love you, Zara. So much," he continues. "I've never felt this way about anyone before, and tonight I want to show you just how much you mean to me."

I can feel my armpits start to sweat. Maybe we should get back to dessert? I look over to the dessert table and that's when I notice that the plate that was covered is now empty.

"What was under the lid?" I mumble.

I think you're about to find out.

Liam's arm emerges from behind his back, revealing a small box nestled in his palm. My heart skips a beat. Another box? I furrow my brows, recalling the box from earlier. Just like that, thoughts of Ronan come flooding in again, muddying the clarity of my mind.

Fuck.

"Zara?" he says again.

Not this game again. I don't want to play anymore.

Just take me home. Please, just take me home.

"Liam—," I finally respond, but he talks over me.

"Will you marry me, Zara?" he blurts out in one breath.

"I—," I don't know what to say. I can't even speak.

"Look, I know this is sudden," he begins, "but it doesn't have to be tomorrow. It can be a year from now." A year? I feel the room begin to spin. "Two even!" he bargains. "I just want to know that you'll be mine. Forever."

His? Forever?

My head feels like it's about to explode and I can feel my dinner start to rise in my throat.

"Liam—," I plead. His eyes are still glued to mine, his hand still out, waiting for mine to be placed in his. For me to accept his proposal. His beautiful, blue eyes still full of hope. Hope that today he will be leaving here an engaged man.

"I'm so sorry—," I shake my head. And his expression dies. All that hope drained from him. Then I storm out of the room.

What am I doing?

I'm not thinking right now, just moving. Doing what my heart is telling me and not my mind. I run down the hall and search frantically for an empty place to escape to. I'm suffocating and I just need to breathe. Liam is in the hall chasing after me. He's yelling something out but I can't hear what he's saying.

I find a door that says exit and push through it. Now I'm on the rooftop. My mind swarming with memories of Ronan, still haunting me. It's like I can't seem to escape him, no matter where I run.

It's freezing out. I look up into the sky and get absorbed by the darkness. The chill of the cold night hits my nerves all at once like a lightening bolt. But I just stand there while I shiver and cry.

Why couldn't I just say yes?

Why can't I just love him?

He's perfect.

"And he loves me," I cry.

I just want to go home. I drop to the ground, tears streaming down my face. Wishing

I could click my heels together like Dorothy in Oz and just be gone. Be home.

The incessant honking of cars below and the roar of LA traffic fills my ears, as planes from the nearby airport fly overhead. I focus on these sounds, taking them in like oxygen. And I visualize home.

I close my eyes tightly, feeling as the ground begins to pulsate beneath me. Small droplets of water fall softly for a second, and then a downpour follows. Soaking me instantly. The rain colliding loudly with the ground. And in the distance, I can hear someone coming towards me.

It's Liam.

I shut everything out, including him. Pushing all the racing thoughts out of my mind, until all the sounds disappear. Until my knees no longer ache from the hard rooftop floor. And the cold rain is no longer soaking my skin.

Then I slowly open my eyes.

"I'm home," I whisper.

I did it.

17

WHEN IT RAINS…

(Zara)

"Zara?" someone calls from inside my apartment. Startling me. But I know that voice.

"Ronan?" I respond. That all too familiar melody is like music to my ears. For a second I forget about everything, and I jolt into his arms.

"Hey," he smiles. "Finally you're home." Ronan holds me tightly, pressing his face desperately against mine.

I've dreamed of this moment so many times. Wishing day after day that I'd come home one day and he'd be here. Just like this. I can't believe he's really here. I soak in his aroma, absorbing the touch of his skin as much as I can before I wake up. Only this time, I think he might actually be real. I take a deep breath, trying to steady my racing heart.

Is it really him?

"Wait, what are you doing here?" All the

emotions I've been trying to suppress suddenly come rushing back. I furiously wipe away the new tears that have now mixed with my old ones. I'm still angry with him. I still haven't forgotten what he did. I'm still hurt.

Boy, have we done some crying today, huh?

"Zara, I—," he begins but I don't let him speak.

"Why'd you come back?" I snap, my voice laced with bitterness. I can feel my anger rising, boiling up inside me like a pot of water ready to spill over.

Why does it even matter? He's back!

It matters to me. He destroyed me.

He left me all alone and didn't say a word.

I'm arguing with myself.

"Zara, I'm sorry—," he pleads, reaching for my hand. But I push him away.

Why should we even hear what he has to say?

My conscience is on my side now.

He didn't even have the decency to say goodbye. How could he do that to me? And now he's popping back into my life like nothing ever happened?

"Can you let me talk?" he tries again.

"I don't want to hear it, Ronan. I don't even care what you have to say."

"Really?" he replies.

"Yes!" I shout. "You broke my heart so

badly, Ronan."

"Zara—," he reaches for me again but I pull away.

"I cried myself to sleep for months, Ronan," I fight back tears. "Months! Just leave." I hang my head in defeat then turn away from him before he sees me cry.

"Zara!" he cries. Tears forming in his eyes.

"Please. Just go," I say sternly.

I don't really want him to leave, but I know it's best that he does. For my own sanity, I can't be around him right now. Not when my head is already a mess because of Liam. Ronan ignores me and grabs me by the arms instead. Pulling me into him, and holding me tightly while he sobs into my hair.

"I'm sorry, Zara," his body is trembling, and his voice shakes as he tries to find the words. "I did come back. I promise I did."

"What?" I take a step back, forcing myself out of his arms. "When?" I don't believe him.

If he did, why didn't he talk to you?

"I went to the party," he tells me.

"What party?" I struggle to recall.

"I saw you with him," his gray eyes are dark.

"With who?" I ask. Then my heart sinks as the recollection hits me. "The Christmas party?"

The kiss.

"Yes," his words are soft. "I left after I saw

you two together. You looked happy enough."

"You were *there*? Why didn't you—?"

"Why didn't I what? What was I supposed to do? Pull you two apart?" he scowls. Then turns away from me.

"I don't know what to say. I—I didn't know," I reach out to touch his arm but he grabs my hand instead.

"I still love you, Zara," he's still speaking so low. Not making eye contact with me.

"*Still*?" I repeat.

Does that mean he always did?

"Yes, *still*. Did you really not know?" he makes a face at me. "I've always loved you. Why do you think I kept coming back?"

"Then why didn't you tell me sooner?"

"I don't know," he begins. "I guess I was afraid. I'd never felt anything like this before. I didn't even know how to tell you."

"Then why did you leave when I kissed you?"

"I don't know!" he exclaims in frustration. "I'm an idiot. I'm sorry that I left like that. Without saying anything—. But I needed to come back," he stops.

"Why?" I press him. "Why now?"

"I need you to come with me," he demands. Urgency in his voice.

"Come where?"

"To Xia," he replies.

“What? Are you crazy?”

“Please, Zara. Just trust me. You’re not safe here anymore.”

What just happened?

My mind is still trying to process the events of the day. And now he drops this bombshell on me?

“Not safe? Are we really going to start with this again?” I’m still trying to wrap my head around the whole 'I love you' revelation.

“Please, just listen to me!” he pleads desperately. “Give me two minutes.”

“Okay, fine! I’m listening,” I give in way too easily. “But then I really have to go. Tell me, what the hell is going on?”

“Okay. Did I ever tell you about the plan to deactivate the light force of every human living on Earth?”

“No! What?” I shout in disbelief.

He explains that every healthcare facility in the world will be receiving millions of shipments in the next few weeks, with contaminated vials mixed in with their regular shipments.

“How will people know which vials are contaminated?” I begin, looking up at him.

“They won’t. I'm going to have to go in there and get them myself. Before it’s too late,” he responds.

“*You?*” I exclaim incredulously.

“Yes, *me*,” he confirms.

“You’re really planning to go alone? Without me?”

“That’s the plan,” he responds confidently.

“Well, change of plans,” I concede, “I'm going with you.”

“I don't know, Zara. I don’t think it’s a good idea,” he shakes his head. “All I need from you is to be as far away from there as possible.”

“Come on!” I insist. “I can help. I work there. I know the place better than anyone,” I make a strong argument.

He knows I’m right.

“I’m going to end up taking you with me, aren’t I?” Ronan rubs his temples in frustration. He already knows I won’t be giving in.

“Yup,” I reply. “So what’s the plan?”

“I guess we’ll both be going,” he throws his arms up in defeat. “And I guess I’ll be teaching you some new tricks,” he flashes me those glorious dimples that I’ve missed so much.

“Ronan, I teleported! All on my own!” I shout. Barely realizing what had just occurred right before I found Ronan. “I teleported to my apartment. All by myself. Just now!”

“Again?” he exclaims, not surprised.

“What?”

“The night of the Christmas party,” he says.

“The Christmas party?” The memory

evades me.

What is he talking about?

I hate this. I hate that no matter how long it's been without him it takes no effort to go back to how we used to be. If I stayed here now, and didn't go, I swear it could be as if those six torturous months never happened and he never left in the first place.

"Zara, can I be honest with you for a second?" Ronan changes the subject.

"What is it?" I get pulled from my thoughts.

"Look, I know you have a new life now. One that I'm no longer a part of. But I can't live without you, Earthling," his words send fiery explosions to my chest.

"Do you mean that?"

"Of course, I do," his eyes pleading for me to believe him. "I really can't, Zara. And believe me I've tried. These have been the longest months of my life without you. And I've lived many *many* months before you." He's really tugging at my heart. But then I remember about Liam.

Liam!

"I can't do this right now."

"I know," he takes a breath. "I know I messed up. But can we at least go back to being friends?"

Friends.

The word makes me want to vomit.

"Can we possibly talk about this later? I have to be somewhere right now."

"Really? Right now?"

"Yes. I need to go talk to—," I hesitate. "To Liam."

"You're leaving me to go see *him*? Right *now?*"

"Yes," I respond. "I'm sorry but I really have to go." I grab my keys to leave.

"Wait!" he tries to stop me. His eyes begging. "It can't wait?"

"I'll be back, I promise. We can finish this conversation when I return," I assure him with a smile. Desperately holding back all the things I want to say.

How I still love him and have not once stopped thinking about him since he left. Or how the thought of being friends with him again kills me. Even though it's better than the pain of not seeing him again.

But I don't say that though.

I just got him back, and I won't lose him again by complicating things. If a friend is what he wants, then that's what I'll be. As long as I can be something.

And as long as he's here.

"Just go," he says.

"Are you upset?"

"No. Yes. No. I don't know," he throws his

arms up again in frustration. "What did I expect? I should have put up a fight and I didn't." He hangs his head.

Don't do this, Ronan, not right now.

"Ronan, please," I stop walking and turn to face him. My heart shatters at the sight of him. His beautiful gray eyes are dark, not the bright eyes I remember.

"It's fine, just go," he sighs. "Whatever it is I'm sure it's far more important than whatever I have to say."

"Liam asked me to marry him tonight," the words spill from my mouth almost as quickly as the blood drains from his face.

"What?" he chokes on his words. "What did you say?"

"I didn't say anything," I confess. "I just—left."

Sound familiar?

"You *left*?"

"Yes. I left right in the middle of his proposal. I don't know what came over me but I ran off and never came back," I explain. "So, that's where I need to go. To fix it."

"To go fix things with *him*," he scoffs.

"Yes," I sigh. "To try anyway. I left so suddenly. I—I still don't even know how I did it."

"Maybe you just needed the right motivation."

His words stick with me.

"I'll be back, okay? We'll finish this then?"

"Okay," he mumbles. "I guess I'll see you when you get back. I'll be here."

"Okay," I grab my bag and head out to Liam's house to see if I can find him.

(102)

She's only been gone for a few minutes and I'm already starting to get upset. Just thinking about her driving to go see him, the jealousy takes over me. And now I can't seem to stop picturing them together.

Flashbacks of the last time I saw her start to play in my mind. Saw *them*. The way he grabbed her when they got out of that pool. The way he kissed her. Those images are burned into my memory forever.

Why can't I just delete those?

I pace back and forth as I wait. Thinking about what I'm going to say to her when she gets back. This isn't the way I wanted things to end with us.

For us to be friends again.

But if friendship is all I can have, then I'll take it. These past months have been the worst of my life. They've made me realize the only thing I really need is to be close to her. I pick up the picture frame that's face down on the coffee table. It's a picture of Zara that I took of her on our trip to Thailand.

November 26th.

"Zara, come back here! Are you crazy?" I shout, my voice echoing across the water. Zara ignores me, as usual. I dive in and swim after her.

"I'm fine!" she hisses.

"That's a six-ton elephant, Earthling. And she has her baby with her," I point out when I reach her.

"I see that. What's your point?" she snaps back.

"She'll kill you in a second if she thinks you're a threat to her calf," I warn her quietly.

"I'm not going to hurt them," Zara rolls her eyes. "What do you think I am? I just want to get a closer look."

"I don't think that's a good idea," I insist.

"Ronan, when will I ever get the chance to see a real-life wild elephant again? I have to do this," she explains, then dives back into the water and swims towards them.

"She's going to be the death of me," I mutter to myself.

As she approaches the mother and her calf, I keep a close eye on Zara. She crouches down and walks slowly towards them, leaving a deep trail of footprints in the mud. The calf notices her first and begins jumping around excitedly, alarming its mother. She quickly spots Zara too.

Here we go.

I'm prepared to get her out of there if necessary, but to my surprise, the mother elephant remains calm and turns away. She seems to trust Zara.

Zara inches closer to the calf, and soon she's playing with it. She holds onto its trunk as it leads her towards its mother, and she follows without fear.

I can't help but admire her courage and her way with animals. And the more time I spend with her, the more I come to realize that she isn't just some clumsy Earthing. But someone incredibly special.

And she's all mine.

Present Day.

(Zara)

When I pull into Liam's driveway, I hurriedly jump out of my Jeep and peak into his garage window to look for his Tesla.

"Yes! His car is here!" I exclaim, relief washing over me. Then make my way towards the front door. He must not have noticed I got here because he's not waiting at the door for me like he usually is.

Or maybe he's upset.

Maybe.

For several minutes, I stand awkwardly at the door. Contemplating whether or not I should ring the bell. Am I being stupid for being here? Should I have given us both some more time to cool off?

Maybe I can surprise him.

If only there was a way I could get inside, I begin to strategize.

"Wait a minute, I have a key!" I quickly dive into my bag, searching for it like a maniac. Liam gave me a key to his house the day I met his father. I can't believe it slipped my mind until now.

This seems like a "just in case" moment, right?

Before I'm able to change my mind, the key is already turning inside the lock. And I let myself inside.

It's dark. But I can hear moaning coming from Liam's bedroom upstairs. My heart is racing, I don't even know what I'm going to say to him yet. But I know what I have to do.

I tiptoe up the steps and follow the sound. Expecting to find a sobbing Liam. I become so filled with guilt with the idea. I begin to doubt my decision.

How could I do this to him?

"I *do* love him," I tell myself. "Right?"

Why is that such a hard question to answer?

Should it be this hard of a question to answer?

When I get to his door, I turn the doorknob quietly, trying not to startle him. The door opens slowly, and he doesn't hear me. In the darkness, I can see movement on his bed.

What is he doing?

"Liam?" I whisper, brushing my hand over the wall inside the room, looking for the light switch.

My finger finds a small knob, and I slide it up. Instantly illuminating the room. And revealing a blonde skank lying underneath Liam.

Naked.

"What the fuck!" I shriek in surprise.

"Zara?" he responds. His eyes are wide and puffy. He jumps out of the bed and hurries to find his clothes.

The blonde is still sitting there, confused and upset. She gets angry and begins yelling at him as she searches for her own clothes. "You have a *girlfriend*?" she screams.

Not anymore.

My heart is completely shattered. I can't believe what I've just witnessed. The bile in my throat rises, and I feel sick to my stomach. I try to speak, but I'm too shocked and disgusted to form words. I turn away, running out of the room. Running away, just as I did a few hours earlier.

Maybe you had the right idea the first time.

My conscience is right. I should have never come back here.

As soon as I step outside, the frigid air suffocates me. Regret clawing at my chest. Why did I even come back here? With shaky hands, I fumble for my car key and manage to start the Jeep. Liam runs out of the house after me. Racing towards my car still half-naked. Only infuriating me further.

I peel out of his driveway, almost running him over. Then I speed onto the highway, not looking back.

"I hate him!" I shout. My mind is still racing and my stomach feels like it's ready to explode. "Oh, no," I urgently pull over on the side of the highway and spill my guts all over the pavement. "I hate him," I wipe my lips. Then I drag myself back to the wheel, just trying to make it home in one piece.

One broken, shattered piece.

I should have stayed home.

Once I'm parked, I'm reminded about Ronan again. But I don't even want to see him. I don't want to see anyone right now. The last thing I want to hear at this moment is, 'I told you so'.

I slip into my apartment and find Ronan sleeping on the couch, watching Ancient Aliens on TV.

Looks like I'm in the clear.

I tiptoe quietly to set my things down in the kitchen. Still trying not to wake him. But someone grabs me from behind, spinning me around. And I drop everything on the ground instead.

"Are you crying?" Ronan studies my face. "What the hell did he do?" As soon as I look him in the eye, I can't hold back any longer. My chin begins to tremble and all the emotions come flooding back.

"I—," I try to speak, but the tears keep coming, and without another word, I throw myself into his arms. "I don't want to see him ever again," I cry.

Ronan wraps his big strong arms around me, holding me tightly. "Sounds good to me."

And there I stay, safe in his embrace. Breathing him in as he makes all of my problems go away. Just like he used to before. And for the first time in six months, I actually feel like everything is going to be okay.

PART 2

(Liam)

What did I just do!

"Fuck! Fuck!" I smack my hands furiously on the steering wheel. "Where are you, Zara?" I squint my eyes, trying to focus on the blur of a road ahead of me.

The Tesla swerves from side to side across the freeway. I'm way too wasted to be driving. But I'm trying by best to keep myself between my own lane. I'm going way too fast though. I'm flooring it and the Tesla is almost flying.

Maybe we should slow down.

"I can't believe I did this shit!" I punch the steering wheel again. "I said the last time was the last time. This isn't me anymore. Why did I have to go to that stupid bar? And take that stupid girl home! Fuck!" I take both hands off the wheel to wipe the tears from my eyes.

What's wrong with me?

My throat begins to burn, and a queasy feeling churns in the pit of my stomach, threatening to erupt. I clutch the wheel tightly, but it's not enough to prevent the violent surge of vomit that engulfs me and my car. As I swerve into the adjacent lanes, I desperately try to regain control of the vehicle and steer back into my own, all the while struggling to keep from throwing up again.

Finally, my stomach is empty and I'm able to open my eyes. Only to find myself in an even worse situation.

"Fuck!" I've veered into the left lane again.

A semi-truck is honking repeatedly for me to get out of his way as we go over the bridge. My reflexes kick in, and I pull the wheel to the right.

Too far to the right.

But it's already too late.

Everything is moving so slowly. I look over and watch as the truck continues onto the curve of the bridge. While I go the opposite way.

The Tesla slices right through the guardrail like butter, flying through the air. I shut my eyes tightly. Images of Zara flashing through my mind. Thankful that hers will be the last face I see.

This is how I die.

The fact that this is the end for me doesn't even elicit sadness. But the thought of Zara's memory of me, does. The idea that she will remember me for this one stupid, irredeemable mistake tears at my heart more than the thought of my own death. I stare out the windshield, watching the ground that was so distant just a second ago, become closer. I shut my eyes and tears stream down my cheeks. Then everything goes black. And I can no longer feel anything anymore.

19

IT POURS.

(102)

They say when it rains, it pours.

I just wish it didn't have to rain on her.

I'd take an entire thunderstorm for her if I could.

Zara trembles in my arms. Although I enjoy her here, I hate that someone made her feel this way. Like her life is over. She stirs in her sleep and I pull her closer into my chest, squeezing her tightly in my arms. Not wanting to ever let her go again. Then I kiss her gently on the head and she sobs quietly until I fall asleep.

November 26th.

"We have to go, Zara!" I call out to her, not wanting her to miss the sunset as the sun starts to dip below the horizon.

"Okay!" Zara waves back to me before approaching the mother elephant fearlessly. My heart clenches in my chest, watching her with a mixture of admiration and apprehension.

She wants to say goodbye to her new friends.

As she reaches out to touch the elephant, it embraces her in its trunk. Relief flooding through me. I don't know how she does it.

"They love her," I smile.

I love that human too.

Zara emerges from the water, her eyes heavy with sleep and glazed from the sunlight. Her skin is radiant and glowing from the sun's warm embrace, and her dark brown hair is forming wet tendrils that cascade down her body.

"You're absolutely breathtaking, you know that?" I tell her, unable to resist her. She just laughs.

"You're just saying that," her cheeks blush slightly. Then dips her head back under just to come back up to spray me.

"I'm gonna get you back for that!" I wrap my arms around her and zap us away.

Present Day

(Zara)

I awaken to the sound of my phone's alarm and find Ronan's handsome face hovering over me. It feels like a dream. I smile as I see the hint of a dimple on his face, but his eyes are still closed, and I don't want to disturb his sleep.

Looks like he's the one that's dreaming.

It's been months since I've slept through the night without interruption, and last night was a blissful exception. I carefully slip out of his arms to check the time, but it's still dark outside. Suddenly, my phone rings again, and I realize it might not have been my alarm that woke me up earlier.

I fumble around in search of my iPhone, and when I find it, I see that Ripley has called me four times.

That's strange.

It must be something urgent. I dial her back, and she picks up immediately, sounding relieved that I've answered.

“Zara, where are you?” she asks, her tone is anxious.

“I'm at home, Ripley. Where else would I be in the middle of the night?” I respond, confused.

“Thank God. She wasn't with him,” she says to someone on her end of the line, and my heart begins to race.

What does she mean by that?

Wasn't with *who?*

“Who are you talking to? What's going

on Ripley, you're scaring me," I interrogate her, feeling more worried by the second.

"I'm at the hospital," she begins, taking a deep breath. "Liam's here, Zara."

"What? Why would Liam be there in the middle of the night?" I can't process what she's saying. Why would he be there at this hour?

When it hits me.

"They brought him in a few hours ago. He's not doing too good, Zara. I really think you should head over here fast," she states urgently.

My mind is racing as I try to understand what's happening. Liam, in the hospital? Not doing too good? The gravity of the situation hits me like a ton of bricks.

"Wait, he's—he's admitted?" I stammer, feeling the panic rising in my chest.

"He's still in surgery. We don't know if he's going to make it," she replies, her voice shaking. "How fast can you get here?"

The phone falls from my hand, and my mind goes blank. I can hear a muffled echo that sounds like Ronan coming from behind me, but I can't turn back. My body is moving without my command.

I slam the door behind me and fly down the stairs. Then I jump into my car and onto the highway, speeding nonstop to the hospital.

"What the hell did you do, Liam?" So many terrible thoughts are flashing through my mind. What could have happened after I left?

Did he hurt himself?

I dismiss the thought quickly and try to concentrate on the road before I get myself killed.

"Did he follow me?" His room reeked of alcohol when I—.

More flashbacks.

The tears are clouding my vision and my judgement. I can't seem to stop crying. I merge to the right, exiting from the freeway. I'm almost to the hospital.

I hit the elevator button furiously, but it isn't moving fast enough. So I run to the employee stairway instead and storm up the stairs. Getting to the 6th floor in a flash as I push my way through the door.

I find Ripley sitting alone in the waiting area of the intensive care unit. I can't even speak. She hears my footsteps and looks up from her phone just as an alert sounds from my bag.

"I just texted you," she tells me.

"Where is he?"

"He just got out of surgery. They're moving him into his room right now for observation."

"Where is he?" I ask again.

"Going up to the 7th floor," she explains. I try to speak but I can't. She just pulls me close, and I fall to pieces in her arms all over again.

Several minutes pass before they finally

permit us to enter the room. As we walk in, we're confronted with a shocking sight. Liam lies motionless on the bed, hooked up to various machines, with a breathing tube down his throat. His entire body is bruised and swollen, making him almost unrecognizable. And I'm finding it hard to even look at him.

"Do we know what happened?" I ask the nurse that's changing his IV.

"What?" she responds coldly. Not even looking at me.

"What happened to him?" I repeat.

"Are you his family?" she questions. "Because if you're not, I won't be able to give you any information."

"Well, technically I'm not—."

"Then I'm sorry. But everything is confidential with Mr. Silverstone. Per his father's orders. Now if you'll excuse me, only immediate family is allowed inside," she tries to shoo me out.

"What?" I get defensive. "Are you kicking us out?"

"I'm afraid so," she responds. "Unfortunately, I'm going to have to ask you *both* to leave, miss."

"But—I'm—I'm his fiancé!" I snap at her.

"His *fiancé*?" Her face goes pale.

"Well, I—," I begin. She looks down at my hand and notices the lack of ring on my finger.

"Hmm," she scoffs. "I'm sorry, miss. But

I've heard that one before. I'm still going to have to ask you to leave."

As I seethe with anger, I am forced to acknowledge that the nurse is right. I have no claim on him. The memory of the girl I found in his bed fills me with jealousy and resentment, and seeing this nurse who bears a resemblance to her only intensifies it. Ripley stands beside me, engaged in a heated exchange with another nurse. My stomach churns with fury.

"Fine! We'll leave!" With a frustrated sigh, I dismiss the blonde nurse and storm out of the room, feeling defeated.

But Ripley, always resourceful, manages to persuade another nurse to let us stay for five more minutes. As soon as the door closes behind the nurse, Ripley launches into a barrage of questions.

"What the fuck was that?" Here we go. "*Fiancé*? Why didn't you just say you were his girlfriend?"

"I don't want to talk about it," I shake my head.

"Like hell you don't," she presses. "You're going to have to explain yourself *right now*."

"Okay," I give in and tell her everything. Minus the part about Ronan. Mainly focusing on the proposal and also the part where I ran off like an idiot.

Thankfully, she doesn't even ask how I got home. Then I explain to her how I had a change of heart, and went back to Liam's and that's when I found him in bed with someone else.

"What a dick," Ripley remarks. Then shakes her head at an unconscious Liam.

"Do you think he got into a car accident?" I whisper softly to Ripley.

"Yes," she frowns. "Kevin texted me from radiology when he saw his scans. He said it was a car accident."

"Do they know what happened?" I question.

"They said he flew off a bridge and had to be cut out of his car. It was completely mangled."

"Oh my God," I gasp. "I did this."

"This isn't your fault Zara," she frowns. Angry at my words. "The doctor's all said he was lucky to be alive. His alcohol levels were crazy. Now we just have to wait and see if he makes it."

"*If* he makes it?" The knot in my throat begins to suffocate me again. I storm out of the room without saying another word to Ripley.

Are we going to make a habit out of running away from things?

I race towards my car, not stopping until I reach it. The rain has picked up again, drenching me in seconds, but I don't care. I slam my fist onto the steering wheel, honking the horn as I cry out along with it.

How can my life fall apart in a day?

When I return home, Ronan is already

gone. And honestly, I'm relieved because I don't have the strength to face him, or to recount what just happened. I drag myself into bed, bury my face in my pillow, and scream into it. The tears come in waves, I lie there and sob painfully for hours and into the next day.

20

WHAT DID I JUST DO?

(Zara)

The next morning I wake up to someone tugging on my sheets.

Why did we get a cat.

My conscience can be so rude when I'm tired.

"I just want to sleep, Binks. Can you call in sick for me?" I mumble, wishing cats could actually make phone calls.

Today I woke up feeling particularly drained and hungover, despite not having consumed much alcohol. My memory is a blur.

"Well unfortunately, I'm not Binks. But I'd gladly do that for you," the culprit replies. It wasn't Binks.

It's Ronan.

Without another word, he picks up my phone from my dresser and dials my work.

What is he doing?

I hear ringing. Why isn't he hanging up? More ringing. Then someone picks up.

"Ronan!" I shout quietly. He can't seriously be calling my job right now. I scramble to my feet, trying to stop him. Then freeze when I hear him speak into the phone. In my voice.

"Hi, Susan. It's Zara from the 5th floor. Yeah, I'm feeling a little under the weather this morning. I don't think I'll make it in today—," he abruptly stops talking.

"Are you fucking kidding me?" I mouth to him. And he shrugs his shoulders innocently. I can hear the person on the other end speaking but I can't make out what she's saying.

Does she believe him?

"Thank you, Susan. Uh-huh, I will," he replies.

"What are they saying?" I mouth to him again but he waves me away.

"Okay. I'll call back later. Bye," he hangs up.

"What the fuck?"

"What happened to Liam?" He's serious now.

That part of last night had clearly slipped my mind. Or maybe I had hoped it was just a guilty dream. But from the look on Ronan's face, I can tell it's not.

"He was in an accident last night. After —," I pause. "That's why I left in such a rush.

God, I should really be there," I mumble to myself, "Hopefully that dumb blonde nurse isn't still there today," The conversation with myself continues.

"It's still early, Earthling," I try to sit up, but Ronan gently forces me back down. "The sun isn't even up yet. I think you should get some rest. You've had a long night," he insists. My puffy eyes and exhaustion from crying make it difficult to see, and I know he's right.

"I shouldn't call off work," I protest. "I've already missed a lot of time, and—."

"Zara," he cuts me off. "You already did, Earthling. 'What's her name' on the phone was more than understanding. She said to take off as much time as you need." Too tired to argue, I give in with a yawn. As I drift off into a deep sleep, I hear him continue to speak. "We have a big day today. You'll need all the rest you can get. We have some serious training to do."

Ronan pulls my head into his lap and runs his fingers through my hair, soothing me to sleep. I'm startled by the soft thud of his head as it falls back onto the headboard, but it also brings me comfort. And I drift away within seconds, all consciousness gone.

(102)

As I watch Zara sleep, I can't believe I'm

back in her apartment again. The nostalgia is overwhelming. Her fragility in my arms always makes me feel so protective and possessive over her. Like she's *mine* and my life's sole duty is to be her armor.

My beautiful Earthling.

"I love you," I whisper, hoping she doesn't hear me. But at the same time, secretly hoping she does.

I brush the back of my hand across her cheek, and she squirms in her sleep. A small groan escapes her lips, making me smile. I caress her hair, just like I used to do when she had nightmares and she drifts away again. The hours pass like seconds, and soon, it's almost noon.

We have to get going soon.

"Zara?" I gently nudge her, trying to wake her. She flips over, still asleep and punches me hard in the nose. "Shit!" I shriek in pain. The taste of metal filling my mouth. I run to the bathroom to clean up the bloody mess, while Zara stays in bed. Rubbing her eyes sleepily when I return.

She's so cute.

"What happened?" she commands in her raspy morning voice that I've missed so much.

"You got me again," I laugh, pointing at my nose.

"Did I do that?" she sighs apologetically.

"It's okay," I laugh. "I'm used to it by now."

Suddenly, she panics. “Where's my phone?”

“Oh, yeah. I guess you'd better call the hospital and see how Loverboy is, huh?” I scoff, referring to the man who has caused her all this pain. The thought of him makes my stomach turn. And my blood boil.

Too bad, he didn’t die.

(Zara)

After fighting with my supervisors for the past hour, I get off the phone with a nurse from the ICU who still won’t give me any information over the phone about Liam.

“Fuck!” I toss my phone on the bed. “Should I even be checking up on him?”

Where’s that skank he was with now?

My conscience is being petty.

“Stop it!” I take a breath. “The guy is fighting for his life, have some empathy, Zara.” I search through my bed sheets to find my phone again and dial Ripley. “Please pick up. Please pick up.” I plead but it goes straight to voicemail. “Damn it!” I pull up my messages and send her a text instead.

Me: “Hey Rip, are you at work? If by any chance you are, can you check on Liam for me? Please.”

I hit send and put my phone away. Then turn back to Ronan who's feeding my cat in the kitchen. He sets Binks' bowl down and pats him on the head. The cat happily rubs against Ronan's legs then goes for the food.

"Thanks for feeding him," I smile wearily.

"No problem," he grins. "He was hungry. And I don't know how long we'll be." Ronan walks over to the front door and picks up his boots that are sitting next to my shoes and starts putting them on. "Are you ready to go?"

"Where are we going?" I inquire. Still a mess. I really need to get a toothbrush in my mouth and a brush through my hair.

"To train," he responds. "I told you we—."

"Well, I need to shower first," I interrupt. "Now take that boot back off and sit your butt back down. Give me ten damn minutes," I storm off.

"Geez. Someone's in a mood," Ronan cringes.

"Excuse me!" I threaten.

I know he hates Liam but is he serious?

"Do you still want to know where we're going!" He yells out to me before I slam the door.

(102)

As she showers, I find serenity in the

silence and start to think about how quickly things have changed. I really thought I'd lost her to Liam, but now she's here with me.

And he's…

"Okay, so this dude basically cheated on her and then almost died to get himself out of it?" I confess the details to Binks. I can't fathom how that plan worked out in his head.

At this point, I feel like it's fair game. He's not a nice guy in my book anymore. Not that he ever really was. But now I have no more guilt over it.

"How could he do that to her?" I rub the cat's head. He vibrates on my chest, but ignores me. I click on the television, scanning the channels in boredom.

Nothing good is on at noon.

Though there's no activity down the hall, her room door is slightly open. I check my watch and realize that fifteen minutes have already passed. I lean back on the couch, attempting to peek into her room.

"Maybe I should check on her?" I suggest to the cat. He doesn't object, so I take it as a yes. With little courage, I rise from the couch and head towards her bedroom. "Here goes nothing."

As I reach the open door, I push it wider and enter the room. My heart races in my chest. The shower continues to run, accompanied by her music. As I approach, I notice that the bathroom door is also open, and I can see her showering through the sheer curtain.

Did she leave it open on purpose?

My nerves momentarily subside as I decide to take a chance. What do I have to lose? I've already lost her once. Can I really lose her again?

I push through the bathroom door and walk inside. I can clearly see the silhouette of her body through the shower curtain now.

What the hell are you doing?

Get out of here, are you crazy!

My conscience is trying to stop me, but I push the little voice aside and keep moving. I don't know if I'll ever have another opportunity like this, but I'm not going to let it slip away.

(Zara)

I press the play button on my music app and set my phone by the shower before jumping into the steam. A rush of cold air sweeps in, and I realize I forgot to close the bathroom door. I turn the knob hotter. Preferring the stinging pain of scalding water to the agony I'm feeling inside.

My mind is consumed with thoughts of Liam. His face. The girl. But then Ronan's face pushes through, and I can't help but smile. This time, I don't push the thought away.

I close my eyes and let myself indulge in daydreams of him. Imagining my fingers running across his lips and his sultry smile cratering those perfect dimples just for me.

Remembering his words from the night before, *"I love you, Zara."*

"I love you, Ronan," I whisper back.

Suddenly, I hear the bathroom door squeak and wonder if someone is in here.

"Binks?" I pull the shower curtain open slightly and peek out. But it's Ronan.

He starts kissing me. And for some reason I can't seem to resist.

What are you doing?

I pull him into the shower with me, fully clothed. And he doesn't pull back. He rips off his socks with one hand, while holding onto the back of my head with the other. His fingers digging into my wet hair as he kisses me more fiercely.

I manage to pull away to take a breath while he peels off his soaked shirt that was pasted like skin on his body. Then he removes his belt and cargo pants. I stare in awe, admiring him. I've never felt this type of intensity for anyone.

"Wow. Is this what all aliens look like?" I'm struggling to catch my breath now. He gives me a bashful smirk, and I can't resist but demand for another kiss.

He holds me tightly against his wet body pressing his against mine. My hand slips into the waistband of his boxer briefs, and with my foot, I pull them down his thigh. Am I dreaming?

"I don't think this is a dream," I say out loud.

And if it is, I think it's time to wake up.

The water cascades down his smooth, sun-kissed skin, making it gleam. I can barely contain myself, and from the looks of it, I can tell he feels the same.

He holds me tighter, his body almost adhering to mine. His lips venture down, tracing my jawline with his tongue, down to my neck. I can't help but let out a soft moan as I grasp onto his back.

But the drenched boxers around my foot prove to be an unwelcome distraction. Frustrated, I wiggle my foot, but they won't budge. His lips meet mine again, and I close my eyes, still trying to rid myself of this sodden fabric. When my trapped foot begins to slide. Causing us both to slip.

Oh, no.

We become entangled in the shower curtain like a burrito. And we tumble to the ground.

"That wasn't part of the plan," he chuckles. Then vanishes.

And I'm left lying naked in a damp towel,

searching the room for him. "Shit!"

I get up and head back to my bedroom, when he sneaks up behind me, making me jump. "What the hell?" I exclaim as I spin around to face him. He's now dressed in clean, dry clothes.

"Hurry up and get dressed. I'll meet you in ten." He kisses my wet forehead, then zaps away again.

"Shit!" I rush to my closet and hastily throw something on.

(102)

Zara's been trying to put on a brave face. I know she doesn't want to talk about how she feels or maybe she doesn't even know how to. But I can see how badly it's affecting her. Her once radiant spirit seems to have vanished. Despite her efforts to conceal her pain over Liam, I remain unconvinced.

"Alright Zara, we have two weeks to get you ready," I begin as she paces around the white room, lost in thought. "Zara, are you listening?"

"Huh? Yeah, uh—sorry. Go on."

"What is it?" I question.

"Bad memories." The somber look in her eyes shatters my heart. Knowing I'm the one that's hurting her now.

"Oh," I sigh. Wishing those weren't the memories she'd remember. "I need you to concentrate."

"I'm trying," she assures me.

"I know it's hard for you, being here. It's hard for me too," I tell her.

"Whatever," Zara scoffs, rolling her eyes at me.

"Excuse me, miss. But if you want to go with me, you'll need to cut that attitude," I remark.

"Really?"

"No," I cave too quickly. "But we do need to start training as soon as possible. Or you're not going."

"How am I supposed to learn invisibility in two weeks? It took me months to learn how to teleport," she snaps back at me. Proving my point exactly.

I shake my head. "Can we begin then?"

"Maybe I should just stay behind," she begins. "I don't know what I was thinking. I'll just slow you down."

"Come on, Zara," I complain. "I know you. I know what you're capable of. You'll nail this in less than two weeks, I know it. Invisibility is easy."

"Yeah. Easy for you to say," she scoffs.

"Can we just try?" I insist. "Trust me, okay?" I grab her chin.

"I do trust you, Ronan."

"Good," I nod in satisfaction.

"But—," she raises her hand to speak.

"But what, Zara?" I chuckle in frustration.

"What if we don't get all the vials?"

"Realistically speaking, the chances are that we may miss some."

"Some?" she gulps audibly. "Well what happens if someone gets a dose from one of the contaminated vials?"

"Zara, relax. Everything will be okay."

"But how can you say that? You don't know that, Ronan."

"Your facility will be one of the last to receive their shipment. That's what I read on their schedule, they're getting new vials in all month, but the ones we're looking for won't be in for two more weeks," I assure her.

"So, you do have a plan then?" she questions, arching her brow at me.

Man, I sure hope I do.

"Of course!" I lie, "I always do." I reach for her hand and grab it. "Come on. Let's get started."

Planning to wing it is not really a plan.

We move into our regular positions. Zara sits confidently and closes her eyes. But this time is different. She doesn't wait for any direction from me, she just starts on her own.

And she knows exactly what she's doing.

Her light appears almost instantly. Shining bright and swaying from side to side. Then she makes it shift colors.

Now she's just showing off.

"I'm impressed," I lean in close and whisper into her ear. She smiles but doesn't open her eyes. "Are you ready for our second lesson?"

"Yes," she nods eagerly, her light flickers in excitement.

"Just do as I say, okay?"

"Okay," she agrees.

"Now breathe. I want you to focus on you."

"On me?" she opens one eye.

"Yes, on you," I concede, and she closes her eye again. "Visualize your body and your mind. Imagine yourself disappearing."

"Disappearing?" she repeats, uncertainly.

"Yes, that's right. Picture it. Now feel your skin dissolve, and watch as the particles float away and disappear. Can you see them?" I speak softly.

"No," she admits, discouraged. Then opens her eyes.

"Keep trying, don't give up," I encourage her. "Focus again and stop doubting yourself."

"Okay," she agrees, taking a deep breath before trying again. "I see it, Ronan," she whispers.

I watch as her arms begin to vanish, the particles of her flesh filling the space around us before dissipating completely.

"You're a natural, Zara," I praise her,

smiling widely as she smiles too with her eyes still closed. “Do you realize that?”

“Am I?” she replies, sounding smug.

“You sure you haven't done this before?” I tease, observing the last bits of her body flutter away.

“Bet you can't find me now,” she chuckles, disappearing completely.

“Zara, come on, stop playing around,” I call out, “Where are you? This isn't funny!”

(Zara)

Holy shit, I’m invisible.

I’ve always wanted to be invisible, but now that I am, I can’t think of a good reason to use my new ability. Who would I even want to hide from?

“Zara!” Ronan is getting frustrated. “This isn’t funny anymore! Are you still here?”

This is so cool. I’ve been following him for the past twenty minutes, and he still doesn’t know where I am.

“Boo!” I yell into his ear. “Can you hear me?”

He jolts his head to the side and throws his hands over his ears. “Dammit, Earthling! Yes, I can hear you. You’re invisible, not mute. I think you might have burst my eardrum.”

"Sorry," I cringe. "How do I turn myself visible again?" This whole invisibility thing is starting to make me anxious.

"Just envision it happening. Anything you want to do, just envision it, then let your mind do the rest," he instructs.

"Anything, huh?"

I close my eyes and visualize my body pulling itself back together from thin air. Then I picture the cloud of color forming again around me, bringing my body back to one piece. After I see my body whole in my mind, I break my concentration and brace myself to see what actually happened.

Slowly, I open one eye, then look to Ronan to see his expression first.

"Did I do it?" I inquire nervously, not wanting to look down at my body. Ronan is grinning stupidly, and I know from his expression that he can see me.

"You sure did," he states proudly. "Like a pro."

"I'm a level 4 badass. Just admit it, I'm a natural at this," I brag. "Pro-fesh-o-nal." I give him a wink.

"All jokes aside, you actually kind of are, Earthling," he agrees. "Uh oh, lost you again. You still here? Or did you teleport on me?" he reaches for me.

I look down, but I can still see myself.

But he can't see me?

“Zara!” he calls out again. Shit. I guess I’m not that professional just yet.

We spend the rest of the day practicing until I’ve almost perfected my technique. Between the mental exhaustion from Liam to the physical exhaustion brought on by Ronan, I am beat with a capital B.

“I'm exhausted, Ronan,” I complain. “Can we go home now? We can train some more tomorrow.”

“Just one more time, please? I want to make sure we don't have any more slip-ups.”

“Fine,” I cave, closing my eyes again. *Poof*. I'm invisible. Then one more *poof*, and I'm back, visible again.

“There. Can we go now?” I plead.

“Fine, you’re so dang stubborn. Let's go,” he concedes, shaking his head at me. “I guess we’ll continue tomorrow.”

“Yay!” I jump up and down, but quickly return to my exhausted character mode.

“Are you hungry?” Ronan raises an eyebrow at me.

“Aren’t I always?”

When we return to my apartment, Ronan orders Xia takeout and it reminds me how much I've missed it since he's been gone.

“This is amazing! I don’t know what I missed more. You or your food,” I admit with a mouthful.

"Oh, so you did miss me then?" Ronan teases, making me blush. I playfully smack his arm.

"I did. I wished every day for you to come back," I confess, looking down at my food. "If I'm being honest, the only reason I practiced my meditations every day was to one day be able to teleport to you." As soon as the words leave my mouth, I regret saying them. "Pretty embarrassing, huh?"

Ronan's face becomes stern. "I'm sorry."

"For what?" I question.

"For leaving. You have no idea how much I wanted to come back to you, Earthling. Every day," he tells me. "Or how long I've wanted to do this," he leans in to kiss me just as my phone rings, interrupting us.

"Damn it. It's Ripley."

"It's okay. Take it," he tells me.

"I'll be quick," I respond, then answer the call. "Hello. How's he doing?" I inquire, hoping for good news.

"I just wanted to call and check in on you, actually," Ripley responds. "Liam's fine. He's stable. We think he may be out of the woods for now."

"That's good news!" I exclaim.

"Don't get your hopes too high," she warns. "He's still not able to breathe on his own. But we're hopeful. His dad even came by—once."

"Oh," I sigh, feeling a twinge of guilt.

"Yeah. How are you holding up?" she questions.

"I'm doing okay," I lie, looking over at Ronan.

"If you're up for it today, I think he may want you here with him, Zara. He's all alone," Ripley suggests.

She's right. I must look like an asshole. I've been so busy with Ronan that I haven't even called once to check up on Liam. After I hang up with Ripley, I gather my things and head out to the hospital, feeling guilty about what almost happened with Ronan in the shower.

In my defense, I really did think it was a dream. I've had steamy dreams starring Ronan as the lead before, but nothing could have prepared me for the reality. Flashbacks of Ronan in my shower send a heat shock to my crotch. I slap myself in the face, feeling guilty for lusting after Ronan while my boyfriend is lying in a coma.

"Boyfriend," I say out loud, the word leaving a sour taste in my mouth. I still don't know if I can get over what he did. I guess I'll just deal with it when the time comes.

What kind of person deals like this, Zara?

"A broken one," I tell myself.

After a quick drive I make it to the hospital in one piece. Not sure how, since I was in a state of dissociation the entire drive.

God, I wish I knew how to get through this.

I walk quietly towards the stairway, avoiding the elevator to avoid people. The last thing I need right now is to run into anyone I know and start playing catch up. My place of employment is the last place I need to be having a mental breakdown at.

Once I reach his floor, I push open the door and find my way to his suite. Or at least I think it was this way. I'm feeling like I don't know this hospital at all anymore. I've worked here for years and I didn't even know we had a private suite floor. So private, that the entire area even requires security access.

"Good thing I work here, huh?" I pull out my I.D. badge and scan it across the keypad, allowing the doors to open.

I enter the deserted floor cautiously, making sure to avoid being seen. "I could have sworn it was one of these," I mutter under my breath, while I search every room.

No matter how hard I try, the memories and emotions I've tried to suppress keep flooding back at the worst possible times.

Will I ever be able to forgive him? Or does this mean I'm no longer allowed to be angry?

I wish there was a guidebook to navigate through the aftermath of a proposal, cheating, near-death experience, and the return of an ex who's also the love of your life - all happening in one night.

It can't be as common as you think it is.

I finally reach the end of the corridor. There's only one door left. I take a deep breath before opening it. “Please be in here. Please be in here,” I whisper to myself.

But he's not here.

“Wait a minute.” My sixth sense begins to tingle, and I think I know where he could be.

I close my eyes tightly and concentrate. I haven't teleported alone since—well, since that night. And Ronan isn't here to ensure my safety.

We got this.

“Come on, Zara, visualize it. You can do it.” I close my eyes for a couple of seconds, but nothing happens. “Did it work?” I open my eyes, still in the same room. “Shit. Let's try again.”

“Are you sure you saw her?” an unfamiliar male voice breaks my concentration.

“Yeah. She came this way. I'm certain,” a female voice responds.

Oh, no. Am I the "she" they're talking about?

Whoever they are, they’re coming this way. And I think they're coming for me.

“Alright, Zara. It's now or never,” I tell myself. The voices get louder, and I know they're about to turn the corner and see me. Failure is not an option this time. “Visualize,” I whisper, closing my eyes again.

Suddenly, the voices become silent.

Did they find me?

I'm afraid to open my eyes.

"I did it!" I high-five myself proudly. Half relieved because honestly I was expecting it not to work.

I'm really starting to impress myself.

I've somehow managed to teleport to Liam's father's house in one piece. But I've landed in a not too familiar room. Now I'm hoping whatever it was that told me he'd be here, was right.

I pause for a second and close my eyes again. "Visualize, visualize," I chant. Trying to practice the new trick Ronan just taught me. But when I open my eyes and look down, I can still see myself. "Shit! It didn't work." I'm still visible.

I guess you're not that impressive.

When I get upstairs, I find a long hallway. Long and lined with tens of doors. "More doors," I groan. But there's a familiar hissing coming from one of the bedrooms that I can identify with my eyes closed after working at a hospital for so many years.

It's a ventilator.

That has to be him.

I follow the hissing sound. Tiptoeing like a teenager sneaking out of her house. Down the corridor as quietly as I've trained. But something catches my eye.

"Wait a minute." I walk past a huge mirror on the wall but fail to catch my reflection. I quickly rush back. My hands on either side of it. Grasping it firmly as I stare into it. And see nothing.

"Why can't I see my reflection?" I whisper to myself. "Did I do it? Am I invisible?"

This is weird.

No wonder Ronan was worried about me.

I manage to peel myself away from the mirror and back to my mission. Back to following the sound. Running off after it until I come to a stop.

The sound is just on the other side of the door now. Right in front of me. I close my eyes and take another deep breath, this time bracing myself for an empty room.

Or am I hoping for one?

Honestly. I don't even know anymore.

I just zap myself inside.

"He's here," I sigh in relief. Feeling a mixture of so many clashing emotions.

Liam is lying on a hospital bed, connected to a number of machines. He's still unconscious and barely looks alive. Seeing him vulnerable like this breaks me all over again. I drop to my knees by his bed and reach for his hand. It's cold.

Sometimes I wonder how a person can still manage to love someone even when that person has caused them such great pain.

Or is something just wrong with me?

Maybe I am broken. Maybe I was broken already before Liam. Before Ronan too. Maybe when my parents died it affected the chemistry in my still developing brain somehow. And now I'm unable to properly form attachments to people. Or maybe everyone is just destined to leave me one way or another.

Like my parents.

Like Lucy.

Like Ronan.

Like Liam.

Maybe I'm just not meant for happiness.

Or love.

I put his hand up to my cheek to warm it. Then kiss his palm, making his pinky wiggle in response.

"What the hell," I gasp. "Liam?" I try again. Wondering if I'm becoming delusional or if I really saw what I saw. "Did he just—? Liam, can you hear me?" I question, rubbing his hand. "Can you feel this?"

I try over and over. But he doesn't move again.

The disappointment brings me back to my knees and I sob quietly by his bed. Holding his hand tightly in mine. Getting lost in the sound of the machines. In the cold room. It smells like a hospital but with a lingering scent of peppermint. I squeeze his hand tightly and continue to cry.

When the door knob begins to wiggle. Without thinking, I react quickly, diving under the bed to hide.

Am I still invisible?

A nurse walks in to check on Liam. She makes her way right up to his bed and stops right beside me. I can see her clearly from underneath the bed. Watching her as she sets her bag down next to Liam and pulls a syringe out of her bag. Then injects it into his IV.

My gut is screaming. Something doesn't feel right. After the nurse finishes, she wraps the syringe in a towel and places it back in her bag. Red flags are going up. Why would she keep a used syringe when there's a sharps container right there? The nurse zips her bag back up and leaves.

What did she give him?

The adrenaline is starting to wear off and I think I might have bumped into something on the way down. My hand is killing me. There's a stinging pain coming from it.

I lift it into the light to see what's causing the discomfort and find blood dripping down my fingers, flowing down my wrist.

"What the heck happened?" There's a giant gash on the side of my hand, running along my pinky. I instinctively clasp my other hand over it to try to stop the bleeding. Then slide out of my hiding spot to find something I could use as a bandage. When I notice a small screw sticking out of the railing under the bed.

Well, there's the little shit that got me.

I snatch a gauze from the nightstand next to Liam and wrap it around my hand. "I think I'm going to need stitches."

(102)

"They're not letting anyone inside without being scanned," one of the anchors on Channel 9 News announces.

"You heard that right, folks. This will be nationwide starting next week," the co-anchor nods with an almost plastic grin. They're talking as if this were the best thing since sliced bread.

"That's all for tonight. Now back to you, Greg, with the weather—." I shut the television off and toss the remote next to a sleeping Binks, who doesn't even flinch. Every channel has been flooded with the same news lately. It's like I can't escape work even on Earth anymore.

I've been trying to keep myself busy while waiting for Zara, but have officially run out of things to do. She's been gone for hours now without checking in, and I'm beginning to worry.

When finally, she stumbles in. And she's

hurt.

"What the hell happened to you?" Zara's cradling her arm tightly to her chest, with blood dripping all over her shirt. "Did you teleport here?"

"I'm fine," she insists, but it's clear she's *not*.

"Who did this to you?" I interrogate her, my blood beginning to boil.

"Who? Why do you always have to assume someone did something to me? Don't you know me?" she frowns. "It was an accident." Zara pulls up a chair and sits down.

"Oh," she's right.

"You think you can fix me up?" she gives me a weary laugh.

"I can't, Zara. We can only heal ourselves. You know that," I respond.

"Guess you can't 'achieve *everything*'," she air quotes.

"Actually, there was someone I knew who could heal others," I raise a brow.

"So, will you help me or not?" she holds up her hand, this time with a smirk on her face.

"That wasn't what you meant by 'fixing you up', was it?" I laugh. Feeling like an idiot.

"No," she chuckles. "I have a suture kit in my bathroom. I was going to ask if you could stitch me up. But—."

"But what?"

"Maybe you could teach me self-healing

instead?" she raises an eyebrow. "Keep me safe from my own self mishaps?"

"Hmm, I don't know if you're ready for that yet," I tease her. But come to think of it, that isn't such a bad idea. This new ability might actually give me a little peace of mind while I'm away.

Especially since she is so damn clumsy.

"Oh, come on!" She pleads. "I'm already wounded. That's the hard part, isn't it? Please!" she continues.

"Okay, okay," I concede, making her hop up and down like a toddler. Blood continuing to drip all over the floor. "But will you please sit? This place is starting to look like a murder scene." I press my finger to her forehead, getting her to sit back down.

"Do I still have to close my eyes?" she asks, with only one eye open.

"No, you don't have to," I laugh. "Not unless you want to."

"No, I want to see this!" she says.

"Okay. You know what to do."

She's so adorable when she's excited.

(Zara)

I look up at Ronan with a quizzical expression.

Is this another test?

"Maybe I do need to close my eyes," I admit, feeling nervous under his intimidating gaze.

"Go ahead," he laughs, not actually seeming intimidating at all.

With my eyes now shut, I focus all my attention on the throbbing pain emanating from my hand. It's not difficult to concentrate on the pain, because it still feels as intense as ever.

Since I can no longer see it, I try to visualize the wound. Then I imagine it being healed. After a moment, I open my eyes excitedly. But to my disappointment, nothing has changed.

"I'm still bleeding, Ronan," I say, feeling let down.

"I can see that," he chuckles.

"Why are you laughing at me?" my annoyance is growing.

"I'm sorry," he becomes serious again. "What were you thinking about? Tell me."

Here he goes again with his Mr. Myagi bullshit.

"I did what you told me," I pout. "I visualized my cut and then imagined it being healed."

"Just like that?" he raises an eyebrow skeptically.

"Well, yeah," I reply, missing his point.

"You're hilarious," he replies. "Like a

magic trick?"

"I'm sorry," I scoff, feeling frustrated. "Are there steps I need to follow? This cut really hurts."

Sometimes I wish he would just tell me what to do instead of making me figure it out on my own.

This is how you learn, dummy.

My conscience taunts me.

"Healing isn't instant, Zara," Ronan explains. "It isn't like teleporting or invisibility. *You* have to heal it."

"*I* have to heal it?" I repeat, contemplating his words. Surprisingly, they make a lot of sense. I think I know what to do now.

Not everything in life is instant. It all takes work and determination. That was something I was forgetting the first time; I got too cocky. The second time, I clear my heart as well as my mind. I straighten my posture and take a deep breath. But now, I keep my eyes open.

As soon as I uncover the wound, blood starts trickling out of it again, but I need to see it. I focus on it intensely, watching as the crimson liquid oozes out of me and onto the floor.

Okay, just heal it.

With my mind and heart clear, I start again. I examine the edges and depth, then imagine the borders coming together and fusing shut. I visualize making it happen. But still, nothing happens.

"Damn it!" I curse.

"You need to relax," Ronan advises me.

"I'm trying," I assure him, but I don't give up. I try again, closing my eyes and doing a little wiggle for good luck.

Come on, Zara. You can do this.

I take a long, deep breath, then exhale slowly. The throbbing in my hand becomes almost rhythmic. I focus on that sound. The throbbing turns to a beating, and then I swear I can almost hear the blood as it runs through my veins with life. The feeling is almost euphoric. I let go and embrace it completely, until my mind drifts away, and I'm no longer here.

"Zara!" Ronan shakes me. "Zara!"

My concentration is broken, and I open my eyes to see my hand, which is no longer in agonizing pain.

"I did it," I gasp.

"You did it," he confirms.

Admiring my now perfect hand, I bounce up and down again, no longer leaking blood everywhere. But Ronan isn't saying anything. He just watches. "You're not celebrating."

"Nothing to celebrate," he grins proudly. "I knew you could do it."

"Is it bad that I want to cut myself again just so I can heal it?"

"Yes! Don't you dare, Earthling!" he

threatens. “Or I’ll take back all the powers I’ve already given you.”

“You wouldn’t.” I counter, narrowing my eyes at him. “You can’t, right?”

“You’re right. I can’t,” he laughs.

“You promise?”

“That’s why I’m here in the first place, remember?” he assures me. “To make sure no one can.”

21

TIME IS TICKING

(102)

As we near the end of our training timeline, Zara has already surpassed most of the guys I know. I can't say I'm surprised though; she's been a quick learner from the beginning. I'm confident in the new partner in crime-fighting that I've created, and it's only taken her less than two weeks to get there. Which is really impressive. Even for me.

"Alright, Zara. Here's your test. Are you ready?"

"I'm ready," she replies.

"Okay, I want you to follow me around. But you have to make sure I can't see or hear you for ten whole minutes this time," I instruct. Her previous record was eight minutes. While she's good at being sneaky, she's also incredibly clumsy. Always tripping over something.

"Ten minutes? Easy," she scoffs. "I followed Binks around my apartment last night for an hour, and he didn't suspect a thing."

Her enthusiasm is contagious, and I can't help but smile. Then, in an instant, Zara disappears, and the entire apartment becomes dead silent. I stand incredibly still and listen closely.

"Come on, Zara. Think stealth," I whisper before zapping myself outside to make things more interesting.

"You're gonna have to do better than that," she startles me. I'm impressed, I didn't even hear her come outside. But not impressed enough.

I zap myself on top of the roof, giving her a few minutes to catch up. But I still don't hear her.

"Boo," I feel an invisible push, and I zap myself back down to the grass.

Now I'm surrounded by trees, and the sound of the leaves rustling in the cool breeze fills my ears. Birds chirping a song above me, and the sound of cars honking on the highway add a magical touch. It's like a symphony. I open my eyes quickly and run, hearing every crisp blade of grass crunch under my boots.

But I still don't hear Zara.

"Is she even following me?" I ask myself. "She can't be this good."

I reach a giant oak tree and move quickly towards it before leaping high into the branches to wait.

"Where are you?" I question, but I still

don't hear anything. Either I've lost her, or she may have given up. I check the stopwatch.

“Fifteen minutes and counting.”

“Boo!” she taps me from behind.

“Hey!” I fall off the branch, and Zara quickly grabs my arm, zapping us back inside before I can hit the ground. “Gotcha, huh?” she smirks.

“You sure did. But I’ve got bad news,” my face gets stern.

“What is it?” she inquires with concern.

“Now I’ve got you,” I tag her on the arm and disappear.

It's been all train and no play lately, so it's time for a little fun. We make ourselves visible only to each other and zap ourselves all over town, playing a friendly game of Alien Tag.

Her idea to name it that, of course.

(Zara)

As the sun begins to descend towards the horizon, the sky turns into a canvas of warm hues. Shades of orange, pink, and red bleed into each other, creating a stunning display of color. The water mirrors the sky, reflecting the colors in a rippling mosaic. The waves gently lapping against the shore, leaving trails of foam that shimmer in the fading light. Ronan takes my hand and holds it in his as we walk along the water.

The sand beneath our feet is cool and damp, sticking to our skin as our toes become entangled in it. As the sun dips lower and lower, the last rays of sunlight shimmer over the water like diamonds, and the world seems to slow down for just a moment.

“Hey Ronan, do you remember telling me once that you knew someone who could heal people?”

“Yeah, why do you ask?” he responds.

“Can you tell me more about them?” I inquire curiously.

“Well, I didn't know them personally. She was a girlfriend of one of my buddies. This was decades ago, and I haven't seen her since,” he explains.

“What happened?” I question, sensing his mood shift.

“He got blown up by an Earth bomb while he was out on a private job,” he informs me. “She disappeared shortly after. I guess the heartbreak really got to her.”

“That’s awful. I’m so sorry about your friend,” I take a breath. Wishing I could just shut up sometimes.

“It’s fine. It was a long time ago,” he assures me.

“But you said she healed him before?”

“Yes.”

“How did she heal him? How did she learn

to do it? And how did she learn that she was even able to do it in the first place?" I say all in one breath. Sometimes I wonder if he's tired of me and my millions of questions.

But that still never keeps me from asking.

"I'm not sure about any of those things, Earthling," he responds. "I never asked."

"You never asked!" I shout. "How could you not ask?"

"I don't know. But no one ever taught her. If that's what you're wondering."

"What do you mean?" I inquire some more.

"No one showed her. She just started healing one day on her own."

"And how do you know that? Thought you didn't ask any questions," I reply, sarcasm in my tone.

"Actually, Rhen offered up that information on his own," he corrects me.

"Really?" I pretend to not believe him.

"Yes," he nods. "He told us she was just a kid the first time it happened."

A kid?

"That's very interesting," I respond.

"Is that all, my curious little Earthling?" he teases.

"Actually, no. One more."

"Go on," he grins patiently.

"What happened to her after?"

"No one knows," Ronan shrugs. "She just vanished. We never saw her again."

"That's such a sad story. I can't even imagine what she must have felt," I sigh. Remembering what it felt like when I had lost Ronan only temporarily.

"Yeah. Losing someone you love is the worst feeling ever," he shares a weak smile, assuring me he shares the same feelings as me.

"Do you think that I could learn that, Ronan?" I ask, my thoughts instantly on Liam. Maybe I could help him.

Ronan stops walking and faces me. Just as the sun finishes setting completely. "Healing isn't an ability that you can just learn like everything else, Earthling. It's a gift. One not everyone will be able to have," he smiles. The smile that makes me feel ten feet tall and like I can conquer the world.

"Noted," I smile back.

Ronan intertwines his fingers with mine again and we continue walking.

He's been making himself visible lately when we're in public. Mostly only places I know we won't be running into anyone I know at. I've really appreciated this because I no longer look like the crazy lady that talks to herself.

"Should we head back home now?" I begin. "It's getting kind of late."

"Why?" Ronan gets caught off guard. "Are you kicking me out of Earth now?"

"No, of course not," I chuckle. "I just—I have to go visit Liam for a bit. See how he's doing today."

"Oh," his expression falls instantly. It doesn't matter how long it's been, he still gets the same every time I mention Liam.

"I'll see you later?" I offer.

"Yeah, sure," he responds a bit more coldly. "Be safe. I'll come by tonight." It seems our old routine jumped right back into place as if he'd never even left.

Well, except for the Liam part.

I instantly zap myself to Liam's father's house the moment I arrive home. This teleporting stuff has literally changed my life. I hated driving. And this sure as hell beats LA traffic. And now that I'm an invisibility master, I no longer have to worry about hiding. I can now be wherever I want whenever I want.

Liam's condition has improved slightly, but there hasn't been any significant progress. As I stroke his hair, I notice the swelling on his face has reduced significantly, and the bruises are slowly healing. However, he hasn't changed much other than that. Today, the doctor spoke with his father about the possibility of Liam never waking up, which was a conversation I wish I hadn't overheard, but I'm also grateful I did because I wouldn't know anything about Liam otherwise.

I pull up a chair next to him, taking his hand in mine and tracing the scars on his wrists and the fading bruises. Without realizing it, tears fall down my face and onto his skin as I plead with him to wake up. I haven't considered what will happen between us if he wakes up, but I know for sure that I want him to.

Will I forgive him?

Will he forgive me?

Will everything go back to normal?

Will I still be able to see him the same?

Do any of those things even matter anymore?

I gaze at Liam's motionless form, his once beautiful face now battered and fragile. My mind races with thoughts about Rhen and whether Liam is too far gone as well. I watch his chest rise and fall in time with the machines, the scent of peppermint lingering in the air. Will this ever get easier? Or is this my new reality that I need to come to terms with?

That he might not wake up.

Suddenly, the door creaks open and I step back, hiding in plain sight. David and a nurse enter the room, their conversation catching my attention. What decision are they talking about? My confusion is mirrored by David's anger and frustration as he lashes out at the nurse.

"The doctor told me it didn't have to be today, dammit!" David shouts.

What are they talking about?

"But the doctor said—," the nurse begins but David cuts her off again.

"Can you just give me some time to think! He is still alive! He is still breathing!" he exclaims. "What's the goddamn rush!"

The nurse backs away from David, clearly afraid. I don't think she'll be coming back. This is the third nurse that has quit this week.

"I—I," she stutters but can't seem to speak.

"Can you just leave," David's voice softens. "Please, just let me get a little more time with my boy. He's all I have left," he begins to cry.

"I'm sorry, sir. I didn't—," her face is no longer fearful, now it's pitiful. The tears must have gotten to her. Maybe she'll stay another day after all.

"Just get out!" David shouts again.

Or maybe not.

"We'll pull the damn plug when I decide!" he continues to yell through the door. "You got that! When I decide!"

Pull the plug?

I zap myself back home quickly, hoping Ronan isn't waiting for me in my apartment. Right now, all I need is to be alone. Alone with just my thoughts that I can't seem to escape from. David's words keep echoing in my mind. *Pull the plug.* But it's too soon for that. Liam can still pull through.

He has to.

"This is all my fault," I berate myself. If only I had said yes to Liam that night.

Then would I be the one making the decision to pull the plug?

No. If I had said yes, Liam would still be alive.

My thoughts add more fuel to the fire.

You should have just said yes.

I shake away the tormenting thoughts before I begin crying again. I need to stop blaming myself for things beyond my control.

Binks is perched on the armrest of the couch, fixated on the blue jay he's been eyeing all week. He may be a house cat, but he was once a wild feline. Before I rescued him from the streets. I scoop him up and take him to the kitchen to eat before retiring to my room. As I look at myself in the mirror, I frown at my puffy and swollen eyes, with dark half-moons lurking beneath them.

"Tomorrow is going to be a big day," I tell myself, anticipating the challenges that lay ahead.

A very big day.

22

HEROES AND ROBBERS

(Zara)

Today's the day. We've trained tirelessly for the past two weeks, me mostly. And now the time has come to prove myself. I really hope I don't fuck up.

"I've never seen myself as a superhero before. But look at me now," I tell Ronan as I model yet another potential super-suit for him. "What should we call ourselves?"

This does make me a superhero, right?

"Next," he boos me, and sends me back in.

This next one will have to do. I fasten my skinny blue jeans at the waist. This was the closest thing to a super-suit I could find. I know it's custom for women to wear skintight leather outfits during these types of events, but I really don't think squeaky leather would be the best idea in our case. Also, leather is not very comfortable.

No wonder the men always wear spandex.

Before I step out for another outfit check, I grab a black hoodie from the floor and pull it over my head. The hospital gets really cold, so I want to stay warm. And that concludes my next superhero outfit.

Ronan is sitting on the couch, flipping through channels while I change in and out of clothes. It's difficult to find the perfect balance between comfort and style. Ronan seems to have an innate sense of fashion, but not all of us are as gifted.

“Are you ready yet?" he shouts from the other room. “The shipment arrives in two hours! We need to be there before so we can prepare and not miss anything!”

“Yeah, I think I'm ready!” I respond, strutting into the living room. “So, do I look badass or like a homeless person? I'm not entirely sure which look I'm going for, but I like this one best. Also, should I wear a beanie or—.”

“You look great. Like Super Bum,” he pulls me into him mid-sentence and zaps us to Silverstone Health.

“God, Ronan! You could at least warn a girl.” I pull my arm away from him and pout. “You made me forget my beanie.”

He smiles at me then zaps it into his hand. “Here, we don’t want that pretty little head of yours getting cold,” he places it on my head then kisses it. "Now come on."

We make our way to the basement supply room, where all shipments are brought in and sorted before being distributed to each floor. We stand in a corner, waiting for someone to arrive, but an hour passes with no one showing up.

"Are we early or late?" I whisper.

"Let's find out," he replies.

We step out of our corner and inspect the area but find nothing that matches the description of what we're looking for.

"Early," I conclude. "So, I guess we wait now?"

"Yup," Ronan yawns.

An hour later a delivery guy shows up. I nudge Ronan to wake him. He nods, indicating that he understands, then disappears into the shadows. I take a deep breath and try to calm my nerves as the delivery guy finishes unloading the boxes and leaves the room.

I wait a few moments, making sure the coast is clear, and then signal for Ronan to join me. He reappears beside me, his eyes scanning the room for any potential threats.

"Remember, the ones we're looking for will have a barcode that starts with the number 4," Ronan informs me.

"Got it," I nod, "let's get to work." We start opening boxes, carefully examining the contents of each one. But all of the barcodes on these boxes seem to start with the number nine.

"None of these start with a number four," I say to myself. Pointing out the obvious. "Are these the right boxes?"

Or maybe we have to open them?

The squeaky wheels from the dolly are approaching. And I run back to hide. The delivery guy is coming back. I wave my arms around, trying to get Ronan's attention. Then signal for him to wait until the guy is done bringing in all the boxes before we start inspecting because the boxes need to be opened.

At least that's what I'm trying to say.

(102)

"What the hell is she doing? Is she waving at me?" I wave back.

Alright, Ronan, I know you were on a time crunch bud, but why the hell did you not teach the girl IM!

My conscience is right. Only God and Zara know what she's trying to say because I honestly have no clue. But I stand back and wait until the delivery guy has left before I go try to find out.

After a few more trips, the shipment is all here. The delivery guy heads to the door and presses a small black button on the wall, which makes a festive chime, and another guy comes in.

“Hey, man! Is that the new shipment?” the new guy, one of the hospital workers, asks. I recognize him, he’s always smoking outside in the mornings when I'm barely getting to work.

“Yeah, it's all here, bro. Are you ready to sign for it?” the delivery guy responds.

“Sure, let me just check them out,” the smoker replies, giving the delivery guy the old finger guns before walking over towards the stack of boxes. The boxes that Zara is still hiding behind.

“Oh no,” I mutter under my breath. He pulls out a knife from his pocket, cuts open one of the boxes, and peeks inside.

“Looks good. Thanks, man. See you next week for the next one,” the smoker adds before he takes off again.

(Zara)

I call Ronan over, and he appears next to me instantly.

“Did you hear what he said? They’re getting another shipment next week,” I exclaim, looking at him expectantly.

“I know,” he replies. Not seeming as surprised as I am.

“You know? What are we gonna do?”

I inspect the box that Joe cut open for me. Everything inside is labeled correctly. I push the box over and open another. Then another. Still no sign of the contaminated vials. I open another and another. Still nothing.

"There's nothing here, Ronan."

"Are you sure?"

"Positive," I reply, frustration seeping into my voice.

"This can't be right," he responds, furrowing his brow.

"Wait a minute—this says shipment 2 of 3," I note suddenly, my heart sinking.

"What?" Ronan asks urgently.

"Ronan, I think we missed a shipment."

"Shit," he swears under his breath.

We both start frantically searching around the room for any sign of the missing boxes.

"There's nothing here," I pant.

"Just like there was nothing here the first time we looked," Ronan's voice heavy with disappointment.

"So, we missed it?" I ask, feeling defeated.

"Let me think for a sec. Where do they take the boxes after they've been inspected and sorted?" Ronan asks me, his mind already working to find a solution.

"The medication rooms?" I suggest uncertainly.

"How many medication rooms does the

hospital have?"

"A lot. It's going to take us forever to check everything."

"Then I guess we'd better get started," he chuckles nervously.

"Let's go then," I sigh. Throwing my hood on over my beanie dramatically. "Alright, Robin, I'll start upstairs on the 7th floor of the main building. You start on the main level here. Then we'll meet back in the middle and head to Building 2 together," I instruct, breaking down the game plan.

"Robin?" he frowns.

"And make sure you've checked every room, okay?" I almost forget to mention, "Not just the med rooms. Sometimes they have a small fridge in the exam rooms with vials inside."

"Okay," he nods. Still acting kind of funny.

Why is he looking at me like that?

"You okay?" I question him.

"Why are you calling me Robin?" he inquires.

"Out of all the things I just said, that's the only thing you heard?" I shake my head.

"Wait—are you calling yourself Batman and me your—sidekick? Because if anyone is Batman, I'm definitely the Batman here!"

"You're insulted that I called you my sidekick?"

"No," he lies terribly. "But I wanted to be

Batman."

"Really?" I put my hand on my hip.

"Yes, really," he argues. "You can be Cat Woman or something."

"Are we really arguing about this right now, Ronan?" I roll my eyes, preparing to take off without him. "I am Batman," I reply in my deepest voice, then disappear.

I begin my search on the top floor, cautiously entering the first room. Quickly realizing that this floor is where the business side of the hospital takes place, as there are only offices and supply rooms.

The first few rooms are stacked top to bottom with filing cabinets, reminding me of the room where I first saw Ronan on this same floor. As I move from room to room, I find the same endless rows of cabinets, all locked. I can't help but wonder what they're all for, or why there are so many. My imagination starts to get the best of me, but I quickly remind myself that I have work to do.

After two more rooms filled with cabinets, I decide to call it quits on this level and zap myself down to the sixth floor, where Liam was staying. But when I get there, I find every room is the same as the last: empty. It seems like this entire floor hasn't seen any patients since Liam. I give up on this floor early as well, but my conscience and I are hopeful that the next floor will yield better results.

I arrive on the fifth floor, where I work, next. I know that we don't typically administer vaccines other than prescribed medications here. But still, I need to check anyways. The first room is clear, but in the next one, I have to wait for two nurses to finish up before I can enter. They don't move fast enough, and just before one leaves, she takes a couple of vials from the box that I needed to look at with her. I let out an inaudible curse, but as soon as they leave, I rush straight to the box and check the label. My heart sinks instantly.

Four.

With a shaky hand, I set the box back down and quickly examine the contents, counting them. It's half-empty. I realize that some might have already been given, and I'm not sure what to do. I don't have time to look for Ronan and tell him what I've found, so my first priority is finding the rest of those vials. I take whatever is left and move on to the next room, determined to clear them all before any more disappear.

I enter our med room, carefully searching every corner. A giant stack of unopened boxes catches my eye, so I quietly dive into that next, mindful of the person in the room beside me. A bad feeling creeps into my gut, and I hope that I'm wrong about what I'm going to find.

But as I turn over the first box, my fears are confirmed. My heart sinks once again.

Four.

The box is nearly empty.

I try to make sense of it. Why are these boxes here when we don't give any shots on this floor? Then I remember the briefing on my last day of work. They were going to start mandatory catch-up immunizations at work the following week.

Did Ripley?

No, she wouldn't.

She promised she would quit before she did that. But did she? I draw a blank. I haven't spoken to Ripley much since the accident, consumed with Ronan and training. Guilt washes over me, but I push it aside. Time is ticking, and people's lives are at stake.

Just as I'm about to move on, the door opens behind me, and Ripley walks in. I'm tempted to ask her all the questions I've been asking myself, but I remember she can't see me. Instead, I move back and stay out of her way until she leaves. As I continue my search, I find three more boxes, one empty and two new.

Panic sets in.

How am I going to carry all of these? I need to think of a plan to dump them quickly and securely. But where? Where is Ronan taking his boxes?

Turns out we kinda suck at this superhero thing.

I might have abilities like a superhero, but I have no idea what I'm doing. So being the amateur that I am, I do what comes to mind first, I put my hands on the boxes and zap myself to Liam's secret room with the slides.

This is your best idea?

He did say no one ever goes there. And well, we know he won't be going in there anytime soon either. That fact saddens me. But this is my best shot. I leave the boxes in a dry corner away from the pool. Hidden behind trees. Then go back to where I left off, searching for more.

On the third floor, I bump into Ronan in the first med room. He doesn't have any boxes, so I'm assuming he found a place to dump them as well.

Probably somewhere better than mine.

"Hey, what are you doing in here?" I exclaim in my best Batman voice.

"Damn it, Earthling. You scared me!" Ronan jumps.

"Where are you putting your boxes?" I ask him quietly.

"I sent them all back to the science lab at the Department of Defense," he informs me. And I cross my arms.

"Thanks for the heads up, pal."

"Shit! Sorry! I forgot to tell you what to do with yours," he looks at my empty hands. "What *did* you do with yours?"

"I dumped them," I admit.

"Where?" he raises an eyebrow.

"I'll tell you later," I laugh nervously.

"Tell me now," he flares his nostrils.

"At Liam's dad's house," I cringe.

The look on his face says he hopes I'm joking. But unfortunately, I'm not as quick-witted as I thought I was.

"You did *what* now?" he raises his voice a little too high.

"Calm down. They're in a safe place, I promise," I assure him. "What did you expect me to do?"

"Well, I could have thought of about a billion other places before taking them to Mr. Silverstone's house," he scoffs smugly.

"We don't have time to point fingers right now or judge each other's not so great ideas. Can we just keep moving?" I shake my head.

"Fine. Let's go."

We find five more boxes in the Psych ward, and he sends them off to Xia before we move on to the pharmacy in the other building.

"How many boxes have you found so far?" I inquire. I know he was in the maternity and pediatrics ward. So my first thoughts are the children and babies. "Did you find any open contaminated boxes?"

"Six," he informs me sternly.

"Six open boxes?" I gasp.

"Six empty," he confirms.

Oh, no.

He goes ahead of me and starts searching the pharmacy first. It's crowded with patients right now since it's the morning shift, so we have to be extra careful. I'm hiding up against the wall at the back of the pharmacy just watching him. The technicians are running around like chickens with their heads cut off.

Why is it so busy today?

I look over the counter at a huge line of people that extends all the way down into the hall. My curiosity has piqued. And I zap over to the waiting area to check it out. The line is wrapped around the building.

What the hell? What's going on?

I turn around to get back into the pharmacy, when I bump into a giant cardboard sign. Almost knocking it over. I catch it quickly, and set it back upright. Then I look around to see if anyone saw. And with my luck, there's a little girl with her mouth wide open staring at me.

Fuck.

I pretend she doesn't see me and turn to go back, but before I do, I examine the sign that almost took me out a second ago. *"Free immunizations. Every Monday!"* It reads.

You've got to be kidding me.

I zap myself to Ronan. But I can't tell him what I saw just yet or they'll hear us. We just need to hurry the hell up. And go.

Ronan is no longer searching when I return. It looks like he's waiting for the commotion to die down before he continues. But after seeing that line out there, I know that's not going to happen anytime soon.

I have no way of telling him that though.

Ronan's mouthing something to me. But I can't understand him. How do I say, "We need to get the hell out of here, asap." in sign language? I don't know. But I also don't have time to play guessing games or charades either. I need to start looking myself.

I squeeze through two pharmacy technicians without touching either one and start on one end of the room. I look back at Ronan. He's giving me the "What the hell are you doing?" look. But I ignore him and continue my search anyway.

This room is full of boxes. The pharmacy here is a lot bigger than the one we have in my building. But so far, all the ones I've found are clean vials. I've half-way cleared the room already when I see Ronan has finally started on the other end.

I guess he finally got the hint and decided to help.

We've almost come to a close when I find another stash of boxes hidden behind a stack of medications. Right away I get a bad feeling about them. One by one I pull out six boxes. Four are empty and two are open. I check the empty ones first. The first box that I turn over reads 97458.

This one's fine.

But when I grab the next one I read 43277. And my stomach begins to turn. Then the next one I pick up is labeled 49088. And it's half empty.

How could so many have already been given?

I close my eyes and turn over the last of the empty boxes slowly. Dreading what I'm about to see because I already know what it's going to say. My eyes open slowly and I scan the barcode.

45562.

My first thought is about the little girl who saw me outside. Will she be receiving one of these today? One that we might have missed?

Or did she get one already?

I grab the other two boxes that are still a little over half full and read the labels. 98865 and 43324. I hold on to the remainder of the contaminated vials and send them off to paradise with the rest of my stash. Then I meet

Ronan and we zap off to the second floor, to finish up together.

Once we're back in my apartment, I don't waste a single second more before telling Ronan everything. About how many boxes I found and how many of them were empty. Then I tell him about the sign.

And the little girl.

"What are we going to do, Ronan?" I question, trying to catch my breath.

"Do about what?" he inquires way too casually.

"About all those people who've already gotten the shots?" I exclaim. "Particularly the kids."

"What do you want us to do?"

"I don't know," I reply. "How do we help them? Can we fix them?"

"I don't know, Zara. Honestly. This is all new to me too. They just started working on a cure in Xia."

"Barely?"

"Yes, it's not as simple as you think. Whoever created this stuff must have been a real dickhead because it's impenetrable. Nothing we've tried has been able to reverse it."

"Does this mean you have someone who has been affected by it?"

"Yes," he explains. "Now we just have to wait."

"Wait? And do nothing?" My breath quickens with anger. "We're just gonna leave them?" Tears begin to roll down my cheeks. Now that I know what I can really do, I can't imagine someone taking it away from me.

"Yes," he states flatly.

"This isn't right, Ronan. We can't just do nothing."

"What do you expect we do then?"

"Well—I don't know," I admit. "What if we just—tell them?"

"Tell them?" he arches a brow. "Tell them what?"

"The truth," I say. "About everything."

"We can't just tell them, Zara. We'd be breaking our treaty."

Treaty? What treaty?

"What are you talking about? What treaty?" I wipe my tears.

"The Department of Galactic Defense holds a treaty with Earth stating that we can only interfere with Earth affairs pertaining to the safety and well being of the Earthling race."

"And?" I press. "Isn't that what this is?"

"That is correct, kind of," he frowns. "But unfortunately we don't have authorization to interfere with Earth Laws."

"Earth laws?" I scoff. "What Earth laws?"

"It's under Code 14. One amendment states that the truth about human abilities is to remain the sole business of those in the position of leadership on Earth."

"Position of leadership?"

"Yes. And they decided long ago that Earthlings shouldn't have knowledge about the light forces they possess nor shall they ever find out about them by the mouth of a foreign people. Not if we want to keep the peace," he explains.

What?

"How can they do this? Who's in charge of deciding what we can and can't know? This is bullshit!" I'm fuming. I can't believe this is real life. This is starting to sound like some type of crazy sci-fi movie. "They can't do this."

"Yes they can. As long as people follow and do what they're told, they can. And they will," Ronan explains.

My mind begins racing. I have so many questions. But I hold back from asking because I already know I'm not going to like the answer. None of this is important right now. We need to fix today's problem first. Which is getting this shit out of our hospitals ASAP.

"I need you to teach me I.M." I change the subject. "This isn't going to work if we can't communicate." He's smiling now. I think he's just glad I'm not grilling him anymore.

"You got it. But first you need to eat," he demands.

"I *am* starving," I concede. My stomach

growling as if on cue.

And we need to get those boxes out of David's house.

23

PUSHING DAISIES

(102)

Our next raid is tomorrow and Zara still doesn't know IM. She's been spending a lot of time at Liam's lately, and we haven't had a chance to train. Time isn't on our side here, and she doesn't seem to realize it. Today is our last chance. We need to do it whether she has time for it or not.

That's if she wants to tag along again.

I have to admit I've been avoiding her slightly as well. Unfortunately, I have some bad news for her. I need to tell her what I found out about her friend Ripley. And it's not something I've put on the top of my to-do list either.

As I wait for her, Zara appears in the living room, surprising me. She looks surprised to see me too. Something tells me she's been avoiding me as well, and I need to find out why.

"Are you here for training?" she asks.

"Yeah, if you're not busy," I suggest.

"No, I'm free now," she responds, putting her bag down. And off we go to Rhelm Zero.

"Instant messaging is a little more difficult than what I've taught you before," I begin, trying to ignore her behavior. "You're going to need to focus."

"Huh?" She looks at me like she just remembered that I was talking and she was supposed to be listening. "I know. Are you sure I still have enough time to learn?"

"Well, if I'm being honest, we should have started practicing yesterday," I mutter under my breath.

"I'm sorry," she looks at her feet. She knows she's been slacking, but I think she's been trying her best under the circumstances.

"It's okay," I assure her. "Let's begin."

(Zara)

"Will I be able to read minds like you can?" I inquire, my attention divided between Ronan and Binks clawing at the glass door to get to the blue jay outside.

"Maybe," Ronan replies, bumping his shoulder against mine. "Not everyone can read minds, just like not everyone can heal others. It's a special ability. I just got lucky, I suppose," he teases. Suddenly making me wonder if he's ever read my mind before. The thought makes me blush, and I can feel the heat on my cheeks.

"Are you okay, Zara?" Ronan looks concerned.

"It's getting warm in here, isn't it?" I fan myself, moving towards the glass door to crack it open and let some air in.

A cool breeze fills the room. Ronan sits on the living room carpet, waiting for me to join him. I kneel down in front of him, crossing my legs, and he takes my hands in his, brushing his thumb over them.

"When I do this, tell me if you hear anything," Ronan instructs me. "Close your eyes and listen with your brain, not your ears."

I follow his instructions, but I don't hear anything. When I open my eyes, Ronan looks concerned. "What's wrong?" he questions, reaching for my hands again.

"I can't do it, Ronan. I don't hear anything," I reply, feeling discouraged. "When do most humans learn this in Xia?"

"Usually around the first or second year of life, but some learn a little later," he answers.

"That doesn't make me feel better," I sigh, feeling defeated.

"Everyone learns at different paces, but in the end, we all end up in the same place," Ronan tries to comfort me. But I don't understand his analogy.

I offer my hands to him again, and he responds with a smile, showing off his gorgeous dimples. “Are you ready?” he whispers. “Close your eyes again. Focus.”

I shut my eyes and attempt to relax, but the bird outside has returned, and is singing louder than ever. It's very distracting, but I try my best to block it out and get in my zone.

“Listen with your mind, not your ears,” he advises.

I direct my attention to the center of my mind and focus there, falling so deeply into a state of relaxation that I lose all sensation. The worries and stresses that had overwhelmed me a moment ago vanish.

A faint ringing begins in my head, growing louder. It feels like tinnitus, but inside my mind. Then Ronan brushes his thumb across my hand, indicating that this is the noise I'm supposed to be looking for. I smile, opening my eyes and still hearing the ringing even though I've broken my concentrative state. Ronan is staring at me with a grin matching mine.

“I did it!” I exclaim. “Now how do I hear what you have to say?”

“You just open up the message with your mind. Let's try that now, ready?” He reaches for my hands again, and I close my eyes. The ringing starts almost immediately, but I still can't access the message. “Focus,” he whispers. “Pretend that your mind is a computer, and you're just answering an email or picking up a phone call."

"Okay," I sigh, determined to succeed.

I concentrate harder, but the yapping of the bird outside keeps distracting me. I shut my eyes tightly, focusing only on the ringing in my head. After a few seconds, the chirping fades away, and I can no longer hear it. I can clearly see the ringing phone in my mind and I reach for it. Attempting to answer it. But before I pick up, my concentration is interrupted by a louder yelp that sounds like Binks.

Oh, no.

"The door!" I realize, jumping up. Ronan follows me as I rush to the glass door, pushing it open to let myself through. I inch closer to the ledge, confirming my fear. Binks lies on the sidewalk, lifeless and broken. "No. No no no." The guilt is overwhelming.

I did this.

"I'll fix you," I pick him up without thinking, holding him tightly in my arms. The guilt and sorrow are unbearable. But I know what I have to do.

I race back upstairs, gently laying Binks on the floor as I sit in front of him, placing my hands over his lifeless body. The tears falling uncontrollably.

"I'm sorry, boy. I'm so sorry. I did this. I wasn't thinking. I'm sorry. I wasn't thinking," I sob, harshly wiping my tears. Binks is still warm, but I can feel the broken bones beneath his skin.

I'll fix you, Binks. I promise I will.

(102)

Zara is carrying her dead cat upstairs and I feel helpless knowing that there is nothing I can do to help her grieve this. All I can do is watch as another thing she loves is taken away from her. However, things are starting to get weird.

"Zara?" I walk over and kneel by her side, but she pushes me away with a strength I've never felt her use before.

"No! Leave him!" she shouts, closing her eyes and wiping her tears away angrily.

What is she doing?

Zara leans forward, her hands moving slowly over the cat's body and combing through its fur. She noticeably takes a deep breath and then places one hand over the cat's leg, which is badly beaten up and broken in multiple places. Her other hand rests over the cat's neck, where I can see he took a hit as well. But I still don't know what she's doing.

"Wait a minute—," I gasp.

Is she trying to...?

I stand back and let her do whatever it is that she's doing. Trying to give her as much space as possible. When I start to see the cat's chest move.

No way.

I move back further, not wanting to break her concentration.

Did he just move?

Am I imagining this?

I rub my eyes, and when I open them, now the broken foot underneath her left hand is twitching. This time undeniably. Then it starts slowly snapping back into place.

“Holy shit.” My eyes widen, but they're glued to the damn cat. Now it's his head that begins to move, turning slightly until it pops back into place. “Holy fucking shit!” I clasp my mouth.

I think he's alive.

Zara opens her eyes and Binks shakes himself completely back to life. He proceeds to take a couple of wobbly steps, then stretches loudly and licks the dry blood off his paws, as if he wasn't dead just two minutes ago. There's no denying what she just did. That cat was one hundred percent dead as a doornail. And now he is alive and kicking.

I walk over and touch him.

“He's alive,” I shake my head. “How?”

Zara hasn't said a word yet. She just sits there, staring at Binks. I can tell she's still in shock also.

Me: "That's my girl."

I say to her mentally.

"Hey! I can hear you in my head!" She snaps out of it and jumps into my arms excitedly.

Me: "Looks like you mastered two things today."

Zara: "How the hell did I do that?"

She responds back.

Me: "Make that three."

Zara: "Can't wait to show off my new tricks."

Me: "I think we're gonna have to keep the 'bringing back the dead cat' thing to ourselves for now. Okay?"

Zara: "Fine."

We both look over at Binks and find him playing with a blue feather the bird left behind. Throwing it in the air and whisking it around as he hops on his hind legs. Then he jumps up on the couch and crouches down on the armrest, ready to pounce.

The bird is on the ledge again. Zara zaps herself to the door quickly and slams it shut.

"I think we've had enough excitement for one day, mister," she scolds her cat.

"What do you say we get out of here? Get some fun in before tomorrow," I make her an offer.

“Are you up for an adventure?” she grins.

Back to the Zara I know.

“With you, always.” I pull her close and take us both far away. Someplace I’ve wanted to take her since the day we met.

24

FALSE HOPES.

(102)

My hands cover her eyes as we touch down softly on the ground. This date has been planned for days to celebrate the end of our training. With Zara by my side, I can finally put all the cash I've saved up from Earth jobs over the years to good use. It's funny, I never thought I'd actually use it.

As I guide her from behind, I make sure she doesn't peek. She has a tendency to be sneaky, but this surprise is worth waiting for. Leading her to the edge of the glass igloo we're standing inside of, I give her a gentle kiss on the cheek before revealing the surprise.

"Okay, you can open your eyes now," I whisper, letting her go.

(Zara)

When I open my eyes, I don't know what to expect. Sometimes I try to imagine where he's taking me before we get there. But somehow the surprise always ends up being way better than whatever I imagine. And this time is no different. I'm completely awestruck.

"Wow," I gasp almost inaudibly. I'm at a loss for words. I press my hands up against the glass, gazing out into the sky.

Snow covers every inch around us. Even as high as the towering green trees. Piles of bright, white fluff decorate every one of them. The sky is streaming with purple lights and speckled with bright shimmering stars. Colorful rays of green crossing through the purple. And just a few feet away from us, a giant reindeer walks past. Stomping through the dusty snow, grunting majestically. It's like nothing I've ever seen before.

This is what heaven must look like.

"This can't be Earth," I gape.

"Do you like it?" Ronan inquires, trying to hide a huge grin.

"Are you kidding me. This is incredible. Where are we?"

Ronan is sitting on the bed watching *me*. He stands up and points up to the sky. "Look! Make a wish."

It's a shooting star. I close my eyes quickly and make a wish. The only wish that my heart really desires right now. For Liam to come back and for Ronan to stay.

Then I go sit on the bed where he was. Calling him back. He grins warmly then comes to lie beside me. Together we gaze out into the sky. Watching as the colors of the streaming lights change from green to blue to purple.

I've never felt anything like this. The way this place makes me feel, is hard to describe. Something I don't think I've ever experienced before in my life. It makes me feel—*peace*.

(102)

"I have a question," Zara begins.

Of course, she does.

"What's your question?" I inquire. Always curious to know what her mind is thinking.

"After we take all these vials, what's going to stop them from creating more? Are we going after the guys that did this next? Are we telling everyone the truth?"

"That's more than one question," I laugh.

And all questions I've been hoping to avoid. But I guess now that she's fighting crime with me, I have to tell her the truth. Tomorrow is the last raid before we figure out what we're going to be doing next. And maybe I need to tell her this isn't going to end as happily as she thinks.

"So?" she continues.

"No. By law, we can't do that," I tell her.

"What?" She's upset. "But—."

"Can we talk about something else just for tonight?" I beg. "We're supposed to be taking a —."

"You mean Code 14?" she cuts me off.

Here we go.

She even remembered the name.

"Can't get anything past you can I," I chuckle. Then sit up, taking a deep breath. This is definitely not the talk I wanted to have tonight.

"I want to know what it means," she insists.

"Under Code 14, as long as Earthlings recognize these self-appointed leaders as *their* leaders and they continue to allow them to make these decisions for them, then there's really nothing we can do."

"Self-appointed leaders? Who the hell are they anyway?"

"A couple of the wealthiest families on Earth. They've been doing it for thousands of years," I inform her.

"But why?"

"I don't know," I tell her. "They argued that if people had that much power, it could destroy the world."

"I guess that makes sense."

"I naively thought the same at first. But it's strange, no other world is as tarnished as Earth," I explain.

"What do you mean?"

"Well, everywhere else where people do have their abilities, it's peaceful. Earth is the only one that's not."

"And you just figured this out now?" she chuckles.

"You're right. How did I ever think suppressing human's abilities could be for their own good? I don't know how I didn't see it before."

"Maybe you wanted to believe Earthlings were better than that. But come on, you never thought Earth could possibly be corrupt?" she questions me.

"Hey, neither did you! And neither does anyone actually. If you didn't get to know me, you probably would have had a hard time believing anything I told you also."

"I don't know—," she shrugs. "Maybe you have a point."

"There have been incidents where others from other worlds have come down and tried telling Earthlings the truth, you know."

"Really? What happened to them?"

"We'd be notified by your leaders of the breach in contract and then we'd never hear from them again. They'd just disappear."

"Un-freaking-believable," she stomps her

foot dramatically. “You guys can’t do anything about it? Like, you can’t just take them all out?” She’s serious.

But she’s missing the point.

“Not if they’re not breaking the law,” I respond. “I told you, as foreigners of this planet, we can’t do anything about your own laws.”

“Wow. That sucks,” she explains. “I guess we really can’t do anything.”

“It does suck. But for now, we’ve found a loophole to where we can confiscate these things they’re using. That’s something at least.”

(Zara)

This doesn’t make any sense.

And this doesn’t seem fair.

“What the hell does that even do exactly?” I start again. This time I’m angry. “Puts a bandaid on this shit? Until when? The next batch?” I shout. I can tell from his expression that I am in fact correct.

“I know it’s hard to understand, Earthling. But there are rules. And we have to follow them,” Ronan tries to explain.

“Yeah, I think I got the rule part down now.” I stand up and try to find an exit out of this glass cage.

Ronan sees my attempt to flee, so he pulls

out some boots and a jacket from his bag and helps me find the door. I slip the boots on and stick my arms into the coat, covering my head with the giant hood lined with fur. Then I push open the door.

The cold chill blows harshly in my face, freezing my nose and causing my teeth to chatter. But I continue outside and Ronan rushes to join me.

"Does everyone follow these *rules?*" I scowl. "I don't understand how just taking these guys out wouldn't be the best solution."

"You can't be serious," he chuckles.

"I am. Taking people's abilities without their knowledge—that's *criminal.*"

"You do have a point there. But that doesn't mean we have the right to kill them either."

"Well, we have to do something. We can't just let them get away with this."

"Earthling, the galaxy is peaceful. We can't just go around killing everyone. Or else we'd be just like them. And like I said, they have their own rules that we have to follow as well. I'm not allowed to take matters into my own hands and cause a revolt, as much as I want to. Unless —," he stops talking. A wide grin growing on his face. I know that look, he's just now thought of something.

"What is it?" I inquire.

"There is one more loophole."

"Really?" I exclaim. "Well, we have to do it!"

"I don't know if you'd be willing, but if you wanted to, there's a clause that states that only someone from their own world is allowed to change the order in which it runs," he explains.

"*Meaning?*" I ask.

"Meaning *you.* You're the answer," he says. "Well, if you want to be."

What.

"Me?" my head spins. "What do I have to do? Tell me more." My adrenaline is already pumping.

Here we go again.

(102)

"Are you sure you want to do this?" Now I'm starting to have regrets about telling her all of this in the first place. What the hell was I thinking? Of course she's going to do it.

"Yes. I have to," she agrees without a second thought.

"Look, Zara. I don't think this is a good idea. I didn't really think this through—."

"Listen!" she cuts me off. "I can't just go on living my life normally now. Knowing all this horrible shit. I have to try to save everyone. It's the least I can do."

"There is one other thing," I add.

"What is it?"

"If I were to help you, I'd get kicked out of the force."

"What. Why?" she stops walking to face me.

"I think the word for it is *treason*?" I laugh.

"Well, I can't let you do that," she begins. "I can do this myself. You've taught me enough. I just—."

"You just what?" I laugh. "I have to help you, Earthling. You can't do this alone."

"Stop calling me Earthling," she warns. "Ronan, I know how much the force means to you. I'd never ask you to give that up for me." She turns away trying to hide her watery eyes.

"Earthling, nothing in this Universe means more to me than you do," I grab her hand, turning her back to face me. "I'd give anything up for you and if this is what you want to do, then I'm all in with you."

"But I—," her chin trembles in my hand.

"Without you, I have nothing, Earthling. My life isn't worth living if you're not in it."

"Do you really mean that?" She can't hold back the tears anymore. And I pull her tightly into my arms just as she unravels.

"Please don't cry, Earthling."

"Don't call me Earthling," she sobs. "I don't want you to lose everything over me."

"But you *are* everything, Zara. You've

given me a reason to live after twelve hundred years. Please, let me do this one thing for you." She pulls her head away from my chest to look up at me and smiles. Her eyes are glossy with tears.

My beautiful Earthling.

I hug her tighter and kiss her head, then she rests it back on my chest.

"Zara, I wanted to ask you something—." I begin, just as my head starts ringing.

It's the Commander.

"Why now!"

"What is it?" she asks, letting me go. "Did someone IM you?"

"It's the Commander. He says it's urgent," I say through gritted teeth. "I have to go. Shit."

"Now?"

"Yes, I'm sorry. If it wasn't urgent I wouldn't be going. But I'll be back, okay?" I plead.

"What am I supposed to do here by myself?" she throws her arms up in frustration.

"It'll be quick, I promise. Go back inside until I get back," I demand. Not wanting her to get into any trouble while I'm gone.

"Okay. Hurry," she frowns. And I zap off.

As I enter the Commander's office, I notice him pacing back and forth. The worry lines and perspiration on his face tell me that something is very wrong.

"Commander?" I clear my throat,

interrupting his thoughts. He halts his pacing and gestures for me to take a seat across from him.

"606 has been captured," he states without wasting any time. I immediately jump from my seat, the chair flying backwards and hitting the wall. I can barely contain the anger rising within me.

"What do you mean he's been captured?" I'm trying to keep my voice steady even though I can barely catch my breath.

"He was on an assignment on Earth when he was ambushed and captured," he explains.

"How!" My voice level is higher than it should be. But I don't think even the Commander dares to test me right now.

"The Earthlings have developed a device that enables them to see us, and we had no idea until of it until now." I feel my anger boiling over inside of me. How could they have let this happen? Who was supposed to be protecting him?

"Do we know where he's being held?" My jaw clenched painfully as I try to keep all of my raging emotion caged.

"Not yet," he replies. "But that's not your concern, 102. We'll take care of him. As for you, all Earth-related assignments are cancelled until further notice. It's not safe for us out there anymore."

Not my concern?

Those words do it for me. They're not going to tell me anything.

"What about our current mission on Earth?" I protest.

"We'll have to let it go for now," he orders.

"But sir," I begin

"That will be all, Sergeant," he cuts me off. "You are dismissed."

I'm livid. I feel like everything I've ever worked for, everything I've given up, is for nothing. Has been for nothing. I've been fighting for centuries for a cause that isn't even real.

As I leave his office, my mind races with questions.

What will happen to Earth?

What will they do about Logan?

I'm not going to let them abandon him. I don't know how, but I know I have to find a way to rescue Logan. And a way to protect Zara.

But for now, I need to focus on keeping my anger in check and wait for the right opportunity to take action.

Patience, Ronan. We can't go back to our old ways.

(Zara)

I think I may be taking a bigger bite than I can chew. But what other choice do I have? Walk away? After everything that I know now. I can't. I know I'm not a perfect person, or the greatest human alive. But I have a conscience. And she wouldn't let me live with myself if I did nothing. What I do or don't do can determine what the future looks like for everyone. Not just me. This is bigger than I am. This is what I have to do.

"You're back!" Ronan joins me again in our glass igloo. But he doesn't look too happy. "Is everything okay?" He doesn't respond. He paces the igloo while he removes his jacket and boots. I can tell he's upset because he's really struggling to get them off. "Is everything okay?" I repeat, waiting for him to talk to me.

"I don't know," he responds coldly. "I don't know anything anymore, Earthling." He's still pacing the room, one hand in his pocket and the other rubbing his forehead.

"What the hell happened?"

"We've just been given orders to evacuate Earth indefinitely," he informs me. "It's no longer safe here for us."

"What! Why?" I exclaim.

"Logan was captured today by Earthlings. I'm not sure by who yet."

"Oh my God. How?"

"They have a new device. They can see us now," Ronan explains.

"What does this mean for us?"

"I don't know. But we're on our own now."

"What do you mean, *we?* I thought you

said you have orders to leave Earth? That it isn't safe for you here," I remind him. And he laughs. "What's so funny? Is this a joke?"

"No, I'm not joking. But I'm also not leaving you, Earthling," his lips pressed to my head.

"What do you mean?"

"I mean I'm not going back," he tells me. "Not without you. And I need to find a way to find Logan."

"Do you have any idea where he could be?"

"No, that's what I need to figure out. How to find him," his jaw clenches. The evident stress clear on his face. "But first I need to get you out of here."

"Me?"

"Yes, you. I need to get you somewhere safe. They're sending out military troops to track down any Light Beings residing or hiding out on Earth. They're having a witch hunt," he informs me, his tone increasingly urgent.

This can't be happening.

"A witch hunt?" I shriek. "But how are we going to find Logan?"

"*You're* not going anywhere," he snaps. "You need to stay somewhere safe. If anything happened to you, Earthling," he stops and grabs his head. "I don't know what I would do, okay? I would never forgive myself if I lost you."

"Okay," I don't fight him. "But what about

you?"

"What about me?" he questions.

"What if something happens to you?" I tell him.

"Nothing's going to happen to me. I'll be fine."

"You don't know that!" I exclaim. "I can help you."

"No you can't!" He forces me to sit.

"Ronan, I have absolutely nothing else to live for anymore besides you. I am going with you, wherever you go. We're going to find him together." I take his hand and pull him close to me.

"Zara, I can't let you do this," he tells me.

"Please, Ronan, let me help you," I insist.

"Zara," he begins. "I know this isn't the best time. But there's something else I've been meaning to tell you."

"What is it?"

"It's about Ripley," he looks away as soon as the words come out. But as soon as I hear her name, I already know what he's about to say.

"I know," I sigh.

"You know? How?"

"I had a feeling." I admit even though I had wished it weren't true.

"I'm sorry," he rubs my arm.

"So, what's the plan then?" I inquire.

"For now we sleep on it. Then tomorrow, we can try to figure out how to save the world," he responds in a tone that says it's not up for discussion.

"Fine," I laugh. "We can figure out how to save the world tomorrow."

"Right now, I just want to gaze up at the stars and forget about everything except this," he smiles at me then pulls me close. If the world ended right now, this is the only place I'd want to be.

With him.

25

WE MEET AGAIN.

(102)

I awaken to a boisterous chomping sound that feels like it's right beside my ear. Zara is already up, standing outside the igloo, feeding a baby reindeer with a carrot. As soon as she spots me, she waves eagerly to get my attention. While continuing to feed the reindeer.

Where did she get carrots from?

While I brush my teeth, the stomping of her boots outside the door interrupts me. Then she barges in seconds later.

"Good morning, sunshine. You slept in. How'd you sleep?" she asks cheerfully.

"I actually slept *great.* I feel so well-rested," I lie. Little does she know I snuck out as soon as she fell asleep. I only got back an hour before she woke up.

"Me too," she beams. "I think it's this place."

"It is. Every time I feel like I need to catch up on sleep, I always come here to recharge. Don't you love that energy?" I stretch my arms out, yawning loudly.

"I do love it. I thought it was just in my head, but there really is an energy, isn't there?" She lies down on the bed, her arm resting behind her head, and her foot bent over her knee. She has one eye closed and is tracing the blue lights in the sky with her finger. I lie down beside her. "Are you behind on sleep because you've been back on Earth with me?" she asks accusingly.

"Maybe," I shrug my shoulders. She's always been on to me about not sleeping when I'm staying over, and now I'll never hear the end of it.

"Then I guess we'll just have to come sleep here more often, huh?" she suggests, and I raise my eyebrows in surprise.

"I think we can arrange that," I concede graciously.

"Can we head back now?" Zara inquires. "I really wanted to go see Liam today." The words burst my bubble.

"Figures," I say with a slight taste of annoyance on my tongue. "I'll get you back home to Loverboy, don't worry."

Maybe a lot of annoyance.

"What's that supposed to mean?" she asks. Striking just as hot.

"Nothing," I respond, biting my tongue. Not wanting to cause an argument when all I want to speak on is the fact that she's been there almost every second of every day for the past *week*. "Why the urgency today? You don't want to give him a day to rest?" I attempt to hide my frustration.

"I just have something I want to try," she responds.

Wait a minute.

"What do you want to try?" I interrogate, sitting up quickly and crossing my arms.

"Nothing," she narrows her eyes at me.

"Oh it's nothing now? Earthling, there's something you need to understand about your new abilities. Especially about the healing," I advise her.

"Why are you bringing that up?" she tries to act like it's not exactly what she was thinking about.

"Quit the act, Zara. I already know what you're thinking about doing," I scold her.

"No, you don't," she sits up beside me. Now equally as annoyed as I am.

"Yes, I do. And I need you to be mindful. This ability is something new to both of us, and we don't know what it could be doing to you yet. Or if it's even safe to be doing," I explain. Hoping she actually listens.

"I'll be fine, Ronan," she rolls her eyes.

“Listen to me—,” I continue. But she doesn’t want to hear it.

“I said I'll be fine. I'm not going to do anything, okay?” she's angry now. She absolutely loathes when I scold her. But I only do it because I love her.

If something were to happen to her because she was trying to save that piece of shit, I'd kill him myself this time.

“Just please, promise me that if you do decide to do something like that, you'll let me know first?”

“I promise,” she rolls her eyes again.

“Now let’s get you home while I figure out what to do next,” I pull her into my arms.

I leave her at her apartment then head home to try to devise a plan. Then I need to visit an old friend to see if I can get some leads on who could have taken Logan.

(Zara)

What did Ronan mean by that? What could possibly happen to me by healing Liam? The thought lingers on my mind for the remainder of the day. I lean over Liam’s bed and hold his hand tightly in mine. The beeping of the machines keeping him alive are comforting to me now.

As I rub my fingers over his face, his eye twitches. I jump back and stare at it.

Did he just blink?

I run my fingers over his face again, and his eye twitches once more.

"Oh my God! Liam, can you hear me?" I whisper into his ear and see his pinky flinch in response.

My hands fly over my mouth, stopping me from shouting. I sit back down and reach for his hand again. Then I flip it around and run my nail over his palm, tickling him.

And his fingers move again.

I stick my face inches away from his and then I whisper to him, "If you can hear me, please wake up."

Wake up, Liam.

But he doesn't wake up.

Disappointment fills me. My head falls to his chest, and I listen to the sound of his heart pounding.

Please, please wake up.

I cry helplessly. I don't know what I expected. My wish to have actually worked? As my tears soak his chest, I continue to sob and pray to a God that I've never actually believed in.

"Please! If you're real, please help him!" I shout to the ceiling. Then wipe my tears away. Knowing damn well that my prayers, like many

I've prayed before, will be going unanswered. "I have to do this myself," I sob quietly.

I take Liam's hand in mine. Then with all the strength I can muster, I try to do to Liam what I did to Binks.

I'm going to fix you.

My concentration is soon broken when Liam begins to jerk forward in his bed. My eyes shoot open and I'm in disbelief.

"Liam?" I gulp.

He's coughing uncontrollably now. The breathing tube in his throat is choking him. His eyes are still closed, and his arms aren't moving, but I can see the tears spilling from his eyes from the strain. He can't breathe.

I look around frantically but don't see anyone coming to help. I know exactly what to do and I know I have to do it fast. Or he'll be dead for real this time.

"Sorry, Liam. This is going to hurt," I tell him before ripping the tube right out. "You're okay," my other hand is on his chest, telling him to breathe.

Once he's breathing again, he lays back down peacefully. His chest still rising and falling, but all on it's own now.

I hear someone running up the steps. I think David might have heard the commotion after-all. The door swings open seconds later and I stand back and stay invisible.

"Liam?" he exclaims, rushing to his side. He drops to his knees, pulling his son's arm down with him. I walk over and kneel down next to David, trying not to get too close. "You're awake," he cries. "You're awake."

Liam is sound asleep again. After David called the doctor and updated him on what happened, he headed straight here. Now he's just informed him that Liam's brain activity seems to have miraculously increased since he was here yesterday. However, we still won't know the extent of the damage until he wakes up completely.

"So, he's going to be okay now?" David questions the doctor.

"We're not completely out of the woods yet," the doctor responds. "But I think with this sudden turn of events, anything is possible."

"He'll be okay," David assures him. "You don't know my son. He's a fighter." He's still standing by Liam's side, holding his hand. The way David looks at Liam with so much pride and admiration, warms my heart.

Is this what parental love feels like?

"Let's hope you're right," the doctor says. "I'm going to head out, Mr. Silverstone. Let me know if anything changes."

"Will do," David responds.

(102)

"Is there any way you can hack into the main server at Xia's Department of Defense?" I question. "I need to get a last log on my buddy, 606."

My regular hacker is out of town, but he's left me in the hands of his younger brother. Who he swears is just as good as he is or *"better"* he claims. I've never had to hack into our own database before, but I have no choice right now. I need to find out where Logan was at last.

And no one is talking to me about it.

"Yeah, man. I got you," he assures me. "But you're going to have to give me a few weeks, though."

"A few weeks!" I nag. "I don't think I have that kind of time." I'm beginning to get frustrated with this new guy.

"This breach is tough. Never met anyone who could crack it yet," the guy advises me. He's nibbling on a tooth pick and pulls on his beanie nervously every time he talks. He looks very young, maybe eighteen or nineteen years old.

This doesn't really seem like a job for a kid.

But I trust Julio. If he says this guy can do it, then I have no choice but to trust him. Julio has been working with me for the past 24 years, I trust him more than any Earthling or being from any other planet.

I never knew he had a brother before, though.

The red beanie he's wearing reminds me of someone. I look around the room as he types. I can smell something rotting. Then I spot a half empty bowl of cereal, with spoiled milk caked at the bottom. It's sticking out from under the unmade bed. One corner of the sheet dipping into it.

"Yuck," I gag.

How is this damn kid supposed to help me?

He can't even keep his own room clean. I continue my tour through the mess of dirty clothes and rotten food scattered all around. When I notice the giant headphones by his computer.

"It's *him,*" I gasp.

It's the halfling kid from the bus accident.

He doesn't recognize me?

Of course, he doesn't. You erased his memory.

"Is everything okay?" the kid inquires when he sees my face drained of color.

"Yeah everything's good," I reply. "We almost done here?"

"Just about," he responds. "*And* done."

"Alright, dawg," I shake his hand. "I'll

catch you later."

Dawg?

I cringe in embarrassment. I'm just trying to act normal. I don't know how much the kid knows about me yet.

"Okay," he shakes my hand. "I'll see you in a few weeks then."

"Have your brother call me when it's done," I add.

"My brother?" He looks like he doesn't know what I'm talking about.

"Yeah," I reply. "Julio is your brother, *right*?"

Is this kid messing with me?

"Oh, yeah! Julio—my *brother*." He's acting weird. "I'll have him call you," he grins.

That was strange.

Did he forget about his own brother?

And why is Julio's brother a halfling?

26

PETRA WITH THE GOOD HAIR.

(Zara)

July.

It's been over a month now since Liam's been back, and he still hasn't said anything. I go visit him everyday but he still seems confused. I don't think he recognizes anyone yet. Including me.

"Hey! How are you doing today?" I ask Liam. Patting him on the thigh.

Liam looks at me with a blank stare and turns to face the window. Watching as a bird in the nest right above his window feeds it's hatchlings. I reach for his hand, but he pulls away.

What the hell is his problem?

"How are you feeling today?" I inquire a second time only for him to ignore me again. I still manage to pull together a grin for him though.

I hear footsteps approaching the door, and we both look over. His face lights up when he sees who it is. It's his new physical therapist.

Wow, he sure looks happy to see her.

I shut the voice up in my head.

"Hi, Liam! How are you feeling today?" she exclaims cheerily as she walks in.

Is she European? I think I hear an accent.

The way she moves is almost majestic. Her slim, muscular body flexes with every movement. She has beautiful, honey-colored hair that's short and curly. It contrasts beautifully against her copper skin tone. And her gorgeous green eyes sparkle brightly as she smiles.

"My name is Petra," she tells Liam. "I'm going to be working with you every week!"

Every week?

"Hi! I'm—," I try to introduce myself but she completely ignores me and brushes me away.

Did I forget to turn my visibility back on?

What the hell's going on?

"You up for a little exercise today?" she asks Liam, making his face light up again. Liam nods to her, struggling to move his lips.

Is he trying to talk?

"Hi! I'm Zara," I cut in successfully this time. I reach my hand out to shake hers, but she doesn't take it.

Can't even look at me, can you.

"Come on, are you going to say something?" she encourages him.

"It's okay! Don't strain yourself," I tell Liam. "You'll have to forgive him, Petra, he hasn't been able to—," I begin saying just before Liam interrupts me.

"Y—yes!" he replies. I look over to him, baffled.

Wow, look at you. You can speak now.

"Isn't that a freaking miracle," I mumble under my breath.

"Good job, Liam!" she applauds him, her curls bouncing dangerously as she hops in place.

Her and her stupid little muscles.

Then she stops and turns to me, the smile on her face disappearing.

"I'm sorry I'm going to have to ask your friend to leave. Is that okay?" She looks over to Liam and smiles again in her cheery elf demeanor.

"Y—yes," he speaks again.

How rude.

"Okay," I respond in a defeated tone. "I guess I'll get going then."

"Bye!" she exclaims. Not looking at me once.

"Okay. Here I go," I continue, hoping for

someone to stop me.

But no one does.

"B—bye," Liam manages to utter.

Wow.

"Bye, Liam," I manage. "I'll see you tomorrow." I wave to him, but he ignores me. His attention is all on his miraculous new P.T.

"Oh, one more thing!" Petra calls out as she runs over to catch me.

"Yes?" I respond.

"I'm sorry. Sarah was it?" Petra questions. And I flare my nostrils with a smile.

"Sure," I say.

"Great," she smiles back. "Sarah, Mr. Silverstone has scheduled Liam's physical therapy daily with me for noon, *every day*. I just wanted you to know that just in case it interferes with your schedule," Petra informs me.

The nerve.

What the hell is her problem? I flare my nostrils again, trying to keep my cool.

"Thank you for letting me know," I force the words calmly. "Could you please let Mr. Silverstone know that I got the message?"

"Sure," she smirks then walks back into the room with Liam.

Bitch.

I stomp down the steps to the front door and can hear laughter upstairs. One thing about me is I can always get the hint when I'm not wanted. I've tried for weeks to get Liam to remember me, but he doesn't. Now I feel like I'm just coming off as the crazy, gold-digging ex-girlfriend.

You'd better just stay away from now on.

"I think I have to," I say to myself.

I toss Liam to the back of my mind and hurry home to try to see if I can catch Ronan before he's off again. He's been so busy trying to get a lead on who could have taken Logan, I haven't seen very much of him lately. It feels like he's gone more now than when he was a Galaxy Defender.

As for me, I've been keeping busy also. Heading out all on my own to Rhelm Zero for training. It's hard for me here sometimes with all the distractions. The white room is a very peaceful place to get away. So, while he's off working, I've been learning many new things. I'm actually hoping to show Ronan a few of them tonight. But there's something I still haven't told him.

I kept some of the contaminated vials.

I'm not exactly sure what for yet. But I took a few from the boxes I'd stashed away at Liam's house. Just before Ronan and I went back to pick them up. Something just told me I needed to keep some, so I did.

When I get home, I hear someone walking around in my kitchen. Then they drop something loudly on the counter.

"Sounds like I'm not the only one here." I run over to see who it is.

"Oh, hi," Ronan answers me. "You're home."

"Where have you been?" I question, my arms folded over my chest. "It's late, honey. You should have been home hours ago. Supper is getting cold," I joke, making him laugh.

"How was your day?" he begins, while taking off his boots. "Learn anything new?"

"I did," I mention proudly. "But I'm not ready to show you yet. Have you gotten any new information about Logan?" I inquire, hopeful. But he shakes his head. "Darn."

"I think I'm getting close, though," he sighs.

He looks tired.

"I was just going to hop in the shower. Find us something to watch on Netflix?" I suggest.

We've both had way too much adventure lately.

"That sounds like a great idea," he exclaims.

I think we could both use a night in. He gives me a warm, two-dimple smile, and rubs my chin with his thumb.

"I'll be quick," I promise.

I close the door to my bedroom and turn on the shower. Before stepping in, I start some music to set the mood. The hot water cascades down on me, offering soothing relief. I close my eyes and let it wash over my hair. The pressure tearing harshly at my sore muscles. Suddenly, I feel as though someone is watching me. I open my eyes to find a woman in my shower.

"What the hell!" I scream. "Who are you? What are you doing here?" I question, trying to cover my naked body.

"You don't recognize me?" the woman asks.

"Am I supposed to?" I respond, examining her. She has beautiful, ebony skin that glistens in the steam, and her long black hair is intricately braided with golden twine.

I reach over to touch her face, but she disappears. I curse and bring my hand back, making her reappear again. "What the hell!"

"Amazing, isn't it?" she grins. "I'm you, Zara."

"What do you mean you're me?" I question her.

"I was you, many lifetimes ago," she clarifies.

"This can't be happening," I rub my head, unsure of what to believe.

I close my eyes tightly, hoping this is just

a figment of my imagination. However, when I open my eyes again, she's still there. "I'm real, Zara," she laughs.

"Okay, what do you mean you were me?" I question her again.

"I lived on Earth many centuries ago. My name is Ravini, and you and I shared a soul once."

"We shared a soul?" I exclaim in disbelief. "Why are you here?"

"I need you to know who you are, Zara," she begins. But before I can ask any more questions, there's a knock on the door.

"Ronan," I say silently.

"Hurry, I'm going to start the movie without you!" Ronan calls out.

"I'm coming!" I reply, turning back to the ghost in my shower. "What do you mean who I really am?"

"Please, I need you to be careful," Ravini warns. "It isn't safe for you here. Someone is looking for you."

"Who is looking for me? And why?" I question, but then she disappears.

Ronan knocks on my bathroom door again, startling me. "I'm pressing play!" he shouts.

"I'm coming!" I yell back, still trying to process what just happened.

I wash up quickly and join Ronan on the couch. However, I can't shake the woman from my thoughts.

"Surely she doesn't mean Ronan," I say to myself.

The next morning, I eagerly await Ronan's departure so I can attempt to contact Ravini again. I practically push him out the door, then lock myself in my room. I sit on the bathroom floor, closing my eyes. Focusing all my energy on summoning her.

Within seconds, a light appears before me and a figure starts to take shape. Transforming into Ravini.

"Ravini!" I exclaim in surprise.

It worked.

"You've found a way to reach me," Ravini responds. "Come, I want to show you something." She extends her hand out pointing with her finger before creating a small bright light. Then the light grows bigger and bigger.

"What's happening?" I question.

"After you," she responds, indicating for me to enter the light first. With some hesitation, I decide to take the plunge and walk in.

The light is blinding at first, but then everything goes dark as the portal disappears.

"Where are we?" I inquire, opening my eyes. I'm still trying to get my bearings.

"We're in Egypt," she informs me before sauntering ahead with her hips swaying gracefully.

As I run to catch up with her, she suddenly dissipates before me, then reappears at my side. "Please, be careful," she warns me. "You and I must never touch, or we could impede destiny."

"What?" I gasp, a little freaked out.

"We're bending time and space to bring you here," Ravini explains. "We shouldn't even be in the same room, but this is an emergency. The fate of Earth depends on it."

"The fate of Earth?" I repeat in disbelief. I make sure to keep my distance from her after that.

"You really have no idea who you are, do you?" Ravini questions. And I shake my head. "Zara, you have a destiny to fulfill. A destiny that I wasn't able to," she continues, walking into a room with a large stone podium in the middle and a large hole in the ceiling above it. Blinding sunlight shining through.

"I think you have the wrong person," I respond hesitantly. "I'm no one. I can't be who you're looking for."

"But you are someone," she waves her arms over the podium.

"Wha—what are you doing?" I stutter. Images flash before us. Clips of me as a young child. Me as a teenager. They're videos I've never even seen before. Then they shut off.

What the hell was that?

"How did you get those?" I'm even more confused now. That was undeniably me. But how?

"You have a gift, Zara. A powerful one. You can heal and revive the dead. And the world needs you now more than ever."

"This is all too much." My head is spinning.

"It's very important that you not trust anyone, Zara," she warns.

"What? Why?"

"Be cautious of who you fall in love with."

Is she referring to Ronan? Or Liam?

"I'm a smart girl," I assure her. "I'll be okay. So, what exactly am I supposed to do to save Earth?"

"You need to give your people the cure. And you need to tell them the truth."

"The truth?" I respond.

"And you need to fight, Zara. Destroy them the same way they tried to destroy you."

"Who's them?" I question her. Does she know something I don't?

The sunlight that's beaming through the hole above us grows brighter, blinding me. I shield my face with my arm and look away. Then it gets dark again. I open my eyes and I'm back on the floor in my bathroom. And Ravini is gone.

"Did that just happen?" I pinch myself to make sure I'm not sleeping. "Ouch! Not a dream.

Okay."

Do I tell Ronan about this?

27

HOME IS WHEREVER I'M WITH YOU.

(102)

I'm praying it isn't too soon for this. But I can't wait any longer.

"I want to take you somewhere," I tell her. "Somewhere I've never taken you before." I hold out my hand and she wrinkles her nose. But she comes into my arms anyway.

"You always take me somewhere I've never been before," she chuckles.

"You are correct, Earthling." I wrap my arms tightly around her. "But this time I really mean it. Now close your eyes," I whisper in her ear.

I really hope she likes it.

I guide her from behind, positioning her directly in front of the house, so she has a perfect view of it. I've been planning this since the week after I met her. I wanted her to have a home here, somewhere I knew she would always be safe.

Okay, I'll admit, I didn't know her that well when I first started this project. And it may sound a little creepy now that I think about it. But I think when you know, you know. And when I first saw her hiding under that table, spying like I was. I honestly just knew.

"Can I open my eyes now?" she complains. She's already getting antsy, but I'm still not ready. I run ahead and open the front door so she can walk straight inside after the big reveal.

"Okay, open them," I respond, holding the door open for her. "Welcome to your very own home!" I shout. But she doesn't say anything. "Zara?"

(Zara)

As I open my eyes, I find Ronan standing at the door of an enormous house. What are we doing here? Whose house is this?

"Welcome to your very own home!" he exclaims.

What? Mine?

I think I've forgotten how to function.

A house? I'm dreaming.

I must be dreaming.

Yup, just give it a second and you'll wake up.

"Zara?" Maybe this isn't a dream. Did Ronan just get me—a *house*? My heart nearly explodes at the realization, but I tame it. This is not a dream. This is real life.

My life.

With tears streaming down my face, I snap out of it and run straight into his arms. The house sits in the middle of what looks like many acres of land, surrounded by mountains and greenery. A vast wooden porch wraps around the entire house, with three small wooden steps leading up to it.

"I can't believe you did this, Ronan," I gush over him as he finishes up his tour of the house. "Where are we exactly?"

"We're in Xia," he responds.

"Xia?" Without another word, I rush back outside, this time through the back door, stopping in the middle of the green field. I inhale deeply—the air feels so clean. When I drop down to my knees, the ground underneath me starts pulsating, like it's alive. Strange birds fly overhead and I can tell we aren't on Earth anymore. I touch the grass—it's soft and moist, and it feels *different*. My eyes close instinctively and I spread my arms like wings, reveling in the cool breeze as it blows through me.

"I think I'm home," I sigh.

"Hold on, Zara. I'm getting an IM," I call out to her from inside.

It's Logan.

That little hacker kid was finally able to track him down and found a way to let him communicate with me. He put out some type of output distress signal from me that only Logan would be able to hear. All Logan had to do was find a way to get something electronic in his hand to receive it. And I'm guessing he found something because he's just now messaging me back.

> Logan: "Hey man, I need your help, we're stuck somewhere. I'm not sure where though. I just managed to escape and stole a cellphone to contact you. They got me, man and they took away my light force or something because I don't have any abilities. But you know me, I was able to get away the old fashioned way."

"This guy," I laugh. If anyone could escape with nothing but brute strength, it had to be Logan.

"Who is it?" Zara demands.

"It's Logan! He's alive!"

> Logan: "Another thing. I got two other prisoners with me, I had to help them out. Here they are. Let me know if you can get some info on them."

He sends me a picture. I glance over them briefly then send a copy to Julio to see if he can get some ID on them. It's a man and a woman. I look at them more closely and can't shake the feeling that they look familiar.

"Zara, do you recognize either of these people? I just sent you a picture."

"Yes," she responds right away, with a puzzled expression on her face.

"You do?" That was easy.

"Why do you have a picture of my parents?" she adds.

Her parents?

I don't know what to say. I just grab her by the arm and zap us back to my place.

"What's going on, Ronan? Where'd you get that picture? And where the hell are we now?" she begins interrogating me as she wiggles out of my grasp. "Is this where you live?"

I ignore her questions and walk straight to the fridge, leaving Zara even more frustrated and confused.

"Hello?" she presses me. "Do you hear me, Ronan? What the hell is going on!"

I hear you, Zara. Just give me a minute to figure out how to tell you either the worst and/or best news you could possibly receive right now. I pull out a bottle and grab two glasses from the cabinet above. Popping off the top, I pour the bubbly liquid into the cups until it overflows with fizz.

"Come, sit down," I tell her. "We're both

going to need this." I hand her a glass, downing my drink first. Then I fill it again.

(Zara)

"What the hell is going on, Ronan?" I begin. "Are you going to tell me why you have a picture of my parents now? Did you do a background check on me or something?"

"No, I wouldn't do that," Ronan tries to respond. "I —."

"Is this about how they died?" I continue with my questions without letting him speak. Then take a sip of the drink he poured me.

Mmm, it's good.

"I have to tell you something, Zara," Ronan begins again. "Please, try not to freak out, okay?"

"Okay—," I raise my eyebrows and take another sip. Something about someone telling me not to freak out somehow makes me want to freak out. But this drink is making me feel more relaxed with each sip.

"What if I told you that those things you see at night that scare you, aren't dreams but really memories?" he explains.

"I'm not following."

"I need you to tell me how they died," he changes the subject back to my parents. "I need to know everything that you know."

"Okay," I agree surprisingly fast for the lack of information he's given me so far.

What the hell is in this drink?

I dig through my memories but don't find much. There's not a lot that I remember from that night. It's mostly just a blur.

"I was only a child, Ronan. I don't know what happened," I explain. "My aunt Lucy said we were in a car crash."

"A car crash? Are you sure?"

"Yes. Lucy said that I was with them," I assure him. "Why?"

"And what happened to you?" he questions me. "How did you survive?"

"Lucy said I got out somehow," I reply defensively. Beginning to question it for the first time myself. "That's what she told me the police report said." I take another sip of my drink. It tastes like kiwi and has a slight fizz.

And it's making me feel nice.

"Do you believe it?" he asks a question no one has ever asked me before.

"No," and for the first time ever I confess to him how I truly felt about it.

"Tell me what frightens you at night."

"Well—in my dreams its also me and my parents. But we're always in the woods. And we're running."

"Running?" How is he getting this

information out of me right now?

"Yes," I reply. "And it's always the same dream. My father is holding me over his shoulder as he runs and my mother is running behind us."

"What else do you remember from your dream?"

"Something is always chasing us."

"Chasing you?" he repeats, trying to understand. "Who is chasing you?"

"I don't know," I confess. "But they're shooting at us. That's when I always wake up."

Images of the dream start to flash clearly in my head as I start to remember. Bullets are flying past us, my father is running in a zig zag pattern to avoid them. Then one strikes my mother. And she goes down.

"Mommy!" I yell for her.

"Are you okay?" Ronan shakes me back to reality. "What happened? It looked like I lost you there for a second."

"I don't know. It felt like I was there again."

"You remembered your dream?" he inquires.

"Yes," I nod. "I got a flashback just now, and it felt so real."

"Is this the first time you've remembered like this?" Ronan questions me.

"No. That's what I wanted to tell you," I beam. "I learned how to go into my memory bank!"

"You did?" he smiles. "That's great! And what did you find?"

"Nothing about my parents' death, which is strange, right?" I explain. "But I did find my reoccurring dreams. What if they didn't die in a car accident, Ronan?"

"Earthling—?" Ronan begins, his voice shaky and his face distraught.

"What is it? Is everything okay?" I begin to panic. "Why did you bring me here? Why do you have a picture of my parents? And what's in this drink?"

"I don't know how to say this but—your parents are alive," the words spill like liquid. Then he covers his mouth.

"What?" I put the glass down, almost missing the countertop.

"They're with Logan," he adds then covers his mouth again.

"What!" I feel like someone just pulled the rug out from under me. The room has gone silent. I see Ronan's lips moving, but I don't hear the words that are coming out of them anymore.

Was Ravini right?

Is all of this really my fate?

A flashback of my dreams plays in my head. What were we running from that day in the woods? And why did my parents leave and not come back for me?

Has everyone been lying to me my entire life?

I snap myself back to reality and Ronan's voice becomes audible again.

"Can you hear me, Zara? I have to go get them," his words echo in my ears.

"Go get them? *You?*" I'm finally able to speak.

"Yes *me*. Who else would go?" he questions.

"Ronan, they're *my* parents. I'm going with you."

"Oh, no you're not," he exclaims. His hands waving around in the air dramatically. "Not this time."

"I have to go!" I retort. "I haven't seen them for almost twenty five years, Ronan. I need answers!"

"And you can get all the answers you need when I bring them back home safely to you," he assures me. Patting me on top of the head. "Here. To *Xia*. Where you'll be *safe!*"

"No!" I stomp my foot. "I need to get them myself. This isn't a debate, Ronan. I'm going with you," I demand. Then zap myself back home to my apartment on Earth.

"Fuck!" Ronan curses. Then follows behind me.

"We can't be here, Zara. We need to go," I inform her but she ignores me as usual.

"I don't care," she snarls.

"Please," I beg. "It isn't safe here, we need to go back to Xia," I insist.

"Don't worry, I'll go. But I need to get some things first. And some *people,*" she mumbles at the end.

"What *people,* Zara?" I flare my nostrils in annoyance. "We don't have a spaceship, Earthling. We can't just take people for a ride through time and space."

This girl!

"Just Binks and my aunt Lucy," she responds.

"Okay," I cave.

"And Ripley," she continues. "Also—*Liam,*" she cringes.

"I draw the line at Liam," I snap back at her. "He's fine here on Earth. He's one of the families, he's already in."

"One of the families?" she frowns. "What about Ripley?"

"Ripley—," I pause. "Well—we don't really have anything left to protect her from now, do we?" I admit. Knowing that was insensitive but true.

"I can't believe you just said that," she glares at me. Sending a chill down my spine.

Yikes.

"I'm sorry, Zara. But I really think that with her connections, she's going to be okay, too."

"But you said that last time!" she cries. "And she wasn't okay, Ronan. She's *not* okay."

"We'll fix this," I falsely assure her. I don't even know if we can yet. "And if we don't, chances are she won't even know it's gone to miss it."

"But you don't understand. Without her light force, when her time on Earth is over, then her clock is really up. There are no more lives left. Her soul is gone."

What. The. Hell.

"Who told you that?" I grill her. Scrambling my brain, trying to recall when and if I was the one that told her. But I don't remember.

How did she know that?

"No one," she responds. "Is it true?"

"Is what true?" I act ignorant.

"Is her soul—dead?" she sobs.

How do I tell her the truth right now? She already looks so emotionally exhausted. Her beautiful, brown eyes now bloodshot, and shadowed by dark circles and can barely stay open. It doesn't look like she could possibly survive anymore bad news.

"We really need to get you back to Xia,

okay?" I plead.

"But, what about—?"

"We can get Lucy and Binks," I concede. "But everyone else stays."

"But—," she begins to cry again.

"Everyone else has family, Earthling. They all need to be with their families."

"No—I," she shudders. I can tell she didn't think this through.

"If you take Ripley, you'd have to take her mother, her father, her sister, her sister's husband." I begin. "And let's not forget Kevin. She would never forgive you if we left him behind."

She furrows her eyebrows.

She knows I'm right.

"Okay, I get the picture. Family only."

"*Family only*," I repeat. The words like music to my ears. I don't know what having a real family is like. But I know that Zara is my family.

And so is Logan.

Binks too, I guess. That fur-ball has really grown on me. But I know damn well *Liam* is not and will never be *my* family.

My head starts ringing again. Logan just sent me over some documents.

What is this stuff?

It's hundreds of pages of research all on the new technology the Earthlings' possess. Attached is also a warning to be very mindful when we get there. That they'll more than likely be expecting us. This means more danger for Zara. Fuck. I'll have to train her extra hard this time. And not just mentally, but physically too. And if this time I don't think she's ready. She's not going.

Me: "Logan, how much time do you think you can spare?"

I send him another message. And he responds instantly.

Logan: "Time moves a little slower here. I can give you a couple of hours, how's that? Two months enough time for ya?"

I think that's more than enough time.

Me: "Yes, see you then. And take care of those prisoners, Lo. I checked them out, they're important."

The line goes dead, and I don't get a response anymore.

(Zara)

I ring the bell at the window and wait for someone who can help me. This place is deserted.

"Does nobody work in the Psych ward?" I mumble to myself just before I spot a guy in blue scrubs leaving a patient's room.

"Hey!" I call him over, waving my hands over my head. He points to himself and I nod.

Yeah, I'm talking to you. Come here.

He runs over quickly, unlocking the door right next to me.

"Hi," he responds quietly, avoiding eye contact.

"Hey, you!" I exclaim. Scanning his I.D. badge. "*Gary*?"

"Yes. How can I help you, Zara?" he grins.

He knows my name?

"Yeah, I was wondering if you could help me. You see, I came to visit my aunt, but I can't remember what room she was in."

"Your *aunt*?" he repeats.

"Yes, my aunt. I think you may have moved her room since the last time I was here."

He blushes then goes into his office. Once he's inside he opens the small window lined with inch thick glass that's next to the door. Poking his head through.

"Hi! Right here. What did you say her name was?" he asks softly. Then glances up at me nervously from his computer. His fingers waiting anxiously over the keyboard.

"Oh, right. Lucinda Meyer," I speak into the window.

"Lucinda Meyer," he repeats as he types, looking back up at me occasionally. Then blushing when we make eye contact.

Why is he being so weird?

"Everything okay?" I question.

"Yup. Lucinda was moved to room 37B," he informs. "*Nine months ago.*" A hint of judgment in his tone.

"Nine months ago?" Shit.

"We tried calling the number we have on file numerous times to advise you before she was moved," he explains. "But no one ever picked up."

Wow, now I look like a complete asshole, don't I?

"There must be some kind of mistake. I'm her only living relative. Maybe the number is wrong."

"Let me check the number for you." He then proceeds to read back the number on file. Reciting my entire *current* phone number.

I cringe.

"Yeah, that's still good for me," I shamefully respond. "It was just a hectic nine months."

"I'm sure it was," he raises an eyebrow at me.

What could have possibly kept you busy for nine months?

"I had a baby," I lie terribly.

A baby?

"A baby!" he beams. "Congratulations! Boy or girl?"

“Uh—boy?” I add.

“Aww, a baby boy. How sweet. What’s his name?” He’s asking way more questions than I had accounted for. Then nearly climbs out of the window. “Where is he?”

“Geez, do you ask all visitors this many personal questions?” I snap. Not knowing how else to end this train wreck.

“I—uh. I’m sorry,” he apologizes. Making me feel even more terrible.

“It’s fine. I’m going to go find my aunt before my sitter calls me,” I continue the charades. “Gonna go show her pictures of her new nephew.”

“O—okay,” he shakes his head in humiliation.

I storm off down the hall, looking for room 37B. When I finally find it, I push through the door. But the room’s empty.

“Damn it!” I curse in frustration.

“Are you looking for Lucy?” An older woman peeks into the room, noticing my dilemma.

“Yes, I am. Do you know her?” I inquire.

“Yeah,” she nods, waving me over. “Come.”

“Okay,” I follow her. Staying close as she leads me into the cafeteria. Then she points to a table where a blonde and four others are sitting, playing cards.

“There’s your girl,” she points to the

blonde.

"Thank y—," I look over to the older woman, but she's already gone. "What the—."

I walk inside the cafeteria by myself and head towards the loud table where all the laughs and cheering are coming from.

"Aunt Lucy?" I call out to her.

When she hears my voice she freezes and turns around slowly.

"Zee-Bug?" she replies. The familiar way she slides her glasses up her nose makes me smile.

No one has called me that in ages.

"Yeah, it's me. Surprised?" I blush.

"You could say that," she grins. "But I'm glad to see you. What are you doing here?"

"I need to talk to you, aunt Lucy," I tell her. "*Alone.*"

"I see," she narrows her eyes at me. I think she gets the message because she gets up to leave. "Alright, ladies, I'll be back in just a few minutes. Please, start without me." She hands the deck of cards over to a red-headed woman with bottle thick glasses. The red-head grabs them and begins shuffling the deck immediately.

"Can we go to your room?" I whisper to her.

"Sure," she nods at me then walks out of the cafeteria. But I stay behind.

"She may be a little longer than that,

ladies. If she doesn't return, you guys got her covered, right?" I whisper to the bunch, being careful that Lucy doesn't hear me. They all nod in understanding. "*Good*," I smirk. Then take off after her.

When I get to her room, I find her waiting for me. I close the door behind me. Checking through the small window on the door that no one followed me back. Then I slide over the curtain to cover it. Lucy is over by her bed, opening up her drawers and searching through them like a mad woman. Tossing clothes all over the place.

"What are you doing? Aunt Lucy, we have to go," I quietly inform her as I walk closer. But she doesn't answer me. She just keeps digging through her things. "Lucy? Do you hear me?" I grab her by the arm.

"These are yours," she responds, holding an arm full of envelopes.

"What are these?" I question her as she hands them to me.

"These are all letters from your parents," she explains.

"My parents?"

"I tried to tell people that they weren't dead. But the bodies—," she dazes off for a second. "I couldn't explain it. It all looked so *real*."

"You mean you knew they weren't dead?"

"Why do you think I'm in here. I'm not crazy."

"Right. Grab your things. We need to go. Like *now*," I urge. The nurse I spoke with earlier is coming up the hall. I can hear the jingle of his keys coming towards us.

"Go where?" Lucy questions me.

"Somewhere far. Far, far away," I tell her.

"Far away?" she repeats.

"Yes. Where they won't be able to find us."

"That sounds nice," she smiles. Then runs off again into her cupboard. Fetching the rest of her things. "We're *going*," she mumbles silently to herself. "We're going."

28

NOTHING IS AS IT SEEMS.

(Zara)

I pace my giant new kitchen as Binks swivels through my legs, causing me to trip occasionally. My aunt Lucy is still sleeping. I had forgotten how strenuous teleporting was at first.

Ronan has been sleeping at his own place now ever since Lucy got here, so unfortunately my nightmares have come back. I've been waiting for him all morning to tell him all the new things I've been dreaming lately. Dreams about my parents.

Dreams that I can still remember when I wake up.

I hear footsteps approaching.

"Ronan?" I exclaim.

"Who's Ronan?" Lucy responds as she comes dragging in. Rubbing her temples as she moans in agony. She's been in and out of sleep for the past couple of days. Hasn't really spoken much until now.

"Does your head hurt?" I ask, fishing for some ibuprofen from my bag. Not sure if it's teleporting to blame or the absence of pills she was forced to take at the hospital. I offer her two red pills.

"It does," she admits. Reaching for the pills.

But before she can grab anything, Ronan appears and swipes them away.

What the hell!

"Hello, I'm Ronan," he comes swooping in with his irresistible charm. "Nice to meet you, Lucy," he reaches his hand out for hers, but she doesn't take it. She steps back instead.

"Who are you?" Lucy interrogates him. "I've seen you before."

"*Ronan*?" I question. "When?"

"A long time ago, I think," she holds her head in pain.

What is she talking about?

She must have him confused with someone else.

"I'm a good friend of your niece," Ronan informs her, flashing her a dimple.

"Oh," Lucy responds. The magic dimple is softening her up. It has that effect. "I'm Lucy," she offers her hand this time.

Those dimples, I tell ya.

"Nice to meet you, I've heard so much about you," Ronan lies to her.

Why is he lying? I've never said a word about her.

"I'm going to go close my eyes for a bit. I don't know why, but I'm awfully exhausted today," Lucy yawns.

"Okay. We'll try to keep it down. Sleep well," Ronan tells her.

"Thank you," she grins weakly. "Must be all this fresh air." Lucy yawns loudly again then retires off to her bedroom.

"So, what are we going to do about my parents and Logan? How much time do we have?" I whisper to him.

"About that—," he raises his brows.

"What now?" I drop my arms at my sides, already pre-annoyed.

"I have bad news," he begins. Rubbing the back of his neck.

Of course he does.

"Are my parents okay?" Is the first thought that comes to mind.

"They're fine," he assures me.

"Logan?" I question.

"They're all fine," he promises. "It's just going to be a lot more dangerous than I thought."

"What do you mean?"

"We may not be able to use our abilities

out there."

"What? How do you know that?"

"Logan think's his light force was taken. But I think they're using a Sonar Deactivation Device," he informs me.

A what?

"So—we can't use *any* of our abilities?"

"No," he sighs. "But we'll still be able to use *these*!" he enthusiastically opens up his palms to reveal nothing.

"Our hands?"

"Yes. Which means we're going to have to train differently now."

Differently?

"Differently, how?" I wrinkle my nose.

"Have you ever shot a gun before?" he inquires, raising his eyebrows.

"Uh—," I shrug then shake my head. "No."

"*Very* differently, then. Come on. We're gonna need to be outside for this." He walks past the mudroom and into the garage. I follow him.

His hand is swiping around at the wall beside him. Then he presses a button, and the ceiling above us opens up. Revealing an array of futuristic weapons. Rows and rows of guns, knives, bows and spears.

Me: "Why are these things in my house!"

I glare at him. "Okay. Different reaction than I expected," he shrugs.

“Why the hell did you not tell me about all of this, Ronan!” I yell. “Was this always here?”

He pushes a second button, and the shelves come down. The glass surrounding them dissolves. He grabs a gun with each hand and then pushes through the door in the back of the garage. Leading to a giant field that’s already lined with targets.

“Ronan!” I have no choice but to follow him out.

“Take your pick,” he smirks as he holds out the two guns.

One is the size of a large assault rifle, and the other is a smaller hand gun. I choose the smaller one because it’s *not* bigger than my arm.

“I’ll take this one,” I gulp.

“Safe choice,” he nods. “Probably for the best, actually.”

Can’t argue there.

Ronan hands me some earmuffs, then we head down to the obstacle course he’s constructed for us. First, he shows me how to load and unload my weapon.

“Here, I’ll help you this one time so you don’t smash your fingers,” he assists me sweetly.

“Thank you,” I blush.

Next he shows me how to remove the safety so that I can finally do some shooting.

“Okay, now that you’re an armed danger to society, please be careful,” Ronan jokes.

"Ha-ha. Very funny," I roll my eyes. Then walk closer to the man-shaped target. Aiming for the red dot right in the middle of his chest.

I know who this one is for.

I think to myself, just before I pull the trigger. The gun fires loudly and the bullet hits just two inches above what I was aiming for.

He's dead.

(102)

"That was very good for your first time! Are you sure you've never shot anything before?" I question her. "You have great aim."

I'm starting to become suspicious actually.

"Thanks," she blushes. "I guess I'm not too bad."

"You're too modest. Are you tired?" I ask her.

Because I am.

"I'm exhausted actually," she replies, as if reading my own thoughts.

"Let's call it a day then," I concede. Then take her back into the garage to show her how to put the guns away properly before heading back inside.

"Can I ask you something and you promise you'll be completely honest with me?"

Zara stops me before letting me in.

"What is it?" I chuckle.

"Are there any more guns in my house that I should know about?" she raises an eyebrow at me.

I scrunch my nose. Quickly debating on whether I should tell her the truth now or just wait to explain later if the occasion ever calls for it.

We can tell her later.

I decide.

"No, just these," I admit. "Why? Would you like me to hide more throughout the house?" I add as I clean my gun innocently.

If I'm right about my suspicions, then we'll be needing those guns at some point. They're going to come looking for her eventually. And when they do, I'll be ready for them.

We both will.

"Maybe it wouldn't be such a bad idea," she responds.

Oh, really?

"Are you serious?" I try to hide my excitement.

"I mean, what if I am in danger? We still don't know why they kidnapped my parents. What if they come back looking for me?"

If she only knew who I suspected she was, then she'd only agree with me more. But I can't tell her yet, not until I'm sure. I don't want *anyone* to know. We don't know who we can trust yet, and she's awfully trusting of people.

The wrong people.

Like Liam.

"You've got a point." I act ignorant. Like it's all her idea. "I'll work on that."

"One last thing, when exactly are we going to go get my parents?" she adds.

I knew this question was coming.

"In two months," I inform her.

"Two *months*!" she exclaims.

"Yes, we have two months to get you ready. And if I don't think you're ready in time, then you're not going," I state firmly.

"But—."

"But *nothing*," I put my foot down. "And that's final."

"That's not fair," she complains.

"I can't risk losing you, Earthling," I tell her. "And I'm not arguing about this either." I comb my fingers through her hair, pulling her face into mine. Breathing her in and holding her close. "I can't *ever* lose you, Zara."

(Zara)

Why is he acting so weird? Did he hear me talking to Ravini that night? Was he there just like he was there watching with Lucy? I shake away the thought and put it to rest. I can trust Ronan. He loves me. He only wants to protect me.

Let's hope so.

Because he's all I've got right now.

"Hey Ronan," I change the subject. "Have you heard anything about a cure yet? For those affected by contaminated vials?"

"No," he shakes his head. "But I doubt they're still looking for a cure."

"What do you mean?" I question.

"Before I left, they were putting all Earth research on the back burner."

"What! Why?"

"I guess they decided Earth just doesn't want to be helped anymore at this point. And they don't want to endanger our own people going out there to force help," he explains.

"Are you serious?"

"Yeah. We can't afford to lose any more men. People heard about what happened to Logan," he sighs. "They're afraid."

"What are they saying?"

"There've been stories going around saying he's already dead. And a big strong guy like him, getting taken out? Everyone thinks they're goners for sure."

"Wow, I can't believe this," I fight back tears.

"Yeah. To them, Earthlings are some kind

of evil monster now. They just can't imagine why humans would kill each other for no reason."

Ronan has a point.

"Can you blame them?" I sigh. "I guess we really are monsters, they're right. There's no excuse for it."

Sometimes I hate being an Earthling. Why do we have to be so evil and heartless? I'm ashamed to be one of them.

"I have to tell you something, Zara," Ronan interrupts my thoughts.

"What is it?"

"I don't know if I should be telling you this, but I don't want to keep anything from you anymore."

"Well now you better tell me," I snap. "What the hell."

"I need you to know something," his demeanor changes. "you're not only important to me, but—."

"Hey, guys!" Lucy opens the door and interrupts us. "I feel so much better. What do we have to eat?"

"Good morning to you," I laugh.

"Good morning, sorry," she blushes when she sees Ronan."

"Good morning," Ronan chuckles.

"Another question, were those gunshots I heard earlier?" Lucy adds. Ronan and I look at each other and cringe.

We forgot about Lucy.

“Yes—sorry,” I nearly slap myself. “We were just working on some target practice.”

“No, no! I don’t want them to come back!” Her eyes widen in fear. “Put those guns away, put them all away! We’re not safe here!”

What the hell.

As I try to calm her, she grabs me by the collar and begins to shake me. “Take me back!”

“What’s wrong, Lucy?”

“I don’t want to run anymore. Please, take me back,” she responds, crying hysterically.

Run anymore?

“Lucy, it’s okay. You’re safe here,” I promise her. “No one will find you here.”

“They will!” She’s unconsolable.

“They can’t. We’re all safe here,” Ronan assures us both. And she finally calms down.

What the hell was all that about?

Is it too soon to tell her we’ve left Earth?

The only thing I’m thinking about now is how all the stories she ever told us were probably true. That all those things we called her crazy for saying, they might have really happened.

Poor Lucy.

Has she been on the run with my parents too? I hold her close as she cowers over my shoulder like a frightened child. Still shaking. I take her back to her room and lay her down.

"I'll call you when the food is ready, Lucy. Just rest," I tell her.

"Okay," she responds. "We'll be okay?"

"Yes. We'll be okay," I assure her. "I promise you, we're safe here." She turns over to sleep and I close the door.

When I get back, Ronan doesn't look like he's missing me. He's busy in the kitchen chopping onions.

"Mmm! Smells good in here," I remark.

"Just you wait," Ronan winks at me.

"What do you think that was all about?" I inquire, running my hands through the faucet to wash them.

"What, Lucy?" he responds calmly.

"Yeah, duh! Did you not see her? She was terrified!"

"Yeah she looked pretty scared. Maybe it's PTSD," he suggests.

"Do you think she's been hiding out like my parents?" I begin to question. "What do you think they did that made someone go after them in the first place?" I rinse the suds off my fingers and dry my hands.

"I guess we have to ask them when we see them. Find out the truth for ourselves," he suggests.

"I just have so many questions. Who am I really?" I start to cry.

"Please don't cry, Earthling." Ronan puts

the knife down and comes rushing to me, pulling me into his chest.

"What were you going to tell me?" I sniffle. "Before Lucy came out."

"Oh, that," he frowns. "Forget it, I shouldn't—."

"Oh yes, you definitely should," I snap. He lets me go and walks away. His hand rubbing his neck.

"I'm still not one hundred percent sure about it."

"Sure about what?"

"What I'm about to say. But I think you need to know who you have a *very* high possibility of being."

"What are you talking about?"

"First, I need you to understand the magnitude of danger you're getting yourself into by simply just returning back to Earth."

"Seriously, Ronan?" I roll my eyes.

"Yes. And what even *greater* danger we're putting you in by letting you come along on his mission with me," he shakes his head.

"But they're *my* parents, Ronan," I remind him.

"Yes, *your* parents who have already been captured *twice*!" he shouts.

"Okay, I get it," he has a point. "Just tell me already. How bad can it be? What did I do, or what?"

"You really don't get it, do you?"

"Get what?"

"If something happened to you, it would not only destroy me, but it could destroy all hope for humanity on Earth," he warns me.

Is this what Ravini was talking about?

"What do you mean?"

"I mean it could be the end for Earth," he repeats. Not really adding more ingredients to the pot. But I already know what he's trying to say.

"She was right," I mumble. "Can I show you something, Ronan?" I don't know if this is a good idea, but I feel like I have no other choice right now and very little time to explain everything. So I'll just show him.

"Sure," he agrees with a questioning look.

"Brace yourself." I close my eyes and visualize. Then send us both somewhere far far away.

"I did it," I grin proudly.

We're back where Ravini took me. The place looks a little more worn down than when she brought me, but I'm assuming I must have just gotten the timelines mixed up. She never did tell me a specific date.

"What is this place?" Ronan looks around in surprise. I'm sure this isn't what he was expecting.

"It's a palace!" I exclaim. "Kind of. It's kind of falling apart now."

The knife Ronan was using to chop is still in his hand, he tries to zap it back but fails. So he sticks it into his belt instead. As he wanders around, his feet brush up the dirt from the dusty floor. Making sand clouds all around him.

"Why did you bring us here?" he questions, looking back at me. "Where are we exactly?"

"Come. I'll show you," I reply, leading him to the room Ravini took me to. Hoping that it's still intact so I can show him what she showed me.

To my delight, the stone podium is still there. And unlike the rest of this place, it looks completely untouched. The sunlight still shining brightly onto it, just like it did when Ravini brought me. I make my way towards it.

"Zara, what *is* this place?"

"You'll see," I grin.

I wave my hands over the stone, just like I saw Ravini do. Then recite the chant I heard her say. The last time I spoke to her, she warned me not to trust anyone. So I'm not too sure how she'll feel about me bringing Ronan here to her ancient home. But it's too late now. I say the last words then a light begins to appear above the podium.

"It's working," I beam. But what appears before us, isn't what I expect. "Oh, no."

It's Ravini.

"Zara," she responds. Then she looks over to Ronan who's still facing the wall, unaware of her presence. She begins to glow crimson.

"Ravini—," what's going on? Did I upset her?

"Why did you bring him here!" Ravini shouts.

Yup. She's angry.

"I wanted to show him—," I try to explain.

"Go!" she screams, making our surrounding shake. And Ronan finally turns around just before she vanishes.

"What the hell was that?"

Just then, all the walls around us begin to tremble. Quivering violently until everything starts to crumble, including the ground beneath us.

Is this an earthquake?

The massive stone pillars that hold up the walls start to break like delicate crackers. Rocks and piles of debris rain over our heads as we try to escape.

Fuck. This was a mistake.

"Zara, where the hell did you bring us!" Ronan pulls me by the arm before a rock falls on me, then tries to zap us back home. But it's not working.

"I—I don't know," I begin to panic. He grabs my hand this time and leads us through a still clear passageway. Pulverized sand covering us as we barely scrape through before the walls collapse behind us.

"How do we get out?" he questions me. "Do you know?"

"Uh—yes. I think so," I reply. Trying to remember the way out. Or if I even took one. "This way." My body begins to move without my permission and I have no choice but to trust it.

Ronan helps me dig our way out of the tunnel that's nearly entombed us and I manage to find another opening. We squeeze through a narrow passageway, feeling the walls tighten on either side of us. The quaking is only intensifying. We're almost out when the doorway in front of us collapses and our way out gets completely obscured by falling rocks. And now we're trapped inside. The last remaining light to the outside disappears, leaving us entirely in the dark.

Now what do we do?

"Zara, why aren't our abilities working?"

"I don't know," I cry. "Shh. Just let me think."

I close my eyes and concentrate, still trying to feel our way out of this rubble but also trying to come up with a temporary solution. My body begins to illuminate. And now the fallen kingdom around us suddenly becomes filled with light.

"How are you doing that?" Ronan is just as surprised as I am. But he follows me down the shaft anyway.

About a hundred yards away, we can see a tiny light shining through the rock, and we speed up towards it. Everything is still falling apart around us. We race through, trying to protect our heads as the tunnel collapses, enclosing us even further. We finally reach the small exit. Then leap through it before it disappears, landing safely onto the warm soft sand. The massive stone structure we were just in is now nothing but crumbles.

"Now what?" Ronan chuckles nervously. When suddenly, the ground begins to shake again. We jump to our feet and run as far away from the debris as possible as the ground begins to sink. Swallowing the remaining rocks entirely before us.

What happened to Ravini?

Ronan's eyes meet mine, and he looks like he's going to be sick. Or kill me.

"What the hell was that, Zara!"

(102)

The sun feels like it's slowly roasting us alive. The sand acting as hot coals under our feet, cooking our soles as we walk. The desert seems never-ending. There's nothing around us, and neither of our abilities are working still. I already feel like I'm on the brink of death when suddenly Zara drops to the ground in front of me.

"Zara!" I shout. Dropping to my knees beside her. Her body is limp. She must be overly exhausted. We've been walking for hours in the blazing heat and I think her body has just about had enough. I swoop her up into my arms and put her head on my shoulder gently so she can rest. "It's okay, I have you now," I whisper softly. But she doesn't respond.

I carry her through the desert for what feels like miles. Until I can no longer take another step and collapse down with her. We both land softly on the sand and it burns our skin. But Zara doesn't even flinch. She still looks completely lifeless.

She's dehydrated.

Suddenly, Zara jumps up out of her sleep in a fright. The heat must have finally got to her.

"What happened?" her voice trembles.

"Stay here, I'll be back," I order her, hoping she actually listens. "I have to go find you some water."

(Zara)

I wake up a third time after continuously

passing out from exhaustion but Ronan still isn't back. It feels like he's been gone for hours.

I wonder where he went?

"I hope he went to find some water," I say to myself. "I'm *so* thirsty." I try to stand, struggling to climb out of the crater of burning sand than I'm in.

"Say *water*?" A small blue creature shouts at me, as it pops out from the sand. "We have water!" it responds. Then disappears again.

What the fuck was that!

"Hello?" I call out. "Little creature!" But nothing answers back.

Am I seeing things again?

When I turn around, I see Ronan coming back towards me.

"Hey! You're up!" he exclaims.

"Did you see that small, blue furry thing?"

"That *what*?" he almost laughs.

"It came out of the ground," I explain.

"Blue furry thing? Out of the ground?" he chuckles. "I think the heat is getting to you. We need to get you out of here ASAP."

Maybe he's right.

Ronan runs ahead, putting his arm out in front of him. Then points his palm to the sky.

What is he doing?

"Need some help out there?" I offer.

"No, I got it," he responds. Still trying to force something to happen. Then after a few attempts, something finally does.

"Wow," I beam. "How'd you do that!" A small ball of light starts forming in front of his palm. Shining dimly for a few seconds then disappears.

"Shit!" he curses.

"What are you trying to do?" I question him.

"I'm trying to make a portal. To get us out of here," he responds angrily.

I think the heat is getting to him too.

"But, we don't have our powers here," I state the obvious, then run to catch up to him.

"We're using power from the sun," he explains as he furiously stomps around the sand, trying to block the sun with his arm as he looks up into the sky.

What?

"Power from the sun?"

"Yeah. Come on," he grunts.

Ronan keeps running further and further away from me and trying to keep up is exhausting. Defeated by this heat, I let him walk ahead without me to figure out what he's trying to do on his own. Meanwhile, I stop in the sand to rest. But my feet are burning beneath me.

"I need to help him find a way out of here," I tell myself.

But how?

I close my eyes and reach out my hand. Trying to do the same thing I saw Ravini do in my bathroom. Then I visualize.

My hand is out, just like Ravini's. My fingers pointing up towards the sun. And I concentrate hard. Almost instantly I begin to feel the electricity as it enters my fingertips and comes ripping back out through my palm.

"Oh, shit," I curse.

I open my eyes and see a bright, round light floating in front of my hand. I force more energy through, and it grows bigger and bigger. I can no longer see Ronan, so I call out to him loudly.

"Ronan! Hurry!" I scream.

I look up into the sky, trying to block the sun's blinding rays from my eyes with my free arm. And that's when I see that it's moving.

It's starting to set.

"Shit." I feel the energy from my arm as it begins to weaken. Then the portal starts shrinking. "Ronan! Where are you!" I yell more urgently. "Hurry! I can't hold it much longer!"

When I look over, I notice a large sand cloud forming over the horizon, coming towards me. Ronan is running through it and to my surprise, the furry, blue gerbil is running beside him also.

Somehow, they manage to outrun the

sand storm, but the cloud of sand is still chasing behind them.

"Zara, how'd you do this?" he exclaims.

"Hurry!" I shout. I have no time to explain. My hands are shaking, and the sun is now halfway down the horizon. Not to mention, the sand storm that's about to swallow all of us alive if we don't get into the portal before it closes.

"Get in! Fast!" Ronan gets to me just before the sandstorm does. Then he jumps through the portal, pulling me in behind him. And together, we're thrown back home to Xia, where we started.

(102)

We barely make it back to Xia in one piece but Zara isn't responsive. The energy it takes to form a portal is strenuous for a person with years of experience. I don't know how she was able to do it, but now I'm worried what it might have done to her.

"Zara!" I shake her urgently. But she doesn't wake up. "Zara!" I shout. Her eyes fly open. "Zara, are you okay?" She doesn't say anything. She just lies there, staring off into nothing. I nudge her on the arm and she finally snaps out of it.

"Hey," she's barely able to speak.

"Are you okay?" I look her over. "What

happened to you?"

"I didn't know that would happen," she explains. "Did you see the blue guy that time?"

"There was no blue guy, Zara," I laugh, shaking my head. "I didn't see anything."

"Are you sure?" she continues. I help her up, and she rubs her head.

"I'm positive," I assure her. "Do you have a headache?"

"Yeah, a little," she mumbles, still pushing on her forehead with the palm of her hand. "I didn't know creating a portal would be so exhausting. I think I need a nap after that." She laughs softly, then stumbles over to her bedroom.

"You sure you're okay?" I frown. Catching her by the arm before she falls over.

"Yeah, I'm sure," she tells me. "But can I have some water?"

"Of course, Earthling," I zap a glass to the night stand beside her. She drinks the glass empty then rolls over and passes out.

"Goodnight, Zara," I whisper to her. "I love you."

This is my favorite way to see her. The sight of her sleeping peacefully and safely makes me happy. I cover her with the sheets then slide into the bed to join her. Caressing her hair while she sleeps.

What blue guy was she talking about?

And how did she know how to make a portal?

I sit there in the dark, having discussions with myself. Now more sure than ever that my suspicions about her may actually be true. This girl might be the real deal after-all. The fragile, clumsy, curious Earthling lying right here in front of me.

Zara—*the chosen one.*

And here I am irrevocably in love with her.

I admire her exquisite features as she sleeps. Listening as she snores quietly. She's so perfect. I'm always so easily distracted by her, but I have urgent work to do. I dig into my mind and try to find the IP address that Logan was messaging me from earlier. It's encrypted, but it's still open. I send him a message quickly.

> Me: "Logan, can you hear me? Are you still okay?"

I send the message and wait for a response. An hour passes and still nothing. Naturally, my mind begins to wander again about all the things that could have gone wrong.

Why isn't he responding to me?

Were they captured again?

Did they lose the phone?

What's going on?

I send another message just for good measures.

Me: "Logan, it's Ronan again. I hope you're safe. If you find a way to hear this or get back to me, I'll be here waiting. There's something important I need you to know about those prisoners you helped escape. But for now, please take very good care of them. They're more important than you think. We need them here alive."

I close the line and shut my mind back off.

What are we going to do?

Everything just got a lot more complicated, and I feel like the clock is running out on us. Things seem to be getting hotter on Earth, and it's only a matter of time now until they come looking for us. But we're safe in Xia. They can't find us here.

As long as we stay here.

Which seems easy, but it's a rather big problem with *this one*. She always wants to go back to Earth for one reason or another.

"I need to come up with a bulletproof plan," I say to myself. "One that will get us safely from here to Mars."

And *away* from Earth.

29

STALKERS IN THE TREES.

(Zara)

September.

"Have you heard from Logan yet?" I ask Ronan, as I empty the last round of my weapon, straight into the bullseye of the target. Making the hay-filled dummy explode. This is going to be our last day of shooting practice before our trip to Mars tomorrow.

"Nothing yet. But if I don't hear from him by tonight, we're still going," he assures me. Then takes his shot.

"Good," I reply. "Nothing's stopping us, I like the energy."

After we finish shooting, I clean out my gun and safely put it away. Then I prop down on the bench in the garage to pull my muddy boots off. I haven't been able to sleep in days, so I feel extra exhausted today.

The thought of seeing my parents again has been weighing on me heavily. It's both bitter and sweet. They've been keeping me up at night, thoughts of what to expect when I first see them again. I've had a handful of positive but also negative outcomes play out in my head. And I don't know which one is more likely to occur. They've just been gone for so long, I don't know what or who to expect.

I feel like I don't even know them anymore.

What if they don't like me?

Not that I really care. Since they abandoned me and all. Although the sting of not being wanted by your parents does hurt a little. That's something I can't seem to shrug even with the countless excuses I've tried to make for them. But I know there had to be a good reason.

I hope there was a good reason.

As I sit there barefoot, I rest my elbows on my thighs, hanging my head between my legs. Ronan notices me and comes over to sit down beside me.

"Are you okay?" he rubs my back.

"I'm okay. Why do you ask?" I sit up to be eye level with him.

"You just haven't been yourself lately," he rubs my chin gingerly.

"What do you mean?"

"You know, the old fun-loving self that was always making inappropriate jokes at inappropriate times to make me laugh."

"I don't make those jokes to make you

laugh," I frown.

He's right. You've changed.

As much as I hate to admit it, he's right. I haven't felt myself lately. I think that Zara stayed behind on Earth.

"So, you're okay?"

"Just nervous," I give him a weak smile. "Since we aren't able to use our abilities out there, will I still be able to heal anyone if they get hurt?"

"Well—," he rubs his neck. "Come on, let's go inside." He's standing at the door holding it open for me like I don't have an option.

"Fine."

We head into the kitchen and find Lucy awake, full of energy and cooking breakfast. The entire house smells divine. The fragrant aroma of buttery French toast and cinnamon fills our famished nostrils.

"Good morning!" Ronan and I chant together.

"Good morning! Are you guys hungry?" Lucy cheerfully offers us.

"Thank you. We're starved!" Ronan responds right away, ready to sit. But I grab him by the arm and drag him into the hall first.

"We'll be right out. We just need to get washed up," I call out to Lucy.

We're all sweaty and reek of gun powder and dirt. Ronan can pull the vibe off but it's not a good look or stench for me. I walk into my bedroom, and Ronan follows, closing the door behind him. He turns back to me, his face pale.

"What's wrong? Why are you acting like that?" I question him, already preparing for more bad news.

"Nothing, it's just about what you asked me outside," he responds.

"About healing?"

"Yes," he nods. "Here's the thing, if anyone dies on this trip, you won't be able to heal them. Or even yourself. We might not be able to get back in time to—."

"Well, I guess we just can't die then," I shrug. Making him laugh. I haven't heard that laugh often enough lately. I think he's been equally as tense as I've been.

"I guess we can't," he agrees.

"I'm going to shower. See you at breakfast," I wink. He flashes me a dimple and winks back, then takes off.

(102)

My hands are trembling uncontrollably as I step onto my kitchen floor. I can't believe she didn't notice how much I was shaking.

I head to the fridge and pull out a bottle of the fizzy drink. Trying not to break the glass as my hands quiver uncontrollably. I manage to pop it open then down the entire bottle. My hands stop trembling immediately. Then I head into the shower.

The hot water prickles my face. I hang my head, wrapping my arms around myself tightly. Trying to mimic the pressure of an anaconda squeeze. I feel like I'm falling apart and I need the physical pressure just to stay together. I haven't been sleeping since we heard from Logan. And I think the exhaustion has finally started to set in. My back falls against the wall and I slide down onto the smooth stone floor, letting the water fall over me like raindrops.

When my mind begins to buzz, and my eyes dart open.

Logan!

Logan: "102, it's 606. Copy?"

Me: "Copy 606. I thought you were a goner. We had already canceled the trip."

I joke.

Logan: "We? Who's we? And come on, man, you know me better than that. Ain't a light-being alive in the entire Galaxy who is stronger, braver, nor more good looking than I am."

I laugh out loud. Even in his worst state, he's still a goofball.

Me: "I have someone helping me. I'll tell you more about it when I see you. How are those prisoners?"

Logan: "Okay, bro. Whatever you say. But this guy better be big and tough because we're going to need some serious manpower if we get caught. You really need to hurry. They almost got us an hour ago. Will you be coming soon? The prisoners are chill, man. No issues here. They've actually been a big help. What's so special about them, anyway? They look pretty regular to me."

Me: "Just look out for them, bro. For me. I'll see you very soon. Share your location with me to save it into my memory bank just in case we get disconnected again."

A message comes in with a location attached right away. I open it up and can see a visual of it in my mind. Now that I know where to go, I close it up and store it away.

Logan: "Got it, boss. See you soon. I'll try my very best to keep us all alive."

He adds then cuts off again.

My mind goes silent. He's gone. I finish up my shower and rush to get dressed. I pull on a gray pair of cargo pants, a black t-shirt, and slide my vest on top. Patting the pockets on my chest to make sure the contents are still inside. The bulges tell me they are.

I pull on a pair of socks and slip my feet into my boots, then take off to Zara's. When I get there, she's already stuffing her face with French toast.

"Thanks for waiting for me," I toss her a fit of sarcasm.

"Sorry," she shrugs and continues jamming syrup-drenched bread into her mouth. Lucy is already gone.

Me: "Is Lucy outside?"

I instant message her. She shrugs again.

"She's gone. We're good," she mumbles as she chews.

"I got a message from Logan," I tell her.

"What! What did he say!" She swallows her food painfully. "Are my parents still with him?" she questions me eagerly.

"He told me where they're at. They're all safe," I assure her. She stuffs the last bites into her mouth then reaches for her orange juice to wash it down.

I grab a plate and stack several slices of french toast for myself. Then drizzle it with syrup. After I pull out a fork from the drawer, I pierce the giant pile and shove a colossal fork-full into my mouth.

"Mmm," I close my eyes in ecstasy. "I hope your aunt Lucy stays here forever. I could eat these every day."

"I'm waiting," Zara glares at me, waiting for more information.

"What? I told you, they're all fine," I assure her. "Your parents being part of the *they.*"

"So, where are they?"

"I have their location. I think we should leave today," I tell her. "After breakfast."

"Today?" she jumps up in excitement. "Let's go then! Come on!"

"I said *after* breakfast," I correct her. And continue eating my delicious meal, peacefully and slowly. She stares at me as I take every bite. But it just makes me eat even slower.

"Please! Would you just hurry!" she shouts.

She's so impatient, this one.

I shouldn't have told her about the last part until after I had finished eating.

After I clear my plate, I stand. Her eyes light up as she watches me head towards the sink with it. Then her expression drops as she watches me walk past the sink and stop at the stove instead. Scooping up more french toast and dumping them onto my plate.

"Oh, *come on!*" she stomps her feet and storms off. "You win. I'll leave you alone to eat in peace. I'm going to change into something cooler. I'll be back."

(Zara)

Okay, I know this is real life, but just because it is doesn't mean I have to look lame. I always wondered why the superheroes in movies dressed up just to fight crime.

I get it now.

I dig through my drawers and flip through the clothes that hang in my closet. Until I manage to pull together something I think looks pretty crime-fighting worthy.

And I think Ronan will approve.

I walk back out to the kitchen to see if Ronan is done eating yet. He turns around as he hears me walk in, and his mouth drops open.

"Is this a joke? Or is this like for real because if you're not making fun of me, your outfit is killer!" he laughs.

The back door slides open, and my aunt Lucy comes barging inside with something wrapped in a towel in her arms.

Did she bathe Binks outside?

She tenses up with surprise when she sees us standing there.

"Hey!" she responds nervously. Then gives us a quizzical look. "Why are you guys dressed the same?"

"Hey," we both look at each other then shrug. Watching her as she sneaks back to her room. In a very suspicious manner.

What's up with her?

"Ready?" I press Ronan. "Can we go now?"

"Yes," he sighs. "Let's go get our guns."

I follow him into the garage, and he

pushes another button under the bench beside the door. The wall above it splits open and reveals another huge compartment filled with even more weapons than the first one.

I glare at Ronan, and he just shakes his head. He pulls out a handful of grenades and sticks them in our pockets. Then pulls out several boxes of ammo. He hands some to me and I stick them into my vest pockets like he does. Ronan packs the rest into his small bag, but first he pulls something out of it and hands it to me.

"What's this?" I unwrap it. "My very own fanny pack!" I shriek, hugging it and pressing it into my face.

"Now you can really be my sidekick," he grins at me.

"Thank you! I love it!" I quickly strap it to my chest just like his and stuff it with even more ammo.

Ronan helps me secure the large gun to my back then adjusts the holster to my hip for the hand gun. Next he bends down in front of me and pulls up my pant leg, wrapping another strap around my ankle.

"What's this?" I question.

"Just another holster for that small gun over there," he points to a miniature gun sitting on the steel table in the garage.

"Cute," I chuckle. After we've been fully loaded with weapons and ammunition, we get ready to head out.

"Are you ready, Earthling?" he reaches his hand out to ask for mine.

"As ready as I'll ever be," I shrug, grabbing onto him one more time. My heart racing as we zap away.

When we arrive on Mars, the heat and dryness of the atmosphere suffocates us instantly. Our feet are already burning through our boots from the hot, coal-like dirt.

"*This* is Mars?" I gape. It looks almost like the desert on Earth except the sand is a darker, burnt crimson instead of brown.

"Yup, this is it," Ronan nods matter-factly.

"So, where are they?"

"This is the last location Logan sent me."

"How long ago was that?"

"It couldn't have been that long ago since it was just before we came," he assures me. "They should only be minutes away."

"*Minutes,*" I air quote.

"Come on. Let's go find them," he rolls his eyes and I follow him.

We trudge through the hard, rocky soil until our legs begin to burn. But we can't find them anywhere. And the sun seems to be taking advantage of our vulnerability as it sizzles and fries our flesh beneath it. We've been walking now for about an hour and still haven't seen a sign of them for miles.

"Are you sure this is where they were at?"

I call out to Ronan as I start to fall behind. I'm so out of breath. But this guy never seems to get tired.

"Yes, these are the coordinates he sent me. Maybe they're hiding somewhere," he tells me.

"Maybe," I pant. In the distance, we hear a vehicle approaching as it tosses rocky gravel beneath it. "You hear that?" I whisper.

"Shh," he quiets me, shoving us behind a huge boulder to hide. We hold our breath as we watch a small robot pass through, surveilling the area. And he has a gun.

What is that thing?

"What the hell is that?" I whisper to Ronan.

"It's a RovTron," he responds.

"A RovTron!" I shriek.

"Shhhh!" he hushes me. "He can hear you."

"Shit," I whisper. "What exactly is that thing?"

"They're like guard dogs," he explains. "But with a machine gun."

"Great," I sigh.

"Yeah. We definitely can't let that thing find us. Not if we want to *not die,*" he makes a joke.

"Very funny," I fake laugh.

"Come on."

"Coming," I follow him.

We turn back around, heading east. Then continue on for about half a mile. When far ahead of us, I catch a glimpse of someone by the hills.

"It's them," I inaudibly say to myself. Then survey the area for the RovTron before taking off towards them. Without even warning Ronan.

"What the—!" he takes off after me.

"Hey!"

"Hey, what are you doing!" Ronan begins to question me as he comes up beside me. "Why are we running?"

"You'll see," I tell him as I continue racing towards the thing I saw.

"It's them!" he says under his breath when he sees, then speeds up to join my pace.

But we only see one person. A very large, bald man. He's running away from us and towards another vast boulder. He looks like he's running from something. I glance over to my right and that's when I see a RovTron coming our way.

He's running from that!

"Demon robot at 4 'o clock!" I yell towards Ronan, who's well ahead of me now. He turns around and spots the RovTron then rushes back to me.

"Don't let him see you! He hasn't got a target on us yet!" Ronan shouts.

The bald man dives behind a big rock and

he's out of sight before he notices we're here.

Ronan finds another boulder and we quickly jump for cover behind it. Our backs up against it as we listen for the robot to pass through. I hold my breath, trying to be as silent as I can. The RovTron drives straight past us. Scanning, but not turning back.

"That was close," I exhale in relief and feel Ronan's clammy hand as he places it over my chest.

"You okay?" he looks me over. Feeling my heart as it pounds furiously beneath his palm. Still racing from the adrenaline that's pumping like fire through my veins.

"I'm good," I pant, trying to catch my breath. "Where'd he go?" We look over towards the other boulder, but we don't see the man anymore.

"Come on, let's go find him," Ronan helps me up, and we start on our search again.

We gaze out into the dry plane. Miles and miles of scorched, red sand stretch for days. But the sun is creating a mirage over the sand and making it look like there's water in the distance.

Or is it real?

"Ronan, that's water, isn't it?" I nudge him.

"Where?" he turns.

"Over there!" I point. He squints his eyes and shields them with his hand, shading them from the harsh sun above.

"I don't think so," he responds. "I can't really see anything." He squints harder and rubs his eyes. "Damn, is this how bad my vision would be if I were an Earthling?"

"Seriously?" I roll my eyes at him. "Come on. I think it *is* water."

We sneak over quietly. While still keeping an eye out for anymore RovTrons. And as we get closer, I confirm my suspicions.

"It *is* water!" I shriek excitedly. And there's a forest of trees behind it.

"Well I'll be damned," Ronan chuckles. "It sure is."

I rush to the water, scooping up a handful, ready to drink. When Ronan stops me.

"No!" he shouts, smacking the water out of my hands. "Don't drink that!"

"What the hell, Ronan!"

"We don't know what kind of contaminants it may have," he explains. "It isn't safe. Come on."

"But I'm—," I begin to argue.

"Do you want to be shitting your brains out right now?" he warns.

"Okay, I'll take your advice this time," I get back to my feet.

We roll up our pant legs then cross over the small pond. The water is only calf-high and heavily polluted. But our waterproof boots keep us clean and dry, thanks to Ronan.

After a few minutes, we reach the mysterious forest. We look back at all the distance we traveled so far then look back into the dark trees ahead. The forest is oddly inviting compared to what we know is back there.

Looking for us.

So we go in.

The dry leaves and branches snap beneath us as we sprint through the forest of trees. Looking around, searching hopelessly for the bald man. Up above us, a bird starts cawing deafeningly. Stealing my attention.

Are there birds on Mars?

I look around, trying to find where the sound is coming from. I follow the cawing and spot a black crow high up on a tree branch. Stalking us.

"Wait a minute," I mutter. As I get closer to the tree that it's standing on, I examine it more closely.

It's not real!

There's a lens in it's eye. It's a robot.

"I need to tell Ronan," I mumble quietly. But before I take off, the bird spots something behind me and starts gawking hysterically.

When I turn, I spot the huge bald man again. This time he sees us. He's hiding behind a tree trunk, motioning us to go over. I throw a rock at the bird first and it flies away. Giving us just enough time to get out of his eye sight.

"Let's go! Now!" I yell at Ronan and he follows us.

We spread out, camouflaging ourselves amongst the trees as the bird flies ahead, trying to find us. I feel like a fugitive being chased down by a helicopter.

The bald man finally loses the bird, and I run towards him again. Ronan is close behind me, making sure I don't get lost.

"Come. This way!" the man says to me, then reaches his arm out to Ronan. "My man!" he exclaims.

"In the flesh," Ronan mirrors his excitement.

"Looks like you managed to find me after-all, huh? Or should I say, I found *you*!" the big guy grabs Ronan by the neck and gives him a noogie on the head.

This must be Logan.

"Surprised, you're still alive out here," Ronan pushes him off. "And didn't get killed by one of those RovTrons running around. You may be big, but you're slow as hell!" Ronan punches Logan on the arm.

A crunching sound up ahead startles them, and we hurry off, following Logan deeper into the forest.

Deeper and darker.

30

DADDY DEAREST.

(102)

Altogether we charge through the dry woods. I stay close behind Zara. Knowing she must be exhausted. And all the stuff she's carrying isn't making this any better with our lack of water and that damn sun out here scorching us dry.

As we run, I daydream about jumping into a cold river and drinking until my belly explodes. Water seems to be a constant thought out here.

"We're here," Logan finally stops. We come up in front of two big rocks that are lying side by side. They're taller than he is. They're about five feet apart, and a layer of tree branches cover the top.

Did he already make shelter? How long did he think we'd take?

"Nice place you got here," I comment.

"We have water, but we don't have any food," Logan informs us. As he speaks, two heads appear from underneath the branches.

It's them.

"606, is that you?" the woman is clearly emaciated and very filthy. It looks like she's been through hell.

"You took a lot longer than we expected," the man beside her who is holding a brown plastic bag says to him. He doesn't look any better than her. "Here, I'm sure you could use this." As he gets to his feet, the bag swooshes in his hand.

It's water!

"We have visitors," Logan informs them. The man reaches his arm out of the cave to hand the bag to Logan when Zara comes running up, knocking them both over. The bag in her father's hand falls to the ground with them. And the water disappears quickly into the soil.

No! Not the water!

"Zara, is that you?" the woman responds, when she finally sees her.

"Zara?" Logan repeats. Looking at me.

"How did you know it was me?" Zara questions her mother.

"Honey, we—," the man begins, but a glass shattering caw cuts him off.

Oh, no.

The sound is coming from above us, stealing all of our attention.

And that's not the only attention it's got.

I spot the RovTron's laser looking for us. The RovTron that's now coming our way.

We all stand incredibly still, trying to avoid the shark in the ocean of trees. The sound of it's tires rolling over twigs and rocks like a bulldozer. We run further east and deeper into the forest. But the RovTron follows us. It's laser still aiming in our direction. Moving rapidly past our heads.

Until it stops.

"Where'd it go?" I question.

"Don't move," Logan warns.

The laser lands directly in the middle of my back. I look over at Zara. She spots it and yells something my way. I drop down to the ground quickly and see the bullets fly over my head. Just missing me. Then I roll off to the side, out of the line of fire and take cover behind a tree. Watching as the RovTron moves past. Not spotting me.

That was close.

It's laser is still moving rapidly from side to side, trying desperately to find me. Find something. I spot Zara running ahead, trying to find cover. The robot's wheels are trekking furiously through the harsh ground, spitting small rocks from it's sides.

I think it's given up on me. The RovTron is now looking for it's next target, it's laser scanning all around. I run off after it, pulling the gun off my back.

The RovTron speeds expertly through the trees as I try impossibly to keep up. It's beam still moving and searching. Then I watch it as it zones in on it's next victim.

Oh, no.

"Zara!" I scream. Just as the laser lands on her back.

This can't be happening.

(Zara)

My heart is pounding through my chest, but the adrenaline that's pumping through my veins has given me a rush of invincibility.

Ronan is calling out to me from behind. I look back, trying to find him. Still running as fast as I can. I'm flying through the trees, but when I turn, my foot hits a large rock and I come tumbling down.

"Shit!" I curse. But just as I hit the ground, the RovTron empties hundreds of rounds over my head. I crouch lower, shielding it. Avoiding the bullets as they fly above me.

When the shots end, I pull the gun off my back and roll over. The RovTron continuing to race towards me. I cock my rifle and aim straight at the middle of the red beam as it searches for me, again. Then I shoot.

Metal sprawls everywhere as I unload my clip on it. Then I drag myself behind a rock to take cover. The flames burn viciously from the robot's remains, causing a giant black cloud of smoke.

"Zara!" Ronan calls out to me. I can see him coming up from behind it, then he stops when he sees where the smoke is coming from. "Zara, where are you?"

"I'm right here!" I wave to him from the ground. My gun is still laid out over me.

"Was that you?" Ronan questions me, noticing the remains of what used to be a RovTron.

"Yes," I pant. "Now please help me up, the adrenaline is gone now and I can't move," I laugh, still anchored down by the weight of my gun.

"Sure," he chuckles, rushing to me. Picking up my gun and pulling me up with it. Then swings it over his shoulder.

"Where's everyone else?" I look around.

"We're here," someone answers me. Logan and my parents come crawling out from their hiding spots and join us.

"That was close. We need to be more careful," my father responds. "Are you okay, honey?"

"Damn, girl, where did you learn how to shoot like that?" Logan comments, throwing a hand up for me to high five it.

“Thanks,” I blush.

“I’m not going to lie, when I realized it was you, I thought my man, Ro only brought you because you were his girl,” Logan continues. “But I have to admit, I never expected you to get down like *that.*”

“Really, man?” Ronan shakes his head in embarrassment.

“No wonder you have this guy head over heels. You got any friends like you?” Logan jokes and Ronan punches his arm.

“How *did* you learn how to shoot like that?” my dad inquires curiously. “And how did you guys get here?”

Before I can answer his questions, we hear a loud rumbling behind us again, and my head turns instinctively to see what it is.

“Shit,” Logan groans. “This isn’t good.” A line of RovTrons come crushing through the trees. Lasers everywhere. There’s five or six from what I can see. Maybe more.

“We have to go,” I quietly inform everyone behind me. “*Now.*”

Here we go again.

(102)

This time I’m not letting her out of my sight. I grab her hand and pull her close to me.

“We need to get out of here quickly. Follow

me," I put my hand out in front of me, and begin to form a portal to get us home. Electricity shoots from my palm, forming a ball of light.

"You did it," Zara grins. The light stays steady and small. I concentrate, trying to make it grow.

"Hurry!" I shout, as I struggle to maintain it.

The rumbling sound from the RovTrons is getting closer and closer. I close my eyes and try even harder to make the portal grow. But the dehydration I hadn't accounted for has me far too weak. When suddenly, I feel the light get more substantial and the energy grows stronger.

"What the—," I open my eyes and see Zara standing beside me with her hand reached out next to mine. She's helping me. Light is shooting from her hand and joining mine.

The light beams are colliding together and forming one big bright ball that's growing larger and larger. Then the light transforms into a portal. And that means it's go time.

"Hurry!" I yell to them.

Just then, one of the RovTron's laser's spots us and begins to fire our way.

"Get in! Now!" I shout.

Everyone is still stuck, staring at the army of killer robots. I think they're in shock. But they all jump to their feet instantly at the sound of my screams and sprint towards us. Her mother goes in first.

"Hurry!" we shout louder as Zara and I struggle to keep the portal open. Logan and her father are still missing.

"Go!" I hear someone cry out. When I look back I see her father as he hits the ground.

"Fuck."

But Logan swoops in behind him and throws him over his shoulder. Racing towards us as he dodges the bullets flying all around him. My arm starts shaking, and I can feel the energy that I'm producing is getting weaker.

"Dad!" Zara screams, looking back in horror as her father struggles to stay on Logan's back.

"Shit," my energy suddenly gives out and I drop my hand to my knees. Panting uncontrollably. Desperately trying to catch my breath.

I can't hold the portal anymore.

But Zara is still keeping it open. Another round of fire sounds and when I look back, I hear another loud groan.

"Oh, no!" This time it's Logan, dropping hard like an ox. Zara's dad tumbles out of his arms and into the path of the RovTrons. Zara's face draining of color when she sees him.

"Dad!" she screams. But before she has time to react, I run off towards them.

I help Logan to his feet first, pushing him to run ahead and leave us. "What are you doing?

Come on," he looks back at me. But I shake my head.

"Go," I order him sternly. He knows he can't fight me on this one, so he does what I say and goes.

I kneel down over Zara's father, throwing his unconscious body over my shoulder. Then I jump into the trees to get cover and take off running as fast as I can. Ducking through branches and hopping over tree trunks trying to lose the RovTrons that are still tracking us.

While I run, I burst into laughter like a mad man. The memory of Zara chasing that dog flashes through my mind.

What a weird time to have these thoughts.

Just then, a bird swooshes overhead, startling me. It nips at my head as it flies over me, cawing furiously to let the RovTrons know it's found me. And in less than an instant, I hear them behind me again.

Looks like our friends are back.

I continue to swivel through the trees but the rays of red beams are closing in on us. I bow my head to stay low and creep gently over the dry leaves. One crunches particularly loud and catches their attention. Then the lasers aim towards me.

"Fuck!" I cry out. I set down the 180 pound man then swing him over my other shoulder. "Here we go again," I take a breath, then wobble to my feet, preparing myself for the run of a lifetime.

About a meter away, I see Zara. Her arm is shaking, and I can see the exhaustion on her face.

I need to hurry. Before we're all stuck here.

I brace myself, then take off faster towards her. Turning back occasionally as I run, to shoot the three RovTrons that are now chasing me.

(Zara)

"What's taking them so long?" I struggle to keep the portal open. "I can't hold this much longer." Flashes of light illuminating the dark forest like fireworks. "Ronan!" I shout. But he doesn't respond.

All of a sudden, my vision becomes foggy and everything turns into a blur.

What's going on?

My hand begins to tremble. I try to keep my arm out as steady as I can, holding it with my other hand to stabilize it. But it's shaking uncontrollably. Loud bangs sound, and my ears begin to ring. The energy that's projecting from my body is beginning to weaken and the light starts to dim. The portal is starting to close.

Fuck.

"Ronan?" an unclear figure approaches me, but I can't make out who it is. Everything is still a huge blur.

What's wrong with my eyes? Why can't I see?

"We're here," Ronan responds.

"Hurry!" I cry painfully. "I can't hold it anymore! It's closing!"

The flashes of light come closer, and one flies across my face, just missing me.

The flashes of lights are bullets.

Bullets are still flying straight at us. Ronan grabs me by the shoulder and shoves me into the portal, just as it's closing. Then one of the bullets hits something.

The sound is almost deafening. I've never heard a person get shot so close. Blood splatters everywhere and gets me on my face. The body that was hit drops, and the portal closes. Leaving it behind.

I fall to the ground beside the other body that made it to the other side with me. But it just lies there motionless.

An unconscious blur.

To be continued.

ACKNOWLEDGMENTS

To my family, thank you for the support you've given me that allows me to follow my dreams.

Made in United States
Troutdale, OR
09/07/2023